Under a Georgia Moon

a novel

Under a
Georgia
Moon

a novel
by
Cindy Roland Anderson

**WINSOME
PRESS**
PUBLISHING

Under a Georgia Moon
Cindy Roland Anderson
©2014 Cindy Roland Anderson
Published by Winsome Press Publishing

Published by Winsome Press Publishing, Farmington, UT

LIBRARY OF CONGRESS CATALOGING-IN-PUBLICATION DATA
LCCN: 2014948726

1. Fiction. 2. Women's. 3. Romance
ISBN-13: 978-0692275955
ISBN-10: 0692275959

Editor: Sadie L. Anderson
Typeset Sadie L. Anderson
Cover Design by Casey Harberston and Zulu Six
Cover Photography by Tomi Kennedy

For my amazing children, Tyler, Nicole, Bryan, Jason and Matthew. I absolutely love being your mother.

Chapter One

Three months. That's all it had taken for Addie Heywood's ex-fiancé to marry Flaxseed Oil Girl. Three lousy months.

Addie swallowed hard as she glared at the invitation, noting Brandon looked almost exactly the same as he'd looked in *their* wedding announcement only a few months earlier. But this time the girl smiling up at him was a blonde—completely opposite of Addie's deep auburn hair.

She'd heard Brandon was engaged, but part of her didn't believe he'd go through with it. That maybe he had commitment issues, and it hadn't just been her...well, her and—according to Brandon and his fanatical health food code—her unhealthy eating habits that had caused him to dump her three weeks before their December wedding.

Her eyes scanned the fancy script and she noted the nuptials had taken place two weeks ago in San Diego. An open house was scheduled for next week at his parents' house. That surprised her. When Brandon dumped her, he'd also dumped their small Idaho town, claiming he wouldn't be back in Daisy Springs anytime soon.

Oh yeah, that was another thing he didn't like about Addie. She was too attached to her family and to Daisy Springs.

Addie glanced up at her big sister, Chellie, and handed her the embellished paper. "I wonder if their wedding cake was loaded with antioxidants and was sweetened with Stevia?"

"Really?" Chellie took the card and narrowed her eyes at Addie. "That's all you're wondering?"

No. She also wondered if the rumors were true and Brandon's wife was now four months pregnant which meant he'd been doing more than sharing organic recipes with another woman while engaged to Addie. She also wondered if his belated nuptials coincided with the first week in March because he planned on going to Hawaii with his new wife— the postponed honeymoon trip they'd booked for Addie and him to take once he finished his bar exams.

"Well." She shrugged and tried not to show the hurt she still felt. "I guess I wonder if the cake tasted good."

Her sister tossed the invitation on the countertop. "Addison, why can't you just talk about your feelings?"

If her sister was using her full name, it meant she was in "mother mode," but right now she needed Chellie to be in "friend mode." That was the whole reason she opted to stop by her house to open the invitation.

"Okay. I *feel* strongly that a wedding cake should not have flaxseed oil or spinach in it." She made a face. "Yuck."

Addie hoped to make her sister laugh, not look at her with pity. She was so tired of pity. Since that fateful day when Brandon announced he couldn't marry her because he'd found someone else more compatible with his obsessive health food tastes, Addie had been the recipient of more than enough stares and whispers from people who felt sorry for her.

Slipping past her sister, Addie served herself a piece of chocolate cake with gooey marshmallows melted under a thick layer of chocolate frosting. Even at the age of twenty-four, if Addie was going to get into her "feelings" and all that, she needed a sugar boost.

"Honey, I'm worried about you." Chellie followed Addie to the table and took a seat next to her. "Please don't keep everything all inside. I'm here for you."

Chellie, fifteen years older than Addie, had three kids to worry about—two of them teenagers—and didn't need the added burden of Addie's problems. Besides, suppressing her feelings was a coping mechanism Addie had learned to use right after her mother died. Instead of facing the hurt, anger and fear, she'd efficiently stuffed her feelings in hidden places. It was like a child who cleaned her room by hiding and stuffing things in closets, under beds and in drawers so on the outside it all looked neat and tidy.

"I'm fine, Chellie." Addie was already finding places to tuck away the negative emotions Brandon's wedding announcement brought to the surface. She took a bite of the cake and closed her eyes to savor the moment. At the same time, she did her best to ignore the fact that since the break up her jeans were starting to feel a little tight. "*Mmm*. I know how I feel about this chocolate cake."

When she opened her eyes again, her sister had that look on her face. The one that said she wasn't going to let it go. "Dad's worried about you too."

Addie swallowed the lump in her throat, along with the cake. She had tried so hard to hide her feelings from him and thought she was doing a great job. "What am I doing that's so worrisome?"

"He said you don't go out anymore and refuse to attend any church single activities."

"Hello. You would've stopped going too if you were me. Need I remind you about the singles retreat I totally ruined for the new youth pastor? Once I spoke up all spiritual thoughts were gone and the poor guy spent the rest of the time trying to get things back on track."

The corner of her sister's mouth twitched. "I'm sure anyone could've made the same mistake."

"Um, I don't think so." Addie felt a hot flush sear her cheeks when she thought about her blunder. While everyone sat around the lodges' cozy fireplace listening to the message, she'd been daydreaming about the new youth pastor who was both single and cute. When he'd suddenly turned to her and asked her to share her thoughts on what he'd been talking about, Addie hadn't had a clue what he'd even said.

Desperate, she'd thought about Sunday's sermon and blurted out her desire to follow God's plan so she could gain immortality. Only it had come out wrong, and Addie had witnessed to the large gathering of young single adults her desire to gain *immorality*.

Letting out a deep breath, Addie glanced up at her sister. "I quit attending the activities because I couldn't take one more guy asking me how my quest for *immorality* was going."

Chellie snorted a laugh before covering her mouth with her hand. When she'd composed herself again, she said, "Okay. I can understand that, but why have you stopped going out?"

"Uh, I think I just explained that." She cut into her cake and lifted it up toward her mouth. "Besides, instead of giving up refined sugar, I've decided to give up men."

While Addie enjoyed the chocolate confection melting on her tongue, her two nephews came into the kitchen with about a half a dozen boys ranging in age from fourteen to sixteen. It was the perfect time to escape her sister's pending lecture about her decision to stop dating.

"Hi, Aunt Addie," her nephews said before diving into the chocolate cake.

"Hey, guys." Addie scooted away from the table to make a quick departure.

Brice, one of her nephew's best friends, moved in front of her and blocked her exit. "Hey, I need to ask you a question."

Addie eyed him warily. Brice was a tad on the arrogant side, especially since he was bigger than most college guys. A comparison Addie regretted making a few months ago since now the kid thought she would go out with him. "Sure. What's up?"

A confident grin stole over his face as he leaned in close. "I was just wondering how the quest for immorality was going."

Ha ha. Very funny. Of course, all of the boys thought it was hilarious, including her nephews.

"You're way too young for an answer, Brice." Addie sidestepped the little twerp and waved to her sister. "I'll see you later." Chellie was too busy reprimanding the boys raiding her kitchen to try to stop her.

Feeling somewhat deflated, Addie drove away from her sister's house and tried thinking happy thoughts. If she couldn't pull off happy-go-lucky girl for her father, it might lead into another Addie-is-depressed conversation. She wasn't depressed. Just a little…under enthused.

She wound through the rural housing development, surprised by the number of new houses under construction. When Chellie and her husband built their house nearly ten years ago it had been surrounded by fields and only a handful of houses. Now, new homes sprung up as fast as the farmers parted out their land.

Daisy Springs, known for its natural hot mineral springs, had suffered from the recession. It had recently gotten a boost in the economy when the new food processing plant had opened up a few years ago. Addie was one of the accountants at the plant. It wasn't her dream job, but at least she wasn't flipping burgers at the local hangout.

Her fingers tightened on the steering wheel as she rounded the corner and saw her favorite house—the house similar to the one she was supposed to be sharing with her husband. Her throat constricted and she blinked hard when she felt the sting of tears. She hadn't cried once today, not even when she'd opened up Brandon's wedding announcement.

Swallowing, she forced her eyes back on the road and told herself how lucky she was not to have such a huge mortgage payment. She and Brandon hadn't seen eye to eye about where they should live after they married. Addie had wanted an older home near her dad in town. Brandon wanted to move to a bigger city like Boise.

The compromise was Brandon would set up his law practice in Daisy Springs and they would build near Brandon's parents' house, which was only a couple of miles away from Chellie. Now three months later, it kind of sucked she wouldn't be living close to her sister and that Addie still lived with her father, but, hey, at least she wasn't stuck doing yard work every weekend.

As she emerged from the neighborhood, she caught the beginnings of a stunning sunset. The fiery orange and red colors bled into wispy clouds that hovered over the snow peaked mountains. It was beautiful, and Addie wanted to capture the image with her camera.

She eased off the side of the road and grabbed her camera bag from the passenger floor. Carefully, she attached the new lens she'd gotten herself for Christmas. It had taken what little she had left of her savings, but was well worth it. Besides, it was more like an investment into the photography business she dreamed of starting one day. It would also work with the professional camera she had her eye on as soon as she could come up with six thousand dollars.

After taking several shots, she put her camera away and climbed back inside her car. Not for the first time, Addie wished she'd followed her dreams and majored in photography. Instead, she'd taken Brandon's advice and gone into accounting. Number crunching was mindless work, and probably the reason for her sugar addiction.

It wasn't her fault she liked eating bad carbs—it was Brandon's. The big jerk.

Thinking of bad carbs made her wish she'd taken a slice of her sister's cake with her. Maybe when she got home she'd make a chocolate cake of her own.

Glancing over her shoulder to check for cars, Addie pulled back onto the road. A mile later, she came to a stop at the intersection, surprised at the heavy traffic on the newly constructed two-lane highway. The processing plant, along with the new hospital, had created the need for the expanded road.

Addie hoped to avoid Daisy Spring's version of a rush hour by stopping at her sister's house before going home. Since the road should be cleared out by now, there had to be an accident or wandering cows. Either way, this was the only route back to town so she merged into the flow of cars as soon as there was an opening.

The sky darkened as she slowly moved forward. Not wanting her dad to worry any more than he already was, she tried to call home. It rang several times before rolling over to voicemail. She ended the call without leaving a message. Her eighty year old father rarely answered the phone unless the handset was right next to him. Listening to voicemail was out of the question.

The congestion started to let up and she increased her speed. The right lane appeared to be going a little faster and Addie turned on her blinker, preparing to merge over.

But a motorcycle filled the gap before she could make the lane change. Instead of flowing with traffic, the motorcycle stayed at Addie's side, keeping her pinned between two oversized pickup trucks. She had to tap on her brakes to slow her Honda back to a slow crawl.

Annoyed, she glanced over at the motorcycle. The driver wasn't some punk like she suspected, but a really good-looking guy wearing a black beanie, a black leather jacket and gloves. A five o'clock shadow darkened his jaw and he seemed a little intimidating—until he smiled. Flashing her a set of straight white teeth, he lifted a hand and pointed to the front of his bike. Did he want her to notice his motorcycle?

A grin tugged at her mouth as she averted her eyes back to the road. It was sort of nice to have someone flirt with her, even if biker boys weren't really her thing. She felt particularly vulnerable right now, so having a guy pay a little attention to her felt good.

The motorcycle kept pace with her as they entered the city limits. Addie looked at him sidelong and he shot her another grin. Again, he gestured with his hand to the front of his bike. *Yes, Mr. Biker Boy, you have a very nice motorcycle.* Addie giggled and lifted her hand to give him a flirtatious wave.

The motorcycle continued alongside her as she approached a stop light. Feeling quite flattered, she crossed her fingers, and hoped for a red light. If they stopped she might have a chance to talk to the guy. Biker Boy was looking better and better to her.

The light turned yellow and she and the motorcycle both slowed down rather than trying to beat the red light. Nervously, Addie glanced over at Biker Boy.

His eyes crinkled at the corners as he motioned for her to roll down her window.

Her heart fluttered inside her chest as Addie pushed the button and leaned toward the passenger side of the window. "Hi," she said, hoping the guy hadn't heard the tiny squeak in her voice.

The man had incredible blue eyes. They twinkled as he revved the engine a little. "Hey, I just wanted to tell you your lights were off. Your car is dark and someone like me might not see you until it's too late."

Addie's face heated. Definitely not the kind of pickup line a girl wanted to hear. "Oh, well, thank you." She flipped on her lights.

Biker Boy nodded his head in approval and winked. "No problem." Maybe now he would ask for her number.

The light turned green and he shot off without giving her a second glance. Addie closed the window and slowly pressed on the accelerator.

She didn't really like guys with motorcycles anyway.

Feeling discouraged and tired, she finally pulled into her driveway. The small bungalow styled house looked cozy and secure. She longed to sneak inside her house, grab a bite of food and go directly to bed, but her dad would be anxious to hear about her day.

She parked in the garage and entered the house through the kitchen. The faint smell of onions and beef lingered from her dad's dinner and she knew he would have a plate for her warming in the oven. She hung her keys on the hook by the door, not sure if she could eat anything heavy right now. A bowl of cold cereal sounded just right. But first she wanted to change into her favorite yoga pants and a T-shirt.

After she placed her purse on the counter, Addie followed the muffled sounds from the television to look for her dad. She found him asleep in his recliner, his head tipped down on his chest. She paused by the door and studied him. His gray hair, or what was left of it, had fallen over his forehead. The flickering light from the television illuminated the deep crevices of his face.

As she watched him, she realized how old he appeared. He looked every bit his eighty years. How much longer would she get to have him around? Tenderness and love for her dad washed over her. The upside of being jilted was at least now she'd have more time with him.

Careful not to awaken her father, she slipped off her shoes and tiptoed toward her bedroom. The floor creaked beneath her feet and startled her dad awake.

"Hi, honey," he said on a yawn. "When did you get home?" She loved the deep, gravelly sound of his voice.

"Just now. Sorry if I woke you."

He smiled and waved his hand. "I needed to get up, anyway." He braced his hands on the arm of the chair and attempted to rise. "I think I'm getting old."

The corners of her mouth tipped up. In spite of his advanced age, his mind was still sharp and his attitude as upbeat as ever. She moved next to the chair and held out her hand. "You're not old, Dad."

He gripped her hand firmly and stood without much assistance. His eyes—the same light brown color as hers—twinkled as he playfully tugged on a lock of her hair. "Not too old with my little girl around." His lips stretched into a smile and he winked. "I'm glad you're home. How was your day?"

Her day had been long, and it hadn't helped that one of the secretaries had gotten engaged the night before. All day, Addie listened to the play by play of the engagement retold multiple times. She also knew the wedding colors, the type of flowers the bride liked and the price range of the dress she planned on purchasing. Plus, there was Brandon's wedding announcement burning a hole in her purse. She should have just tossed it.

"It was okay." She avoided looking in his eyes. "It's tax season so that should say it all." Technically, since she was the lowest ranking accountant, Addie didn't have much to do with the crazy tax season but it was a solid excuse for having a bad day at work.

When her dad didn't make a comment, Addie met his concerned gaze. "Chellie called," he said softly. "She told me about the wedding announcement."

To her horror, the sting of tears pricked her eyes. "Oh." She blinked rapidly. "I'm okay." A tear spilled over her bottom lash and she wiped at it with the back of her hand. She couldn't fall apart now.

"I'm sorry, baby," he said with just a hint of a southern accent.

Even though her dad had been raised in Georgia, he'd lost most of his accent long ago. Every now and then it came out, especially when he was offering words of comfort. He held out his arms and it only took Addie a second before she leaned in to embrace her father. With her face pressed against his chest, she cried, feeling like a little girl all over again.

Life wasn't fair. But she already knew that. When you're eleven and your mother gets so sick she can't even hug you good-night, the reality of pain and suffering becomes very apparent.

As much as she hurt right now, nothing could compare to seeing her mother fade away to nothingness and then leave her for good.

After a few minutes Addie stepped back, embarrassed by her emotions. Her daddy always used to tell her "If you hurt, cry a river, build a bridge, and get over it." Apparently seeing Brandon's wedding announcement had hit her like a rogue wave and knocked out the bridge she had built to get over him.

"Sorry." She sniffed and gave her dad a shaky laugh. "I really don't know why I'm crying."

He studied her for a few seconds, love evident in his eyes. "Honey, you've been holding that in for quite some time now." He took her hand and led her to the couch where they both sat down. "I know the past few months have been hard on you, so that cry was long overdue."

Her dad was obviously not aware of the many nights Addie had cried herself to sleep. Lately, things had been better and she thought she was done shedding tears over Brandon. Honestly, part of her had been relieved when he had called off the wedding. The two of them hadn't acted like most engaged couples—like the ones who can't keep their hands off each other and are constantly stealing kisses, making everyone around them uncomfortable.

The reminder of their strained relationship made her want to forget everything about Brandon. "I feel better now." She glanced up. "I think I'm just tired and hungry."

She started to get off the couch, but her dad grabbed her hand and held her back. "I'm glad you feel better, but I'm worried about you."

"Because you talked to Chellie?"

"No. Because for the past couple of months I've waited to see that spark of life come back into your eyes." He rubbed his rough thumb over the top of her hand.

"It hasn't. And now you've cut yourself off from socializing with young people your age."

That's because the young people her age were looking for a relationship. Addie wasn't prepared to go there again. "I'm just not ready to date right now, Dad."

"Okay. But I think you need a change of scenery. Your aunt Janie has been asking you to come to Georgia and stay with her for a while now. I think you should go."

It'd been so long since Addie had visited Georgia, and Aunt Janie would spoil her with all kinds of good southern food. Still, she was reluctant to make the trip because every time she talked with her aunt, she kept mentioning all the nice boys Addie should meet, especially her closest neighbor Chase Nichols.

Addie remembered meeting Chase not long after her mother had passed away. He had been arrogant, teased her about having red hair and had hated that she was two inches taller than him. Sure, he'd been cute, and, according to her aunt, he was even better looking now, but if he was that annoying at fourteen, she could only imagine how much worse he'd gotten.

"That would be fun. Maybe sometime in the fall I can save enough money to buy a ticket."

"Why not now?" One of her father's bushy brows lifted. "I thought you still had two weeks off and a voucher you can use anytime?"

Yes. Theoretically, Addie had two weeks of unpaid vacation starting next Friday, due to the aforementioned belated honeymoon. Since her boss had already arranged to have a free college intern step in for Addie, he had made it clear she wasn't needed at the office.

She hadn't been eager to fight his decision since the whole situation was humiliating enough. And the roundtrip voucher was one of the only things she didn't lose money on when Brandon dumped her.

"I do, but I thought I'd just hang around here and organize the basement or something." By the look on her father's face, she knew that had been the wrong thing to say. She sounded completely pathetic. Correction, she *was* completely pathetic.

Letting out a defeated breath, she said, "I'll give Aunt Janie a call to see if she's up for a house guest."

A spark lit her father's eyes. "I talked to her this morning and she already has your favorite room ready for you."

"I'm still calling her so she doesn't get any ideas of setting me up with her neighbor." Addie fished her phone out of her pocket. "I'm not interested in meeting any men."

Her father let out a deep chuckle. "You'll ruin her fun, but go ahead and tell her."

Addie leaned her head on her dad's shoulder. The familiar scent of his aftershave gave her a sense of reassurance that things might be okay. "Thanks for understanding."

"You're welcome." He slipped an arm around her shoulders and gave her a gentle squeeze. "You know, sweetie, it'll all workout. And when you meet the man you really are meant to be with, this'll all seem like nothing."

She closed her eyes briefly. The last thing she wanted was another man in her life. There was nothing wrong with staying single. "Yeah, I guess. But I'm in no hurry."

She stood and held out her hand to help her father off of the couch. "I'm going to go change my clothes before I get something to eat."

"Sure, honey. I'll get your food out of the oven."

"Thank you, Daddy." Addie let go of his hand and padded down the hall to her bedroom. The minute she opened the door, she stopped dead in her tracks and stared at her wedding dress, still hanging on the closet door. Oh yeah, she forgot she'd pulled it out last night, determined to take pictures of it and sell it on eBay.

That was before she had opened Brandon's wedding announcement.

Her eyes started to sting again, but she blinked, swallowed down her emotions, and moved the dress inside her closet. Selling her dress could wait another day.

Closing the closet door, Addie grabbed her laptop and sank down on her bed. She was going to book her flight before she chickened out and stayed home to organize the basement.

She logged on and quickly scanned over her email. There was the usual amount of spam, notifying her of specials at her favorite stores. A few of the messages were from church, probably inviting her to the next activity. Feeling more guilty than embarrassed at the moment, she opened one of the messages and then wished she hadn't. The next activity was going to be a surprise wedding shower for a couple Addie remembered always being together, holding hands, whispering and stealing kisses. Ugh. She was so not going.

Skipping the other church related mail, she scrolled to the most recent message. It was from the company she'd purchased her new camera lens from. The subject announced in bold letters a photography contest with a grand prize totaling ten thousand dollars.

Excitement shot through Addie as she clicked open the message and read the details. The recipient of the winning photograph would take home a professional camera with all the accessories, including memory cards, and two additional lenses.

If she could win the contest, this could be her chance to finally go for her dream. While Addie's current camera was great, it wasn't ideal for the kind of quality of work she'd like to have with her own studio. With the right equipment, she could work out of her home until she built a clientele, which hopefully wouldn't take too long. Daisy Springs didn't have a professional photographer. Yet.

Feeling more hope than she had in a long time, she dropped her gaze to the bottom of the message and found the rules as well as the deadline. She had three weeks to get the perfect picture. Her mind whirled as fast as the high-speed shutter setting on her camera as she thought of possible locations and subjects. She loved doing landscape but it was still pretty brown outside. Spring rarely came early in Idaho, but the South would be a different story.

Mitchel Creek, Georgia was a picturesque town about thirty minutes outside of Macon. With large plantation type homes dotting the rolling hills and a quaint little main street lined with antique shops and boutiques, Addie should be able to capture the perfect image.

Opening a new tab in her browser, Addie typed in the airline name and clicked on the link to their website. After logging into her account, she booked her flight for the following Friday.

Next, she found her cell phone and texted her travel plans to her aunt. Unlike Addie's father, Aunt Janie—his younger sister by eight years—had embraced the latest technology, including smart phones and texting.

A few minutes later her phone dinged and she read the excited message from her aunt. Before Janie could mention anything about setting Addie up with her good-looking neighbor, Addie quickly sent her stipulation that she wasn't interested in dating anyone. Period.

The reply she got back was very short, and not as reassuring as she'd wanted.

Sweetie, you don't need to date anyone you don't want to. I can't wait to see you. Hugs!

Addie decided not to clarify her stance because she was sure about one thing: she did not *want* to date. At least not for a very, very long time.

Chapter Two

Chase Nichols, dressed for work in a button-down shirt, tie and khaki colored slacks, leaned against the door jamb of Janie Caldwell's kitchen. His mouth watered as the tantalizing smell of freshly baked cinnamon buns drifted his way. With great anticipation, he watched Miss Janie drizzle icing over the warm bread.

"Chase, are you sure you don't mind picking up Addie?" she questioned without glancing up at him.

Chase would do just about anything for one of her cinnamon buns. "Miss Janie, I told ya I don't mind, and I'm gonna be in Atlanta, anyway." His neighbor baked the best breads and pastries in the entire South, making Chase a frequent visitor.

"That's right, you and the boys have a…" Janie looked up and furrowed her brow. "What'd ya call it?"

"A gig."

"Right. A gig." Janie finished with the icing and reached for a spatula. "Well, Addie's plane comes in early afternoon on Friday. Is that gonna be a problem?"

Chase pushed away from the door jamb. "That'll be perfect. We're only playin' one night and it happens to be Thursday." Chase grinned. "We're still not good enough for the weekend crowd at this club."

Janie swatted her hand in the air. "What? That's crazy. You boys sound wonderful to me. Y'all will get your big break. Just wait and see."

Every time somebody brought up the failed attempt of *Chasing Dreams* to break into the country music scene, Chase felt an almost desperate feeling inside to stop time. He was twenty-eight, and now that he had a college degree, and a good career in graphic arts, the next step should be marriage. But while the other members of their country music band were content playing a couple of weekends a month, Chase couldn't let go of his dream. He wanted one more chance to make it big—even if it meant going solo.

"Miss Janie." Chase walked toward the counter. "The guys are happy doin' a few gigs a month." He took the plate from Miss Janie's outstretched hand. "Thank you." He tore off a corner of the roll. "Besides, Drew and his wife are expectin' another baby, and he complains about being away from his family as it is. Same with Jackson, now that he's married."

Jackson McCall, his best friend since the fourth grade, had gotten married six months earlier. His goals had been the same as Chase's until he met his wife Sydney. That realization still stung.

Janie gave him a calculated look before her lips stretched into a big smile. "And do you have any marriage prospects?"

Chase smiled, trying his best not to show his irritation. He would get married. Eventually. As soon as the right girl came along.

"No, ma'am. No one yet."

Janie's grin widened. "Well, maybe my Addie will turn your head. She's a pretty little thing and needs to have her heart mended."

Chase was in the process of taking his first bite, but paused midway. *Addie?* As in the Addie he was supposed to pick up?

"Your niece? What happened to break her heart?"

Janie crossed her arms over her ample chest and narrowed her eyes. "Her fool fiancé broke off their engagement two weeks before the wedding. Although it's a good thing it happened before she married the scoundrel."

Chase was mildly curious about what caused the break up, but didn't ask for clarification. He knew there were always two sides to every story, and he remembered Janie's red-headed niece. She'd been hot-tempered, even at the age of eleven. "Yes, ma'am. That is a good thing."

"He didn't deserve her anyway, so I'm glad it didn't work out." She eyed Chase again, a speculative gleam glinting in her dark brown eyes. A look he knew all too well when someone was trying to set him up.

Chase wasn't interested in Janie's fiery niece, and he seriously doubted she would be interested in him. Shoot, the last time he saw her, she'd been a couple of inches taller than him. Man, he'd hated that. And the girl rubbed it in whenever she got the chance. His growth spurt came the following year, but the redhead never returned for a visit. He was tempted to ask Janie how tall her niece was now. While Chase's height was above average, he was still just six feet with his boots on.

"Well," he said, needing to change the subject. "I need to get to work. Why don't you give me her cell so I'll have a way of callin' her."

Janie wiggled both eyebrows. "You want her number?"

Not for what you're thinking. "Well, yeah. I just figured that would be the best way to contact her at the airport." He shrugged. "Or, I can just hold up a sign with her name on it."

"Perfect idea. I'll make the sign tonight and you can take it before you leave for your gig thing."

"Yes, ma'am. I'll be by to pick it up the mornin' before we leave." He took the rest of the roll and handed Janie his plate. "Thanks for feeding me."

"You're welcome." She grinned as she followed Chase out the door. "Oh, I'll still text you Addie's number."

Chase waved a hand. "That'd be great."

"Have a good day."

"You too." He climbed in his truck and headed to work, telling himself not to worry about his neighbor's matchmaking ideas. Out of all the girls he'd dated, not one of them had ever been a redhead. They weren't really his type.

* * *

Chase tucked the bright colored sign Miss Janie made for him in between the airport's vinyl chairs. His idea of a sign didn't entail sparkling glitter. He didn't plan on using the sign, not when he could just as easily text, but Miss Janie was so excited about it he knew he had to at least bring it inside. As it was, he left the balloon bouquet in his truck.

Since Miss Heywood's plane wasn't due for another ten minutes, Chase leaned back in his chair and closed his eyes. He might as well catch a few Z's while he waited. The performance the night before had been great and they'd played until two in the morning. Before going to his hotel room, he'd stayed up even later talking with a pretty girl. Chase called it a night when the girl invited him for a sleepover.

Even if he had been tempted—which he hadn't been— his mama raised him to respect women. With four sisters, Chase took it upon himself to protect them from guys that usually had only one thing on their mind.

Luckily, two of his sisters were happily married. The other two—the twins—were the youngest and were making him crazy. They were beautiful. They knew it, and they knew everyone else knew it too.

He couldn't wait for them to graduate high school in a few months. Although he wasn't a proponent of marrying young, he sort of hoped the twins would find good husbands their first year in college like his other sisters had.

He shifted in the hard seat and tried not to think of where that would leave him—the oldest and not married. His parents, especially his mother, would be all over him like a tick on a hound dog, harassing him for being single and trying to set him up with every eligible girl in the state of Georgia.

No thanks. Being the only son in a houseful of girls made him leery of marriage. His sisters' emotions were all over the place. He was an expert on PMS and he'd had to buy more feminine products over the years than any guy should ever be subjected to. In spite of Jackson's insistence that the benefits of marriage far outweighed the hormonal mood swings, Chase was content focusing on his career for now.

A mother with two young boys took the empty seats next to Chase. Right away, an unpleasant odor wafted up from one of the kids. Chase decided to skip his nap and quickly vacated his seat. He walked over to the monitors and was surprised to see Miss Heywood's plane landed early.

A few minutes later, an influx of passengers approached the baggage-claim area. Chase moved toward the one designated for the flight number Miss Janie gave him. He leaned against a column and studied the passengers, looking for a redhead.

He doubted he would be able to identify Janie's niece by sight, especially since he'd been too busy worrying about work and whether or not the talent scout was going to show up at their performance last night to even track her down on Facebook.

If his phone's battery wasn't in the red zone, he could've done a search while he waited. Hopefully, it would hold out long enough for a text message—otherwise he'd be holding up the girly-looking poster board. He glanced back by his seat and saw it was still tucked in between the chair. His phone better not die.

As soon as the luggage started circulating, the passengers crowded around the conveyer belt. They were all crammed in so close together it made it difficult for anyone to remove their bag once they spotted it.

Chase watched the process over and over, but noticed one girl was having a hard time getting close enough to reach her bag. She was cute, at least from what he could tell. She sure looked good in her jeans and a turquoise colored top that hugged her generous curves. Under the airport lights, her long hair looked thick and shiny. The color was similar to his sister's chestnut mare Roxie.

He squinted, wondering if he could call the hair red. To him it looked more brown than red, so he doubted it was Janie's niece. Her hair color was something he could never forget. Whenever she'd teased him about being taller than him, he'd made some wisecrack about her fire engine red hair. She hadn't liked that very much.

Another surge of passengers flooded the already crowded space. Chase knew it was futile but he still scanned the newcomers, hoping to spot Janie's niece. So far the only woman he'd found with red hair was very pregnant and holding the hand of a little boy.

Deciding he better let Miss Heywood know he was here, he pulled out his phone and quickly typed in a message that he'd wait for her at the base of the escalator. He sent the message and was frustrated when a second later the screen went blank and his phone powered off. He couldn't believe he'd forgotten to pack a charger. It was stupid to not have an extra one in his truck.

Hoping the message had actually been sent, he continued to people watch. Once again, he spotted the girl in the turquoise shirt. She'd made progress, and Chase watched as she inched forward and squeezed between two men, reaching out to grab a large roll-on duffle bag with a bright pink ribbon tied to it.

She struggled to get the piece of luggage off of the carousel, but was unsuccessful as she lost her hold and stepped away. A big linebacker-looking guy moved in, and Chase thought he was going to help her. Instead, he about knocked her over as he snatched up a mammoth boarding case.

Shooting the man an annoyed glance, the girl held her position as she watched her bag slowly circle around. Figuring he had some time to find Miss Heywood, and since his mama raised him to be a gentleman, Chase made his way over to the girl and hovered directly behind her.

As they waited for the bag to come full circle, she slowly glanced around, like she was looking for someone. Chase swallowed and tried not to stare. She was more than cute. She was beautiful.

Her gaze briefly passed over his face, and his mouth lifted up at the corner when her light brown eyes came back and took a second look at him. He noted a spark of awareness flicker in her eyes before she returned her attention to the revolving bags.

With her back to him, the duffle bag moved into view. Hopefully Chase would be able to offer his assistance. He might even be able to find out where she was visiting, and, if he was lucky, get her phone number too.

* * *

Addie could feel the handsome stranger's eyes on her, and she desperately wanted to steal another peek at him. She might have sworn off men, but she hadn't sworn off looking at them. And this one was very nice to look at.

She fidgeted with her purse strap, forcing herself not to look back over her shoulder. His medium blond hair, with natural highlights women pay big money for, was cut for that just-crawled-out-of-bed look guys could get away with. His eyes were a light mossy green color framed by thick, dark lashes.

As a photographer, she was drawn to faces and could pick up details quickly. She'd had only a cursory glance, but it had been enough to know he was a pretty boy. Generally, she didn't like to date men who were prettier than her. If she hadn't boycotted the idea of dating, she'd have made an exception for this guy.

Remembering her purpose, Addie spied the hot pink ribbon on her bag as it drew closer. If she couldn't get the duffle off this time, she'd have to try to find an airport worker to help her. So much for southern gentlemen living here—not one person had even glanced at her while she struggled to retrieve the heavy bag.

Maybe Aunt Janie's friend from her church could help her. That is, if he'd even showed up. She had no idea what he looked like, but Aunt Janie said not to worry about it because she'd given him her cell phone number, plus she'd made a lovely yellow sign with pink glitter.

The man would also be holding a bunch of balloons. Since Addie hadn't noticed anyone with those items, she figured he wasn't here yet.

Actually, she hoped he wouldn't show up. It was going to be so awkward driving two hours with a man she didn't know. She would much rather rent a car and make the drive herself, but Aunt Janie wouldn't hear of it. She called late last night to say her car was acting funny and she'd made arrangements to have an old friend of hers pick Addie up since he had business in Atlanta.

The person next to Addie stepped in front of her and snatched up a backpack. With the coast clear, Addie braced her legs and reached for her bag. She yanked as hard as she could but her bag didn't seem to move. Ugh. She shouldn't have packed so many shoes. She tried again and let out a frustrated moan as the strap slipped from her fingers.

Suddenly she felt someone reach around her to grasp the handle of the bag. A citrusy male scent swirled around her, making her a little dizzy. Her rescuer smelled really good.

"Let me help you with that, ma'am," a nice tenor voice said in a perfect southern drawl.

His voice melted over her like butter on a bowl of piping hot grits. Addie turned slightly to see who it was and almost started to hyperventilate. It was the pretty boy with the incredible green eyes. He smiled at her, revealing straight, white teeth. At this close proximity, Addie smelled the minty gum he chewed.

She wanted to put her hand over her heart and murmur something like, "I declare" and then swoon. Instead, she backed out of his way so he could get her bag for her. "Thank you," she managed to mutter.

He lifted it effortlessly, and she noticed his well-developed biceps strain against his short sleeve. "This is the only one, right?" he asked, giving her another heart-stopping smile.

"No. I mean, yes. Just the one. Thank you."

He flashed his teeth again. "You're welcome."

They moved to the side, and Addie found herself staring into his green eyes, unable to think of anything else to say. The corner of his mouth lifted. "Do you need help carryin' this to your car?"

Wow, she loved the way he talked. He should be wearing a sign, warning women that his slow, southern drawl was lethal. Of course the women here probably didn't appreciate his accent the way a girl from Idaho would.

"I don't have a car." She nervously moistened her lips. "I'm hoping a man is going to pick me up."

One of his eyebrows crept upward.

That didn't come out right.

"Not pick me up as in *pick me up*." She gave a short little laugh. "Just pick me up for a ride…to my aunt's…the guy she, um, asked to pick me up." She sounded like an idiot.

"Ahh. So I'm guessin' you don't know who this man is?"

"No." She bit her lip. "He's supposed to be holding a yellow sign my aunt made and carrying a bunch of balloons. So far, he's a no-show. I guess I can always rent a car and drive to Mitchel Creek."

The man's eyes narrowed slightly. "Did you say Mitchel Creek?"

"Yeah. I take it you've heard of it?"

A small grin edged up one side of his mouth. "I sure have." His smile broadened. "Actually, I'm headed that way. Would you like a ride?"

Wow, he was smooth, but still…she wasn't that kind of a girl or that stupid. "Uh, no thanks. I'll just wait until my aunt's friend comes with the sign."

"You sure?" he asked. "I don't mind."

His sexy accent was so tempting that she actually considered accepting before coming to her senses. "Yes. Thank you, though." Besides, the man was a complete stranger. He could be some creepy guy who tried picking up unsuspecting women at the airport. "Thanks for helping me with this," she said, gesturing to her bag.

His eyes crinkled slightly, and he gave her another great smile. "You're welcome."

She followed him with her eyes as he walked off. Most creepy guys weren't that cute. Maybe he was just the Boy-Scout type who liked helping others. Once he disappeared behind a crowd of people, Addie searched the busy airport for her would-be ride. Feeling slightly worried, she slipped her phone out of her front pocket to check for messages. One look at the blank screen reminded her she forgot to turn it back on.

A lock of hair fell across her eyes when she dipped her chin to power up her phone. She tucked the errant piece behind her ear as someone moved in front of her. She eyed the cowboy boots, peeking out from jeans and scanned up the mystery man's jean-clad legs. He held a yellow sign with her name written in pink glittery letters. *Finally*. Her ride was here. "Oh, I'm so glad you're here."

The sign lowered, revealing the pretty boy. "So am I," he drawled.

Chapter Three

"Y*ou?*" Addie said in disbelief. "You're the friend my aunt sent?"

A slow, mischievous grin tipped his mouth. "Yes, ma'am."

She stared at him, wondering if he was telling her the truth. "But…she said an *old* friend of hers was coming to get me."

"I am an old friend of hers."

Addie made a quick perusal of her surroundings, searching for an older gentlemen holding helium balloons. For all she knew Pretty Boy here could've stolen the sign since she'd mentioned it earlier. "If you are who you say you are then where are the balloons?"

"I left them in my truck."

A likely story.

He started to laugh. "Look, I didn't knock anyone off, if that's what you're thinkin'."

It had been what she was thinking. "Then where did you get that sign?"

"From your Aunt Janie."

"How did you know her name was Janie?"

That little smirk was back on his handsome face. "Because she's known me since I was a kid."

"Oh, really." Addie leaned in close. "Then what's her last name?"

"Caldwell."

Drat. How did he know that? Unless, of course, he was telling the truth. "I'm going to need to call my aunt just to be sure. Could you give me your name?"

"Are you sayin' you really don't remember meeting me?"

"Well, yeah. You just helped me get my bag but I don't remember us exchanging names."

He grinned. "I meant before today. Chase Nichols? That doesn't ring a bell?"

Addie's mouth dropped open. "You're Chase Nichols?" Her eyes skimmed over every inch of him. He was a lot taller and so much hotter. "You used to be short."

Again, the smirk. "I had a late growth spurt."

Obviously. Still stuck at five four, Addie hadn't grown another inch since her thirteenth birthday. She had, however, increased in other areas that men usually found attractive. She had to hand it to Chase since his eyes hadn't once drifted down below her neck.

"Why didn't you say something earlier?"

"I hadn't figured it out until you mentioned Mitchel Creek." He shrugged. "Sorry, but I couldn't resist teasin' you."

"Are you telling me you really didn't know it was me and you just decided to help me out of the goodness of your heart?"

"Yeah. Besides, you've changed since I last saw you." This time he did look her over. But it was quick, and he didn't linger on any particular part of her body. "I remember your hair being a different color."

"Yes, what was it you used to call me? Flame Brain?"

His lips pressed together, like he was trying to hold back a laugh. "I was fourteen and you kept referrin' to me as Frodo."

Okay, her name calling had probably hurt much more than his taunts. Guys were pretty sensitive about their height and she actually liked her red hair, especially now that it had darkened to a gorgeous shade of auburn her sister tried to mimic from a bottle.

"If I promise not to call you anymore names, do you think we could leave? My feet are killing me."

His eyes slid down to her four inch heels. Shoes were her weakness, well, that and sugar.

"I don't know how you can walk on those things." He reached out and easily took her bag, then weighed it with one hand. "This thing is heavy. Are you hiding a dead body in here?"

"Yes, because security would have never picked up on that."

He laughed and slung the bag over one of his solid shoulders. Addie followed close beside him. "You know you don't have to carry it. It has a handle and wheels."

"I'm good."

Yes he was. Which is why—despite his handsome looks and that killer accent—she wasn't looking for a spring fling...or any kind of romance. The point was she wasn't interested in dating. Still, looking, just looking, wouldn't hurt.

Walking alongside of him, she covertly studied Chase's profile. Nice jaw line and nose. Her gaze traveled down, noticing his tan, muscled arm, sprinkled with light brown hair. The contrast against the white tee he wore only seemed to emphasize his masculinity. Hmm. She still couldn't believe this was the same annoying boy she'd known as a child. Her Aunt Janie hadn't been kidding when she'd said Chase was incredibly handsome.

Before she could look away, he glanced at her. Shoot, she hadn't meant for him to catch her ogling him. "I can take my bag now, if you need me to."

A smug grin crossed his face. "I got it, but thanks." They came to a set of automatic doors that slid open to the parking garage. Chase paused. "After you."

"Thank you." She slipped past him and caught the scent of his yummy cologne. For some reason it made her feel all jittery inside. She tended to say stupid things when nervous. Which might prove to be a problem since in a matter of minutes it would be just the two of them. Alone.

Addie told herself she had nothing to be nervous about as they both moved steadily toward a crosswalk. Chase was her aunt's neighbor. An acquaintance. No big deal.

They paused while a couple of cars crossed in front of them. Chase looked down at her. "Miss Janie's pretty excited to see you."

"I can't wait to see her. I wish she could've picked me up." The second the words were out of her mouth, she realized how ungrateful they sounded. "Not that I'm not glad you picked me up, because I am. Grateful that is. You know, since her car broke down and all."

"Her car broke down?"

"You mean it didn't?"

"Not that I know of."

Chase appeared as confused as she felt. Had her aunt made up the whole car trouble thing so she could get the two of them together? "Aunt Janie texted me last night to say her car was giving her trouble and she didn't dare drive to the airport."

"Hmm, she asked me a few days ago if I would pick you up since I was already going to be in Atlanta."

He lifted one shoulder up. "Maybe she just doesn't like driving in big cities."

Addie knew her aunt was pretty fearless and wouldn't be intimidated by a bigger city. Did Chase really not guess this whole thing had been a set up?

Before Addie could say anything, he placed his palm against her back to nudge her forward. "I'm over this way."

He dropped his hand as soon as they started walking again, but Addie could still feel the warmth from his touch and the tingly sensation that had spread from the contact spot. *Uh-oh. Don't go there girl because that was not attraction.* It was awareness of another human being. Nothing more. She reminded herself she was here for two weeks to relax and get the perfect shot for the contest. She didn't have time for a relationship, especially a long-distance, rebound relationship. That had disaster written all over it.

They stopped next to a big black pickup truck with lifted wheels and shiny chrome running boards.

"This is it." Chase pulled out his keys and unlocked the doors with a push of the button.

He hefted her heavy bag into the back seat of the truck while Addie made her way to the passenger side. She opened her door, preparing to climb in. Even with her four inch heels, she might need a step ladder to get into the thing. "Whoa, this is a little high."

"Oh, hey," Chase said. "A friend of mine broke the handle so it makes it hard to climb in. Just give me a sec and I'll come help you up."

"No, that's okay." Addie hadn't meant her comment as a hint she needed help. "I got it." She placed her purse on the floor and stepped up on the running board.

Colorful balloons hovered in the middle of the truck. Addie cringed with embarrassment as Chase leaned over and parted the balloons just in time to see her first failed attempt as she stumbled back, nearly twisting her ankle.

"Please let me help you," he said. "I don't want you to get hurt."

Oh brother. She could climb up into a truck. She was from Idaho where most kids could drive a stick shift by the time they were twelve. "Don't worry about it. I'm fine."

Determined to climb in without any help, Addie anchored her palm on the seat, and grabbed onto the dash. She probably should take her shoes off but didn't want to waste time. She almost had it but the bottom of her heel slipped and she started to fall back. Then she felt warm hands on her waist and was so startled she gasped and lost her balance.

The next thing she knew, Chase held her against his firm chest. "Are you always this stubborn?" he asked, a hint of that smirk back on his face.

It wasn't every day Addie found herself in the arms of handsome, well-built man, and for a few seconds she was speechless. Heat from his body spread through her like an Idaho wildfire. *Oh, wow, he smells really good.* That thought only seemed to fuel the flames. She had to do something to douse these feelings.

"I'm not stubborn." She twisted and wiggled her feet for him to put her down. "I'm just independent."

Chase lowered her to the ground and smiled. "I wasn't tryin' to rob you of your independence, Miss Heywood. My mama just raised me to open doors for women and to help ladies into cars or trucks." He held out his hand, palm up. "May I?"

If any other guy had used that line on her, she would have laughed right in his face. But Chase's southern drawl and serious eyes made it sound completely sincere.

"Thank you." She placed her palm in his and ignored the sensation of the skin to skin contact.

She snatched her hand back the second she was securely in the vehicle. She didn't know if Chase felt the same crazy, electric attraction she experienced, and she wasn't about to try and find out. He stood there watching her, but she resisted the urge to look at him again and busied herself with putting on her seatbelt. Finally, he closed the door and came around to the driver's side.

Tired from the day's travel, Addie blew out a big breath and leaned back into the seat. The feelings would pass, and even if they didn't, she had no intention of spending time with Chase Nichols. Hopefully, the two hour drive to Mitchel Creek would go by quickly, especially if she kept everything light and fun. Then she wouldn't have to see him for the rest of her trip.

* * *

Chase started the engine but didn't attempt to back out. With Addie sitting in the passenger seat, he had nowhere to put the balloons. He couldn't safely drive with them in the middle.

Using both of his hands, he parted the balloons down the middle to find Addie watching him. "These are gonna be a problem. Any suggestions?"

Her lips curved up into the first genuine smile, making a dimple appear in her right cheek. "My nephews like to suck on the helium and then sing like The Chipmunks."

Chase laughed. "Yeah, but we've got a half a dozen balloons here and between the two of us we'd have a whopper of a headache by the time we finished up."

"You sound like you're speaking from experience."

"I am. Jackson and I thought it'd be real funny to make prank phone calls with helium-induced voices. It was funny—until the headache hit, and my mama made us spend our own money to replace my little sister's balloons."

"Is Jackson your brother?" Addie asked.

"Close enough. He and I have been best friends since grade school."

"I guess we can just deflate them. Or—" She pointed to a family with a bunch of kids getting into a Suburban. "—Maybe they'll want them. Kids love these things."

She unlatched her seatbelt, opened the door and slid out before Chase could offer to help her down. By the time he reached her, the little family had the balloons and was thanking Addie.

As soon as the family climbed into their SUV, Addie turned to Chase. "I can't believe how adorable those little kids sounded with that accent." She grinned, nudging him in the shoulder with her own. "They probably don't sound any different to you."

When Chase had spent a few months one summer in California selling solar panels, people were constantly commenting on how much they loved his accent. To him, they were the ones who spoke differently.

"I like your accent too," he said, stopping at the truck. He did love the way she pronounced everything.

"I have an accent?"

He attempted to lose the twang. "Of course. And all of you guys out West sound alike."

She arched a chestnut-colored eyebrow. "That was pretty good."

He shrugged. "It's a hidden talent."

The smile she gave him made the dimple reappear. "Even though my dad is from the South, I've never been able to talk with a drawl, so I won't even attempt to try."

"Maybe you'll pick it up while you're here."

"Maybe." Their eyes held for a few seconds before she turned toward her door. "I guess we better get going."

Chase moved next to her and held out his hand to help her up. Addie hesitated, and her eyes flickered down to his open palm. She moistened her lips and slowly placed her hand in his.

Heat pooled in his gut at the touch of her warm skin. The rush of awareness he felt was similar to the feel of performing in front of a live audience. Both were something he liked. A lot.

Once she was seated, Chase closed her door and rounded the front of his truck. He hadn't counted on feeling like this, and wasn't quite sure what to do about it. One thing was for sure, Addie was no longer the annoying brat he'd met thirteen years earlier. Still just as stubborn, but now it was kind of cute.

After climbing into the driver's seat, Chase started the truck and followed the exit signs. He pulled in behind a line of cars waiting to pay for parking and glanced over at his passenger. A lock of her auburn hair covered her face as she tipped her head down to study her phone. He hoped the underlying tension between the two of them didn't make the long drive home uncomfortable.

"If you see a text from an unknown number that would be from me."

Addie glanced up at him. "You texted me?"

"I tried, but my phone died."

She glanced back down and scrolled through her messages. "I don't see it."

"Good thing Miss Janie made the sign, right?"

Her lips curved up as she met his eyes again. "Yes, it is."

The car behind them tapped on its horn, and Chase released the brake to move forward a few spaces. "Cell phones don't do a whole lot of good if they're dead."

"What kind of phone do you have?"

He slid her a glance. "The same as yours, just without all the bling."

She laughed and held up her sparkling turquoise colored case. "Admit it, you're jealous."

"Nope." He moved forward and pulled out his wallet. "I'd want it to be purple."

"You're in luck. I'm pretty sure they had it available in two different shades of purple."

Chase withdrew a ten dollar bill and lowered his window. "I think I'll pass." He slipped the ticket in the machine and waited for the total.

"Oh, hey, let me pay for the parking," Addie said.

"I got it." He ignored her protest and fed the cash into the slot. His change popped out and the red crossbar lifted before Chase exited the parking garage.

"Please let me pay for it." Addie held out a twenty dollar bill. "This will cover the parking and a little gas."

Chase shook his head. "Don't worry about it."

"I insist." She placed the money down on the center console.

When he could tell she was going to be persistent, he came up with an idea. "Do you have your charger?"

"Yes."

He withdrew his phone and handed it to her, along with the money. "I'll trade the price of the parking if you'll charge my phone." He glanced her way and shot her a grin. "Please?"

She hesitated and then accepted the phone and money. "Okay, but what about gas?"

Chase made a left turn and headed for I-75. "I was already in Atlanta, Addie. I'm a friend of your aunt's, so let me just be a nice guy and call it good."

A few seconds ticked by. He wondered if her stubborn-independent side would argue with him.

Finally, she nodded her head. "All right. Thank you." She pulled out her charger, plugged it into the USB adapter, and connected his phone. "There you go."

"Thanks." They passed a chain of fast-food restaurants. "Hey, are you hungry?"

She sat with her back angled against her door and clasped her hands tightly in front of her. "Not really. I'm saving up for one of my aunt's cinnamon buns."

"Yeah, those are pretty good."

"But if you want to get something, you should stop. Just know that I'm buying."

He shook his head. "Are you always this difficult?"

"Yes, at least that's what my family is always telling me."

He laughed and merged onto the freeway. "Tell me about your family. I believe you mentioned a couple of nephews. The helium-sucking ones."

"I have an older sister and she has three children. Josh is sixteen. My sister is about to pull her hair out whenever he wants to take the car. Josh is a little on the impulsive side."

"Bryan is fourteen and the family clown," she continued. "I love being around him. He makes me laugh every time I see him. And then there is Stephanie." Chase could hear the smile in her voice. "She's eleven going on twenty. She is all girl and so cute. My brother-in-law, Derek, doesn't look forward to the day when she can date."

Chase knew all about worrying about the girls in his family. "I'll bet. My daddy gets the shotgun out every time one of my little sisters goes out on a date."

"He does not."

"Okay, but he always threatens to if anyone dares to disrespect his girls."

"I'll have to mention that tactic to Derek." She angled her body so her back was in the corner of the cab again. "How many sisters do you have?"

"Four, and they're all younger than me. I'm the only boy."

"Poor baby."

He snorted. "You got that right! Do you have any idea what it's like to live in a house full of hormonal women?"

"Hey, I'm one of those hormonal women."

He chuckled. "Is that so?"

"Well, I'm a woman."

"Yeah," he said, taking a quick look at her. "I kind of noticed that."

After a few seconds of silence, she gave him a nervous giggle. "Your poor sisters. Are you always such a tease?"

"Isn't that what brothers are supposed to do?"

"I wouldn't know." She yawned through the last word. "I only have the one sister." She yawned again. "Sorry, I didn't sleep well last night."

Chase wasn't sure if she was telling him the truth. Maybe she was just done talking to him. But when he glanced over and caught her stifling another yawn, he noticed the fatigue written on her face. "Hey, your seat can recline. Why don't you try to sleep some?"

"No. I'm fine."

"I really don't mind. Why don't you at least close your eyes and try to relax."

She hesitated. "Maybe for just a few minutes."

He reached out to turn on the stereo. "Do you want a little music?" She nodded and Chase tuned into Tim McGraw singing a soft ballad.

"Mmm," she said in a quiet voice, "I love Tim McGraw."

"You and 'bout a million other women," Chase said dryly. But it was good to know she liked country music.

It didn't take her long to fall asleep, her breath slow and even as she snuggled against the seatback. Chase focused on the road ahead, but had a hard time concentrating on anything other than the pretty girl sleeping in his truck.

She sighed in her sleep, drawing his eyes to her face. Long, dark lashes fanned across her smooth skin. Her full lips parted slightly, creating warmth in the pit of his stomach. He had the strongest desire to test the softness of her mouth.

Swallowing, he turned away and put a stop to his wayward thoughts. He'd just met her, and he was thinking about kissing her?

The last time he'd felt such a strong instant attraction was with Hayden. But the two women were nothing alike. From what little he knew about Addie, it seemed cruel to even compare them.

Chase's mood darkened slightly when he thought about Hayden and all the trouble she'd caused him. He almost laughed out loud when the next song on the radio was Lady Antebellum singing "Lookin' for a Good Time." The lyrics boldly stated to not promise anything more than one night. Jackson had teased Chase that the song was all about Hayden Barclay. Sadly, he was right.

Leaning forward, Chase pushed the CD button, playing a mix he'd burned of his favorite artists. He rolled back his shoulders to release some of the tension, remembering the first time he ever saw Hayden. His first year in college, his band Chasing Dreams had entered the Battle of the Bands contest at the Georgia State Fair. Before the competition started, the MC introduced Hayden Barclay, the newly crowned Miss Mitchel Creek.

Chase had his back turned away from the stage, sipping from a bottle of water and trying to mentally prepare for their performance. The wolf whistles and Beau's rasping "whoa" made him turn around. His heart tripped over itself when he saw her. And, like every other male, he was instantly besotted with the dark-haired beauty.

Her midnight blue eyes and her lilting laugh had him mesmerized. His gaze swept over her curvaceous body, hugged by a silvery-blue, sequined gown with a plunging neckline and the back scooped out, revealing flawless skin, kissed by the Georgian sun.

Jackson told him to get his eyes back in his head and focus. They were the first band scheduled to play and once they finished, Chase could ogle her all he wanted.

During the performance, Chase caught her watching him from the front row of the audience. He turned up the charm, giving her a smile and a wink while he sang and played his guitar. During the rest of the competition, he kept his eye on her until the last band played and they announced the winner. Chasing Dreams had taken second place and Miss Mitchel Creek had sought out Chase to congratulate him.

They had talked for over two hours where he found out she and her family had recently moved from South Carolina. Chase thought he'd met the girl of his dreams. Luckily, he'd found out how wrong he'd been before it was too late.

His cell phone vibrated against the console, cutting into the dark memory. "Hey, Mom," he whispered, trying not to awaken Addie.

"Why are you whisperin'?"

"I picked up Miss Janie's niece from the airport, and she fell asleep."

He heard the background noises of the kitchen. His mother was a southern woman through and through. She loved cooking, food, her family, and the Lord. "That's right. I forgot about that. Well, I just wanted to know if I should expect you for supper."

Chase's mother counted on all of her children to be home for supper—however, weekends were different. "Sorry, Mom, but I have a date."

He was taking out a girl Jackson's wife had set him up with. Sydney was forever trying to set up the other two band members who weren't married. Beau Jacobsen, their drummer, gladly went out with every girl Sydney sent his way. Unlike Chase, he was ready to get married. Tonight's date was a total favor to Sydney. Since the girl was visiting from Florida, Chase knew this one date couldn't amount to much.

"I should just stop cooking on the weekend," his mother said with a deep sigh. "Both Ashlee and Taylin are going out as well."

His mother would never stop cooking. "*Nice.* You and Daddy can have a romantic dinner for two."

"True," she said with a soft laugh. "I'll see you later, sweetie."

"Bye, Mom."

Chase secured the phone on the gel dash pad where he could view the screen. His agent was supposed to get back with him today about whether or not the talent scout had showed up for last night's performance. So far he hadn't heard anything which meant the rep probably hadn't come. Chase could only hope the talent scout would show up at their gig next weekend.

Breaking into the country music scene wasn't coming easy. It had been hard enough getting someone reputable to represent Chase, but it was proving to be even more difficult to get someone to listen to him.

If he lived in Nashville, he could hit all the open mic clubs and possibly get noticed that way. Even then, he knew the chance of getting a recording contract was pretty low. Still, as slim as the odds were, he couldn't give up.

But in order to move to Tennessee, he had to get a job, and it couldn't be as a waiter, which was typical for most musicians. Although he lived at home, he paid his parents rent, helped with utilities, and still had another three years before his student loans were paid off. It was a good thing Chase loved his chosen vocation as a graphic artist. He just hated the company he worked for.

He'd interned at Barclay Industries while he and Hayden were dating. After he graduated, Barclay offered him a fulltime position. Since Hayden's daddy, Whit Barclay, owned the company, Chase thought it was a brilliant move. By the time he knew differently it was too late to leave without detrimental repercussions to his career. Even leaving now was risky, but it was a risk he was willing to take.

After spending time researching businesses in Nashville, Chase settled on one corporation he wanted to work for. Nashborough Marketing represented the majority of the top companies involved in the music industry, including the record label Chase wanted to get a recording contract with most: TJ Music. Tate Jepson, the owner of TJ Music, had a reputation for being fair yet aggressive. Chase figured if he landed a job with Nashborough as a graphic artist, it would bring him that much closer to getting a foot in the door with TJ Music.

It all seemed like the perfect solution, except for one major complication. Nashborough and Barclay were rivals, often competing for the same accounts.

They had a history of bad blood that started when Barclay Industries had been headquartered in South Carolina. There had been some scandal of corporate espionage involving Barclay employees, but Nashborough could never prove their claim and Whit Barclay and his company had been cleared of any wrongdoing.

It would be very tricky getting an interview with Nashborough without letting his current employer know about it. Getting a good letter of recommendation would be even tougher, but Shanna, his secretary for the past two years, promised to help him any way she could.

So far, she was the only one who knew about his job search. It had only been fair to confide in her since she'd told him many times he was the only reason she hadn't quit her job, and if he ever left Barclay she would too.

Glancing over his shoulder, Chase switched lanes as he approached the Mitchel Creek exit. He wondered if he should wake Addie or just let her sleep. Taking a quick look at her, he grinned and decided to wait.

She was really out, not even bothering to brush away a few strands of her silky, auburn hair that fell across her eyes. He was tempted to do it for her.

Gripping the steering wheel tight, he kept his hands to himself and sang along with the song currently playing. The lyrics were about holding on to the memories of all the firsts of falling in love and finally having your last first kiss.

Chase had never really thought about it that way, but it was true. Someday he would kiss a girl and know it was his last first kiss.

Chapter Four

Somewhere in the back of Addie's mind she knew she was asleep and needed to wake up. She heard the soft echo of someone singing. It sounded nice, especially in the floaty haze of her dreams. Sighing, she snuggled down into her bed. A loud thumping noise jarred her from her sleep. Then someone started shaking her bed. "Hey, stop it," she mumbled, struggling to open her heavy eyes.

Someone chuckled, but didn't stop vibrating her bed. "Sorry. Construction zone."

"Huh?" she said and forced her eyelids open. Where was she? She straightened up and looked around, trying to get her bearings. She was in a truck. The man driving the truck was grinning at her and it all came back in a rush. Chase Nichols.

"I should've taken another route," he said. "I forgot they were tearing this road up."

Wiping her hair out of her face, she glanced out the window and immediately recognized the area. She hadn't meant to sleep so long. "We're here already?"

Chase laughed. "Goes by fast when you're sleepin', doesn't it?"

"Sorry." She'd only intended to close her eyes for just a minute. Raising her hand to her face, she surreptitiously felt for any drool.

"Don't be sorry." He turned at the next left, the road smoothing out. "I'm glad you were able to sleep. Living with your aunt will require a lot of energy. That woman puts most everyone I know to shame. She's up at the crack of dawn and I don't think I've ever seen a scowl on her face."

It was true. Aunt Janie was the happiest and most energetic woman she'd ever known. It would feel good to be with her again. *But the crack of dawn?*

"I am *so* not a morning person," Addie said. "But I guess I'll have fresh cinnamon buns to lure *my* buns out of bed."

Chase laughed. "I guess you will."

He made another turn, bringing them onto Main Street and the heart of the business section of the historic town. Addie had forgotten how magical and quaint Mitchel Creek was with its brick sidewalks and aged storefronts that seemed to transport you back in time.

"This is so incredible." Like a true southern town, most of the shops sold either antiques or food.

"Yeah, it is," Chase said as he came to a stop at the only traffic light. "Growin' up, I always wanted my parents to move back to Atlanta because it seemed so old fashioned here. But now I love it."

"So this is where you want to settle down?"

"Yeah." He shrugged. "Unless the Lord has other ideas for me."

Addie shouldn't be surprised by his mention of his faith. Aunt Janie had emphasized Chase was a regular at church and sometimes participated in the worship music. Still, having a guy talk about God so openly was refreshing.

She wanted to ask him how he'd know what the Lord wanted him to do since she usually was so clueless, but decided she didn't want to delve into such a serious conversation. She might have to admit she'd recently been dumped by her two-timing fiancé.

The light turned green and Addie looked at the stores to see if she could find the fudge shop her aunt had taken her to that year after her mother had died. "Aunt Janie used to take me to this great candy store that sold fudge. I just can't remember what it's called."

Chase pointed out his window. "That would be A Little Sugar."

Addie recognized the antiquated store front with large jars of colorful candy displayed in the window. "Now that place has very pleasant memories. Especially for a sugar-aholic like me."

"We can stop if you need a fix."

"Hmm. Tempting, but I better not. I'm trying to cut back."

He glanced over at her. "Why?"

Because my stupid ex-fiancé left me for Flaxseed Girl. "I've been told I eat too much of it."

"Well, shoot, here in the south sugar is practically part of the five food groups."

"Sweet." She grinned at him when he looked her way. "No pun intended."

He laughed at her stupid joke. "I'm sure Miss Janie will keep you from goin' through withdrawals. And you're on vacation so you should be able to indulge."

Okay, if he kept talking like this Addie might actually allow herself to really like him. "You're right. Thank you."

He looked at her sidelong and winked at her. "You're welcome."

Yeah, and if he kept being so charming she might even do something crazy like ask him out.

They left Main Street and Chase turned onto a winding road that led to her aunt's. Just on the outskirts of town, a large antebellum home came into view. "Wow, that house is so beautiful."

Chase slowed down so she could get a good view of the plantation home with stately white pillars surrounding a porch that was bigger than Addie's little house in Idaho. The home had four chimneys and too many windows to count.

"The Mitchel Mansion was once part of a huge plantation," Chase said as they made a slow drive by. "When I was a kid, they used to give tours of the house, but when it changed hands a few years ago, the new owner's limited public access to Christmas time only."

"Oh, I bet it's beautiful." She craned her neck to get one last look at it. "Too bad I wasn't into history twelve years ago. Aunt Janie always wanted to take me but I never wanted to go."

"You could always come back for Christmas."

Addie sat back and sighed. "I could never leave my dad, and he refuses to fly anywhere."

"There are other houses nearby that you might be interested in seeing." He cleared his throat. "I could—"

Addie's phone cut Chase off mid-sentence. Not wanting to miss a call from her dad, she glanced down at the caller ID screen to see Aunt Janie's name.

"Do you need to get that?" Chase asked.

"I don't know. It's Aunt Janie. I'm sure she's dying to know how her little plan worked."

Chase shot her a quick look. "Her plan?"

"Yes." She silenced the phone without answering it.

They would be to her aunt's house in a few minutes so it wouldn't hurt to have Aunt Janie sweat it out a little. "I'm sorry you got roped into her matchmaking scheme, but she's convinced that you and I are supposed to hit it off and live happily ever after, even though I've told her over and over that I'm not interested in dating right now."

He was quiet for a few seconds and Addie worried she might have offended him. "It's not because of you. I mean you haven't even called me Flame Brain once."

The corner of his mouth lifted. "Well, since you haven't called me Frodo, maybe we can be friends?"

"Sure. I can handle being friends." At least she thought she could. It might get a little tricky if her attraction toward him didn't go away.

He pressed on the brakes and came to a rest at a stop sign. Then he turned toward her and held out his hand. "Friends?"

Addie licked her lips and nodded her head as she tentatively placed her palm against his. "Friends." She hoped he didn't notice the breathless tone of her voice due to the zingy heat coursing through her body.

Her phone chimed an incoming text and she quickly withdrew her hand to read the message. "I better put her out of her misery and tell her we're almost there," she said with a nervous laugh.

Chase made a right turn, and neither of them said anything for the next half a mile until they came to her aunt's long driveway. So many emotions came flooding back as Addie caught sight of Aunt Janie's house.

The Caldwell home looked as if she'd stepped back in time. Enclosed by enormous oak and magnolia trees, the historic Victorian home that was built before the Civil War took Addie's breath away.

A large sign hung across the wide wrap-around porch to welcome her. A few more balloons were tied to the front porch banisters. Aunt Janie was bouncing up and down, waving wildly at them.

"It looks like your aunt is excited to see you," Chase said with a low chuckle as he rolled to a stop. "I think you better go give her a hug."

Filled with love for her sweet aunt, Addie started to open the car door.

Chase stopped her. "Hey, what're you doin'?"

She gave him a quizzical look. "I'm going to give her a hug." Hadn't he just suggested that?

He turned off the engine. "Well, you need to wait until I open the door for you."

Really? "Really?"

"Yes, ma'am." He winked and got out, walking around to the passenger side. He opened her door and gave her a lazy grin. "Besides," he said, holding out his hand, "if my mama found out about my lapse in manners, she would tan my hide."

"Oh," Addie said with a smile. "Well, I don't want that to happen." She took his offered hand and was proud of herself for not being too effected. "Thank you. I'll be sure and tell your mother she raised a very nice, well-mannered son."

He held onto her hand for a second longer before releasing it. "I'd appreciate it. I think just the other night she accused me of being completely uncultured."

"Why? What'd you do?"

"I started to eat before everyone had been served."

Seriously? Note to self: Do not have dinner at the Nichols's house.

"Ooh! You're here," a familiar voice squealed. Addie turned to find Aunt Janie closing in. "Oh my gracious, Addison Mae. You come over here and give your aunt some sugar."

Ah, sugar...now she knew why she loved it so much. Her aunt was perfectly plump and being wrapped in her soft embrace felt like a warm bath on a winter day. Addie inhaled the scent of vanilla and cinnamon that clung to her aunt's clothing and hair.

"Aunt Janie, I love you." It felt so good to be here. So normal.

"I love you too." Aunt Janie pulled away and started for the house. "Y'all come on in. I have fresh cinnamon buns I just pulled out of the oven."

Addie and Chase exchanged a conspiratorial grin. Then he leaned in close and whispered in her ear, "So, Addison Mae, sugar is an essential thing in the South, *hmm*?"

She laughed and started for the house. Chase walked close beside her, making her acutely aware of him. Yeah, she was aware of him, but that was completely different than being attracted.

She cast a furtive glance his way. Okay, maybe she was a little attracted to him. Still, even if she was, she was not about to get involved with another guy, especially with someone who looked like Chase Nichols. Good-looking men tended to attract women whether they were engaged or not, and she did not need another man breaking her heart.

She sneaked another peek at him. Oh boy, he really was cute. And a natural at flirting. That combination was a big red flag to keep him at a distance.

Addie slowed her pace as she climbed the porch steps. Chase paused in front of her, holding the screen door open.

She avoided looking at him when she passed through the door, but couldn't ignore the faint masculine scent of his cologne.

"Come on back here, baby," Aunt Janie called from the kitchen.

Thankfully, the heavenly aroma of baking bread dominated the air as she entered the house. Addie slipped her shoes off and then followed the tantalizing smell into the cozy kitchen. Although the home had been remodeled several years ago with granite countertops and top of line appliances, Aunt Janie had maintained the authenticity of the nineteenth-century home, complete with pine cabinets and antique furniture from the era.

On the countertop sat a plate of glazed cinnamon buns. "Addie, honey, you and Chase come on over here and sit down," her aunt said, picking up the platter. "I just finished icing these."

Addie drew in a deep breath and grinned. "I've dreamed about this moment ever since I booked my flight."

Chase's lips twitched, his eyes filled with amusement as he pulled out a chair for her and motioned with his hand for her to take a seat. He lightly touched her back as he helped her scoot close to the table.

Addie could only count a few times when a car door had been opened for her—they had all been prom dates. Nobody had ever pulled her chair out for her. Well, not unless she counted the time when a boy who liked her in junior high had pulled the chair out from under her, making her fall very unladylike to the ground.

"Thank you." She felt slightly self-conscious as Chase took a seat across from her. Suddenly the setting seemed a little too intimate.

She prayed Aunt Janie wouldn't bring up the real reason she was here. To heal from a broken heart and get out of the funk she was in.

Addie relaxed when her aunt asked questions about her dad and Chellie's family. She ate two cinnamon rolls while giving details about her nephews and niece and all their shenanigans. To her relief, nothing was ever said about Brandon and his recent wedding.

With her stomach full, she was ready to ask Chase a few questions about himself. Before she got the chance, Chase pushed back from the table and stood up. "Well, ladies, please excuse me. I need to make a showing at the office before headin' home."

He's leaving?

He met Addie's gaze and flashed her a grin. "I enjoyed meeting you. I hope to see you again."

The tiny little flutter in her belly was a reminder to keep herself immune to Chase's southern charm. Friends. They were just friends. Besides, he probably said that to all the girls.

"Me too. Thanks for the ride."

"You're welcome." Chase's eyes regarded her warmly before he turned and walked out the door.

Chapter Five

The next morning, sunlight filtered through the curtains, brightening Aunt Janie's already cheerful yellow room. Addie smiled, snuggling down into the cocoon of blankets and the soft pillow-top mattress.

This room was her favorite and probably hadn't changed very much in the past hundred years. The intricate hardwood floor had been beautifully restored. The crown molding, painted a glossy white, accented the soft yellow walls. Most of the antique furniture in the house had belonged to the Caldwell family for generations.

Addie sat up and stretched and pushed back the yellow and cornflower blue quilt her aunt had stitched by hand. Climbing out of bed, she shivered when her bare feet hit the cold wood floor. Pulling them back up, Addie felt around in the bed until she found her soft fleecy socks.

What a relief to be able to wake up without any responsibilities looming over her. Even better was the fact she wouldn't have to go to work or answer questions about how she was handling Brandon's recent marriage.

Addie took a quick shower and then dressed in a pair of comfortably worn jeans and a fitted yellow cotton tee before going downstairs. Aunt Janie had told her to sleep in as long as she liked and had promised to save a couple of cinnamon rolls for her. Glancing at the clock, Addie bit her lip. It was already noon. But then she remembered the two hour time difference and felt better. Technically—if she went by Idaho time zone—it was only ten o'clock.

The lingering scent of baking bread made her stomach rumble as she descended the stairs. She rounded the corner and entered the kitchen. Warmth and security filled her when she saw Aunt Janie sitting at the table, her head bent down as she read a magazine. Her aunt's trendy short hairstyle, tinted a few shades darker than her natural color, made her appear much younger than her seventy plus years.

She glanced up and grinned. "Good mornin', sugar. Did you sleep okay?"

Addie laughed. "Don't you mean good afternoon?" She slid into a seat next to her aunt. "I'm sorry I slept in so late."

Janie's warm hand covered her own. "Baby girl, you needed the sleep." She stood up and moved to the kitchen counter. "I saved you a couple of cinnamon rolls. Do you want hot chocolate or milk to go with them?"

"Cold milk sounds wonderful. Thank you."

While her aunt poured the milk, Addie bit into the bun. The warm icing dripped down her fingers. "Mmm. This is so good."

Her aunt chuckled and placed the glass of milk on the table. "I'm glad you like them." Aunt Janie sat back down. "Now, let me tell you about my plans today."

"Okay." Addie licked the icing from her fingers. "But remember I don't want you worrying about me. Honestly, if I get to sleep in, eat cinnamon buns and go exploring today, I will be a happy camper."

A smile lit up Janie's face. "Well, sugar, I think that sounds like the perfect vacation. I'll make sure you get fresh cinnamon buns every day."

Addie took a small bite. "Yes, but by the time I leave I'll have to pay the airline for my extra weight." *And start an exercise program*, she thought cynically.

Her aunt eyed her critically. "You could use some extra weight. You're too skinny as it is."

Addie smiled, but didn't take it too seriously. According to her aunt, anyone without a double chin was too skinny. "So, what are your plans for the day?" Addie asked as she reached for the glass of milk.

"The church my friend Hazel attends is in need of a new sound system. I volunteered to help make pies today. They're being auctioned off, along with other baked goods for a fundraiser later on this evening." Janie glanced at her watch. "And I'm late. I don't expect I'll be home until around seven. You can come with me if you want, or you can just hang around here for the day."

Addie was anxious to explore her aunt's yard. The gorgeous landscape would be fun to photograph, and hopefully there would be a shot good enough for the contest. "I think I'll stick around and play with my camera. Your yard looks so incredible."

"Thank you." Janie studied her for a few seconds. "I feel badly about leaving you all alone. Why don't you let me call Chase to come over and visit with you."

"No way." Addie shook her finger at her aunt. "In all the excitement of arriving last night, I didn't get a chance to scold you for being so sneaky. Your car was not giving you trouble. Chase told me you'd asked him to pick me up a couple days earlier."

A spark of mischief lit Janie's eyes. "I wasn't being sneaky, just clever."

"Ha! All your cleverness was for nothing. I told Chase I'm not into dating right now and we both agreed to be friends."

"Maybe he's just not your type. There are plenty of nice young men I could introduce you to."

"Not interested."

"Addison, stop being so difficult. Our new youth pastor is a very eligible bachelor and I've been telling him all about you."

Addie started to laugh. "If you knew my history with eligible clergy you wouldn't be so eager to introduce me."

"What happened?"

"I'm not telling you, but if you try to set me up with him I'll have to confess how I single handedly trashed a spiritual retreat by making one simple mistake."

Aunt Janie narrowed her eyes. "I see you're just as stubborn as you used to be."

"So I've been told."

"Well, sugar, that is just fine by me." She stood up and kissed Addie on the head. "I'll just call Chase and let him know he can stop by as a friend."

"Aunt Janie!" Addie sat up straight. "Don't you dare call him."

Her aunt slung her purse over her shoulder. "Oh, all right. I won't call him."

"Promise?"

"Cross my heart," Janie said, making an X with her finger over her chest. "You have fun and call me if you need anything. I'll have my cell phone tucked in my apron." She turned to leave but looked back over her shoulder. "By the way, the pulled pork from last night is in the fridge. I made fresh rolls this morning so you can make yourself a sandwich whenever you're hungry."

"Mmm. I can't wait."

Janie grinned. "I'll see you later."

Addie waved good-bye and enjoyed every single bite of her early lunch. The sugar rushed through her blood stream, energizing her to get moving and outdoors. One glance out the window told her it was a beautiful day.

Before she went outside, she quickly jogged up the stairs to fix her hair. Since she had already slept away the morning, Addie didn't want to take the time to straighten her hair. She parted her hair in half and made two thick braids. To avoid looking like she was twelve, she quickly put on a little makeup.

With one last look in the mirror, Addie grabbed her camera case and headed downstairs. The screen door on the back porch creaked as Addie pushed it open and stepped outside. A warm breeze slid over her skin, the fragrant scent of the flower blossoms tickled her nose. The big yard stretched out before her, encompassing nearly two acres. It was incredibly beautiful and she wasn't sure where to start.

She followed a narrow brick pathway that wound through the yard and spied part of the white gazebo in the corner of the yard. As a child, she had dreamed about having her wedding reception in this very gazebo. The weeping willow trees, silhouetted in the background, created a perfect romantic setting. Roses and azaleas surrounded the structure, their vibrant blossoms contrasting against the white paint.

When she saw the purple wisteria cascading from the lattice, she stumbled to a stop. All at once the familiar pang of sadness assaulted her and she felt her eyes burn with emotion. *No!* She was not going to think about Brandon. Not today. There was no way she would wallow in her self-pity any longer. Besides, why ruin perfectly good make-up over her idiotic ex-fiancé?

Addie's gaze returned to the gazebo and, despite her best efforts, she conjured up a vision of herself wearing a white wedding dress, holding a bouquet of flowers picked from her aunt's gardens. Getting married and having children had always been one of her dreams.

But in order to have children, she needed to have a husband. And in order to find a husband, she needed to date. Men. But who?

The image of Chase Nichols and his beautiful green eyes flashed in her mind, bringing a smile to her lips. Just the thought of him caused warmth to spread through her as if the sun had just broken through the clouds.

Yeah, he was cute, but riding home with a guy from the airport did not constitute as dating. Plus, there was the whole he-lives-in-Georgia-and-I-live-in-Idaho obstacle. All this deliberation about dating was giving her a headache. So, in true Scarlet O'Hara fashion, she decided not to think about it right now.

Determined to enjoy her day, she continued forward, past blossoming sweet alyssum, brilliantly colored tulips and purple and yellow pansies that grew in the many flowerbeds placed strategically around the yard.

The gazebo came into full view and Addie stopped, raising the camera to her eye. Branches from one of the weeping willow trees brushed against the white gabled roof of the structure. It was easy to visualize what it would have looked like in another era.

As she captured the image, Addie could envision the grounds swarming with women dressed in rich, colored silk gowns and matching parasols, their billowing hooped skirts swaying as they glided across the expanse, sipping sweet tea. While men, wearing new Confederate uniforms, clustered together, optimistically discussing the war as they prepared to go and fight against the North.

The Caldwell house had never been invaded by the North, but the family had still suffered along with everyone else in the South. Addie remembered her aunt telling her about her husband's family.

With their men off fighting, the fear of an invasion had made the Caldwell women bury all of their valuables for protection. Although they claimed to have unearthed all the buried riches, it was rumored that one of the wooden boxes had never been recovered. Every time she came to visit her aunt, Addie had dreamed of discovering the lost treasure. If only she knew where to look.

A light wind rustled the canopy of leaves above her. The sun created a lacy pattern of shadows on the grass as it penetrated the large trees. Shielding her eyes, Addie gazed up, admiring the way the new leaves shimmered in the light. Wanting to capture the amazing beauty, she found a shaded area on the grass and lay down, angling her lens up at the sky and lost herself in getting just the right shot.

* * *

Chase snapped his helmet on and guided his bicycle out of the garage just as his cell phone started vibrating in his pocket. One look at the caller ID made him wish he'd left his phone inside. It was his secretary which could only mean one thing: Mr. Barclay was looking for him.

"Hey, Shanna. What's up?"

"The boss man is looking for you and naturally he called me."

Chase could hear the irritation in his normally easy-going secretary's voice. "Sorry, do you know what he wants?"

"No. I'm at the mall with my sister. All he said is have Chase call me immediately."

"I really am sorry. I know he has my cell number."

"It's not your fault. For whatever reason I'm the one on his speed dial."

Chase apologized again and ended the call. Wondering what his boss wanted, he scrolled through his contacts. Whit Barclay's number was right below his daughters.

Dating the boss's daughter and then breaking up with her hadn't been the smartest career move. At least Chase had allowed Hayden to make the claim that she'd broken up with him. He supposed—aside from being a talented graphic arts designer—that is why he still had a job.

He pressed Whit's number and waited for the man to answer.

"Chase, thanks for calling me back so quickly." Chase heard voices in the background. He had no doubt Mr. Barclay was on the golf course. "Listen, I'm having a few clients over to the house this evening and want you to be there. Five o'clock for cocktails. Dinner will be at six. Hang on, Son."

Chase could hear him tell someone to hold the phone for him. Then he heard the distinct whack of a golf club hitting a ball. Whit cursed and angrily asked for his phone back. Whatever excuse Chase was going to use to try and get out of this party died on his lips. Mr. Barclay liked winning at everything—especially golf. He would be in no mood for Chase to decline the invitation.

"You still there?" Whit asked in an irritated voice.

"Yes, sir."

"This is a formal event so wear a tux. By the way, you'll be escorting Hayden."

The phone went silent. Mr. Barclay had given his order and hung up.

Chase slipped the phone back in his pocket. *Hayden is back home?* He'd been relieved when she moved to California the year before to pursue an acting career. Hopefully this was just a visit. He wasn't in the mood to play any of her games, and somehow he knew Hayden was behind the invitation.

Feeling aggravated, Chase straddled his bike. Why couldn't Hayden just let go? It's not like she really loved Chase. She just didn't like to lose any more than her father.

He pulled out his phone again to access his music, but before he got a chance his phone chimed an incoming text. If it was work related, he better answer it so Shanna didn't have to track him down again. At least one of them should enjoy their weekend.

There were actually two messages. One from Miss Janie and the other from Lexie. He opened the one from Lexie first.

Hey, my roomies and I are making homemade pizza tonight if you want to stop by for supper. Try to come because I miss you. Love Lexie.

Love? Obviously Lexie hadn't taken him seriously when he'd told her a couple of weeks ago they needed to see other people. Lexi was pretty and sweet and he'd sure liked kissing her, but he wasn't in love with her.

When they'd first started dating, Lexie told him upfront she wasn't looking to get married for a long time. It had been exactly what Chase needed to hear because he wasn't in the market for a wife either.

He wasn't ready to make a commitment to her or any other girl right now. Before he decided to settle down for good, he wanted to see if he could really give his music career a chance. Once he married, he knew he might never have the opportunity again. Drew was increasingly adamant that they cut back on performances because of his growing family. Even Jackson seemed less enthusiastic since he'd married Sydney.

Despite what Lexi told him, after they'd been dating for a little over a month, she'd started dropping hints about them being completely exclusive.

Chase flat out asked her what she'd meant by that and Lexie confessed she'd like to see if they could make their relationship more permanent. She'd even suggested moving in together.

Chase had been shocked. He and Lexie met at a church retreat and the extent of their intimacy had been a few hot make out sessions. Without feeling too guilty, he'd ended the relationship amicably. It looked like he'd been too nice.

Rather than make a less than friendly reply, Chase simply deleted the message. If Lexie persisted in trying to start things up again, he'd have to be more direct.

Next he opened the message from his neighbor and smiled.

Chase, thank you again for picking up Addie. You've always been such a polite, considerate boy, and I knew I could count on you to get my niece to me safely. She's a real sweetheart and I've missed her. I hated leaving her home all alone today. If you get time, maybe you could stop by and say hello. Hugs.

Shaking his head at her not-so-subtle attempt at matchmaking, he keyed in a response, telling her he'd try to stop by. Not wanting to get interrupted again, he hastily accessed his playlist, placed the ear buds in each ear and pocketed the phone. Then he pedaled off before anyone else attempted to get a hold of him.

Although Janie was considered his neighbor, there was still a good half a mile in between their houses. As he approached her driveway, he decided he wasn't in the mood to talk with Addie right now. Maybe after a good long ride he'd feel less stressed.

The first mile, Chase concentrated on the music, especially the guitar solos Brad Paisley was so famous for.

The gifted musician had been Chase's idol for as long as he could remember. While Chase could never claim to be as good as the popular country music artist, he knew he was pretty talented. He was banking on Reggie getting the talent scout to one of his performances so he could prove he had what it took to be successful.

Before he knew it, Chase had come to the mini mart on the outskirts of town. Crossing the road, he brought his bike to a stop and climbed off. He took off his helmet and ran his fingers through his damp hair. He felt better already.

After locking one of the wheels to a bike rack, Chase went inside the gas station and purchased an electrolyte fortified water along with a Georgia chili dog. The weather was too nice to be cooped up inside so he took his purchases and found a spot at an empty picnic table outside.

Chase took a big bite of his chili dog and pulled out his phone. He was hoping to hear back from Reggie today. Since Thursday, Chase had only gotten his voicemail. He'd left several messages with his agent, but hadn't heard anything from the busy man. If he didn't hear something soon, he'd take a trip into Macon to catch Reggie at his office.

There wasn't any new texts but he had one missed call from Hayden. The hotdog lodged in his throat as he debated about listening to the message or just deleting it. Whatever she had to say, Chase was sure he'd hear about it at the party tonight. Unless maybe she was calling to say she wouldn't be able to be there.

He took a long drink of water and finally decided to go ahead and listen to the message. Hayden's sultry voice was familiar and sounded just as seductive as she had the last time they'd talked.

Hey, Chase. You need to call me right away. I promise you won't regret it. Talk to ya later.

Not regret it? When it came to Hayden, Chase had too many regrets to count. He deleted the voicemail and took another bite of his hotdog.

Trying to ignore that part of him that wanted to find out what Hayden wanted, he opened his Facebook app and searched for Addie Heywood. There was only one result and it wasn't the girl he'd met yesterday. He typed in her full name which still only came back with one result that definitely wasn't her. He was surprised. Didn't everyone have a Facebook account? Even his mother had joined the social media site.

He finished his chili dog while scrolling through the newsfeeds. A recent post by Hayden seemed innocuous enough so he clicked on it and read all about her supporting role in a new television drama that would start shooting the pilot in six weeks. Until that time, she was home for an extended visit and wanted to reconnect with old friends.

Yeah, Chase was pretty sure he wasn't going to be one of the many guys who'd be lining up at her house to "reconnect." If he knew Hayden—and he did—the invitation would mean much more than just a friendly little chat to catch up.

An alert sounded that he had a Facebook message. *Fantastic.* It was from Hayden. He wasn't sure he liked that others could see he was currently logged in. Hopefully, Hayden didn't know he'd actually been reading her latest post.

Her message was pretty much the same thing he'd just listened to only she added a little teaser. A teaser Chase couldn't ignore.

Chapter Six

Tossing his trash in the garbage can, Chase walked away from the picnic table and did something he'd vowed to never do again. He called Hayden Barclay.

The phone rang several times before she answered.

"I got your message," he said abruptly.

"Well, hello to you too." Her voice was husky and velvety smooth. At one time he'd found her voice sexy. Now he knew it was all just part of the act.

"Hayden, you've left me two messages to call you back so I'm callin' you back."

Light laughter filled his ear. "Oh my, somebody's in a grumpy mood. Maybe I should tell Daddy to find me another escort tonight."

Chase's fingers gripped the phone tight as he closed his eyes and mentally counted to three. The temptation to tell her to go right ahead and then hang up was too strong. "Hello, Hayden," he said flatly. "I'm returning your phone call."

"That's a little better."

Biting back a reply, Chase ground his teeth together and waited to hear what she had to say. After several seconds, she let out a dramatic big breath. "I can see you're still upset with me."

Upset? Is that really how she remembered their last conversation? "Let's not rehash the past, okay?"

"Good idea."

"Great. Now, what did you need to tell me? Something to do with TJ Music?"

She laughed again. "You're going to have to be a lot nicer than that if you want to hear what I have to say."

Chase couldn't do this. Nothing she had to say—not even if it meant helping him further his music career—was worth this kind of headache. Before he could tell her goodbye, she said, "And Chase, you do want to hear what I have to say."

Pinching the bridge of his nose with his thumb and forefinger, Chase checked his anger. If Hayden had connections to Tate Jepson, this could be his big break. "All right." He dropped his hand and took a deep breath. "I'd like to hear more about your connection with Mr. Jepson and how I can meet him. Please."

Hayden's voice was animated as she told him all about the parties she'd attended since moving to California. The names she dropped were intended to wow him, and, grudgingly, he had to admit he was impressed. It looked like Hayden had finally landed in the Hollywood limelight.

Lucky for him, the weekend long yacht party Hayden had attended just before coming home also had Dana Jepson, Tate Jepson's only daughter, aboard. The two became friends and when Dana mentioned her boyfriend was opening for the country music sensation Phillip Jacob's, Hayden told Dana all about her boyfriend Chase and how he'd be just as good if he could ever get noticed.

The word boyfriend immediately sent an icy chill down Chase's spine and doused his excitement like he'd just jumped into a cold river. "I'm not your boyfriend, Hayden."

"Goodness, Chase. Is that all you heard?"

"No, but you told her I was your boyfriend, like we're still together."

"So, what's the big deal? I would've sounded completely pathetic if I'd told her we'd broken up."

"Fine." Chase decided it wasn't worth arguing the point. "It's not like she's going to ever know we aren't together."

Hayden laughed. "Actually, she's going to be at Daddy's party tonight. If things go well, I know I can get Tate himself to show up at your next gig."

"What do you mean by *go well*?"

"Let's just say I'd like you to play the part of an adoring boyfriend. It shouldn't be too hard since you were so attentive before I left."

The muscles in Chase's chest tightened until he felt like he could hardly breathe. Regardless of how incredible this opportunity might be, nothing could be worth getting involved with Hayden again. The power she held over him was like some kind of fatal attraction. No matter how many times she betrayed him, somehow she always could lure him back. Not this time.

"Hayden, I've already got a girlfriend." The words just slipped out before he had time to think about it.

"Oh please, I know you and Lexie broke up weeks ago."

Chase glared at the phone. What? Did she find it so hard to believe he had another girlfriend? His male ego—along with self-preservation—made him blurt out, "That's true but it's because I've met someone else. Actually, I've known her since I was fourteen. We liked each other then, but we were both too young." He winced at the mild deception. At least the part about them both being too young was true. "She's recently returned to Georgia, and when we reconnected it was like things just clicked."

There were several seconds of silence. Well, other than the annoyed heavy breathing coming through the speaker. Finally, Hayden snorted a laugh. "You're making this up. What's her name?"

Chase didn't even hesitate. "Addie. Addie Heywood."

For a few heartbeats, more irritated breathing filled the silence. "If she loves you, she won't mind you pretending for one night I'm your girlfriend. If Dana finds out I wasn't telling her the truth, she'll have a heyday telling everyone."

"If she's a friend, she'll understand."

"We're not actually friends, Chase. She's my competition, and she thinks my boyfriend can sing better than hers."

"Tell her we broke up."

"No. That's humiliating."

Chase rolled his eyes. Hayden must have been up to her old tricks, spinning one story after another. "You said one night, which means we'll be breaking up as soon as the party's over so what does it matter?"

"It just does." Hayden sniffed and Chase wondered if she was crying or just *acting* like she was crying. "Dana won't be the only one in the business at the party tonight," Hayden continued. "There are gonna be a few cast members from my new show, as well as the producer, and Daddy wants to see if Barclay Industries can get some new clients. He won't be happy about his little girl being made a liar."

If Daddy knew how deviant his *little girl* was, lying would be the least of his worries. "Look, I'm in a relationship with a girl I don't want to hurt. Pretending we're back together isn't going to go over very well."

"One night," Hayden said tightly. Now she sounded ticked off. "I'll break up with you and we'll never have to speak again."

"What about your dad? I'm not sure he's going to be too happy to find out we're suddenly back together and then we break up again."

"Well, actually, I've been telling Mama and Daddy that we've been secretly seeing each other for a few weeks."

"What?!" Chase exploded. Why would Hayden lie about that? Didn't she have enough men in California? He barley refrained from swearing at her and hurling the phone across the grass. "Why would you tell them something like that?"

"I didn't tell them on purpose. A couple of weeks ago Mama had come out to see me for the weekend. This guy I'd dated a few times didn't take our break up very well. While Mama was in the ladies room, he came over and begged me to take him back. I told him no and that I'd gotten back together with my old boyfriend. Mama overheard me."

"Hayden, this is ridiculous. I'm not doing it."

"I thought you were smarter than that. It's not a big deal, and this could be your ticket to Nashville. Think about it, Tate Jepson could show up at your next gig." She sniffed. "Daddy doesn't like it when I'm unhappy. I'd hate to have you end up without a job or any references."

Chase wanted to bang his head up against a brick wall. He knew better than to talk to Hayden, yet the lure of a chance at achieving his dream in music had made him stupid and greedy. "If we go through with this charade and then you break up with me, how do I know Tate will even show up?"

"Because, before you leave tonight, I'll make sure Dana calls her father and he sets something up with your agent."

This was crazy. Even crazier, Chase needed to convince Addie to be his girlfriend. At least until they could come up with a reason to break up too.

"Fine. One night."

"I know I'm the actress, but you'd better hope you're acting is convincing. I have a reputation, you know."

Yeah, he knew all about her reputation. "Whatever. I'll see you in a few hours."

Chase ended the call before she made another request. He stalked over to his bike and unlocked it, then he snapped on his helmet. As he took off for the Caldwell house, he hoped Addie Heywood was as nice as she seemed yesterday and would agree to help him out.

The ride back seemed to take forever, but finally he cycled down the long driveway. Parking his bike next to the porch, he took off his helmet, and grabbed his water bottle, draining the final few ounces.

Wondering how this would all play out, he slowly climbed the steps. He had no idea how to broach the subject with Addie. The whole scheme sounded insane, and he had no idea if he had the courage to actually go through with it.

Crossing the porch, Chase rapped his knuckles loudly against the door. He leaned his shoulder against the house and waited for Addie to come to the door. An underlying tension tightened his stomach as the seconds ticked by.

He waited a little longer before pressing his finger on the doorbell. He listened to the chime but didn't hear any movement from inside. There was a chance she hadn't heard the knocking or the doorbell.

Pulling his phone out of his pocket, he considered sending her a text, letting her know he was here for a visit. He slid his finger across the screen to unlock the screen, and noticed he had a new message from Miss Janie. Maybe she was going to tell him Addie wasn't here after all.

Chase, in case Addie doesn't answer the door, try checking out back. She said something about exploring the yard today.

Either Janie was clairvoyant or providence was on Chase's side. Pocketing his phone, he made his way around the house and ducked through the lattice archway to the back yard. His mother would love to have a yard like this, but they didn't have as much property as the Caldwell's and most of their land was for his sisters' horses.

Following the brick pathway, Chase squinted against the sun and slowly scanned the lawn. He spotted Addie lying on her stomach with a camera pointed up at the trees. *What is she doing?*

Uncertain of what she was taking a picture of, Chase quietly drew a little closer. He tipped his head back to see what her target was. Leaves fluttered in the soft wind but he couldn't see anything else she might want to capture.

After she took several shots, she angled the camera to the right and stared through the lens. Chase continued to watch her, knowing she was completely oblivious to his presence. There was a good chance she would swing the lens around and catch him staring at her. Not quite sure how to let her know he was there, he finally just cleared his throat and said, "Hey."

Addie emitted a startled scream and sat upright. "Oh, my heck." She flattened her palm against her chest. "You scared me to death."

"Sorry," Chase said with a chuckle. "Didn't mean to scare ya."

Addie narrowed her eyes. "Uh-huh."

He hoped she wasn't really mad at him. "I guess I should've made a little more noise."

"Uh-huh," she said again as a teasing smile slipped across her face.

Man, she was cute. Braids and all. "What're you doing, anyway?" he asked, taking a seat next to her on the grass.

"Just messing around with different lighting and angles."

"You must be pretty good. I don't believe I've ever considered takin' a picture from that angle," he teased.

"Well," she said, nudging him in the shoulder, "if you decide to try it, just make sure nobody sneaks up on you."

He laughed. "Duly noted."

"So, uh, what brings you over here?"

"I rode my bike over to say hey."

Her lips slanted upward. "Well, you did say *hey*." Then a look of concern flashed across her face. "Did my aunt call you to come over here?"

"No. She just texted me to say you were home alone. I was out riding my bike and decided to stop by to see you." *Oh, and I need you to be my pretend girlfriend.* Even in his head it sounded crazy. She would probably slap him and run for the house.

"I can't believe her. She better not send anymore unsuspecting men over here. She mentioned she had other guys she'd like me to meet, including some bachelor youth pastor."

"Pastor Dave?"

"She didn't give me any names."

"Hmm, he is single and my little sisters think he's hot."

Addie gave him an exaggerated eye roll. "I do not want to spend my entire vacation dodging my aunt's matchmaking schemes."

And there was the opening he'd been looking for. "So, what if I came up with a plan that would keep Miss Janie off your case?"

"I'd say sign me up. What's your idea?

Chapter Seven

Nervous energy buzzed through Chase, making his mouth a little dry. He wished he had a bottle of water, or at least some gum. "Just hear me out before you say no."

"*Okaaayyy.*" She drew out the word as a wariness flickered in her eyes.

Chase did his best to explain about Hayden, their previous rocky relationship which hadn't ended very friendly, and how Hayden's father was his overbearing boss who'd ordered him to be his daughter's escort at the party tonight.

Addie seemed to understand or at least appeared to be compassionate to his plight, especially when he told her about Hayden's demands.

"So, let me get this straight, she's threatened to tell Daddy to fire you if you don't act the part of the doting boyfriend?"

Chase almost told her about the other part of the deal that might get him an audience with Tate Jepson, but decided to keep that part to himself.

"Yeah, but I was stupid and told her I had a girlfriend and I wouldn't do it."

"You have a girlfriend?"

"No, but I panicked and said I do." Chase looked up and gave Addie a half smile. "I kind of told her you were my girlfriend."

"Oh."

"So," Chase said, deciding to hurry up and make the deal before she took off running. "I was thinking that if you and I pretended to be dating then I can avoid Hayden and you can avoid being set up with all the guys Janie has in mind."

Addie didn't say anything for several heartbeats. Chase finally dared to look her in the eyes and was surprised to see her smiling at him. "Hmm, so tonight you'll have to pretend to be Hayden's boyfriend while pretending to be my boyfriend?"

Heat crept up his neck. When she put it that way it sounded so ridiculous. "You know what. Just forget it. I'll man up and let the consequences fall where they may."

"Hold on, there. Let's not make any rash decisions." She nudged him in the shoulder. "We both know Aunt Janie isn't going to back off until I go out on at least one date whether it's with you or Pastor Daniel."

"Dave."

"Whatever. The point is she won't stop trying to set me up. She even mentioned another guy I might like to meet that works at the assisted living place her friend Hazel lives in. So, since you and I are friends, and if you really don't mind faking our undying love for each other, let's go for it. It will make both of our lives much easier."

He studied her for a few seconds. It wasn't going to be hard pretending to be into her. "Are you sure?"

"Positive." She stuck out her hand and Chase felt some of the tension leave his shoulders.

He placed his hand in hers, and the second their palms met he could feel heat travel the length of his arm. "Thank you for doing this."

Her eyes flickered down at their clasped hands and Chase realized the tricky part about pretending to fall for Addie would be to not let it really happen.

"No, thank you," she said, pulling her hand back to her lap. "I can't tell you how relieved I am."

"Do you think Miss Janie will be too disappointed when we decide to only be friends at the end of your stay?"

"Maybe, but she'll get over it." Addie lifted one shoulder. "Besides, she couldn't possibly expect anything more to happen in two weeks."

Her words eased Chase's conscience. "Okay, should we plan our first date?"

"Sure, what do you want to do?"

"Do you like to ride?" Chase asked

She tilted her head to the side. "Ride as in a bike or a horse?"

"Both, really."

"Bicycles. Yes." Her eyebrows drew together and she shook her head. "But I'm not very fond of horses."

"That's too bad," Chase said, hoping he might be able to persuade her later on. "There are some really beautiful places to go horseback riding."

Addie shivered and shook her head. "I'll have to take your word for it. Unless it's attached to a merry-go-round, I try to avoid horses. Bad experience as a child."

"What happened with horses?"

"Something I don't ever care to repeat."

"Now you have to tell me the story."

Addie glanced his way and squinted. "Fine, if you insist."

"No." Chase shrugged. "But I'm very intrigued."

Her face relaxed and she gave him a sweet smile.

"Okay, so my sister took me and my nephew to a place near my dad's house. It's a small farm that gives children the opportunity to get to know and ride horses. Since I was older I got to go first. My nephew was mad he had to wait and pulled a fit, startling the horse. It took off with me barely hanging on and then bucked me off."

Ouch. No wonder she was scared. "Were you hurt?"

"Yeah, I broke my wrist in two places. My sister loves riding and still feels bad about my fear of horses." She held out her left arm and pointed to a scar. "They had to surgically repair my wrist."

Chase scooted a little closer, taking a hold of her wrist. "I'm sorry," he said, lightly running his finger over the thin scars. Touching her soft skin did crazy things to his insides.

He heard her take a quick breath. "I'm okay now."

Raising his eyes, he met her gaze. "But still not gonna get back on a horse?"

A small smile surfaced as she shook her head and withdrew her arm from his grasp. "Nope. My sister wanted me to try again, but my dad said the old adage, 'If you fall off the horse, get right back on,' didn't apply to me."

He grinned and tried to figure out her family dynamics. How could her sister be married and have children that weren't that much younger than Addie? "Can I ask you something personal?"

She narrowed her eyes slightly. "You can ask. I might not answer, though."

He chuckled at her honesty. "Well, your sister is obviously much older than you…" He didn't really know how else to ask his question, but Addie understood what he was curious about.

"We're fifteen years apart. My mom didn't think she could have any more children." She held up her hands. "At fifty-three she got a surprise. Me."

"That's awesome. Do you live near your parents?"

The smile faded from her face and, too late, Chase remembered her mother had passed away. *Smooth, Nichols.*

"No. My mom died when I was eleven. Since Chellie was married, it's just been me and my dad." He saw her lips quiver slightly before she forced them up into a smile. "We're close and I feel blessed to be able to spend so much time with him. On top of that, I've been able to save money."

"You're lucky. I still live at home, but my parents make me pay rent. It's kind of a hint I should be living on my own by now."

Addie smiled. "My dad said he'd pay me to keep living with him. I feel bad about leaving him alone for so long, but he says he's too old to travel."

"That's too bad. I'll bet he misses having someone to cook for him."

Her grin deepened, carving the dimple in her cheek. "Actually, he does all the cooking. He's almost as good as Aunt Janie."

"Nice," Chase said with a laugh.

His phone beeped, alerting him to a new text message. He pulled his phone out of his pocket and nearly groaned out loud. "I better get home so I can be ready. Apparently my boss is sending a car over to get me and I can't be late."

"Wow, you get to ride in a limo. What a nice guy."

"Right, it's probably so I can't escape and leave early."

She laughed and Chase stood up and held out his hand to assist her. She hesitated for a second before placing her palm against his.

The same feelings of awareness rushed through him and he guessed by the guarded look on her face, Addie must be feeling it too.

Slowly, he let go of her hand. "Will I see you at church tomorrow?"

"Yes. We should be there."

"I'll talk to you after the service and we can plan our first date."

"Okay. Have fun tonight."

Chase cast her an annoyed look.

She grinned. "Well, as your new girlfriend. Not too much fun."

"That's better." He took a step backward. "Thanks again."

"Don't thank me yet. For all you know I could be a very demanding girlfriend."

"And I just might be a very attentive boyfriend." He winked. "We might be good together."

She shook her head and laughed softly, her eyes never leaving his. Chase took another step backward, waved and then turned and walked away. He had a feeling the next two weeks were going to be fun, and he intended to play his part very well.

* * *

Addie stood at the kitchen counter, rolling out her pie crust. She kept messing up by making it too thin in spots. She blew out a breath of frustration. Getting the dough smooth and round was hard work. Hopefully it would look better after it baked.

Aunt Janie had come home just before seven. She'd brought home some extra pie filling, and wanted to know if Addie was interested in making a pie.

It was pie. Of course she was interested.

Besides, she would just do about anything to get Chase out of her head. She squeezed her eyes closed and remembered the feel of his fingertips sliding softly across the scar on her wrist, leaving a trail of heat along her skin. Even now, the memory made her breath hitch.

A tiny hole appeared in the center of the pie crust. Unhappy with how it looked, she put the rolling pin to the side and pinched the dough together. "So, Chase stopped by to see me today," she said, smoothing the dough with her fingers.

"He did?" Janie sounded innocently surprised. "Did y'all have fun?"

Addie wanted to scold her aunt for forcing Chase on her, but decided she better proceed with the agreement she and Chase had come to earlier. "Actually, it was a lot of fun."

"Really?" Aunt Janie practically squealed. "I'm so pleased."

Her aunt's enthusiasm was the perfect catalyst to go through with Operation Fake Boyfriend. "He's really nice, and so cute." This part of the plan was easy because it was all true. "He said something about talking to me after church tomorrow. I think he might ask me out."

"Oh, how exciting!" Aunt Janie rounded the counter and clapped her hands. "What are you going to wear tomorrow?"

Addie failed to hide her smile which only made everything look completely legit in Aunt Janie's eyes. "I don't know but something pretty." This was actually kind of fun.

"Once the pies are in, let's go and look through your things." Janie reached out and snagged one of Addie's hands. "Your nails are in serious need of a manicure. Since we don't have time to go into Macon, I'll give you a mani-pedi after your bath this evening."

"I don't want to try too hard. He'll think I'm desperate." She rolled up the pie crust and put it over the fruit. It looked more like a five year old had made the pie but hopefully it would still taste okay.

"Nonsense," Janie said, pinching off some excess dough. "Men in the south like pretty, demure women."

"Who said anything about me ever being demure?"

Janie laughed. "I just thought I'd throw that in there." She winked at her. "Besides, if you want to woo Chase Nichols, food would be a good way to do it. That boy just *loves* my buns."

"Aunt Janie!"

Her aunt put a hand over her mouth, trying to suppress a giggle. "I think that came out wrong. I meant cinnamon buns."

Addie put her hands on her hips. "Demure, indeed." She picked up her finished pie and placed it on the baking sheet next to her aunt's perfect cherry pie. "Mine doesn't look very good."

Aunt Janie patted Addie on the back. "Well, sugar, it's what's inside that counts, anyway."

With the pies in the oven, they went upstairs and looked through the few dresses Addie brought. They settled on a pretty, off-white, lacey dress that came just above Addie's knees, along with a pair of four inch apricot colored pumps.

Aunt Janie was a regular customer of a charming store that sold jewelry in every color imaginable along with matching colored purses.

She had quite a collection of necklaces to choose from, and Addie picked out a beautiful cluster necklace with multi-teal colored stones, accented with gold.

She felt pretty. Sexy, even, but not—thank goodness—demure.

Later that evening while they were watching a re-run of *Downton Abbey*, Aunt Janie painted a pale peach color to Addie's freshly manicured nails. On the end table next to where Addie sat was an old photograph of her great-great-great grandparents. They were standing on the porch of the home her father and aunt had been raised in, which was no longer in the Heywood family. She looked around the room, wondering why there weren't any old photographs of the Caldwell house. There was a more recent picture of the house in the entry way, but nothing in the eighteen hundreds.

"Aunt Janie, do you know if there are any old pictures of your house, like maybe around the Civil War?"

Her aunt stopped and gave her a curious look. "Hmm. I do believe there might be a few pictures in the attic. Why?"

"I'd like to see what the house looked like back then." She shrugged. "And I love studying old photography."

"You're welcome to look, sugar."

"Maybe sometime this week we can look in the attic together?" Addie made the suggestion mainly because she didn't want to go up in the attic all by herself. She hated spiders.

"Sorry, honey. I haven't been up there for a few years." Aunt Janie started on another nail. "And if I did go up, you'd have to call the fire department to get me down."

Darn. She was going to have to go up there all by herself. "Okay, but I think I'll wait until it's light outside."

"Maybe you could ask Chase to help you look around."

Despite the plan to become his pseudo-girlfriend, every time her aunt mentioned his name, Addie's heart seemed to take off. "I don't want to bother him."

"Oh hush. He'd love to help you, not to mention he'd get to spend more time getting to know you."

Oh, boy. Aunt Janie was really getting excited about a relationship that was doomed to go nowhere. Addie probably needed to put a damper on her aunt's excitement. "Aunt Janie, I'm not looking for a long-term boyfriend."

"I know." Her aunt grinned. "Besides, Chase is more husband material than a boyfriend."

Oh, well, that makes all the difference.

"Please don't tell me you've told him that."

Her aunt clucked her tongue. "I declare, of course I wouldn't. A lady would never throw herself at a man."

"Then what would you call texting him to come over and see me?"

Janie bit her lip and looked up. "Who told you that?"

"Chase mentioned it." ·

"I kept my promise and didn't call." Janie winked again. "You never said anything about not texting."

Addie rolled her eyes. "Well, from here on out let Chase and me make our own plans. No more meddling."

"If y'all are making plans then my work is done."

Oh, they had plans all right. And after tonight's conversation, and seeing how determined Aunt Janie was to make a match for Addie, she was more than ready to participate in the little scheme Chase had come up with.

Commence Operation Fake Boyfriend right now.

Chapter Eight

Chase entered the living room as he finished knotting his tie. "Morning, Mama."

"Good morning." His mom's eyes softened as she slipped on a white sweater. "You look handsome this morning."

"Thanks." He kissed her on the cheek. "You look beautiful, as usual."

Her lips parted into a smile and tiny laugh lines crinkled around the same green eyes he'd inherited. "Thank you." She picked up her purse and moved to the front door. "I wish your sisters would hurry up." She glanced up the staircase. "I'm going out to the car. If they're not down here in two minutes, they're missing breakfast and can catch a ride with you to church."

Chase grimaced. The last thing he wanted to do was get stuck with them. He opened the door for his mother. "I'll make sure that doesn't happen."

"By the way, I spoke to Janie this morning and invited her and her niece over for supper. You're gonna be home, right?"

"Yes, ma'am." A smile accompanied his reply. "I wouldn't dream of missing it."

"That's what I thought." She winked and stepped outside.

As the door closed, his two seventeen year old sisters rushed down the stairs. They weren't identical twins, but so close it was sometimes hard to tell them apart.

Taylin was about an inch taller than Ashlee. Both were blonde and beautiful. And did he mention vain?

"So," Taylin said, striking a pose. "What do you think?"

She was way too cute for his comfort. Chase knew her boyfriend, Ryan, was home for the weekend from college and that the guy would like what he saw. "Nice," Chase said reluctantly.

"Nice?" Taylin's eyes narrowed. "I know I look better than nice."

She did and it made him wish she were still ten-years-old.

"Like what you think matters," Ashlee said with a dramatic eye roll. "Ryan will think she looks hot and that's all that counts."

Chase eyed Ashlee's clothing. As usual, her skirt was just a little shorter and her shirt a little tighter. She had a few more curves than Taylin and she liked to show them off. "Both of you need a sweater. It's chilly outside."

Taylin laughed and quickly checked the weather on her phone. "Nice try, bro but it's going to be in the seventies today."

She started for the door, but Ashlee lagged behind. "You're helping out with the worship music today?"

"Yeah, Jacks and I are doing a few numbers."

Ashlee twirled a strand of her long hair. "Is Beau gonna be there?"

"Nope, he's in Florida visiting his mom for the weekend."

"Oh." She chewed on her bottom lip. "If I promise to be good can I come to your gig next Saturday?"

His little sister was madly in love with Beau Jacobsen, one of Chase's best friends and the drummer for their band.

No matter how many times both he and Beau discouraged her, she wasn't letting go.

"Sorry, Ash. The answer's no."

She stomped her foot. "Why?"

"First of all, you're not old enough to get into *Gracie's Haven*. Second, Beau is too old for you, and third, Beau has a girlfriend."

"In a few years our age difference won't matter. His girlfriend's a flake, and you and I both know I could pass for twenty-one. I won't be drinking so they'd never have to card me if I came in with Sydney."

"Still not gonna happen."

"Please? Pretty, pretty please?"

Before she could pester him further, the door swung open and their father, Charles, stuck his head in the door. "Come on, baby girl. Your mama is fixin' to leave without ya."

"I'm not done bugging you," Ashlee whispered to Chase as she headed out the door.

"I'm not changing my mind."

"We'll see about that." She flashed him an annoying smile and then proceeded to sweet talk their father into allowing her to see Chase's upcoming performance as long as she was with Sydney.

"I'll have to think about it," Charles said opening the back door. "Now get in the car or we're gonna miss seeing your brother today."

Before climbing into the backseat, Ashlee turned triumphantly to look at Chase, put her fingers to her mouth and blew him a kiss.

"Brat," he muttered, making Ashlee's smile widen. Chase knew his parents and they'd never allow Ashlee to go.

Still, it bothered him how manipulative Ashlee was. One day it was gonna land her in trouble. Worse, it reminded him of Hayden's behavior.

A hot ball of anger lodged in his gut when he thought about last night's party. Hayden hadn't come through on any of her promises. Tate Jepson's daughter had failed to show up at the party, and Hayden had clung to Chase tighter than the revealing dress she'd worn.

The whole night had been a disaster, at least for him. Hayden hadn't done anything to dispel the notion they weren't really back together, and had ignored Chase's reminders that he had a girlfriend.

On the bright side, at least Hayden's parents had been too busy schmoozing the Hollywood producer and his wife to pay any attention to Chase's obvious displeasure at being forced to spend the evening with Hayden.

Whit was very pleased with himself and wasn't bothered when Chase called it an early night and left in the same limo that had picked him up long before the party ended.

Hayden was furious. She'd promised to follow through on her threat to get Chase fired if he didn't stay longer. At that point, Chase hadn't cared what she did or said, and told her so. It only made her angrier.

Pushing thoughts of his ex-girlfriend out of his mind, Chase grabbed his guitar case and headed out the door. He was meeting Jackson at the church before services started to go over the songs with the other musicians slated to help with the worship music today. It would be nice if their band *Chasing Dreams* could do the whole thing but with Beau out of town and Drew staying home to help his very pregnant wife with the kids, the other band would have to do.

The drive to the church wasn't long. With his window down, and the beautiful weather, he was able to ease some of the tension in his shoulders. The one thing that was still stressing him out a little was the deal he'd made with Addie Heywood.

Now that he'd decided to blow Hayden off, he didn't need Addie as a girlfriend. She still needed him, and he was happy to help her out, but what scared him was how appealing he found the idea of being Addie's boyfriend to be.

* * *

Addie stepped out of the car, her stomach a ball of nerves. No matter what she told herself, she still kept thinking about Chase with his messy hair and irresistible green eyes.

As she crossed the parking lot, a light breeze blew a strand of hair across her face and stuck to her lip gloss. She pulled the hair free and hoped she had remembered to bring the tinted gloss with her so she could reapply it if necessary. She had spent a long time on her makeup and hair this morning. Longer than a real girlfriend would take, let alone a bogus one.

The effort had been worth it because, even though it was vain to admit, she looked good. She smoothed a hand down the skirt of her lacy dress, feeling feminine and pretty. Her apricot colored heels clacked against the sidewalk as she and Aunt Janie approached the church doors. Before they could go inside, a striking brunette and a good-looking, dark-haired male stopped to say hello.

"Hey, Miss Janie. Is this your long lost niece?" the guy asked. He had a goatee and dark brown eyes, making him look like a cross between Brad Paisley and Tim McGraw. The messy hair looked just as good on him.

Why can't women get away with that look? Getting ready would be *so* much easier.

"Sure is." Her aunt turned to Addie. "Honey, this is Jackson McCall and his lovely bride, Sydney."

Jackson? This had to be Chase's best friend.

"Hi." Addie held out her hand.

He took her hand and shook it firmly, a glint of mischief sparkled in his brown eyes. "Hello, Addie."

What was it with these southern boys? They were all prettier than most girls Addie knew back home.

Sydney placed her hand on Addie's arm and smiled. "It's nice to meet you. Chase mentioned he picked you up for Miss Janie."

Okay, so Sydney is probably prettier than her husband.

Jackson started to laugh. "Yeah, he did." He put his arm around his wife, still chuckling. "Wish we could've been there."

Addie wondered what Jackson found so amusing. She considered asking him, but changed her mind when the speakers crackled through the open door, and a deep southern voice welcomed everyone to church, encouraging them to take a seat.

"Oh man, I've gotta get in there," Jackson said. He kissed his wife on the mouth and then hurried inside the church.

"I'm guessing your husband is participating in the music today?" Aunt Janie asked.

Sydney looked longingly toward the doors where Jackson had just disappeared inside. "Yeah, I love it when they get to play here. It's a much sweeter environment to be in."

The music started, surprising Addie. Back home the only music was the choir made up from their little community. Here it was a live band.

"Oh my, we're late," Aunt Janie said, stating the obvious.

Oh good. Next to having a root canal, making a late entrance was Addie's favorite thing to do. Naturally, Sydney wouldn't have a problem going in late. She was probably used to having people's eyes follow her all around.

"Would y'all like to sit with me?" Sydney questioned, moving quickly toward the door. "I've got some seats saved."

Aunt Janie grabbed onto Addie's hand. "We'd love to."

They rushed inside and followed Sydney toward the front. Sydney slid onto an already occupied pew, and Addie took a seat beside her with Aunt Janie sitting on the end. Sydney reached over and hugged the pretty woman she sat next to.

"Thanks for saving me a seat."

"Sure thing, honey. I hear you had car problems this morning."

"Yeah, Jackson came home and got me but we made it back just in time."

Addie loved listening to the two women talk with their soft southern drawls. She was curious who the family was that had saved a seat for Sydney. With all their fair hair they didn't look related.

"That's Chase's family," Aunt Janie whispered as the pastor greeted the congregation. "I'll introduce you to them after services."

Addie discreetly took a look at the Nichols family. Chase's mother was slim, her skin virtually free of wrinkles. She didn't look like she could possibly have grandchildren. The man next to her had to be Chase's father since the two resembled one another closely. Beside him had to be the twins. With their long, blonde hair they looked like angels—mischievous ones judging by the way they flirted with the cute guy sitting next to them.

It suddenly occurred to her that if Jackson took part with the music today, Chase might do the same thing. She didn't have time to ask Sydney or her aunt as the congregation quieted and the lights dimmed with a spot light shining on a grand piano. Addie recognized Jackson McCall behind the keys, and listened as he began playing one of her favorite Tim McGraw Christian songs.

After the long piano intro, soft lights shone on each one of the other band members. Chase stood in the middle, holding a guitar. He looked pretty good just standing there in his button up shirt and tie. Addie forced herself not to sigh out loud when he started to sing.

She had no idea he was this talented. His clear tenor voice had a raspy, rocker tone to it. Goose bumps prickled her skin and her tummy tightened with awareness. At the chorus, he added his guitar to blend in with the other instruments. The cuffs of his shirt were rolled up and she could see the muscles in his forearms flex each time he strummed the guitar. Oh, how she wished she had her camera with her.

She'd love to capture the image of Chase singing and playing his guitar. He was incredible and Addie might have fallen a tiny bit in love with her pretend boyfriend.

The music was powerful and Addie was as spellbound as the rest of the audience. When the song came to an end, there was a stillness, a reverence that only faith filled music can bring. The pastor gave his message, but Addie couldn't concentrate on what he said. Her eyes were focused on the lead singer up on the stage. Even when the handsome youth pastor made a few comments, Addie barely noticed the guy.

Chase sang another number she wasn't familiar with but the last song was a popular song that had crossed genres to mainstream radio. Addie was mesmerized by both the lyrics and the musician. She was so tangled up in emotion that when it ended she felt like she couldn't breathe.

Aunt Janie reached over and clasped Addie's hand. "You okay, sugar?" she whispered.

Addie swallowed and nodded her head. "That was beautiful."

Her aunt gave her hand a gentle squeeze as the meeting closed and the congregation buzzed to life. Sydney patted Addie on the back and excused herself, making her way up on stage to greet her husband. Addie watched and was a little envious at the couple's obvious love for each other, if the lengthy kiss Jackson gave his wife was any indication.

Trying to look for Chase, but trying not to appear to be looking for Chase, Addie caught a glimpse of him before he was swallowed up by a crowd of girls. She stifled the niggling feeling of jealousy. He wasn't hers. She needed to remember that.

Aunt Janie prodded Addie out of her seat and introduced her to Chase's family. "Addie this is Amanda and Charles Nichols, Chase's parents."

"Hello," Addie said shaking Mr. Nichols' hand. "It's nice to meet you both."

"Thank you," Mrs. Nichols said, taking Addie's hand next. Rather than shake it, she clasped it between her hands and smiled. "Chase told us all about you."

He did? Addie was dying to know what he'd said. Amanda released her hand and glanced behind her. "I'm sorry I can't introduce you to our girls. They're already off socializing." She faced Addie again. "You can meet them when y'all come to supper this evening. Is that still all right, Janie?"

"We're planning on it." Janie placed a hand on Addie's shoulder. "Addie made a delicious apple pie we can bring for dessert."

What? Her pie had looked worse this morning. And when had these eating arrangements been made?

"Wonderful." Amanda winked. "Chase loves apple pie."

"So do I," Charles said, sounding very much like Chase. He patted a fairly flat stomach. "As you can probably tell."

Chase's parents said their goodbyes and exited the row of pews. Addie really liked them, and they seemed very friendly towards her. Unlike the first time she'd met Brandon's parents who both had made it very clear Addie wasn't good enough for their son. It hurt to know they'd probably been thrilled when Brandon had dumped Addie.

Aunt Janie tugged on Addie's hand and introduced her to other friendly members of the congregation. While she smiled and said hello, Addie continued to surreptitiously look for Chase. He was probably still encased by the throng of girls on the stage.

Slowly, Addie and her aunt made it out of the pew and into the aisle, giving Addie a perfect view of Chase up on stage. Sure enough, a whole gaggle of pretty girls were talking with him. He looked like he was having a great time and not at all concerned about his would-be girlfriend watching.

"Addison," her aunt said, tapping her on the arm. "Stop scowling and go on up there to say hello."

"I'm not scowling." At least she hoped she wasn't. "And I'm not going up on the stage." *Chase can do the chasing, thank you very much.*

"Oh, stop it now and go on up there."

Suddenly, Addie didn't feel like playing this game. Chase said he would come and find her, but he wasn't in any kind of hurry. "Would you mind if we just went home? I don't feel all that well and I think I need to eat something." Preferably something loaded with sugar.

Aunt Janie's eyebrows drew together. "Sure, honey. I had wanted to introduce you to Pastor Dave but I guess it can wait until next week."

Addie caught sight of the youth minister. He was kind of cute, and had just as many girls surrounding him as Chase did. Neither man needed Aunt Janie to set them up with her jilted niece.

"How about we just stop by and say hello to him on the way out?" Janie said, nudging Addie toward him.

"That's fine."

Addie just wanted to escape. Her head hurt and she was seriously doubting her decision to date a handsome, popular guy like Chase. Sure, they were only going to pretend to date, but it would still involve actual dating. She glanced back up at the stage. Unless he'd changed his mind.

She should just grow a backbone and tell her aunt she wasn't going out with any guy, no matter how persistent she was.

Aunt Janie politely wiggled in between the group of girls talking with the youth minister. She dragged Addie next to her. "Pastor Dave, I'd like you to meet my lovely niece, Addison Heywood."

The pastor had the bluest eyes, emphasized even more so by his tanned skin. He flashed a white-toothed smile as he took Addie's hand. "Hello, Addison. It's nice to finally meet you. Your aunt has told me all about you."

I seriously doubt it. "I'm not sure if that's a good thing or not."

"It was all good, trust me." He held onto her hand for a few seconds before slowly releasing it. "How did you like today's services?"

Shoot, she should've paid better attention. "I loved it. The music was amazing. I mean, wow—so incredible."

"The music is pretty fantastic."

"Not that your message wasn't good because it was, um…very inspiring." *Please don't ask me specifics. Please.*

His lips twitched. "Thank you. Making an announcement about our upcoming retreat can sometimes come across as boring."

Oh. He'd made an announcement, not given a sermon.

"Nope. Not boring." Addie could feel her cheeks reddening. "I'm sure you'll have a great turnout."

"Especially if there's good music, right?"

Was that a trick question? Had he mentioned the band would be playing? "I really enjoy music."

The skin around Pastor Dave's eyes crinkled and he chuckled lightly. Yeah, the guy was definitely a hottie.

Speaking of being hot, Addie was feeling way too flushed. She really needed to go home, or at least outside for a breath of fresh air. Glancing around, she realized Aunt Janie had abandoned her. Licking her lips, she brought her gaze back to the minster's amazing blue eyes. "Well, it was nice meeting you, Pastor Dave."

"Please call me Dave."

"Okay, it was nice meeting you, Dave." Addie took a step backward. "I better go find my aunt. I'll see you later." She made a slight turn and hurried toward the exit only to slam into someone standing in the aisle.

She squealed. Yes, squealed and fell backward. Except she didn't fall. The person she'd hit grabbed her around the waist and pulled her close so her face pressed against their chest. She sucked in a lungful of air and knew immediately it was a man who had just caught her. And boy did he smell good.

Chapter Nine

Tipping her head back, Addie stared into Chase's light green eyes. "Hey, there," he drawled.

"Hey," Addie said, feeling a little dazed and breathless. What was it about this guy that rattled her so much? "Sorry about nearly running you over."

His fingers tightened around her waist and the smile he gave her doubled her already racing heart. "I'm glad. As fast as you were leaving, I would've had a hard time catching you."

Did he want to catch her? Frankly, she wondered how he'd managed to get away from his adoring fans in the first place.

"Addison," Pastor Dave said, coming up beside them. "You dropped this." He held out Addie's sparkly iPhone.

Realizing she was still in Chase's arms, she stepped back and took the phone. "Thank you."

"You're welcome."

The minister looked at Chase and an amused expression crossed his features. Addie followed his gaze and noticed Chase did not look particularly happy. "Chase, you did a wonderful job with the music today. It was very inspiring," Dave said.

"Thank you, sir." Chase's words were clipped and formal. He addressed the pastor like he was much older than him when in reality the two men had to be close to the same age.

"I know Addison enjoyed it as well," Dave said.

"I'm happy she liked it."

Um, hello. I'm still here. She glanced back and forth between the two men. Dave still had a smirk on his face and Chase's lips were pressed tightly, like he was ticked off at the minister. He couldn't be jealous, could he?

"Well," Addie said, making the men look at her. "If you'll both excuse me, I need to find my aunt."

Chase's scowl disappeared and his lips curved into a smile. "Actually, Miss Janie asked me to take you home. She had something come up and had to leave."

"She left me?" Addie looked around incredulously. Her tenacious aunt was not very subtle. "Did she say where she was going?"

Chase lifted up one shoulder. "Something about needing to stop by the retirement home. She said she wouldn't be long."

Yeah, just long enough for us to be alone together. Addie wasn't sure why she was irritated. It would fit in perfectly with the plan she and Chase had come up with. Still, when it came to manipulation, she liked having the upper hand.

"Okay. I'm ready when you are." Addie glanced at Dave. "I guess I'll see you next week."

"Next week it is," Dave said, putting his hands in his pockets. He flashed a decidedly wicked grin for a man of the cloth. "Unless I happen to see you sooner."

Was that a hint he'd like to call on her or something? Before she could make a reply, the pastor leaned in a little closer. "Miss Janie is helping me plan the menu for our retreat. I need to follow up with her on a few things so I may stop by her house."

Addie wasn't sure whom that clarification was for: her or Chase. Dave's amused gaze was pinned directly on the cute musician standing next to her. "Oh, well, in that case, I guess I'll see you when I see you," Addie said.

Dave chuckled. "Sounds like a plan. Y'all have a good day."

"Thanks." Chase didn't sound very thankful as he picked up his guitar case with one hand and placed his other hand at the small of Addie's back to guide her out of the chapel. He didn't say anything until they were outside. "I'm parked over here." He moved his palm from her back and pointed to the east side of the building.

As they approached his truck, Addie glanced over at Chase. He still seemed so annoyed. "Sorry you got roped into taking me home. Aunt Janie just can't seem to help herself."

"I don't mind." His scowl deepened. "But now that you've met Pastor Dave have you changed your mind about our plan?"

Addie bit her bottom lip to keep from laughing out loud. Chase was definitely acting like he was jealous. "No. He's not my type."

Chase was quiet for the remaining few steps it took to get to his truck. He pulled the keys out of his pocket and unlocked the doors. Then he turned to look at Addie. "What is your type?"

Truthfully, Addie had no idea. It's not like she'd had a ton of dating experience. Brandon had been her first serious boyfriend. Clearly, he wasn't her type. "I'm not sure," she answered honestly. She hated how vulnerable she sounded.

The creases on Chase's face softened. "I wouldn't worry too much. You'll know it when you meet the right guy."

"I hope so." So far her track record hadn't been very stellar. Feeling silly, she turned to open her door.

"Let me help you up." Chase held out his hand to her, and Addie braced herself for the skin to skin contact. She might not know what kind of guy was her type, but she knew she and Chase had chemistry.

Her dress was a little short and she exposed more of her thigh than she'd intended once she was seated in the truck. But like the gentlemen Chase had proved he was, his eyes only flickered down for a brief second before he stepped back and closed the door.

While Chase went around the truck to the driver's side, Addie tugged on the hem of her dress and tried to calm down. Her heart pounded like she'd just sprinted across the parking lot. For a few seconds, she entertained the thought of Chase being her type. She definitely was attracted to him.

He opened the back door and put his guitar on the seat. Before he could close it, a trio of his groupies surrounded him, and Addie changed her mind. Guys who attracted girls like this were off-limits. Brandon had frequently attracted female attention whether Addie had been with him or not.

"Chase, I didn't get a chance to tell you how incredible you were today!" one of the girls said. She was pretty and looked exactly like Chase's type. Blonde, skinny and had even more curves up top than Addie did. In fact, she looked very similar to her niece's *Barbie*. "Your cover is even better than the original soundtrack."

"Wow, thanks." Chase's face glowed with the praise.

The other two girls offered similar compliments but *Barbie* moved in for a hug. "I just know you're gonna be famous someday. Just don't forget me, okay?"

Addie tamped down her irritation at the girl's cheesy line and the lingering hug. No wonder Chase didn't have a girlfriend. He wouldn't be able to limit himself to just one. The girls lavished Chase with more compliments and promised to come to his next performance.

Addie tuned them out and pulled out her phone to check her messages. There was another email from the camera company about the photo contest. She really needed to focus on her purpose here in Georgia, which wasn't dating Chase or any other guy. If she wanted to move forward with her plan to open her own photography studio, then she had to win the contest.

Since there weren't any other new messages, Addie closed the app. She was suddenly feeling a little homesick and missed her family. The Facebook icon was still on her home screen, and Addie was tempted to reactivate her account just so she could stay connected with her nephews and sister.

The choice to leave the social media site had been made one night after dozens of people had commented on a post someone had left about Brandon's new girlfriend. People were trying to be kind, but Addie hadn't needed any more sympathy or advice. Now that Brandon was married, maybe she could open a new profile. Chellie would be happy since she'd view it as Addie's entrance back into the social scene.

Addie wished she could call her sister, but Chase's fan club had wrapped up and he was climbing into the truck.

"Sorry," he said, giving her a sheepish grin. "I shouldn't have kept you waiting."

"No worries." She lifted one shoulder up. "Besides, they're right. You were pretty amazing. I had no idea you were that talented."

He looked genuinely pleased by her compliment. "Thanks." He started the truck and shifted into gear. As he pulled out to head for Aunt Janie's, Chase lowered his window and glanced over at her. "You okay with the window down?"

"Sure." She lowered her own window as they slowly passed by a row of cherry trees just starting to blossom. If the weather stayed this warm, the trees would be in full blossom before she left. "This weather is amazing. Back home, we're still getting snow."

"Seriously? Last year we were hit by some freak snow storms that made me glad we don't get snow that often."

"I don't mind if it snows in the mountains this time of year, but in the valley I'm ready for spring to come."

Chase glanced at her as he came to a four-way stop sign. "Do you ski?"

"No. I'm one of those annoying snowboarders." That was another thing Brandon had found distasteful about her. His family often went skiing to different premier resorts in both Idaho and Utah. Addie had never been invited since she was a lowly snowboarder.

"Annoying?" Chase lifted one eyebrow. "I've tried both and snowboarding was a lot more fun."

She smiled. "Where do you go skiing around here?" Addie had yet to see any mountains.

"There isn't anything in Georgia." Chase looked back at the road and moved through the intersection, heading for Aunt Janie's. "We go to a resort in North Carolina. It's about a five hour drive from here. My friends and I usually go once a year and spend the entire weekend on the slopes."

"Does Jackson go with you?" Addie remembered the loving couple, and doubted his friend went on skiing trips now that he was married.

"Yep." Chase gave her a quick glance. "Jackson said he and Sydney met you."

"Yeah, Sydney is really sweet."

Chase laughed. "She's amazing. I honestly don't know how Jacks landed her."

"They seem like they're in love."

"Disgustingly happy."

Addie was surprised how cynical Chase was. Maybe he resented his best friend being taken away from him. "What's wrong with being in love?"

"Nothing. It's just not something I'm looking for right now."

There was no reason for Addie to feel disappointed by his comment. If anything, it should make her feel relieved. Still, there was a part of her that wondered if she wasn't the type of girl men fell in love with.

Fearful her emotions would be evident in her voice, Addie swallowed and looked out the window. After a few seconds of marked silence, she noticed a sign for the annual Macon Cherry Blossom Festival. Aunt Janie had mentioned they could drive into Macon one of the days to see some of the sights.

"Did I say something wrong?" Chase asked.

Addie quickly shook off her insecure feelings. "Of course not." She turned back toward him. "I just saw the advertisement for the cherry blossom festival. Have you ever been?"

"Yeah, my dad's side of the family came from Macon so we go every year." Chase made a right turn, bringing them onto the back road to her aunt's house. "We could go, since you're supposed to my girlfriend and all."

He was teasing her, probably trying to lighten the atmosphere. "Speaking of girlfriends. How did it go last night?"

Chase pressed his lips together and stared straight ahead. "Hayden doesn't seem to care if I have a girlfriend or not." He chuckled dryly. "I shouldn't be surprised. Fidelity has never been one of her strong points."

Wow. Wrong thing to ask about. The atmosphere just went from slightly uncomfortable to extremely tense. "I'm sorry."

He turned down Aunt Janie's driveway, his hands gripping the steering wheel tightly. "I'm the one who should apologize."

Addie waited for him to finish, but he didn't say anything else until he came to a stop. "Look, I can't promise Hayden won't try to cause some kind of scene, so if you want to back out of our deal I'll understand."

The muscles in Addie's tummy tightened. This was the second time he'd mentioned backing out of the deal. Maybe he wanted to call it off and just didn't know how to say it nicely. Before she could offer him an out, he turned to look at her, a tentative smile playing at his lips.

"But I'd really appreciate it if you didn't...that is, if you'd still be willing to go out with me a few times. Please?"

Um, yes, and can I be the mother of your children too? "Sure. And don't forget you'll be helping me out." She grinned. "Pastor Dave really isn't my type."

His gaze narrowed slightly. "He seemed to really like you."

"He was just being nice."

Chase laughed. "There's nice and then there is *nice*."

Addie tried not to smile too brightly, but the way his southern accent drew out the word *nice*, Chase almost sounded jealous. Not sure what else to say, she was glad when her phone chimed an incoming text.

"Ten bucks it's my aunt making sure I got a ride home." She glanced down at the screen. "Yep." Another message popped up. "Ooh, even better. She invited you to stay for lunch."

"Sweet," Chase said. "I love when she feeds me."

Although she was tempted to say she was still stranded at the church, Addie quickly typed in a reply that, yes, Chase had taken her home and that he would stay for lunch.

A few seconds later her aunt sent another message. "Aunt Janie needs us to go turn off the oven. She'll be home in about fifteen minutes."

"Let's go." Chase started to exit the truck, but paused when Addie went to open her door. "Hey, what've I told you about opening your own door?"

Addie let go of the handle. "I forgot."

He smiled, his eyes crinkling at the corners. "See that it doesn't happen again."

"Yes, sir," she said, giving him a two-finger salute.

He laughed and climbed out of the truck. When he opened the door for her, Addie was self-conscious of her short skirt and quickly swung her feet over to step down on the running board. One of her apricot colored stilettos slipped off and fell to the ground. Chase picked it up then leaned over to place it on her foot.

Boy was she glad she'd shaved her legs this morning. She pointed her foot slightly as Chase skillfully slipped the shoe on. Her breath caught as his fingertips lightly skimmed across her ankle before he stood up.

His green eyes had taken on a different intensity as he held out his hand. Warmth snaked up her arm and settled inside her stomach when her palm met his. Addie stepped down, but Chase didn't let go of her hand right away. Slowly, she lifted her face until their eyes met. The air around them popped with a tangible energy.

No wonder Cinderella married the prince. Well, that and the fact he was handsome, rich and would get her out of indentured servitude. Addie never dreamed having a shoe put on your foot could be so...sensuous.

Dropping his hand, she drew in a quick breath and gave him a shy smile. "I guess we should probably go in."

His lazy grin set off a flock of butterflies in her stomach. "I guess we should."

They walked side by side, not touching, yet Addie could almost swear she felt the heat from his arm. Something had just happened between them but she wasn't ready to examine what that was. They entered the heavenly scented kitchen and Addie placed her purse on the countertop.

"What can I do?" Chase asked, placing his hands low on his hips.

Just stand there and look gorgeous? There was something hot about a guy wearing a tie and a dress shirt—a shirt Chase filled out extremely well. She dragged her eyes away and retrieved three plates from the cupboard. Turning around, she held out the dishes. "If you could put these on the table that would be great." Her voice sounded as flustered as she felt. Hopefully, Chase hadn't noticed.

His mouth quirked up in a half grin. "Sure."

He moved toward her and took a hold of the plates, but Addie didn't let go of her end. She couldn't. She was too caught up in staring into his amazing eyes. This close up, she noticed a thin blue circle around the edge.

"Did you know your eyes are outlined with blue?"

Had she really just said that out loud?

"I wear contacts."

"Oh." She held in a sigh as she visualized Chase wearing glasses, looking like some sexy-professor-scholarly type. Drawing in a mouthful of air, she let go of the plates and braced herself against the countertop. "I, uh, guess I'll turn the oven off."

He held up the dishes. "I'll go ahead and set the table."

"Thank you." She picked up the oven mitt. "I'll turn off the oven." Shoot, she'd already said that. And why had she picked up the oven mitt? "Um, maybe I'll take the chicken out."

A slow smile spread across his face. "Good idea."

That delicious southern drawl of his made her feel dizzy. Addie turned away from him before she said anything else stupid, like asking him about the tiny scar she noticed on his chin. Heat rushed out when she opened the oven door. She pulled out the roasted chicken and set it on the stove. Removing the oven mitt, she grabbed three glasses out of the cupboard and swiveled around to face him.

Chase took two of the glasses. "Something sure smells good."

"Don't look at me. I only know how to cook things with S-U-G-A-R in them."

"Ahh. I remember that." He placed the glasses next to the plates. "But don't you mean bake?"

"I can't believe you know the difference."

"Hey, I'm very good in the kitchen." He lifted one eyebrow up. "And remember I grew up in a house full of girls. They taught me a lot of things most guys might not know."

"I'll bet." Addie handed him the last glass. "I hope you use your knowledge for good and never evil."

He grinned wickedly. "Of course."

"Uh, huh." A tiny smile escaped before Addie whirled around to get the silverware. She was going to have to be so careful around this one. His likeable factor was a ten out of ten. "So," she said when she turned back around. "Where do you work?" She laid the fork and knife next to the plate, pleased with how normal her voice sounded. "I think I remember you saying something about an office."

"I work for a large marketing firm as a graphic artist and web designer." He took the remaining silverware out of her hands, placing it next to the last plate.

"Do you like it?" she questioned, taking a seat at the small table. His job sounded much more creative and fun than accounting.

"Well, you already know how I feel about my boss." Chase scooted his chair next to Addie and sat down. "But I do like what I do. Plus, it's a job I can do anywhere and allows me the freedom to put in my own hours, especially if we have a gig booked."

"Oh, yeah," Addie said, sliding her finger along the edge of her plate. "I think I heard you tell your fan club you have one this weekend." She desperately wanted to be invited to hear him. As his girlfriend, shouldn't it be a given?

Sitting back a little, he regarded her with an amused smile. "My fan club?"

"Yes. You remember the swarm of girls hovering around you after church today?" Great, now she was the one that sounded jealous. She shrugged. "I'd just like to hear you guys perform before I go home."

"We're playing at a local bar this weekend, and I'd love for you to come."

A bar? She gave him a hesitant glance. There were a few bars in Daisy Springs, and none of them were establishments Addie would ever go to. Like The Tin Can, a popular bar on the outskirts of town with a lighted billboard featuring the names of the girls that would be dancing that weekend. "Uh, I don't know…I…"

His smile faltered. "You don't have to come if you don't want to."

"I don't drink."

"Neither do I." He reached out and fingered the napkin that edged his plate. "Sydney doesn't either and she'll be there."

"Are there dancers?"

He quirked a brow. "People usually like to dance, but you don't have to. Syd usually just orders dinner and watches the show."

Addie couldn't imagine someone as refined and beautiful as Sydney McCall in some sleazy bar.

"Gracie's Haven is an exclusive club, and has amazing food. But you really don't have to go," Chase said with a definite apology in his tone.

Ohhh. So it was more like a nice restaurant.

Addie felt stupid, and reached over and placed her hand on top of his. The intent was to reassure him, not make her heart try to pound its way out of her chest. "I'm sorry. I really do want to come. I'm just from a little town in Idaho and the bars there are the kind you see in the seedy side of town with dark windows and lighted signs with enticing messages about the scantily clad entertainment they provide."

One corner of his mouth lifted. "I promise I would never take a lady to a place like that." He turned his hand over so their palms were pressed together. "So you'll come with me?"

"Yes, I'd like that." Her words were soft and airy due to her shallow breathing. Chase's touch was seriously impeding her respiratory efforts.

"You can sit with Sydney." Chase had slid his hand around hers and was now making circular motions with his thumb in the center of her palm. Addie could hardly think straight.

"Who?"

"Sydney." Chase grinned. "You sat with her in church. She's married to my friend Jackson."

"Right. I did meet them. And I still can't decide who's prettier—Sydney or her husband."

Laughing, Chase laced his fingers with hers. It didn't look like he was going to relinquish her hand anytime soon. "That's a good one. I can't wait to tease Jackson about being prettier than his wife."

Addie gasped. "Please don't tell him I said that." She tried to tug her hand free, but he kept hold of it.

"Don't worry." His green eyes softened. "I promise I won't say anything."

"Promise?"

He nodded his head slowly. "Cross my heart."

Only he didn't cross his heart. His eyes were locked with Addie's and he still held her hand. Neither of them moved, until she heard her aunt's car door slam. Addie pulled her hand free just as her aunt came in the kitchen.

"Sorry I took so long. Did y'all have fun?"

Chase stood up and chuckled softly. "I know I did." He looked at Addie, tilting his chin down. "You?"

"Um, yes. We were just discussing the difference between the bars here and the bars in Daisy Springs."

Her aunt raised an eyebrow. "You've been to a bar in Daisy Springs?"

Addie's face went hot. "Well, no. I..." She could hear Chase laughing at her. The least he could do is help her explain. "I'm going to hear Chase play next weekend in a bar, only he explained to me that it's more like a nice restaurant. That's what I meant. I don't go to bars. I've never stepped foot in one. And I—"

Aunt Janie held her hand up. "Okay, sugar. I get it. You're not a barroom maid." She patted Chase on the arm. "Didn't I tell you she was a nice girl?"

"Yes you did," he drawled, grinning at Addie with an impish glint in his eyes.

With her aunt's back turned to her, Addie stuck her tongue out at Chase, making him laugh even harder.

Chapter Ten

Chase held his guitar as he sat perched on the end of his bed. His fingers plucked at the guitar strings, creating the melody he'd had in his head since seeing Addie this morning at church. It was easy to picture her in the lacy dress she'd worn, including the high heeled shoes that had left an impression on him. Up until today, he'd never found feet to be so sexy.

Strumming a few more chords, he heard a loud rap on his door. "Chase," his sister Ashlee yelled. "Mama wants you upstairs to wait for your guests."

He glanced at the clock, surprised to see it was time for Addie and her aunt to arrive for supper. It was easy to lose track of time when he was in the zone.

"Coming," he hollered back as he carefully laid his guitar on the bed. He crossed his bedroom floor and opened his door. Ashlee had already disappeared.

She was pretty mad at him right now since he'd nixed any hope of her coming to their gig this weekend. All it had taken was a few well-placed concerns voiced to his mother to silence Ashlee. Once their mother made up her mind there was no changing it. Ashlee was smart enough to know this but she was furious with Chase. She'd even gotten Taylin on board the I-hate-Chase train. While his sisters would be polite to Addie, he was afraid they might purposely sabotage the evening by bringing up some of the stupid things he'd done in the past.

Chase found his mother in the kitchen. She had her back to him, drizzling melted butter over the top of rolls fresh out of the oven. She glanced up at him when he walked in. "Hey, sweetie."

"Mmm, supper sure smells good," Chase said, peeking over his mom's shoulder.

He started to reach for a roll when his mother swatted his hand. "Chase Nichols, you know better than that."

"Yes, ma'am, I do." He kissed his mom on the cheek. "By the way, did I ever thank you for making sure I had good manners?"

She looked at him askance. "No. In fact, I think you've complained about it your whole life."

"Well, just for the record, thank you. I've appreciated it the past the couple of days."

She turned and gave him a soft smile. "Well, I'm glad I did something right."

The doorbell chimed and Chase couldn't hold back his grin. "And that would be our guests."

She arched an eyebrow. "You really like this girl, don't you?"

Chase didn't have to pretend too hard that he was into Addie Heywood. Truthfully, he didn't have to pretend at all.

"Yeah, I do." He gave his mom another smile and jogged out of the kitchen. "Be right back."

Just as he made it to the entry way, his father opened the door. "Hayden, how are you?" he heard his father say.

Chase's blood chilled. *Hayden?* It was too late to backtrack to the kitchen. Hayden spotted him and waved, her generous mouth tilting up in a seductive smile he was all too familiar with. "Hey there, Chase."

"Come on in, Hayden," Charles invited warmly, closing the door behind her.

Chase's footsteps faltered as he stifled a groan. Now that she was inside, it would be difficult to get her to leave. He stepped in before his dad did something worse like invite her to stay for supper.

"Did you need something?" Chase didn't bother hiding the irritation in his voice.

His dad looked at him with both eyebrows raised high on his head as he walked by and left them alone.

Hayden ignored Chase's obvious aggravation and sidled up close to him. "Well, hello to you too." She scrunched up her nose, her lips pursed into a pout. "Can't a girl stop by to say hey?"

His scowl deepened. "Hayden, what're you really doing here?"

"I told you." She reached out and wrapped her fingers around his arm. It reminded him of a snake coiling around its prey. "I stopped by to say hello. After last night, I missed you." She slowly circled her finger on the bare skin just below his rolled up sleeves.

Chase could feel the muscles in his jaw tighten as he ground his back teeth together. He stepped away from her, making her hand drop to her side. "I left early because Tate's daughter never showed up, and after I left, you were supposed to make sure your parents—and anybody else you've misled—knows that we aren't together."

"Dana did show up." There was an edge to her voice. "It was humiliating trying to explain why you weren't still by my side."

Chase didn't know whether or not to believe Hayden. Even if it was true, he wasn't getting sucked into Hayden's game again. He couldn't believe he'd agreed to the whole thing in the first place.

Besides that, Reggie had texted him early this morning that a rep from a smaller record label, Country Sounds Music, might show up at Gracie's Haven this weekend.

Hayden moved in close again, brushing her body against his. "If you play your cards right, she can still get her daddy to listen to you." She looked up at him through her thick lashes, and her lips parted in an invitation.

He didn't want to kiss Hayden, and felt somewhat comforted by the fact that her touch didn't set him on fire anymore.

He jerked the front door open. "I'm not interested."

Her eyes narrowed. "I'm sure you don't mean that."

Chase sucked in a deep breath. He needed to redirect the path of this futile conversation. "Hayden, I already told you I'm seeing someone right now. I like her and I don't want to blow it."

He moved outside, relieved when Hayden followed him. "Who is she again?" Her voice sounded unnaturally high.

Chase pulled the door closed and started toward Hayden's red sports car. "Her name is Addie."

"And when did you meet her?"

"I told you that I've known her since I was fourteen." He really hoped she didn't press him for more details, and decided to be as honest as he could right now. "Look, Addie and her aunt are coming for supper. I really don't want you to be here when they do."

She eyed him for several long seconds. Her lips had been pressed flat but now were curved up into a subtle smile. "I'd really like to meet her."

"No." Chase pointed to her BMW. "I'll walk you to your car."

Hayden held his gaze a few more seconds before she shrugged. "Fine. Let me get my keys." She opened her purse and fished around for a few seconds, taking her sweet time.

Chase heard a car and lifted his face to see if it was Janie and Addie. The next thing he knew, the contents of Hayden's purse were dumped at his feet.

"Oh goodness," Hayden said. "I can't believe how clumsy I am."

Chase had no idea how she'd landed an acting job because she was a terrible actress. As he bent down to help gather up the scattered items, Janie and Addie turned into his driveway.

* * *

Addie saw Chase crouched down next to a very pretty girl that couldn't possibly be his sister. Her long, dark hair was a dead giveaway, considering Chase's twin sisters were blonde. They both stood up and watched as Aunt Janie slowly inched her sedan toward the Nichols's house.

"How sweet," Aunt Janie said. "Chase is waiting for you."

"With another girl," Addie said dryly. A knot of jealousy twisted her gut, and she wondered if the pretty girl was Hayden, or just another member of his fan club.

"Well, then do something. You need to get out there and fight for your man."

"He's not my man." Not really. They'd put on a good show for her aunt earlier—laughing and flirting with each other—but Addie wasn't sure what had been real and what had been pretend.

"Nonsense." Janie brought the car to a stop. "I saw the way you two were getting along this afternoon."

Chase started moving toward the car, a deer-in-the-headlights look on his face. Addie didn't know if it was because he'd been caught or if he was begging her to help. Aunt Janie opened her car door, and Chase's good manners made him detour away from Addie's side to assist her aunt.

"Hey, Miss Janie," Chase said, holding open the door as she climbed out of the car. "Do you need any help?"

"No, thank you." Janie retrieved the pie holder from the middle of the seat. "I'm worried the coconut cream won't be any good if I don't refrigerate it right away. I'm just gonna run this inside to your mama."

"Yes, ma'am." Chase closed the car door. "Just walk right in."

While Aunt Janie made a beeline for the house, Chase skirted around the rear of the car to the passenger's side. Addie noticed the dark-haired girl followed his every move like a cat tracking a mouse.

"Hey there," Chase said once he opened Addie's door. "I'm glad you're here."

"Thanks." Addie slid out of the car without his help, leaving the pathetic looking apple pie she'd made on her seat.

"Do you want me to carry that in?" Chase said, pointing to the pie.

"We can get it later." She closed the door behind her and glanced at Chase. She wasn't exactly sure what she was supposed to do. Did he want her to play the role of his girlfriend or what?

"Chase," the pretty girl said, moving next to him. "Aren't you going to introduce me?" Her alto voice, combined with the genteel southern accent, came across as provocative and sultry.

The surly look Chase shot the brunette tipped Addie off that no matter how pretty the girl was, Chase didn't seem to like her.

The girl rolled her eyes. "I'm Hayden Barclay." She held out her hand with her knuckles up like she was royalty.

Addie wasn't sure what she was supposed to do. Shake her hand lamely by taking a hold of her fingers or give her a fist bump. She hoped Hayden didn't expect her to kiss it. "Hi," Addie said, lightly gripping the girl's fingers. "I'm Addie Heywood."

Hayden's perfectly plump lips curved up as she kept a hold of Addie's hand and leaned forward. "Chase and I used to date so I know all of his secrets. Maybe you and I can get together and I can give you a few tips."

From the corner of her eye, Addie could see Chase's eyes narrow with anger. He looked like he was about to interfere, but she was a big girl and could handle Hayden Barclay all by herself. "Thanks for the offer, but I'm enjoying discovering his secrets all on my own."

A hard look crossed Hayden's face, and she squeezed Addie's fingers tighter. "I doubt you'll discover everything. The offer is still open if you change your mind." Her voice was tinged with a game-on attitude.

Addie tugged her hand free. "That's really sweet of you." She smoothly moved next to Chase and slid her arm around his waist. His body tensed for a fraction of a second and then, thankfully, he played along and wrapped his arm around her shoulder. "It was nice meeting you, Hayden," she said, snuggling closer to Chase.

Hey, if she was going to play the girlfriend, she might as well enjoy it. Plus, it didn't hurt that he smelled absolutely yummy.

Hayden's eyes flickered from Addie to Chase. "I'll let you know what Dana says, but we'll probably be at your next gig. See you then." With that, she spun around on her heel and walked toward her car, her hips swaying seductively from side to side.

Addie glanced up to see if Chase was following his ex-girlfriend's departure, but found him looking at her instead. "Thank you." His eyes seemed to hold much more than gratitude. "You were very convincing."

Right. This isn't real.

"Just doing my job."

Two lines creased his forehead. "Is that—"

Hayden's car roared to life, cutting of his words. She revved the motor, almost as if it screamed out in protest for her. Both Addie and Chase watched the little red sports car peel out of the driveway, the tires squealing against the asphalt.

Somebody has a temper.

As soon as the car disappeared, Addie stepped away from Chase. "Nice girl."

He grunted a laugh. "Yeah, right." Chase eyed her for a second, a small smile playing at his mouth. "So, you're gonna enjoy discovering my secrets, huh?"

The way he said it almost made it sound scandalous. Still, Addie was pretty sure she would, indeed, enjoy it. "Speaking of secrets. Who's Dana?" She really hoped she wasn't another ex-girlfriend.

The levity in his face vanished. "A friend of Hayden's. I've never met her before but she's got connections in the music industry."

"Could those connections help you?"

He shrugged and looked away. "Maybe."

Addie sensed he wouldn't give her any more. This discovering secrets thing wasn't going to be as easy as she thought.

"I guess we should go inside."

Chase didn't respond right away. Then, he turned back toward her. "Dana is Tate Jepson's daughter. Tate owns one of the hottest record labels in Nashville." He pressed his lips flat and a muscle flexed in his jaw. "While Hayden said she'd make trouble for me with her father if I didn't go along with her little scheme, she also sweetened the deal by saying Dana could get me an audience with Tate."

He met her gaze. "I was stupid and went along with it."

Addie appreciated his honesty, and understood why he'd done it. She only wished she'd been as brave when it came to making her own dreams come true. Part of her wondered even if she did happen to win the photo contest and the camera, would she have the guts to really open her own studio?

"Trying to further your career isn't stupid."

"Anything involving Hayden is stupid." His face hardened. "And now she's coming to the show on Saturday. I doubt she'll bring Dana with her, and is only coming to make more trouble." His eyes flickered to Addie's. "Sorry, but you'll most likely be her target."

For some reason Addie looked forward to the challenge. "So I get to play the part of your amazing girlfriend a little longer?"

A small smile surfaced on his handsome face. "You *were* amazing." He laughed and shook his head. "Man, the way you put her in her place was priceless."

"I know, right?"

He reached out and lightly tapped her under the chin. "Humble too."

Addie laughed, hoping to hide the crazy emotions his touch created. "Should we go inside? I'm excited to meet your sisters."

"Yeah, but I should warn you that they're both mad at me right now, so ignore whatever they might say about me."

"Even if it's good?"

He laughed. "I doubt they'll have anything good to say other than I'm overprotective and annoying. I wouldn't put it past them to share some of the stupid things I did when I was young."

"Hmmm. This might be very enlightening. I think I'm going to like talking with your sisters."

He eyed her warily. "Don't encourage them."

This time it was her turn to laugh. "Of course not." She headed for his house, but paused when he hadn't moved. "You coming?"

"Yeah." He stepped toward her aunt's car. "Just let me grab your pie."

Dang. She hoped he'd forgotten all about the pie. After he retrieved the foil-covered tin, Addie offered to take it from him. Maybe she could trip on something and accidentally drop the poorly put together dessert.

"I got it," Chase said as he gently prodded her forward. He opened the front door and allowed her to enter before him.

Addie stepped inside the beautiful two-story, Georgian Colonial styled home and marveled at the simplistic beauty of the foyer. The wood floor was stained dark, the wide planks rough around the edges as if they'd been hand-hewn. Before her stretched a winding staircase that ascended gracefully to the second level.

Overhead, a large chandelier hung, illuminating the pictures of Chase's family that covered the wall along the stairs.

"Your house is beautiful." Addie turned to look at Chase, wanting him to take her on a tour. She found him peeling up the edge of the foil. "Hey, no peeking." She grabbed at the pie, but he evaded her efforts by lifting it higher.

"Why?" he asked with a chuckle.

Addie pressed closer, and tried to reach around him to get the pie. "Because, it doesn't look pretty."

Chase held the pie further away. "Let me be the judge of that."

"No. I'm serious." She made another grab for the pie tin, bringing her body flush with his back. In an instant, she became aware of his hard muscles and the breadth of his shoulders. Tendrils of warmth spread through her, rendering her immobile.

Slowly, Chase looked back over his shoulder so their noses almost touched. "C'mon," he said in a low voice. "It can't be that bad."

Her mind scrambled to stay on task and not focus on his soft lips. "Fine, but don't you dare say one word."

"Addie, any man with a lick a sense would never criticize a woman's cooking."

Interesting. Brandon frequently made unfavorable comments about her culinary efforts. "Um…okay."

A door slammed shut and both of them turned their attention to the top of the stairs. Two giggling girls rapidly descended the winding staircase. Addie stared at the beautiful blondes. If she didn't know better, even this close up she would've thought they were identical.

They came to an abrupt halt on the bottom step. One of them arched a brow, her sky blue eyes glittered with interest. "Are we interrupting something?"

Addie felt her face go hot as she untangled herself from Chase. "Nope."

"Kind of," Chase said at the same time.

Addie shot him an annoyed look but Chase only winked at her. "Addie, these two are my little sisters." He pointed to the one who had spoken. "Ashlee."

The girl daintily waved her fingers in a greeting.

"And this is Taylin."

A curious smile spread across her pixie-like face. "Hey."

Addie knew she wasn't ugly, but compared to the Nichols girls she felt like the plain wallflower nobody wants to dance with. "Okay, so what line in heaven did I miss when they were making gorgeous, blue-eyed blondes?"

Both girls seemed genuinely pleased by the compliment until their brother gave a cynical laugh. "Please don't make their heads any bigger—they obviously missed the line with humility."

Their smiles disappeared as they glared at Chase. Taylin leaned forward. "Just because you missed the "nice brother" line, doesn't mean you have to be so rude."

Whenever Addie's nephews and niece started arguing, she usually tried to lighten the mood before the argument could escalate into something worse. And in spite of Chase's sarcasm, she knew how much he loved and worried about his sisters.

She leaned toward the girls. "Just ignore him. He's only acting that way because he wants to protect you two. You're both so beautiful and it scares him."

She shot a quick glance back at Chase. "I never had a brother. You're lucky."

The girls looked at each other and then back at Addie. Taylin's slender shoulder rose up. "I guess it is kinda sweet how protective he is of us."

"A little annoying," Ashlee said. "But sweet." She gave her brother a cheesy grin.

Chase glanced from sister to sister and smiled. "Well, uh, thanks."

Taylin sauntered past her brother and patted him on the shoulder. "Yep. You're a regular knight in shining armor."

"My hero," Ashlee said with a smirk.

The girls burst out laughing and disappeared around the corner.

"There's gratitude for you," Chase said dryly.

Addie giggled. "Someday they'll appreciate you."

"Doubt it." His eyes landed on Addie and a grin replaced his frown. "Thanks for trying to make me look good, though."

Yeah, like you need any help in that area. She leaned over and patted him on the arm. "I got your back."

Chase captured her hand as it fell away. "Hey, nobody has to see the pie if you're really stressed out about it."

The soft tone of his voice, coupled with their entwined fingers, vanquished any stress about the marred pastry. "It might not look the greatest but Aunt Janie made the crust and the pie filling and that's what counts, right?"

"I'm sure it's not that bad, but how about I serve the pie with a big scoop of vanilla ice cream right in the center?"

"You would do that for me?"

His lips curved into a soft smile. "Yeah." He tugged on her hand, bringing her much closer. "I'd do that for you."

She lifted her eyes and met his gaze. He studied her for a few seconds, as if trying to discern her thoughts. She hoped he couldn't actually read her mind or he'd know how much she wanted him to kiss her. Heat flared between them and his focus shifted to her mouth.

Addie wasn't sure if she felt disappointed or relieved when Chase's sister, Ashlee, came back into the foyer. "Y'all coming to supper or what?"

The spell broken, Chase glanced over at his sister. "We're coming."

Addie swallowed as he led her into the dining room, suddenly feeling very nervous. She wasn't exactly sure why, but she wanted Chase's family to like her.

Chapter Eleven

The aroma of baking bread wafted through the screen door of the Caldwell home as Chase climbed the porch steps. He read a note taped to the door, and followed the instructions to walk right in. Every Monday morning, Janie invited some men from the Senior Citizen Center to come to her house for coffee and some home baked goodies. Today it smelled like Miss Janie's famous cinnamon rolls. Addie should be happy.

The deep southern voices of the older gentlemen echoed from the dining room as Chase entered the house. His empty stomach rumbled involuntarily as he followed the delicious scent coming from the kitchen. The moment he stepped into the dining room, a few of the men looked up to see who the latecomer was.

Miss Janie sat next to Harry Burns, a retired postman Chase had known his whole life. Janie's eyes lit with surprise when she spotted him. A small smile formed on her lips as she raised a welcoming hand. "Well, good morning, Chase. This is a nice surprise."

He smiled, doubting her surprise was genuine. He and Addie made it fairly obvious they liked each other during and after supper last night. Chase didn't know how much of their flirting was real—at least on Addie's part. He didn't need to pretend he liked her.

"Morning," he said, crossing the room. He felt a stab of disappointment when he didn't see Addie.

"Ain't you a little young to be here, son?" Mr. Burns asked. Then he grinned widely and winked. "Or are you here to see that little gal with the red hair?"

Janie pushed back from the table. "Addie's hair isn't red. It's auburn. And of course Chase is here to see her."

This elicited a few cackles from the other men sitting around the table. Janie pointed to the kitchen. "She's icing the last batch of cinnamon buns. Go on in, sugar. I'm sure she'll be happy to see you."

"Just don't go and eat all those rolls up. We're still hungry," Harry called as Chase exited the dining room.

He found Addie drizzling icing over the hot bread. She had her hair pulled up in a ponytail and wore a pair of jeans and a fitted light blue tee. When his shoes hit the tile floor, Addie lifted her face and her eyes widened with surprise. "Chase. I wasn't expecting you." She appeared truly astonished to see him this morning, staring at him and unconsciously dribbling icing onto the dark granite countertop.

He pointed his finger at the puddle of white confection. "Uh, Addie…"

She blinked and looked down at the mess she'd just made. "Oh, shoot." She stopped squeezing the bag and laid it down on the counter.

"Sorry," he said with a laugh. "I didn't mean to distract you."

A faint blush colored her face. "I thought you were coming by after work." She looked down at her blue shirt and tugged at the hem. "I must look a mess."

"I think you look cute."

That earned him a glare. "Liar."

He moved closer to the bar. "Okay. You look gorgeous."

She gave him an exaggerated eye roll and reached for a spatula. "Flattery will get you nothing but a cinnamon bun." She lifted an iced roll from the pan and deposited it on a plate. "You did come in for one of these, right?" she asked, sliding the plate over to him.

"Well…" His eyes made a lazy perusal of her face. "Among other things."

The color in her cheeks deepened, making him wonder if she remembered the moment he would've kissed her last night if Ashlee hadn't interrupted them. "Do you want anything to drink?"

Chase wished he could play hooky from work and hang out with her all day. He could hardly wait for their first official date tonight. "I better not. I've got a meeting with a new client in an hour. I brought by Claire's bike for you."

"Oh, thanks."

He laughed at the look of dread on her face. Last night she'd told him about the photo contest and how she liked photographing landscapes, but usually found her best settings off the beaten path. Since Addie was afraid of horses, Chase suggested riding a bike to give her a scenic view of the area. "You did say you'd rather ride a bike than a horse."

"That's true, but you also remember I haven't ridden a bike for like ten years, right?"

"They say you never forget how to ride a bike."

"That's not what I'm worried about." She bunched her brows together. "Did I tell you I don't like to exercise?"

"No." He laughed again. "You don't have to ride the bike, Addie. There are other ways to explore the back roads."

She shook her head. "No, riding a bike is a good idea. It's hard to get inspired about an area if I'm in a car."

Glancing up at him, she offered him a smile that showed off her dimple. "Thank you for bringing the bike over."

"You're welcome." The kitchen clock chimed once on the half hour, reminding him he needed to get going. "Can you walk with me out to the truck?"

"Sure." She lifted the pan of iced cinnamon rolls. "I just need to take these out. Apparently, Harry likes these as much as we do."

"He did seem a little territorial."

Addie raised an eyebrow. "A little?" She walked a few steps and then looked over her shoulder. "Let's just say I'm glad Aunt Janie only does this once a week."

All eyes turned to them as they entered the dining room. Janie took the pan from Addie. "Thank you, darlin'. These look wonderful."

"Yes, thank you," one of the men said, reaching for another roll.

"You're welcome." Addie stepped away from the table, motioning for Chase to follow her. "I'm gonna walk Chase out to his truck. I'll be back in just a minute."

Mr. Burns snorted. "I bet it'll be longer than a minute." He wiggled both of his eyebrows up and down.

Miss Janie gave Harry a playful swat. "Hush, or no more rolls for you." She glanced back over at Addie and Chase. "Y'all just take your time."

Chase held the door for Addie, and ignored the other comments from the men as he closed the door behind them.

They walked toward his truck, and Addie pointed to his cinnamon roll. "You haven't eaten that yet?"

"I'll take it to go and bring the plate by later on."

"Just make sure it's clean," she joked, "I also get dish duty."

Chuckling, he opened the passenger door and put the plate on the seat. "I promise to return it clean." She followed him to the back of the truck, stopping beside him as he lowered the tailgate.

"You better let me do this." Addie placed her hands on the back of the truck. "I don't want you to ruin your clothes."

Chase tucked his tie in between the buttons of his shirt. "Nah, I won't get dirty." He nimbly climbed up into the bed of the truck and pulled the bike to the edge.

She reached for the back tire. "Well, at least let me help you get it down."

Together they managed and Chase jumped back down. He clapped his hands together to get rid of any dirt. "I hope this works out okay. I made sure the tires were good."

Addie balanced the bike. "It'll be perfect. Thank you. Tell your sister I'll take good care of it."

Chase smiled. "Claire's expecting a baby, so she won't be using it anytime soon. Plus, she and her husband live in North Carolina so she left it at home on purpose."

He reached back inside the truck bed, pulling out a bike helmet. "This is Taylin's. She never used it and I have no idea if it'll fit, but she said you're welcome to use it."

"That was sweet of her." She took the helmet and hooked it on one of the handles. "Tell her thanks."

"I will." He lifted the tailgate and Addie moved over to help him click it in place. They turned and faced each other. Addie was near enough that Chase caught the scent of cinnamon and sugar. "Are you still up for dinner tonight?" he asked.

"Yeah, what time should I be ready?"

"Syd is expecting us at six. I'll come by around five-thirty if that's okay?"

"Sure." She gave him a soft smile. "I'll see you then."

Chase really didn't want to leave, but he needed to get to work. Before backing away, he noticed tiny crystals of sugar clinging to Addie's bottom lip. Without thinking, he reached out and brushed a few of the crystals away with his thumb. "Looks like someone's been into the sugar this mornin'."

Her eyes were filled with apprehension, wonder and something else he couldn't quite define.

Lowering her lashes, she shrugged. "I can't seem to help myself."

He knew the feeling. "Ah, something I can definitely relate to." She lifted her eyes again and offered him a shy smile. Before he gave into the temptation to sample her sugary lips, Chase backed away. "Have a good day, Addie. I'll see ya later."

* * *

Trembling inside, Addie watched him drive away. She felt as warm and gooey as the inside of a cinnamon roll. Sighing, she licked her lips and tasted the evidence of her poor self-control. And speaking of poor self-control—that was twice now that she would've let Chase kiss her.

Careful, Addie, she reminded herself. *This is only pretend.*

Sighing again, she made her way to the back porch, the wheels of the bike crunching in the gravel as she steered it behind the house. After securing the bike on the back porch, she entered the kitchen.

Feeling a little out of sorts, she started washing dishes and tried to erase the memory of the look in Chase's eyes when he'd brushed his warm thumb across her bottom lip. Did he know what he was doing to her? For that matter, did she even know what was happening to her?

Slipping another plate into the hot water, Addie wished she could wash away her feelings as easily as the white frosting disappeared from the dish. She didn't want to like Chase. A new relationship, long-distance or otherwise, wasn't in her plans. Obviously, Chase wasn't looking for anything either. So why were they going out tonight as a couple to hang out with a married couple?

It's not like they were in danger of blowing their cover or anything. Aunt Janie hadn't threatened to set her up since orchestrating her ride home from church with Chase. As far as she knew, Hayden wouldn't be seeing Chase until his gig on Saturday, and Addie would be there as his date so they were covered there.

Reaching for another plate, she dunked it into the water. She needed to remember Chase was her pretend boyfriend. She needed to stop thinking about him as anything else and concentrate on her goal of starting her own studio. Just because her breath caught whenever she thought about those incredible green eyes, his great smile and his sexy southern accent…well, none of that mattered, right?

She let out a sarcastic laugh and shook her head. Who was she kidding? Looks like she was interested in chasing Chase—maybe even catching him.

After finishing the dishes, Addie went upstairs to her room and grabbed her camera. She knew she could spend the next couple of hours seeing more of her aunt's property. Her bike riding exploration would wait another day. Quietly, she slipped past the dining room. Aunt Janie and her gentlemen friends seemed to be having a great time and she didn't want to interrupt them. She also didn't want any more embarrassing comments about her love life from Mr. Burns.

Addie left a note on the counter for her aunt, letting her know where she would be. Instead of going to the gardens near the gazebo, Addie made her way to the edge of the property that abutted a forest of Georgia pines. As a child, the woods had seemed spooky to her and she'd avoided this side of the property the few times she'd visited her aunt. Even now as an adult it still seemed eerily quiet.

Amongst the tall pine trees, Addie noted a variety of flowering shrubs that were in full bloom. Careful not to trip on the thick ground cover, she made her way toward the large holly tree. The uniquely shaped green leaves were heavily laden with bright red holly berries. She'd always thought this would make the perfect Christmas tree since all the decorating you'd need was a string of white lights.

She took several shots, including a few close-ups. When she backed up to get a wide view, she was excited when a male red Cardinal landed on one of the branches. The bird held still for a few seconds, giving Addie plenty of time to get some great pictures.

She spent the next thirty minutes in the wooded area before venturing back to Aunt Janie's yard. Near the south end of the property sat a tiny cabin that had been the temporary housing of her uncle's family when they'd first settled the property before the Civil War. Now it was used to store garden tools.

The little cabin was more dilapidated then she'd remembered, but it had character and she got some great pictures of it, especially on the side with a flowering dogwood tree. After spending another hour traversing the yard, she made her way back to the house for lunch.

Although the temp was in the low seventies, Addie was hot and sweaty from all her exploring. She entered the kitchen for a drink of water and was surprised to find a stranger seated at the kitchen bar. The woman, who appeared to be as round as she was tall, stared at Addie, her eyes filled with distrust. A frown puckered her already wrinkled dark skin.

"Who are you?" the woman questioned hotly.

Addie briefly looked for her aunt before answering the demanding question. "Hi, I'm Addie Heywood. Janie's niece."

The woman's gaze narrowed. "Hmmph. Your hair's changed color. I remember a little red headed gal that likes to eat sweets."

Obviously this woman knew her well. "That would be me." Addie smiled. "And you are?"

"Hazel Morris."

The name sounded vaguely familiar. "Nice to meet you, Hazel." Addie held out her hand.

"That's Miss Hazel to you, young lady," Hazel said, her frown deepening.

Oh, that jogged her memory. The last time Addie saw Hazel the woman had been thirty pounds thinner and had shiny black hair instead of short curly gray hair. But she had been just as grumpy back then as she was now.

"That's right," Addie said, dropping her hand. "I remember you now. You used to make the most amazing fudge."

The woman snorted. "And you used to eat it as fast as a hot knife in butter. She eyed Addie critically. "I'm surprised you're not fat."

That was a compliment, right? "Thank you, Haz...uh, Miss Hazel."

"I suppose you're looking for your aunt."

Addie moved to the fridge and retrieved a bottle of water. "Actually, yes. Where is she?"

"She had to take that rowdy bunch of men home since that old coot Harry Burns left his lights on and killed his battery dead." Hazel pushed her chair away from the bar. "I'm supposed to feed you dinner."

Addie knew by the tone of Miss Hazel's voice that feeding her was the last thing she'd like to do. Hungry or not, her lunch could wait until Aunt Janie was back. "Oh, please don't get up," Addie said, before the grumpy lady could heave herself out of the chair. "I really appreciate the offer but I'm not hungry right now."

Instead of being grateful, Hazel sank back in her chair and glared at Addie. "In my house you eat when it's dinner time whether you be hungry or not."

Good thing I'm not in your house. Addie kept the snarky reply to herself and tried to use diplomacy. "Before I go take a shower, is there anything I can get you, Miss Hazel?"

Wow, while the woman didn't actually smile, she at least wasn't frowning any more. "Yes, thank you. I'd appreciate more of Janie's sweet tea."

Addie opened the fridge and found the pitcher of tea. She poured Hazel a glass, and was surprised when the woman thanked her again. "Anything else?" Addie asked.

Hazel looked to be contemplating another request, but finally shook her head. "No, thank you. You go on and take your shower. You look a mess right now."

Biting her tongue, Addie hurried out of the kitchen. Honestly, she didn't know how her cheerful aunt could be friends with such a grouchy person. On the way to her room, Addie noticed the cord hanging down from the attic stairs. Since she was already dirty, maybe now would be a time to look through the attic for old photos. Maybe one of them would inspire her to take the winning picture.

After putting away her camera equipment, Addie went out in the hall and stood beneath the attic entrance in the ceiling. She tugged on the string, and the aged stairs groaned as they unfolded. A cloud of dust swirled in the air, making Addie sneeze. Before climbing up the narrow staircase, she waited for the dust to settle.

"Girl," Hazel said, making Addie jump. "What're you doing?" She stood in the foyer with her hands on her hips, a deep scowl on her face. "You nearly scared me to death."

"Oh, sorry. Before I shower, I decided to look for some old photographs Aunt Janie thought might be up here."

"Well, don't you go fallin' and gettin' hurt now. I sure ain't gonna be climbing those skinny stairs to help you."

"I'll be careful. And I'm sorry about scaring you, Miss Hazel."

Addie couldn't be sure, but she thought Hazel Morris might be smiling. "I'm fine." She waved her hand. "Holler if you need help. I can always call the fire department."

"Okay. Thank you."

The woman waved again before going back to the kitchen. Addie put her foot on the first step, and determined it to be solid. The wooden stairs creaked as she slowly climbed upward. She continued to look all around her, afraid to find a spider waiting to greet her.

At the top, an uncovered light bulb hung from the ceiling. She pulled on the chain, flooding the attic opening with light.

Cobwebs clung to the rafters, swaying gently from the air flowing up the stairs. It was fairly clean, considering nobody had been up here in over ten years. Just to be safe, she continued to scan the area for spiders and other creepy things.

The cardboard boxes Aunt Janie told her about were pushed up against the bare studs and Addie prayed that nothing would run out when she pulled them away from the wall. The bottom of the box scraped against the wood floor as she drew it toward the light. To her relief, nothing stirred except more dust.

She rifled through it carefully and found a variety of old magazines. Most of them were past issues of *Good Housekeeping*, dating back to the 70's. Another box contained more magazines, old property tax information and faded receipts from different stores. The musty smell of old paper made her wrinkle her nose and she pushed the box back against the wall.

In the next box she struck gold. There were at least a dozen black and white photographs of the yard, several of which had a few people posing that Addie didn't recognize. There were quite a few of downtown Mitchel Creek and the old chapel that was now a museum. Beneath another stack of magazines, Addie found a framed picture of Aunt Janie's house, taken from the side of the property where the gazebo stood.

She rubbed a layer of dust from the corner of the glass and saw a 1929 date stamped in faded gold letters. Addie felt a tad disappointed when she didn't find anything close to the era of the Civil War.

"Addie? Are you okay up there?" Aunt Janie called from the bottom of the attic stairs.

"Yeah." She scooted to the opening and poked her head out. "Just looking for pictures."

Her aunt looked over her shoulder and hollered, "She's fine, Hazel." She glanced back at Addie. "She was worried you'd hurt yourself."

"Nope. I only have a couple more boxes to look through and then I'll be down."

"Okay, sugar. Hazel and I are going to our book club meeting. We're just gonna be down the road at the Jensen's house so if you need me all you have to do is call."

Addie loved how active her aunt was. She didn't have time to grow old. "Okay, thanks. And have fun at your meeting."

"Sure thing."

Moving back to finish her search, Addie went through two other cartons without discovering any other pictures. Satisfied with her find, she pushed the box toward the stairs. It took some finagling but Addie managed to get the box of old photographs down. After putting the attic stairs back up into the ceiling, she picked up the box and carried it down to the kitchen table.

The pictures were easier to inspect in the natural lighting. She soon discovered some of them had writing on the back, and was disappointed to find out many of the pictures were taken on the grounds of the Mitchel Plantation. So far nothing had inspired her.

She picked up the frame containing the one picture she knew was of her aunt's house. Holding it flat, she blew a light coating of dust from the glass, and noted a hairline fracture running across the middle.

The frame itself was also in poor condition, and a corner of it broke off by her simply holding it. If her aunt wanted to protect the picture from any damage, the glass and frame would need to be replaced.

Knowing it was over eighty years old, she carefully removed the backing from the frame. Underneath she found the mat, yellowed and cracking. Gently, she peeled away the old mat and found there was another layer or possibly two. Her fingers tingled with anticipation. It was common to place another photo over an existing one. Many great finds had been made from this very thing.

Once again, she carefully repeated the procedure of parting the aged paper. The second photo was of the house again, only it was of the front porch. The type of photo paper was clearly from an earlier era, maybe from around the eighteen hundreds. Excitement bubbled when noted another photograph underneath this one. Praying it would separate as easily as the others, she carefully pulled at the corner. Slowly and meticulously, she peeled the old paper apart.

To her astonishment, in between the photos she found a thin piece of yellowed paper with spidery handwriting, fading from age. The remaining photograph was of a young woman, posing on the front porch and dressed in clothing from the late nineteenth century or early twentieth century. She was really quite beautiful and had a soft smile playing at her lips instead of the usual stern look that was so commonly found in older photographs. Was she the author of the letter?

Thoroughly intrigued with the single piece of paper, Addie arranged each photograph on the dining room table in the order they had been found. Picking up the fragile paper, she tried to decipher the elegant handwriting.

Dearest Lydia,

As I write this letter, I can scarcely keep from weeping. Robert has not returned, nor have I heard from him in the past six months. This wretched war has no doubt claimed his life, leaving me a widow at the age of nineteen. The Yankees have burned Atlanta and I believe 'tis only a matter of time before they invade our peaceful little town. You will remember the day I hid mama's valuables? I'm afraid of remaining here without a man to protect me or my sweet little Margaret. I've taken everything I can carry and escaped from here, except the treasure you most valued. It will remain hidden until you are able to claim it. Dearest, never give up hope. Find comfort in the word of the Lord. In times as these remember the passage of scripture that has comforted me. The gospel of John 4:11-14. Is this not the evidence that all will be well? I will try to have courage and pray that we will meet again. If not in this life then in the next.

Love your sister, Marianne

Addie re-read the letter as a thrill of excitement rushed through her veins. If this Lydia or Marianne was related to the Caldwell's, it would prove the rumor of the buried riches surrounding the house to be true.

Dying to tell somebody about her discovery, she debated about texting her aunt. She decided against interrupting her meeting, especially since Hazel would be put out with Addie for being inconsiderate.

Addie scrolled through her contacts, realizing she didn't really have any close friends. Most of the girls from high school had either married or moved away, and she hadn't kept in contact with the few friends she'd made in college. Truthfully, once she and Brandon started dating, they'd hung out with his friends.

She went to her favorites screen and pressed her sister's number, only to get voicemail. A minute later a text came from Chellie saying she was on a field trip with Stephanie's class and would call Addie later if it wasn't an emergency.

Unless finding out I'm a loser counted as one? Addie quickly replied that it wasn't an emergency.

Blowing out a depressing breath, she acknowledged her lack of friends was entirely her fault. She'd stopped going to church activities and never socialized with anyone at work. Suspending her Facebook account had isolated herself even more. It had taken her aunt's dogged persistence to get Addie to go out with a guy. A guy she only pretended to date while actually dating him. It didn't help that she was extremely attracted to him either.

She groaned and lay her head down on the table. Aside from the fact that Chase was a hot country rock star and had a sexy southern accent, could her loser status be the reason she was so drawn to him? At least one good thing would come from their fake relationship. Once she got home, she was determined to make new friends and start dating again. She might even track down Biker Boy and ask him out.

Feeling a little better, Addie cleaned up the pictures. She put the letter and old photographs in a manila envelope and then carried the box back upstairs. Placing the envelope on her dresser, she lowered the attic stairs and returned the container of pictures back where it belonged.

Back in her room, she glanced at the clock and saw Chase would be coming in only a few hours. She tried not to get too excited about seeing him again, and reminded herself what the status of their relationship was: Friends. Nothing more.

Chapter Twelve

Chase loosened his tie as he left his office. He took the stairs two at a time, eager to leave and pick up Addie. His shoes echoed against the marble floor, making the security guard look up from his desk. Chase waved his hand as he passed by. "See ya later, George."

The older man grinned, his white teeth gleaming against his black skin. "Have a good night, Mr. Chase," he said in a low gravelly voice.

"You too." He waved and stepped out into the sunshine, glad to be free of his office. He picked up the pace and started to hum a tune he'd had in his head. It died on his lips when saw Hayden waiting for him next to his truck.

Her heavily glossed lips curved up into a seductive smile. "Hey there, handsome."

Chase ignored her greeting and proceeded to unlock his truck. "What are you doing here?"

Hayden moved next to him, her arm brushing against his. Physical contact had always been one of her tactics to getting her way. "I've been thinking about you all day and wanted to take you out to supper."

Chase stepped away. "Sorry, I've got other plans."

"What kind of plans?"

He almost laughed out loud. The entire time they'd been dating, she never let him ask about her plans. Of course, that's because she was cheating on him.

"Not that it's any of your business, but I've got a date with my girlfriend." Irritation flashed in her eyes, and Chase had to admit feeling a small measure of satisfaction. "If you'll excuse me, I don't want to be late."

Hayden didn't move. She eyed him for several seconds, her mouth slowly lifting into her signature smile. "I know your girlfriend said she would enjoy discovering all of your secrets, but I've discovered one that I know won't make my daddy too happy."

"What are you talkin' about?"

"Well," she said, closing the distance between them. "Daddy asked about us today. He seems pleased we're back together."

Chase's chest tightened with anger. "I thought you would've told him by now that you broke up with me."

"I didn't want to do anything to make him angry with you." She lifted one shoulder up. "You know, in case you need a good reference for the job in Nashville?"

A cold feeling of dread knotted his stomach. How had she found out about Nashborough? Chase knew Shanna would've never divulged his secret, especially to Hayden. No one else knew about the application he'd filled out. Although he'd talked to his parents about finding work in Tennessee, he hadn't told them about the lead on the job yet. Not even his best friends knew.

"I wouldn't want Daddy to fire you if he found out you've been looking for a job with one of his biggest competitors."

Swallowing back his anger, Chase tried to keep calm. Hayden was like a shark and if she smelled blood it would only increase the frenzy.

"What do you want, Hayden?" He crossed his arms over his chest, and leaned against the truck. "Another date?" he asked cynically.

Her eyes remained cool and detached, the smile still there. "Maybe." She turned and casually sauntered toward her car. Opening her door, she glanced over her shoulder. "Enjoy your night."

Before he called her an offensive—although fitting— name, he jerked open his door and climbed in behind the wheel.

The cab of the truck was stuffy, and he felt like he couldn't breathe. He quickly started the engine, and cracked the windows, turning the air on high. The radio blasted his CD demo and he turned it off, needing a second to think.

In the side view mirror, he spotted Hayden's car approaching him on the driver's side. She expected him to look at her, so he kept facing forward as she slowly passed by. Only when she exited the parking lot and merged into traffic did his grip on the steering wheel loosen.

What had he ever seen in her? It was hard to believe that at one time he'd been so blinded with love, or what he thought was love, that he'd actually wanted to marry her. He'd even bought the ring.

He adjusted the air vent to blow on him more directly and pulled his tie off. Divine intervention had saved him from making that mistake. He'd come home early from a business trip, and decided to make a surprise visit to her apartment in Macon. When she hadn't answered the door, he'd used the key she'd given him and walked in, catching her in a compromising position with another guy.

This time she couldn't lie or talk her way out of the situation, although she tried, even blaming Chase for being gone.

Shortly after their breakup—which Hayden claimed she had instigated—she left for California. The hold she once held over him was shattered, and Chase felt free.

Now she was back, trying to mess with his life again. The question was why? What could possibly be her motive, other than to cause trouble?

Feeling frustrated and stupid for getting tangled up in Hayden's web of lies in the first place, he shifted the truck into gear and started for home. Before he exited the parking lot, his phone buzzed an incoming call. He smiled when he saw who the caller was. Jackson could always make him laugh. "Hey," he said, easing onto the street. "What's up?"

"We're planning tonight's entertainment and Syd wondered if strip poker would scare your new girlfriend off?"

Chase grinned when he heard Sydney scold her husband. "I never said anything about stripping."

"Sure you did, babe. Just a few minutes—"

Chase heard a scuffle and a lot of laughter. Then Jackson came back on the phone. "Sorry, my mistake. Syd was talking about stripping *after* everyone goes home."

Sydney protested loudly again, but Chase could hear the amusement in her voice. Jackson liked to tease, and usually his teasing went a little too far. He hoped Addie would be able to handle it.

"Maybe I'll just take Addie out to eat," Chase said. "You're notorious for scaring women off, especially on first dates." He pulled out of the parking lot and headed for home.

"I'll be good," Jackson said. "I promise."

"I'll make sure he behaves, Chase," Sydney hollered loud enough for him to hear. "If not, he's sleeping in the guest room tonight."

"That's just cold," Jackson said.

"No teasing Chase's date. I mean it, Jackson." Sydney's voice sounded firm. Whether or not Jackson heeded his wife's warning remained to be seen.

"Dude, listen to your wife. For once."

"What? I'm not that bad."

"Yes you are." Chase snorted. "Do you honestly think Sydney would've gone out with you again if I hadn't talked her into it?"

Jackson chuckled softly. "Yeah, I guess I do owe you for that one."

Sydney's family had moved into the area a few years earlier, and the first time Jackson saw her he'd fallen in love. Sydney, however, wouldn't give him the time of day. She'd just come out of a bad breakup and wasn't interested in dating. It took nearly three months for her to finally agree to go out with Jackson.

Their first date had been at Chase's house. A few couples had gathered in his basement to eat pizza and watch a movie. Jackson sat close to Sydney, holding her hand. When the lights turned off for the movie to start, he yelled out, "Hey, don't touch me there."

Everyone laughed and, knowing Jackson, didn't take him seriously. A few minutes after the movie started, Sydney excused herself to use the restroom. She never came back.

Jackson begged and apologized for a solid two weeks without making any progress. Chase had finally been able to talk with Sydney, asking her to give Jackson one more chance. They were married eight months later.

"By the way, Beau might come over. He and Kara are fighting again so you might have a little competition."

"I hate when they're fighting," Chase grumbled as he made a left turn. Beau compensated by flirting with any girl he was near. "Maybe I'll bring Ashlee over. He'll be so busy dodging her he won't have time for anything else."

"Now that could be funny. See ya soon, buddy."

Chase ended the call, feeling a lot less stressed. Rolling back his shoulders, he focused on the email his agent sent him right before leaving work. A smaller, but successful record label liked Chase's demo CD and planned on coming to their gig at Gracie's this Saturday. It might not be what he wanted, but it would be a step in the right direction.

Excited about the prospect, Chase turned on his CD and sang along as he made his way through a line of traffic backed up by road construction. When he finally made it through, one glance at the clock told him if he stopped by his house to change clothes, he'd be late picking up Addie. He hated being late, especially if someone was waiting on him. Since the Caldwell's property turnoff was before his house, he decided to swing by there first.

A few minutes later he pulled up to Janie's house. He popped a piece of gum in his mouth and climbed out of the truck. He crossed the yard and made it to the porch in record time. If someone was watching him they'd know how eager he was to see Addie again. Not wanting to come off desperate, he waited a few seconds before ringing the doorbell.

Addie opened the door so quickly it made him wonder if she'd been watching for him. "Hi there." She smiled, carving the dimple in her cheek. "You're just in time to help me carry our dessert."

"We're bringing dessert?" he said, entering the house and following close behind her to the kitchen.

She glanced back at him, her hair swaying across her shoulders. "Yeah, I texted Sydney and asked if I could bring anything. Lucky for us, when Aunt Janie made her delicious coconut cake for her quilting circle, she made an extra one."

"That is lucky," Chase said, spotting the coconut laden cake on the countertop. "Are you sure we have to share?"

Addie flashed him a smile. "You have no idea how torturous it's been to not taste it."

"I'm impressed with your self-control."

Chase remembered the telltale signs of her taste testing this morning when he'd wiped away the sugar from her lower lip. Checking for any signs of coconut, his gaze dropped to her mouth. He quickly forgot about trying to find any incriminating evidence, his thoughts going in an entirely different direction. His eyes flickered back up to meet hers, and electricity crackled between them.

After a few heated seconds, she gave him a shy smile. "Okay, I confess I did snitch a tiny bit of frosting, but I just covered it up with more coconut."

He laughed and scooted the cake toward him. "Maybe I should let you drive while I guard the cake."

"I don't think so. I saw the way you were looking at that cake."

Well, at least she hadn't mentioned the way he'd been looking at her. He'd had to use every ounce of willpower he possessed not to let his gaze linger on the teal colored tee that hugged every generous curve she'd been blessed with.

"I can't help it. It's one of my favorite things and my mother won't ever make it because she thinks the frosting is too rich." He carefully lifted the cake platter. "If you ever want to do something really nice for me then make me a coconut cake."

She wrinkled her cute nose and grabbed her purse, leading him out of the kitchen. "I've tried to make one before and it looked even worse than the apple pie."

"That pie was good."

"Good food is all about the presentation. If you really want me to bake you something then cookies are my specialty."

"What kind?" he asked as he balanced the cake with one hand and opened the door.

"Whatever your favorite is." She breezed past him and he caught a tantalizing scent that smelled as good as one of his mama's magnolia trees.

He closed the door behind him and followed her to his truck. "I love any kind of chocolate chip. Regular, oatmeal or pumpkin."

"Well, my friend," she said, standing by the passenger door. "I promise before I go home I'll make you chocolate chip cookies. Which kind will just have to be a surprise."

"Promise?" He kept his tone light, although his insides twisted at the thought of her going home.

"Absolutely."

With a grin, he leaned forward and opened the truck door. "I look forward to being surprised." While balancing the cake with the other, he held out his hand and helped her up into the truck. Once she was situated, he handed her the cake. "You sure you can handle this?"

"I'll do my best."

He chuckled and closed the door.

* * *

Addie watched as Chase rounded the front of the truck. While she could handle not snitching from the cake again, she wasn't so sure about her growing feelings for her pretend boyfriend.

They'd definitely had a moment in the kitchen that had generated as much heat as a beachside bonfire.

It wasn't her fault, though. The guy was totally irresistible. He looked so good in the fitted button-down shirt. She glanced down at her own clothing, wondering if she should've dressed up a little.

"I just realized you're wearing a dress shirt and slacks," she said, once he slid in behind the wheel. "I think I'm underdressed."

His gaze skimmed over her before returning to her face. "I think you look great. And I was going to swing by my house to change clothes and grab my guitar."

"Your guitar, huh? So are you going to sing for me?" Ever since hearing him in church, she'd been dying to hear his voice again.

He gave her a lopsided grin and started the truck. "Well, I sorta hoped you'd sing with me."

Her eyes widened. "I don't sing. I mean, I can sing, but not in front of people."

Chase chuckled. "Just kidding. Jackson wanted me to bring my guitar. We usually like to mess around whenever we can."

"Whew. That's good." She placed a hand over her racing heart. "For a minute there I thought I was going to suddenly develop a massive headache—you know the kind that would require you to take me home."

Chase looked at her sidelong. "You wouldn't fake a headache, would you?"

"Um, yes."

The edge of his mouth twitched as he turned the truck around and started for his house. "Okay, so no singing in public.

No riding horses. You like sugar and baking cookies but dislike exercising. Anything else I should know?"

"Yellow is my favorite color and I don't just like sugar, I love it."

He laughed. "Got it." He made a right turn and shot her a quick look. "By the way, how was your day today?"

Addie thought about the mysterious letter she'd found pressed between the old photographs. Aunt Janie had been so excited to share the news with her quilting circle this evening. She was convinced the rumors about buried treasure were true. "So great. You won't believe what I found today."

"What did you find?"

Addie told him how she'd found the letter, and summarized what it said. He laughed when she told him her aunt's obsession with finding the lost treasure. "Knowing Miss Janie, she'll probably find it."

"Wouldn't that be awesome."

"Very." Chase pulled into his driveway. "So, did you get a chance to go exploring on the bike?"

Addie shook her head. "That's on tomorrow's agenda. I want to get an early start before it gets too hot."

"Yeah, it might reach seventy five. Scorching."

"Shut up. It's still in the forties at home."

"I'm just teasing. Heck, if it drops into the fifties I'm complaining about how cold it is."

"In Idaho, if it hits the fifties, girls are laying out, getting an early start on their tans. It doesn't matter if there's still snow on the ground."

One side of his mouth curved up. "Snow and bikini's. Sounds fun."

She rolled her eyes. "You're such a guy."

Grinning, he killed the engine and climbed out of the truck. Addie slid the cake platter onto the seat, waiting for him to open the door. She kind of liked his genteel manners, and knew she'd miss it when she went home.

"You know," Addie said, as he helped her out of the truck, "when I go back to Idaho, I'm probably going to sit in my car waiting for someone to open the door for me."

He looked at her with something she couldn't describe. Maybe a combination of frustration and longing? Slowly, one corner of his mouth drew up. "Then don't go back."

Addie sucked in a startled breath and tried to read Chase's face. He was teasing, right? He winked. Of course he was teasing.

"Or," she said, patting him on the chest, "I could just take you home with me." Through her flattened palm, she felt the rapid beating of his heart.

"I just might take you up on that offer."

Oh boy, the way he said it, with that slow, southern drawl, sent a shiver through her. Her heart raced and the whole idea sounded completely sane—staying in Georgia or taking him home. It scared her a little. She dropped her hand and tried to be nonchalant. "Well, either way…you've totally spoiled me. Thank you."

"You're welcome." His eyes lingered on her for a moment longer before he took her hand and led her inside his house. A tantalizing aroma circulated in the air as he closed the door behind them. Still holding her hand, he guided her through the entry way, passing by the kitchen.

His little sister, Taylin, stood by the stairs leading to the basement. "Hey," she said as her eyes lowered briefly to their joined hands. "What're y'all doing tonight?"

"Going to Syd and Jackson's house for dinner," Chase said. He squeezed Addie's hand before releasing it. "I'll be right back."

He jogged down the stairs, leaving Addie alone with Taylin. His little sister leaned against the wall, watching Addie intently. "You look great. I love your hair straight." Then she pointed down and grinned. "Love the shoes."

Addie stuck out one of her teal cut-out pumps in front of her. "Thanks. Shoes are sort of a weakness I have. I believe I own almost every color possible."

Taylin grinned and pushed away from the wall. "I knew I liked you." She looked back over her shoulder as she headed for the kitchen. "Do you want anything to drink?"

"Sure," Addie said, following behind her. "Ice-water sounds great."

While Taylin got her a drink, Addie took a seat at the bar. "Are you doing anything fun tonight?"

"Are you kidding?" Taylin rolled her eyes. "I have a stupid paper to write for English, a history test to study for, and, on top of that, I volunteer once a week at the Christian Youth Center and the activity I'd planned for the girls I mentor fell through."

She slid the glass of water toward Addie and took a seat next to her, acting like they were old friends. Without Chase or her twin sister around, Taylin didn't seem as snide. "The lady that was going to come and teach the girls about using the right kind of make-up, canceled on us today." She heaved a deep sigh. "I have no idea what I'm gonna do now."

Before she knew what she was doing, Addie volunteered herself. "I could help if you can't find anyone else."

Taylin's eyes lit with hope. "Seriously?"

Addie tried to downplay her skills as a makeup artist. "I mean, I'm not a professional or anything, but I took a class so I can offer glamour shots when I open my own photography studio."

"You do glamour shots? Because, that would totally be cool!"

Technically, no, but she'd experimented with her sister and some of the teenage girls in her neighborhood. "How many girls are there going to be?" Addie wasn't sure there would be enough time to do make-up and take pictures too.

Taylin's eyebrows knit together as she concentrated on doing the mental math. Chase came up the stairs, carrying a guitar case. Addie stared and felt her pulse leap. He looked good, wearing a pair of distressed jeans and a simple T-shirt that emphasized well-developed biceps.

"Ready?" His lips curved as he met her gaze.

"Hang on, Chase," Taylin said. She put her hand on Addie's arm. "If everyone comes, we have a total of six girls. Think it'll be too many?"

Addie shook her head. "No, if you're willing to help, I'd love to do it. Will the girls be able to bring their own make-up? If that's a problem, I can pick up a few new things to use."

Taylin grinned. "Most of them won't have anything, but Ashlee has a ton of make-up she's never opened."

Chase moved to the bar, resting his guitar case on top. "What did my sister just rope you in to doing?"

Taylin stood up and moved around to stand next to her brother. "I didn't rope her in to anything." She bumped him with her hip. "Your girlfriend just saved me." She stepped back toward the staircase. "Thanks again, Addie. You're awesome."

"No problem."

"Chase can give me your number and I'll text you all the info."

"Sounds good." With a wave, Taylin disappeared down the stairs. Addie pushed her chair out from the bar and stood up next to Chase. "Ready?"

"Yeah." Amusement lit his soft green eyes. "So, what did my sister just talk my *girlfriend* in to doing?"

"I'm going to help Taylin at the youth center by taking glamour shots of the girls she mentors."

"She's right. My girlfriend is awesome."

"Ha ha." Addie picked up her ice-water and took it over to the sink. She was starting to feel guilty about all the people they were deceiving about their relationship. Worse, the lines of reality were starting to blur for her as well. After dumping the water out, she placed the glass on the counter and turned around to find Chase watching her. "We both know I'm not really your girlfriend."

"I don't know. You're a girl and you're my friend." He lifted his guitar case with one hand and came around the bar to stand next to her. "Sounds like a girlfriend to me."

Addie couldn't help smiling. "You're so clever."

Chase grinned. "I know." He took her hand and led her outside. She liked the feel of his hand. She liked the clandestine smiles he sent her way, and she liked the idea of being Chase's girlfriend. Probably a little too much.

Chapter Thirteen

Addie stared at the McCall's house in disbelief. The two-story Colonial brick home was massive with a four-car garage flanking one side and an enclosed glass solarium on the other. Either the newlyweds were loaded or they lived with their parents.

"Wow. Nice house," she said with awe.

Chase snorted. "It was a wedding gift from Sydney's grandmother."

"Wow. Nice grandma."

"Tell me about it."

Addie took in the incredible landscaping and wished she would've brought her camera. She glanced over at Chase. "And just the two of them live here?"

"For now." He leaned forward and rested his chin atop his knuckles on the steering wheel. "I know Jackson is planning on filling it with children. He came from a large family of boys, a small home and hardly any money. But his parents are the most wonderful, down-to-earth people you'll ever meet."

"Judging from the size of the house, I'd say Jackson and Sydney could have a dozen kids and still have room to spare."

He sat back and looked at her with a smile. "Syd has one brother. I think her idea of a large family would be three or four kids." He shrugged as he opened his door. "I guess they'll figure it out as they go."

Addie stared back at the house as Chase came around to help her out. Having only one sister herself, she agreed that three or four kids would be a large family. She wondered how many kids Chase wanted. Then she wondered why she even cared. They were just friends. But as he opened the door and held out his hand, his words echoed in her head. *"I don't know. That sounds like a girlfriend to me."*

Their eyes met as she placed her palm against his. Warmth started at the contact spot and spread up her arm. She took in a fortifying breath and stepped out of the truck, eager to break the connection. Touching him made her imagination run wild.

Before she knew what was happening, her heel caught on something and pitched her forward. She squealed and threw her arms out, grasping onto Chase. He stumbled back, but kept her firmly in his arms.

"Sorry." She dragged her eyes up to meet his amused expression.

"I don't mind." His mouth quirked as he rubbed a hand across her shoulders. "I kinda like having you in my arms."

Yeah, she liked it too. She shouldn't, but his solid embrace and the heady scent of his cologne made it nearly impossible to think straight. His hands moved to her waist, as if the magnetic force drawing them closer wasn't enough. Addie wasn't sure how much longer she could fight the powerful pull he seemed to have on her.

"Okay, you two," Jackson said, coming out of nowhere. He placed one arm around each of them. "No PDA in my front yard."

Chase groaned, looking a little annoyed. "Right."

Jackson just grinned, keeping his arms around them as if in a group hug. "Well, at least that's what my mother-in-law is always tellin' me."

"Like you ever listen to her," Chase mumbled.

Jackson laughed and moved out of their way. "Yeah. You're right."

Chase shot his friend an annoyed look as Addie turned around and retrieved the cake from the truck. She closed her eyes and tried to get a hold of her emotions. Kissing Chase was not part of the plan. She couldn't get any more involved with him—any deeper than she already was. Her return flight to Idaho was a like a ticking clock and before she knew it her time would be up, and so would their ruse. If she wasn't careful, she'd be returning to Idaho with more than a broken heart. It would be shattered.

She twisted back around just as Sydney came outside. "Hey," Sydney said, slipping her arm around her husband's waist. "I didn't know y'all were here."

Jackson turned and circled his arms around his wife, his hands clasped behind her. "I was just coming out to see if they needed help with anything."

Chase snorted. "Yep. You know Jackson. Always tryin' to be helpful."

Sydney's brows drew together at the sarcastic tone in Chase's voice. "Jacks—"

Her words were cut off when Jackson leaned down and kissed his wife. Thoroughly.

"Hey," Chase said indignantly, "I thought you said no PDA in your front yard." He glanced over at Addie with a can-you-believe-this-guy look on his face.

Jackson pulled away from his wife, a wicked gleam in his laughing eyes. "Yeah, but like *you* said, I rarely listen."

Sydney let out a deep sigh. "Do I even wanna know what y'all are talkin' about?"

No! Addie wanted to shout. Couldn't they talk about something else? When Sydney looked her way, Addie shook her head, pleading with her eyes to drop the whole thing.

She could've hugged her when Sydney held up her hands. "You know what, I don't even wanna know."

Chase gave Addie that smile of his, making her heart do a little flip-flop. He took her hand and led her toward the front door. "You're right, Syd, you don't wanna know." Then he said with a laugh, "But maybe you can ask your husband about advice he should be taking from his mother-in-law instead of quoting her."

Addie stifled a giggle when Sydney asked, "What does my mother have to do with this, Jackson?"

While Jackson sputtered, Addie squeezed Chase's hand. "Your quick thinking just got Jackson in trouble."

"I know," Chase said with a grin. "Doesn't it feel good?"

More like satisfying. "Yes, but I'd watch my back if I were you."

Chase chuckled as he held open the door for her. "See, you already know Jackson so well."

* * *

"So," Jackson said, once he and Chase were outside. "You and Addie looked pretty cozy."

Chase finished scraping the grill and looked into his friend's mischievous eyes. "We were. As usual, your timing was impeccable."

Jackson sniggered and nudged him out of the way. "Sorry, but I couldn't resist." He ignited the gas grill and turned to Chase with a grin. "It's not like y'all can't pick up where you left off."

Moving to the patio table, Chase took a seat and let out a deep breath. As much as he hated to admit it, kissing Addie wasn't the smartest idea. He had a feeling once he did, he'd want to do it again and again. "It's probably a good thing you came out when you did. I've been trying to take things slow."

Jackson lifted a skeptical brow. "You, women and slow don't really go together."

"Hey!" Chase laughed. "I've matured in the last couple of years."

"C'mon, Chase. I know you and you like kissing women. Don't deny it."

"Okay, I won't deny it. But I have changed. I *do not* kiss every girl I go out with."

"You better move fast, Nichols," Jackson teased. "Idaho Girl is going home soon."

Something sharp gripped Chase's stomach. Addie was leaving soon. The more he thought about it, the more it bugged him. "Don't remind me."

A smile tipped Jackson's mouth. "I think you're falling in love with her."

Was he? Chase ran a hand through his hair in frustration. "If I am, I have a big problem. I doubt she'll live anywhere else but Idaho. And if I move anywhere, it'll be to Nashville."

Jackson closed the lid to the grill for it to preheat. He stuck his hands in his pockets and shrugged. "Man, I don't know what to tell you. Love isn't something you ever plan on. It just happens. And you two seem really good together."

"I think it's a little premature to call this love."

But what if it was love? His feelings for her were different from anything else he'd ever experienced.

Yes, he was incredibly attracted to her, but as stupid as it sounded, he felt like he'd just found his best friend.

"I don't know," Jackson said. "I fell in love with Syd the first time I saw her."

Before Chase could comment, the loud rumble of a diesel engine announced Beau's arrival. Jackson grinned and pointed a finger at Chase. "Just ask yourself how you'll feel if Beau starts moving in on Addie."

He already knew how he felt—and it irked him. Chase stood up. "We better go inside. I need to protect Addie from Beau."

Jackson started to laugh. "You've got it so bad."

By the time Chase and Jackson made it into the kitchen, Beau was already hitting on Addie.

Letting out a long wolf whistle, Beau slid into the chair next to Addie, eyeing her with intense interest. "Please tell me you're my date."

Women found Beau irresistible. Even Chase's own sisters had commented on his sex appeal. Beau was tall, muscular and shaved his head bald. However, Ashlee said it was the "hot" kind of bald. Whatever that meant.

"Nope," Chase said as he crossed the kitchen floor. He thumped Beau on the arm and grinned. "She came with me." He moved behind Addie, placing both his hands on the back of her chair.

Beau looked at him curiously, his lips twisted into a grin, emphasizing the soul patch he wore just below his lower lip. "Ah, man. So what I'm gonna be, the fifth wheel?"

Jackson came in and the two men bumped fists. "I guess you and Kara didn't kiss and make up?"

"Don't think that's gonna happen this time."

Jackson patted his friend on the back. "I think it's time to move on"

Beau gave a derisive laugh. "I think you're right." He swung his head around and looked at Addie. "By the way, I'm Beau Jacobsen." He held out his hand.

"Addie Heywood." She shook his hand.

"Addie?" Beau said.

Chase knew the moment his friend made the connection as a look of understanding crossed his features.

"Wait a minute." Beau pointed his finger at her. "Are you tellin' me you're the niece from Idaho that Chase had to pick up?"

"Yes," Addie answered hesitantly. "That's me."

"I know you're not what Chase was expecting." Beau laughed as he slid his gaze toward Chase. "Bet you're glad you changed your mind about making me pick her up once you saw her, huh?"

Nice one, Beau. Chase felt his neck flush with embarrassment as Addie tipped her face up to look at him with questioning eyes.

Jackson put his arm around his wife. "And you thought *I* was gonna cause trouble?"

Sydney crossed her arms in front. "Addie, don't listen to a thing these boys say. I swear when they get together they are worse than a bunch a teenagers." She pointed a finger at Beau. "You better be nice, or you won't get any of the dessert Addie brought."

"If she's the dessert then I'll shut up right now."

Jackson snickered and Sydney elbowed him. "That goes for you, too."

Chase should've known his friends would be annoying. He reached for Addie's hand and pulled her to her feet. "We're gonna get started on the hamburgers." He grabbed the plate of meat, leaving Beau and Jackson laughing.

Keeping a hold of her hand, Chase stomped over to the grill. "Sorry about that."

She squeezed his fingers and he felt her gaze on him. When he finally looked at her, she smiled. "What are you sorry about?"

They stopped in front of the grill and he felt the heat radiate as he opened the lid. "Beau and his big mouth."

"So," she said, holding the platter of meat. "Do I get to hear the story?" Her voice was laced with laughter.

Using the spatula, Chase transferred one of the patties to the grill. It sizzled as the flames shot up around the meat. Then with a sigh he met her eyes. "I guess."

He loaded the rest of the meat on the grill and closed the lid. "I wasn't that excited to pick you up. I remembered this red-headed bratty girl who was taller than me. Beau was razzing me about it and I threatened to make him pick you up."

She set the empty plate on the table, looking at him incredulously. "So, you really didn't know that was me when you helped me with my luggage?"

Chase shook his head. "I really didn't."

She tilted her head and smiled. "I think that it so sweet. Your mama really did raise you to be a gentleman."

He grinned. "I hope I would've helped anyone, but to be perfectly honest, I was attracted to you the minute I saw you." Jackson's words flashed in his mind. *"I fell in love with Syd the first time I saw her."*

Addie took a step toward him. "Is that so?" Her voice was soft and flirtatious.

"Yeah." Chase took her hand and tugged her to him. He couldn't help it. Whenever she was near him all he could think about was touching her.

She studied him for a few heartbeats, and he wondered what she was thinking. Unfortunately he didn't get the chance to ask her. Jackson and Beau burst outside, laughing like a couple of hyenas.

Chase cast his friends an irritated look, which only added to their fun.

"Don't mind us," Jackson said, wearing a playful grin while tossing a tomato in the air and catching it again.

"Just pretend we're not even here," Beau said, standing so close they could smell his aftershave.

"Like that's gonna happen." He eyed the two men and was tempted to push them both into the pool.

The door to the house slammed shut. Sydney stepped out, her hands to her hips. "Jackson McCall!"

Jackson sobered up at the sound of his wife's voice. "What?" He tried to appear innocent.

"I thought I told y'all to stay inside," she said as she marched toward him.

He pointed a finger at Beau. "He suggested we take over the cooking.".

Flattening his palm against his chest, Beau said, "Me? You're the one who said it looked like things were getting way too hot." He smirked as his eyes flickered over to Chase and Addie.

Sydney made an irritated noise in the back of her throat. "Jackson…"

Placing the tomato on the table, he straddled one of the chairs, barely holding back a laugh. "I meant the grill. The grill was getting hot."

"Uh-huh," Chase said dryly. He handed the spatula to Beau. "Go ahead and take over. Just don't burn mine."

* * *

The second Beau took over the cooking, he looked over his shoulder and gave Addie a wink. "Wanna help me?"

Addie could tell Beau was just trying to annoy Chase. Judging from the look on his face, it must be working. "Um, do you really need me to?"

"No," Chase said, taking her hand. "Beau doesn't need help." And then under his breath added, "At least not with cooking."

Laughing, Beau turned toward the grill and lifted the lid. "Talk about sizzling hot." He slid another glance in Addie's direction and winked again.

Chase shook his head. "Just ignore him." He gave Addie's hand a squeeze and led her to the table where Sydney and Jackson sat.

Sydney let out a loud sigh. "Can't y'all act like grown men for a change?" She leaned next to Addie and whispered in a loud voice, "And they say women are hormonal?"

Jackson snorted. "Hey, I grew up in a houseful of men and trust me testosterone is nothin' compared to a hormonal woman."

There was an elongated pause of silence.

Jackson cast an innocent look at his wife and held up his hands. "Just sayin'."

The side of Sydney's mouth twitched. "What exactly are you implying, Jackson McCall?"

"Nothin', baby. I'm just glad I'm a man. The Lord knew we wouldn't be able to handle it like you women. Right, Chase?"

Chase laughed. "Yeah. Women are definitely more equipped to handle their—" He made quotation marks in the air with his fingers. "—fluctuating hormones."

He must have noticed the look of disbelief Addie exchanged with Sydney because Chase quickly added, "That was a compliment."

"Thank you," Addie said smugly. "But I'm glad I'm a woman. I'd much rather be the one with the hormones than have to be the man who has to deal with me and my *fluctuating* hormones."

All three men busted up laughing.

"Score one for the girls," Beau said, saluting her with the spatula.

"I knew I liked you," Sydney said, giving Addie a high-five. "By the way, the guys have a gig on Saturday. Please tell me you're gonna come?"

"I'm planning on it," she said, sounding like she and Chase were really a couple. Her eyes flitted over to him, and she found him watching her with a look full of appreciation.

"Good, you can sit by me," Sydney said, drawing back her attention. "I hate going by myself. Drew's wife, Kellie, doesn't come that often, especially since her baby's almost due. She was the perfect person to be sitting by, too. Not too many men want to try to hit on a pregnant woman. I'm hoping that between the two of us, we can limit the amount of pick up lines we'll get." She held out her left hand. "It doesn't seem to matter to some men that I'm wearing a wedding ring and makin' eyes at the keyboard player."

Jackson leaned over and kissed his wife. "Yeah, it makes me crazy watching how all the men look at you. I think we need to start workin' on getting you pregnant so they'll back off."

Sydney blushed. "I can't believe you just said that." She playfully smacked him on the arm. "My mother would keel over with a heart attack if she heard you talkin' like that."

He raised his eyebrows mischievously. "Why? We're married, aren't we?"

Sydney narrowed her eyes again and whispered, "You know, it's gonna be a little hard to accomplish that when you're sleepin' in the guest room."

Jackson grinned. "Honey, I'm sorry. I'll keep my mouth shut the rest of the night."

Sydney's mouth curved up into a tender smile, her eyes filled with obvious love for her husband. "Sure you will," she said with a soft laugh.

Observing the couple, a pang of envy shot through Addie. She could feel their love radiating with the looks they gave each other. She wondered if she would ever get to share that kind of love with someone.

Glancing away, she found Chase still watching her, his mouth lifted into a half grin. With a slight tug on her hand, he pulled her to his side. It was crazy what was happening to her. She was falling for him hard and fast, feeling very much like the first time she'd gone skiing, gaining momentum with each second, careening out of control down the mountain, and crashing at the bottom.

She had injured herself, twisting her knee and ending her day on the slopes. By the time she left Georgia, what condition would her heart be in?

Chapter Fourteen

With her shoes and socks in her hand, Addie rushed down the stairs. She just about plowed over Miss Hazel. The tiny black woman placed her hand over her heart. "Where's the fire, girl?"

"The kitchen?" Addie quipped, teetering on the bottom stair.

"Doubt it," Hazel said with a hearty laugh. She put her fists to her hips and looked Addie up and down and raised one eyebrow. "I thought you were going for a ride with that Nichols boy. You can't go out dressed like that."

Addie frowned, looking down at her clothes. What was wrong with the way she was dressed? She had on red, knee-length basketball shorts from her days at high school and a white fitted T-shirt that said, "100% REDHEAD and I've got the ATTITUDE to prove it."

Aunt Janie came out from the kitchen, wiping her hands on her apron. "Oh, don't you look cute."

Hazel snorted. "If you say so."

"I declare, Hazel. What's wrong with the way she's dressed?"

Not really liking where this conversation was going, Addie tiptoed to the entryway and sat on one of the chairs to put on her shoes and socks. It's not like Hazel knew her *that* well.

While she tied the laces of her Nikes, she peered through the screen door to see if Chase was here yet. He'd called about an hour ago and said he was getting off work early to take her on a bike ride to a park where she could get some fantastic pictures. He was also bringing a picnic along so to come hungry.

Just thinking about seeing him again made her stomach do a little dance that wasn't from lack of food. Something had changed in their pretend relationship last night that felt more real than anything she'd ever experienced before. The night could've ended perfectly with a kiss both of them wanted if Chase's little sister Ashlee hadn't called him, needing a ride home from a party she should've never been to in the first place.

The minute his sister called, and Chase found out who she was with, his big brother mode kicked into high gear. Addie found it very endearing how concerned he was, enough that when they pulled up to Aunt Janie's house, he allowed Addie to open her own door and hop down without his assistance so he could go rescue Ashlee.

The twins, she found out last night from Chase, were very opposite in many ways. Taylin was a straight A student, volunteered at both the youth center and the hospital once a week and had her sights set on becoming a doctor. Ashlee, on the other hand, was graduating from high school but with a much lower GPA. She spent most of her free time shopping, and had no idea what she wanted to do other than marry Beau Jacobsen.

Addie had been worried about the girl, and told Chase to text her with an update. An hour later he sent her a message, telling her that Ashlee was home safe. He was glad she'd been smart enough to call him when the college aged boy she'd snuck out with took her to a party that wasn't the typical kegger with red plastic cups. Chase had been ticked off when he saw all the drug paraphernalia scattered around the room, and called the cops with an anonymous tip as soon as he had his sister. He'd apologized about cutting their date short, and said he'd make it up to her.

She heard the crunch of Chase's truck tires on the gravel driveway as he came to a stop. Although she wasn't thrilled with the idea of going for a bike ride, she figured it wouldn't be too bad. Riding a bike was easy. At least it was the last time she'd ridden one. Like ten years ago.

She stood at the doorway and watched him climb out of his truck. Dressed similarly to her, he looked cute in a pair of black basketball shorts and a white Hard Rock Café T-shirt. With little effort he got his bicycle out of the back of the truck and wheeled it over to where hers sat waiting for them.

Not wanting to get caught spying on him, she retreated back to the entry way. She sneaked a peek in the mirror that hung on the wall to check her appearance one last time. Janie and Hazel came in and caught her primping just as the doorbell chimed.

"Addie, you look adorable," Aunt Janie said, passing her by to open the door.

Hazel harrumphed disapprovingly, mumbling something about girls dressing like boys. Maybe Addie should go change. What if Chase didn't like what she had on? She tugged on the bottom of her T-shirt as Chase stepped inside.

The minute their eyes met, she relaxed a little. The approval she read in his gaze boosted her confidence. After exchanging pleasantries with Janie and Hazel, he took a step toward her. "Hey," he said, his eyes sweeping over her again. "Ready to go?"

She picked up her camera bag. "Yep."

A smile tipped his mouth as he reached for her hand and laced their fingers together. "Let's go."

Aunt Janie grinned with delight. "Y'all have fun."

"We will," Addie said, following Chase out the door.

With one foot on the top stair, Addie overheard Hazel say, "I can't believe it! They're dressed exactly the same. It's not proper, Janie."

Maybe Chase hadn't heard—or not.

He started laughing. "Should I be offended or you?"

"Me." She stopped next to the bikes. "Miss Hazel doesn't like the way I'm dressed."

Chase stepped back, keeping a hold of her hand and slowly scanned her from head to toe. He squeezed her fingers and gave her a wicked grin. "I like the way you're dressed, Miss Attitude."

"Thanks." She held onto the bike for support. That delicious southern drawl of his made her knees weak. "My sister gave me this shirt. Do you think she was trying to tell me something?"

"Probably."

"Hey!" She pulled her hand out of his and playfully tapped him on the arm. "Since when have I shown any attitude?"

He lifted an eyebrow and took her camera bag. "I don't know. I seem to recall you and Sydney having a conversation about hormonal men."

"Your memory is a little sketchy, Nichols," she said, as Chase secured her camera in a backpack containing their picnic. "We admitted women are hormonal. You men just have to deal with it."

He chuckled. "Like I said…attitude." He removed the bike helmet that hung from the handle of her borrowed bike and held it out in front of her. "Do you need any help with this?"

While Chase had looked completely adorable wearing his helmet, she knew she would probably look like a dork.

She took it anyway, not sure what end was the front. "Which way does this thing go on?"

His mouth hooked up on one side as he took the helmet out of her hands. "Like this." After placing it on her head, he tipped up her chin to clasp it together. She probably could do this part by herself, but decided not to say anything, thoroughly enjoying the close proximity and the yummy scent of his cologne. Dipping his head, he bent closer. "I don't want it to pinch you."

She probably wouldn't feel it if he did. Her body felt as if she floated on air as his fingers brushed against her throat. Her hand itched to caress his jaw, wanting to feel the shadow of whiskers growing there. His mouth was just a breath away and suddenly her heart went haywire.

A sound from the house reminded her they were not alone. Then she heard Hazel whisper loudly, "Are they kissing?"

Oh good. Commentary from two old women was just what anyone wanted. She held her breath and hoped they wouldn't say anything more.

"I can't tell from here," Janie said.

Chase snapped the clasp shut and moved slightly back. Catching Addie's gaze, he smiled and whispered, "It's not a bad idea, though."

"What's not a bad idea?" she asked coyly.

His eyes crinkled and he chuckled. "You know exactly what I'm talkin' about, Miss Attitude."

She did know. And even though it would make things ten times more complicated, kissing him sounded like an absolutely wonderful idea. However, hearing two grown women giggling from inside the house sorta put a damper on the whole thing. "We have an audience," she whispered.

"I know." He stepped away and grabbed his helmet. "Wanna help me?"

Addie didn't think her heart could handle another close encounter. She gripped the handle bars and tapped the kickstand out of the way. "We better not give them anything else to speculate about."

He laughed and put on his helmet. "Ready?" he said, strapping on the backpack.

"Lead the way," she said, pushing off to follow him.

The two of them pedaled leisurely onto the road. The late afternoon sun warmed the air sliding over her skin. The high temp topped out at seventy two with a few clouds here and there, making it a perfect day. It felt great to be outside, and riding a bike was fun and relaxing.

At least until they came to a hill.

Addie's breath became labored and embarrassingly loud as they pedaled up the incline. The nice leisurely bike ride had just changed into something that resembled exercise. The hill wasn't that big but she had serious doubts as to whether or not she would make it up without dying. How could she be this out of shape?

"You okay?" Chase questioned after they crested the top of the hill. He wasn't even winded.

Addie tried to slow her breathing down. "Fine," she huffed. "I'm just not used to the altitude."

A slow grin spread across his face. "Nice try. I hate to break it to you, but the altitude here should be helpin' you out."

Some gentlemen he was!

"Well, then it's the humidity. It can't possibly be that I never exercise and I'm out of shape." This was completely mortifying.

He didn't even try to hide his amusement. "You're right—it has to be the humidity." Glancing over at her, he had that wicked gleam in his eyes again. "Because there is nothin' wrong with your shape."

She felt her cheeks go hot, probably making her already flushed face even redder. "Thanks for trying to make me feel better, but it's clear I need to get out more."

"You're doing great."

Yeah, right. The road leveled out for a good half a mile, and Addie thought she might just make it. She still couldn't hold a conversation with Chase, which he found amusing. Luckily he was nice and didn't ask too many questions, only pointed out different landmarks.

They came to another hill and Addie adjusted her gears, hoping to find one that would magically make it easier. Nothing helped. Her breath became more labored, and sweat trickled down the sides of her face. Her extra strength deodorant better work or this whole date would be ruined. Despite her efforts, she fell a little more behind with each second.

Chase looked back over his shoulder, concern written all over his handsome face. "We're almost there. You're gonna make it, aren't ya?"

No! Her thighs were on fire and her chest hurt. "Yes," she wheezed, "but please tell me you brought your cell phone. I may need you to call my aunt to come and pick me up." At this point, she had no pride left.

"I brought it," he assured her with a wry grin.

He could laugh all he wanted, but there was no way she was coming back the same way.

Her foot slipped on the pedal and she seriously considered just stopping right there to die.

"It's downhill the rest of the way," Chase said, slowing down to let her catch up.

Positioning her foot again, she pumped for all she was worth, cresting the top just when she couldn't go another inch. Stretching out her aching legs, she took advantage of the momentum, coasting the rest of the way.

Chase pedaled backward, coasting alongside her. "I sure know how to show a girl a good time, don't I?"

"Uh-huh," she said, sucking in another breath. All she could think was he better have packed something really good to eat.

After a few minutes, Chase pointed up ahead. "There's the park."

Finally. They pedaled the last few yards and stopped. Addie planted both feet on the ground and straddled the bike. She wondered if she could walk. Her legs felt like Jell-O.

"Chase?" she said, taking off her helmet and hanging it on the handle bars.

He swung off of his bike, barely breathing hard at all. "Yeah?" He turned to look at her as he removed his own helmet.

"I cannot go back up that hill."

He snickered and shrugged off the backpack. Reaching inside, he pulled out a bottle of water. "Do I need to call my friend? Jackson's always willing to help." He offered her the water.

Her fingers curled around the cool bottle, wet from condensation. "Are you kidding? He'll never let me live this down." She twisted off the lid, taking a long drink. But they were going to have to call someone because there was no way she was getting back on that bike.

"Can't we call my aunt?" she questioned, swinging her leg over the middle bar and engaging the kickstand. Setting the water on the ground, she removed the band from the ponytail and finger-combed her hair. Her head was all sweaty and the slight breeze felt wonderful.

"We'll figure somethin' out." He ran his hand through his own hair. It wasn't fair. The guy looked incredible.

"I know what my next New Year's resolution is going to be," Addie said, twisting her hair back into a ponytail. "Start an exercise program."

"You do realize it's the second week of March. January is ten months away."

She flashed him a smile. "I know. That'll give me plenty of time to work up to it."

He chuckled and lifted the backpack up, slinging it over one shoulder. Together they walked to a secluded area shaded by a tree. Chase pulled a blanket out of the pack and spread it on the ground.

The first thing Addie did was take off her shoes and socks. She dumped some of the water to cool off her feet, grateful they didn't stink. "Sorry I'm so pathetic." She sat down on the blanket, wiggling her toes blissfully. "Ahh, that feels so amazing."

Chase joined her on the blanket, his eyes dipping down to her bare feet. "You're not pathetic." He lifted his gaze, giving her a crooked smile. "You're just not accustomed to the *altitude*," he said dryly.

"Very funny."

"I brought food. Will that help?"

"Let's hope."

"Do we need to start with the dessert?" he asked, unzipping the cooler. He pulled out a clear plastic tray with fat, flaky croissants, stuffed with a delectable chicken salad.

Her mouth watered and for once she opted for the main course instead of dessert. "I think I need the protein more than sugar right now."

Chase placed a croissant on a plate, along with Sun Chips and a small cluster of red grapes. "Thank you. This looks delicious," she said accepting the plate. "Did you pack this all by yourself?"

He started to fix a plate for himself. "I did. With the help of Kroger's deli."

"I'm impressed." She took a small bite of her sandwich.

"Well," he said, raising the croissant to his mouth. "That was the goal. Of course, I probably should've gotten us here by another means of transportation."

She grinned at the teasing note in his voice. "But I made it, didn't I?" *Barely.* But unlike her former fiancé, this man seemed to find her apathy for exercise sorta cute.

He laughed and dug into his food. Addie enjoyed watching him eat so enthusiastically. She hated to keep comparing him to Brandon, but her previous boyfriend was so obsessed with the quality and type of food that he rarely enjoyed anything he ate. Come to think of it, food had become such a source of contention between the two of them Addie was surprised she hadn't developed an eating disorder.

With Chase, it was different. She loved how comfortable she felt around him. It was like they'd been friends forever. He was fun to be around, easy to talk to and so cute he made her breath catch whenever their eyes met.

They talked about his work, and his upcoming performance on Saturday. He wasn't too stressed about the music rep, only hopeful he'd actually show up.

Neither of them brought up Hayden, which was fine with Addie. She was still eating and didn't want to ruin her appetite.

Chase finished his meal first, and put his hands behind his head, stretching out on his back while she told him about her day of washing windows and thoroughly dusting all of the wood furniture. He listened with his eyes closed. When she stopped talking and he hadn't moved, she wondered if he'd fallen asleep.

Taking a drink of water, she watched his chest rise and fall evenly. Reaching out with her foot she nudged him in the side. "Are you asleep?"

He kept his eyes shut and grinned. "No. I'm just resting my eyes."

"You *were* asleep." She tapped him with her foot again. "Am I that boring?"

He captured her foot with his hand and opened one eye. "You? Boring?" He gave a deep chuckle. "Hardly."

The warmth from his hand sent her heart into overdrive, even more so than the arduous bike ride had.

Chase kept a hold of her foot and turned on his side, resting on his elbow. "You have cute feet." He ran a thumb across her skin, leaving a trail of heat and shorting out her brain.

"Thank you."

He tickled the bottom, making her pull away giggling. "Stop that."

"That's for waking me up."

She threw a grape at him. "You said you weren't asleep."

"I'm kidding." He sat up beside her, their shoulders touching. "Ready for dessert?"

"I honestly don't know if I could eat another bite right now."

One eyebrow lifted.

"I'm serious. Can we save it for later?"

"Sure." He pointed to a small bridge next to a covered pavilion. "We could take a walk, maybe see if you can find something worthwhile to take a picture of."

The late afternoon sun shone behind a set of wispy clouds, making the lighting perfect for outdoor photography. "Good idea." They cleaned up, and Chase took care of the trash while Addie put her shoes and socks back on.

Although her legs felt like rubber, she stood up, shook out the blanket and then folded it. Chase handed her camera bag to her before stuffing the blanket inside the backpack. He slipped his cell phone in one of his pockets and used the bike lock to secure the pack to the bikes.

"Ready?" He reached for her hand and slid his fingers between hers.

Oh boy. One touch from him and her thoughts scattered like the seeds of a dandelion in the wind. She hooked the strap of her camera bag over one shoulder, and nodded. "Lead the way."

Chapter Fifteen

Heading toward the pond, Chase slowed down his pace, sensing Addie may not be very steady on her feet. "Are your legs feeling any better?" He still felt bad about forcing the bike ride when he knew she wasn't that excited about it.

"I'm still a little wobbly." She looked at him with a wry expression on her face. "Clearly I need to start exercising more. My sister is always after me to go on power walks with her. I guess when I get home I'll start going with her."

His stomach tightened when she mentioned home. He didn't want to think about what would happen when she left. Something had shifted in their relationship the night before, making it feel more than just an agreement between friends. He remembered the words of the song he'd started writing last night when couldn't sleep.

It was only supposed to be make-believe but nothing's felt more real.

Your laugh, your touch, each moment we've shared; I know what they make me feel.

The rest of the lyrics hadn't come that easily, probably because he felt so conflicted about what was happening between them. The timing was all wrong.

"Well," he said wryly. "If not power walks, you can always take up bicycling."

"Shut up." She laughed, and bumped his arm with her shoulder. "I know I'm pathetic."

"No you're not." He cut her a sidewise glance. "Cute, yes. Definitely not pathetic."

"Flatterer."

"I have to do something to make up for the torturous bike ride." He grinned, and gave her fingers a squeeze. "Besides, truth is never flattery."

"Ahh, thanks, but you've already redeemed yourself by promising me dessert." She glanced up at him. "By the way, what is for dessert?"

"It's a surprise."

"It must be good if you're holding out on me."

He laughed. "I believe we've already established your love affair with sugar, so you're kind of easy to please."

"You know me so well." She let go of his hand and opened up her camera bag. "Will you do me a favor?"

"Go get the dessert right now?"

"No." She pointed toward the pond. "Look at how the trees surrounding the bridge filters the sunlight."

Chase followed her line of sight. Towering poplars banked the bridge, allowing just enough light to make the water appear as if it had shimmering gold sprinkled across it.

"It's beautiful," she said, attaching the lens to her camera. "The only thing left to do is to find some hot-looking guy to pose for me."

Glancing around, Chase lifted one shoulder. "Sorry, I don't see anyone."

She smiled and aimed the camera right at him. "Oh, wow. I just found one."

While Chase had never been shy in front of an audience, posing for Addie seemed intimidating. "Now who's the flatterer?"

"Remember," she said, lowering the camera. "Truth is never flattery."

He shook his head. "I'm not really dressed for pictures."

"Actually, it'll appear more natural, and with the angles I'll be taking, the focal point won't be your clothes."

When he hesitated, she gave him some kind of look that must have made her father spoil her rotten. "Come on, please? Pretty, please? With sugar on top?"

It was the smile and the dimple that did him in. "Oh, all right. Tell me what to do."

Addie was surprisingly good at what she did. Artistically, she knew what she was looking for and directed Chase in various positions on the bridge and down by the water's edge. Most of the pictures were of his profile. They ended with him on the bridge. Addie had him looking out over the water while leaning on the railing.

"Okay, this last one try to look contemplative and brooding."

He didn't have to reach very deep for those emotions. The more time he spent with this girl, the more his goals of Nashville blurred.

"Perfect." She moved in for some close-up's. After taking several shots, she lowered her camera. "Done."

"Hey, don't I get to see them?" Chase asked when she disassembled the lens from the camera and stowed the equipment in the bag.

"Not yet." She slung the strap over her shoulder and joined him on the bridge. "Let me upload them on my computer first so I can edit them." She leaned against the railing with him and looked up into his eyes. "I think I got some amazing shots. Thank you again."

"You're welcome." Part of him wanted to ask about the photography studio she hoped to open one day, but then it would bring up her inevitable departure for home.

He didn't want to ruin the moment—because they were having a moment. A regular occurrence each time they made eye contact. "I hope you get your winning photo, with or without me in it."

"Me too." She smiled, making her dimple appear again.

Unable to resist, he lifted his hand and lightly ran a finger down the crease in her cheek. "I love your smile and that killer dimple."

"You do?" She seemed surprised and almost shy.

His thumb brushed the corner of her mouth. "I do."

His gaze drifted to her mouth as an invisible force drew them closer. Chase shouldn't kiss her. It would only complicate things. Their eyes met again, and that's all it took for him to make up his mind. He slid his hand behind her neck and dipped his head to meet her waiting lips. The perfect moment was ruined when his cell phone belted out Brad Paisley's *Start a Band*.

Ah. C'mon. Chase blew out a breath, resting his forehead against Addie's as the music continued. He drew back, shook his head and pulled out his phone. "Dang Jackson."

Addie took a step away, a dazed look on her face. Chase could almost swear he heard her mutter, "Dang right."

"Hey," Chase answered, cursing himself for not shutting off his phone.

"What're you doing?" Jackson asked as if he was bored and just wanted to shoot the bull.

"Ah, nothing much. I was just about to kiss Addie when you called." Although he knew better, the words just slipped out.

Addie dropped her chin and put a hand to her forehead, "What have you done?" she murmured under her breath.

Jackson hooted with laughter. "Are you kidding me?"

"No."

"I can't be that good. C'mon, what're you really doing?"

"Not kissing, that's for sure."

Addie's head snapped up, and he winked at her as Jackson let out another loud laugh. She seemed to have a good sense of humor, and hopefully wouldn't hold his impulsiveness against him. Having the upper hand on Jackson was such a rare thing, and he couldn't help himself.

"How do I know she's even with you," Jackson said. "Let me talk to her."

Chase lowered the phone. "He doesn't believe me and wants to talk to you."

She pointed a finger at her chest and mouthed, "Me?"

"You don't have to if you don't want to. In fact, I'll just hang up."

Humor lit her eyes and she shrugged, taking the phone. "Hey, Jackson."

She rolled her eyes as two pink spots appeared on her cheeks. Chase strained to listen, unable to hear the conversation. Good thing Addie was feisty enough to handle Jackson's sense of humor.

"Yes. Yes you did," she said with mock seriousness. "Your timing is terrible." She shook her head, rolling her eyes again. "Um, I'll let you tell him."

Chase took the phone from her. "See? I told you. Now can you leave us alone?"

"No," Jackson said with a laugh. "Syd is gone and this is the most fun I've had all day."

The guy had way too much time on his hands. "Bye, Jackson."

"But…"

Chase ended the call. "I give him five seconds before he calls back." He held up his fingers and started counting. "…three, four, five." Brad Paisley started singing again.

Addie sniggered. "He is so predictable."

"Tell me about it." Answering the phone, Chase tried to sound annoyed. "What?"

"You really should turn off your phone, or at least stop answering it when you're tryin' to kiss a girl."

"Thanks for the advice. I'm taking it right now." He ended the call and then pressed the button to turn off the phone. "If I don't shut it down, he'll just keep callin' back."

"Yeah, I kinda get the feeling he's like a dog with a bone," Addie said dryly.

Chase slipped the phone into his pocket. "Exactly." Reaching out for her hand, he tugged her close. "Where were we?"

A grin stole across her face. "I think—"

"Me first! I get to go first," a little boy shouted as he raced onto the bridge with two other boys right behind him. The leader held a bag of bread crumbs no doubt intended for the ducks gliding on the pond.

"I think," Addie said, leading Chase toward the grass. "We're relinquishing our spot."

A man and woman, presumably the kids' parents, apologized as they passed by Chase and Addie. "Sorry," the dad said. "We didn't mean to kick y'all off the bridge."

"We were just heading home," Addie said. "Enjoy the ducks."

"Why does it seem like the park just got busier?" Chase asked, noticing their secluded picnic area now had a family of five, plus what looked like two sets of grandparents.

"Probably because it did."

"For a while there it felt like we were the only two people here."

Addie shot him a wry look. "It did until Jackson called, and then you told him we were...you know."

"About to kiss?"

"Yes, I can't believe you told him." She groaned and laughed at the same time. "Him, of all people."

"Sorry about that. I think nearly kissing you rattled my brain and I wasn't thinking clearly."

Another giggle escaped. "Right."

"I'm serious."

She looked at him askance. "You know you enjoyed that just as much as Jackson did."

"I'd enjoy kissing you a lot more."

"I don't know." She untangled their hands and skipped ahead, glancing back at him over her shoulder. "You may have missed your opportunity."

Judging by the flirtatious tone in her voice, Chase figured he still had a shot. He jogged to catch up to her and found her staring at the bikes.

"You know, I told myself to buck up and ride back home." She blew out a big breath, shaking her head. "But I know I won't make it."

He pulled out his phone and powered it up. "Call Miss Janie to come and get us and then I'll bring the truck back to get the bikes."

"Really? You don't mind?"

"I really don't mind." He held it out to her. "Just don't answer if you hear Brad Paisley again."

She laughed and took the phone. "Trust me. I won't." She tried calling both her aunt's home and cell phone without much success.

Puffing out a sigh of resignation, she handed him the phone back. "I have no pride left at this point. I'll ride as far as I can and then walk the rest of the way."

Chase smiled and tapped her under the chin. "How about I just ride back and get the truck?"

Her brown eyes studied him for a second or two, then she shook her head. "Okay, I guess I do still have some pride left because there is no way I'm letting you ride back while I sit here and wait for you." She walked over to the bike and started to unhook the helmet. "I made it here, and I can make it back."

She was a good sport. Most girls he'd dated in the past would've made him suffer by complaining non-stop. "I think I have an idea," he said, taking the helmet from her. "But it involves callin' Jackson."

"You can't call Beau?"

He shook his head. "Beau's in Atlanta for the day."

Weighing her options, she glanced back and forth between the bike and the phone. "Okay." She sucked in a deep breath as if to fortify her decision. "Call Jackson."

Chase pressed down on the speed-dial for his friend. After only a couple of rings, Jackson answered. "Did you kiss her?"

"Hey, Jacks," Chase said, ignoring the question. "I need your help."

There was a momentary pause and Chase wondered if he'd lost the connection. "*Okaaayyy,*" Jackson finally said, drawing out the word. "But it's not too complicated. Although techniques vary, simply pressing your lips to hers usually does the trick."

Chase chuckled, despite trying not to. "Not that kind of help."

"So how was it then? The first time I kissed Syd—" He gave a low whistle. "Well, let's just say I was as happy as a tornado in a trailer park."

Unable to hold back another laugh, Chase turned slightly away from Addie. "I don't know yet."

"What? Why not? Seriously, bro, I'm getting a little worried about your skills."

Ignoring the comment, Chase continued, "Look, I need you to come to Mullis Park to pick us up. It seems we both have a flat tire."

Addie looked at their bikes and then back to Chase, narrowing her eyes a fraction. He held up his finger and mouthed, "One minute."

"Sure," Jackson said, humor lacing his voice. "Do I need to give you time to—"

"Just come and get us, will you?"

"Okay. I'll be over in a few minutes. That should give you—"

Chase ended the call before Jackson could razz him anymore.

"You do realize we don't have flat tires, right?"

"Yeah," he said with a grin. "But by the time Jacks gets here we will." Digging through the backpack, he found his keys and squatted down next to the bikes. Using one of the keys, he let the air out of each of their tires.

"Clever boy," Addie mused.

"Thanks." He stood and brushed his hands against his shorts. "I'm not sure how long Jackson will take. We can eat dessert while we wait, or..." He shrugged his shoulders. "I don't know, we could explore missed opportunities."

A small smile appeared on her lips. "Hmm, I *hate* missed opportunities."

Before Chase could process the coy remark, her smile widened. "But right now I really want that surprise dessert you promised."

He grinned, lifted the backpack, and sifted through it until he found the pink and white striped box from the candy store *A Little Sugar*. "Close your eyes," Chase said, keeping the box hidden from Addie's view.

"For the record," Addie said, closing her eyes. "You are by far the most creative boyfriend I've ever had."

"Thanks." He heard the teasing tone of her voice, but part of him wanted her to be serious. He wanted this all to be real. "Now, hold out your hands."

She immediately obeyed. "I really hope you've outgrown your boyhood prank days and you aren't going to smash a pie in my face or something."

He laughed. "Don't give me any ideas."

"Just keep in mind I won't hesitate to seek swift retribution."

"I think I'm safe." He placed the box in her hands. "Okay, you can look."

Her eyes fluttered open and she squealed. "You bought me fudge!" She hugged the box to her chest. "Thank you."

"You're welcome."

She sat down on a bench, and patted the seat next to her. "Come over here and we'll split it."

"You don't have to share." He slid in next to her, his thigh pressing against hers. "I bought it for you."

"I want to share." She opened the box and peeled back the white wax paper. "Do you still have that plastic knife?"

"Nope. I tossed it with the other trash."

Using the wax paper the candy was wrapped in, Addie picked up the fudge and tried to break it in half.

Chase reached out and took it from her, then held it up to her mouth. "Just take a bite."

She bit into the chocolate and let out a tiny moan of satisfaction. When he offered her more, she shook her head. "Your turn now," she said, taking the candy and giving him a taste.

They traded off until there was one last bite. Chase held it up. "It's all yours."

"I shouldn't." Her lips parted into a smile. "But I will."

Instead of letting him feed her, she plucked it out of his fingers and placed it in her mouth. She closed her eyes and let out another moan of pleasure. "So good." Her eyes flickered open, and she met his gaze. "Thank you."

"You're welcome."

A horn honked, and they watched Jackson's red truck come to an abrupt stop.

"Looks like our ride is here." Chase stood up and Addie joined him as they watched Jackson cut the engine, jump out and saunter toward them. "Hey, y'all," he said.

"Hey," Chase said, feeling a little wary. The sardonic smirk Jackson wore could only mean he had something up his sleeve.

Stopping in front of the bikes, Jackson methodically stroked his goatee as he studied both of the deflated tires. He shook his head, making a tsk-tsk sound with his tongue. "Wow, a flat tire on both bikes. That's like the *kiss* of death on a date." He emphasized the word kiss.

Chase fought back a smile. "Yeah, thanks for coming to get us."

"Hey, it's no problem." Jackson tucked his fingertips in the front pocket of his jeans. "That's what friends are for. Heck, if I didn't come...well, I wouldn't blame you if you just *kissed* our friendship goodbye."

Schooling his emotions, Chase grabbed a hold of his bike. He'd started this whole thing, and he didn't want to egg Jackson on by laughing.

"Where's your wife?" Chase asked, hoping to sidetrack him. He had a feeling Jackson was just getting started with all the "kiss" puns.

"She's at her parents' house." He shifted his focus on Addie. "Syd asked me to tell you since the band will go over early to set up at Gracie's, she'll come pick you up at six." He smiled with probably the same look the cat had on his face right after eating the canary. "She's pretty excited and said she could just *kiss* you for agreeing to sit with her."

The corners of Addie's eyes creased and she pressed her lips together as if trying to suppress a grin. She obviously didn't miss Jackson's play on words either.

"I'm looking forward to it."

Jackson raised an eyebrow and chuckled. "I'll just bet you are."

Her lips twisted up before she turned away and coughed. Chase knew she was desperately trying not to laugh. One laugh and Jackson might never stop. Grasping the handlebars, she started to roll the bicycle toward the truck.

Jackson stepped in front of her and took a hold of the bike. "Here, let me get that for you."

"Thank you, Jackson. If you weren't married, why, I just might kiss *you-ew*," Addie said with a lot of attitude and a very poor southern accent.

It cracked Jackson up. "Sorry. I'm taken." He pointed to Chase. "But I reckon he wouldn't mind a kiss."

Chase rolled his bike to a stop and groaned. He'd created a monster. "I should've just called my dad."

Jackson gasped dramatically, appearing to be insulted. After leaning the bike against the tailgate of the truck, he reached his hand over his shoulder and patted it haphazardly. "Oh, man, I can't get a hold of it…can you please pull the knife out of my back?"

Regardless of their efforts, Chase laughed and a giggle bubbled out of Addie.

Jackson grinned and lowered the tailgate. "Do y'all wanna come over and watch a movie with us?"

Does this mean he's done? Chase exchanged a glance with Addie and she shrugged her shoulders. "Maybe," he said, as he jumped up in the truck to pull the bike inside.

"We can watch one of Sydney's favorite movies." Jackson lifted up Addie's bike. "It's that one with Drew Barrymore. *Never Been Kissed.*"

Guess not. Jackson was just getting started.

Chase gave him an eye roll and jumped back down. "We'll see." He took a hold of Addie's hand and pulled her to the passenger side of the truck. He opened the door and whispered, "I'm sorry. I should've never said anything. Just try'n ignore him."

"Uh-huh," she said under her breath as she slid in the middle of the front seat.

Chase sat down next to her and pulled the door shut as Jackson climbed in behind the wheel. Addie was sandwiched in between the two men.

"Excuse me." Jackson reached across the middle to open the glove box. He pulled out a bag of silver-foiled covered chocolate. "Anyone want a Kiss?" he asked in a droll voice.

Addie snatched the bag out of his hands. "Yes. I love chocolate."

Chortling, Jackson turned the ignition on and the stereo blared Faith Hill singing *This Kiss*. The track was just starting on the chorus. Grinning from ear to ear, he said, "If y'all don't like this song, I can change it." Without waiting for an answer, he pushed another button. *Kiss a Girl* by Keith Urban played over the speakers.

Chase had to give his friend credit. He'd come up with some great stuff on such short notice.

Jackson sang along with the lyrics as he put the truck in gear. "I wanna kiss a girl. I wanna hold her tight. And maybe make a little magic in the moonlight." He raised his eyebrows comically.

Addie let out a big breath as she dramatically lolled her head against the seatback and turned her face toward Chase. Her lips stretched into a smile and then the two of them burst into laughter.

Jackson had won. Only then did he turn the volume down.

Chapter Sixteen

By the time they reached Aunt Janie's house, the sun had lowered beyond the horizon, leaving the sky a brilliant color of purple. As the truck bumped down the driveway, it jostled Addie into Chase's side. He had a hold of her hand, loosely covering her fingers, but his grip tightened, as if he wanted to keep her close. She didn't mind, and stayed right where she was.

"Y'all sure you don't wanna come by the house?" Jackson asked, shifting the gears down as he pressed on the brakes.

Addie liked the McCalls, but she felt too keyed up to watch a movie right now. There was the matter of "missed opportunities" humming between her and Chase, an almost palpable electrical energy that seemed to grow with every passing second.

"Nah," Chase answered. "It's getting late, and I have to get up early in the morning for work." He gave Addie's fingers another gentle squeeze. "But maybe another night?"

It seemed so natural to make plans for a movie night. Like they were really a couple.

"Sounds good." The truck rolled to a stop. Jackson cut the engine and opened his door. "I'll have Syd give Addie a call. It's the ladies turn to pick out a movie."

"Is that okay?" Chase asked, helping her down from the truck.

"Sure. That sounds fun." She liked the way Chase looked at her. As if he liked the idea of her picking out a movie for them to watch as much as she did.

As the guys transferred the bicycles to Chase's truck, Addie inched toward the house. She needed to use the restroom and definitely wanted to brush her teeth.

"Thanks," Chase said, patting his friend on the back.

"No problem." Jackson pivoted toward Addie, a silly grin on his face. "Did you get your Kisses?"

He just can't leave it alone. "Nope."

Jackson swung open the door to his truck and leaned across the seat. He pulled out the bag of candy and tossed them to her. "Here you go."

"Thanks."

"Make sure to give Chase a few of your kisses."

She knew he wasn't talking about the candy, and she was half tempted to throw the bag back in his face. But it *was* chocolate so she hugged it to her chest.

"Bye, Jackson," she said sweetly.

Chuckling, he waved, climbed into his truck and drove away.

"Sorry about Jackson." Chase glanced over at her. "He doesn't know when to stop."

"Really? I hadn't noticed," Addie said dryly, making him laugh.

"If you're not too mad at me," Chase said, looking a little contrite, "do you want to sit on the porch swing and talk for a while?"

Addie didn't want the evening to end yet, so she let him off the hook. "I'd like that." She took a step backward. "I just need to run inside for a minute."

They started toward the porch, and their arms brushed. Instantly, the electric pulse arced between them. "I won't be long," she said, opening the door.

Chase took a seat on the swing. "I'll be waiting."

The screen door slammed behind her and she rushed up the stairs. Sort of. Her legs were a little wobbly. She hoped she wouldn't be too sore tomorrow. After tossing the bag of Kisses on her bed, she stepped into the bathroom and caught her image in the mirror. It surprised her. She looked different somehow. Happy. Could it be the exercise?

Or was it something else?

Whatever it was, it looked good on her. She took care of business and then she brushed her teeth. Twice.

Aunt Janie still wasn't home when Addie stepped out onto the porch. The full moon illuminated Chase, making it unnecessary to turn on the porch light.

"Hey," Chase said, giving her a smile that tickled her stomach. He stopped the swing with his foot and patted his hand on the seat beside him. "Come and sit by me."

Her bare feet treaded softly across the wooden porch. After brushing her teeth, she had removed her shoes and socks and changed into a clean, white T-shirt. She'd also used a little of her vanilla and brown sugar scented lotion on her arms and legs.

"No fair," he said as she sat down next to him. "You changed your shirt." He leaned in close. "And you smell good."

Dang. She'd kind of hoped it wouldn't have been that obvious. "Will it make you feel better if I go put back on my attitude shirt?"

He laughed, curling his fingers around her hand. "No." With the toe of his shoe, he pushed back, rocking the swing in motion. "But if the shirt fits…"

She gave his shoulder a playful nudge. "I do not have an attitude…much."

"You're right," he teased. "Besides, I think the problem had more to do with the *altitude*."

"And here I thought Jackson was the comedian."

He looked at her sidelong. "Yeah, I guess he was kinda funny."

She hadn't meant to bring up the whole "kiss" thing. It made her appear too eager. Nervously, she changed the subject. "I think I'm going to borrow Aunt Janie's car tomorrow and stop by that house we rode by. You know, the one with the amazing wrap around porch?"

"It's also the one with all the No Trespassing signs."

"What?" She glanced up at him. "How did I miss those?"

He grinned. "I have no idea."

She bit her bottom lip. "I planned on asking permission anyway, but maybe it's not a good idea to even try."

He slowly circled his thumb over the top of her hand. "I know the owner. Mr. Hanks is a grumpy old guy, but he likes me. When I used to deliver the paper, I was the only one who ever made sure the paper landed on the porch instead of the sidewalk."

"Really? Do you think he'll remember you if I tell I'm your friend?"

"Maybe." He studied her for a few seconds. "Tell you what, I have an early meeting in the morning, but should be done around eleven. What if I take the rest of the day off and take you to meet Mr. Hanks? I'm sure he'll say yes, and then after we can go somewhere to eat."

"Are you sure?"

"Yeah." He gave her a mischievous smile. "Besides, I would never want to be responsible for anymore missed opportunities."

His implied message made her heart beat wildly. "You wouldn't?"

"Absolutely not." His tone was seductively low.

They leaned closer, and Addie's gaze drifted to his mouth. Every nerve ending was alive with anticipation as he lowered his head. It was like being at the top of a roller coaster just before it plunged straight down, leaving you breathless.

Her eyes fluttered closed, and she felt his warm breath next to her mouth. Then, under a Georgia moon, Chase kissed her. Lightly at first, like he was savoring the feel of a first kiss. Then he shifted and the pressure on her mouth intensified.

He was very talented—and not just as a musician. His kisses mirrored the way he spoke. Slow and soft. Perfect.

The most intoxicating warmth engulfed her body as his lips skillfully moved over hers, and Addie finally understood what Faith Hill was singing about—centrifugal motion, perpetual bliss and all that. She had never felt like this. Never been kissed like this.

Chase drew back, his breath uneven. Still lost in the blissful, floating sensation, Addie met his eyes. "Wow…that was amazing."

"Yeah. It was." A playful smile spread across his face. "Wanna do it again?"

She grinned and nodded her head, leaning into him as his mouth met hers in another long, slow kiss. Heat trailed up her arm as he slid his palm along her skin, bringing her closer. A soft sigh escaped as he deepened the kiss, and Addie became lost to everything around her. She was flying—floating, and she never wanted to come down.

At length, they reluctantly parted. Her eyes fluttered open and she shivered.

"Cold?" he asked, his voice rough with emotion.

Was he kidding? She felt so warm she could instantly melt an ice cube on her skin.

"No. No, I'm not cold." She drew in a shaky breath. "In fact, I doubt I'll ever be cold again."

Deep laughter rumbled in his chest as he hooked his arm around her neck and pulled her close. "You know what?" he asked, pressing a kiss into her hair.

"What?"

"I think I just had my last first kiss."

With her thinking still clouded, her mind struggled to make sense of what he'd just said. She tried to recall the exact wording when headlights illuminated the porch as her aunt's car pulled into the driveway.

Chase stood up and pulled her up beside him. "Well, Miss Attitude, looks like we're not alone anymore."

She melted into his side. No they weren't alone anymore. And after that kiss, she never wanted to be alone again. What was she going to do?

Chapter Seventeen

Chase tapped the ballpoint pen on his desk and wished this morning was already over. He stared at the computer screen in frustration. The program wasn't loading correctly and the last thing he wanted to do was shut everything down and reboot his computer. Mr. Barclay had requested a few changes after this morning's meeting, and it was taking longer than it should have.

Glancing at the clock, he realized he wouldn't be able to pick Addie up at eleven. He reached for his phone to text her he'd probably be a half hour late. The good news was Mr. Barclay announced he was leaving for a last minute business meeting in South Carolina, and wouldn't be back until Monday. So, in addition to cutting today short, Chase planned on taking all day Friday off as well.

Sending off the text, Chase let out a frustrated breath and reached for the bottle of water he had on his desk. No longer cold, the warm liquid slid down his throat, leaving a funny, plastic aftertaste.

He replaced the lid just as Shanna knocked on his door and stuck her head inside his office. The look on her face didn't bode well. Chase wondered if she'd figured out how Hayden had learned about his job application for Nashborough. The two of them had talked earlier, and Shanna assured Chase she hadn't told anyone other than her husband. Chase believed her and made sure she knew that, but his secretary was upset and wanted to find out how the information had been leaked.

"Hey, Chase." She slipped inside his office and closed the door behind her. She clutched a white piece of paper to her chest and looked at him with a worried expression.

"Is everything okay?" he said, standing up and coming around to offer her a chair.

She shook her head and remained standing. "Just remember, don't shoot the messenger." She offered him the paper along with a strained smile. "Mr. Barclay wanted me to give you your itinerary."

"My what?" As he scanned the contents of the paper, his stomach lurched. This had to be a mistake. The E-ticket said he was scheduled to fly out for South Carolina this evening and he wouldn't be returning until late Sunday night. "I don't understand?" he said, raising questioning eyes to his secretary.

One of her shoulders rose up. "I know. I don't either, and I'm sorry."

Laughing mirthlessly, he laid the paper on the corner of his desk. "I can't believe this. I have a gig on Saturday night."

Shanna put a finger to her lips to quiet him down. She leaned forward and whispered, "Look, I need to give you a heads up. I overheard Mr. Barclay talking with someone…well, actually, it was more like arguing. But they were discussing you and the trip to Hilton Head."

Chase sat on the corner of his desk and ran a hand through his hair. He had a sinking feeling in the pit of his stomach. Somehow Hayden was behind this. "What did he say?"

"The only thing I caught was the fact he promised to make sure you were gonna be there."

"Great."

"One more thing," Shanna said with trepidation. "I think I know how Hayden found out about Nashborough." Tears filled her eyes. "I did tell someone else about your job search. A few days ago I got my hair colored. The girl who does it knows me well, and knows how frustrated I am with my job and that the only reason I haven't left is because of you."

She sniffed and Chase grabbed the box of tissues off of his desk and held it out to her. "Whatever it is, Shanna, I'm not mad at you, okay?"

"Thanks." She took a tissue and dabbed at her eyes. "The coloring process takes a while, and we got to talking about my job. While she shampooed and rinsed my hair, I told her if you got the job in Nashville, I planned on quitting and staying home with the kids for a few months until I decided what to do."

Twisting the tissue in her hands, Shanna continued, "I didn't see Hayden come in, but when I went to the register to pay, I saw her sitting in the next booth over, getting her hair done. She didn't even look at me so I figured she hadn't seen me. I'm sorry, Chase, but she must have overheard me talking."

"It's not your fault, Shanna." Chase wanted to ease the woman's conscience. "At least now we know Hayden isn't some computer genius who hacked into my laptop."

That won him a tiny smile. "You really thought that was an option?"

Despite how messed up everything was, Chase laughed. "No. I figured she would've paid someone else to do the hacking." Glancing down at the itinerary, the smile on his face disappeared. "Now I just have to decide what to do about this. Maybe I'll just wait until Mr. Barclay leaves. He's always more relaxed if he's away from the office."

"I hate to tell you this, but he wants to see you in his office right now."

This just gets better and better. "Well, I guess here goes nothing."

Shanna hesitated for a moment. "I really am sorry, Chase. Let me know what I can do to help you."

"I'll be okay." Chase gave her an encouraging smile. "On the bright side, since I won't be here, you should take tomorrow off."

"Thank you, Chase. I think I will." She opened the door and together they exited his office. "Good luck," she whispered before returning to her desk.

Uttering a silent prayer, Chase walked down the hall to the opulent office at the end. His stomach tightened as he rapped on Whit Barclay's door. He might have to go on this business trip, but he was coming home in time for his gig.

"Come in," Whit barked in his familiar, no-nonsense way.

Chase pushed the door open to find his boss poised with a golf club, preparing to hit the tiny white ball. The elaborate putting green occupied a fair amount of office space. Whit took his golf seriously, trying to hone his putting skills on a daily basis.

He paused mid-stroke and flashed his white capped teeth in a showy smile. "Hang on, son." He lowered his eyes and concentrated once more on his task. With perfection, he tapped the ball, making a hole-in-one. He chuckled and came around to stand in front of Chase. "Now if I can do that in Hilton Head, I'll be a happy man."

Ah, yes. Hilton Head. Chase couldn't wait to find out what was going on. "Speaking of Hilton Head," Chase said, choosing his words carefully. "In this morning's meeting I understood that Kyle was going along with you since the Winter's account belongs to his team. I'm not sure why you need me to be there."

Whit gave an imperceptible tilt to his head, his gaze narrowing slightly. He clearly didn't like to be questioned. "Kyle is still planning on taking the lead. You'll need to sit in on a couple of meetings to justify the expense, but business isn't the reason you're coming along." He smiled, but it came off more as an irritated grimace. "I'm taking you on this trip, son, to give us a chance to talk. Hayden's hinted you might want to speak to me formally and thought a little fun and relaxation with our family would be the perfect ice-breaker."

What? Chase barely held back a snort of disbelief. Fun and relaxation coupled with the Barclays was an oxymoron. And if Whit thought Chase wanted to talk to him formally, it meant Hayden was back to her usual manipulating self.

"I don't quite follow you." He kept his gaze fixed on the man in front of him. Intimidation wasn't something Chase liked all that much and maintaining eye contact was his only line of defense. "Hayden and I aren't dating anymore. I thought you knew that."

Anger flashed in Whit's blue eyes. "What I know is that my little girl has been seeing you under the radar for the past month." He leaned in close, once again going for intimidation. "She's been given the impression you might be providing her with a new piece of jewelry. I hope you haven't been toying with her."

Toying with her? Chase stared at him with disbelief. This had to be a really sick joke—at least he hoped it was. In desperation, his eyes briefly scanned the room, looking for any sign of the practical joker. The office was eerily quiet. Well, except for the pounding of Chase's heart. His gaze returned to Whit's irate face.

Drawing in a deep breath, Chase rubbed his hand over the back of his neck and tried to think of a way to tell his boss about his daughter's deception without actually calling her a liar. "There must be some kind of misunderstanding, sir. Hayden and I haven't been dating since before she left for California."

Whit's eyes reduced to thin slits. "There is a misunderstanding. One you need to fix." His lips flattened in anger. "This trip will be the perfect opportunity."

Unbelievable.

Chase swallowed back a sarcastic reply. "You're right. And I'll be more than happy to speak to Hayden and get this settled." He narrowed his own eyes. "But I'm returning Saturday morning. I have a gig at Gracie's Haven, and it's been on the calendar for months now."

The muscle in Whit's jaw tightened. Chase had no idea what would happen next. He waited, never backing down from his stance.

"Fine." An icy tone edged Whit's voice. He picked up his putting iron again. Hopefully he didn't plan on using it on Chase. He leaned on the golf club and said, "We leave this evening. I'm not sure what's going on, but I intend to get to the bottom of this, understand?"

Perfectly.

"Yes, sir."

The man gave him one more cold glare before turning around, effectively dismissing him. Maybe it would've been better to have been fired. Chase placed his hand on the doorknob, twisted it and pulled back.

"Chase?" Whit's hard voice made him pause.

Chase looked over his shoulder. "Yes?"

"I'm looking to promote one of my team leaders as director of marketing. I'd hate for anything to lessen your chances."

Was that a threat? "So would I," Chase said evenly.

"Good." Whit's lips twisted into a smile. "We'll talk more about it later. See ya tonight."

Shaken and angry, Chase stepped into the hall. What kind of game was Hayden playing? And what did she expect to happen? That he'd somehow see the light and ask her to marry him? Not only was Hayden obsessed, she was also delusional.

Passing Shanna's desk, she glanced up sympathetically. "Everything okay?"

Behind Shanna, Whit's assistant paused at the copy machine, seemingly waiting on his answer. "Yeah." He glanced at the clock on the wall. He wasn't sticking around here another second. "But I think I'll head on home to pack for my *business meeting*." He couldn't keep the sarcasm from spilling out.

Shanna nodded her head. "Okay. Do you need me to do anything?"

"Yes, please. Mr. Barclay has agreed to let me come home early so I'd like to come home late Friday night or early Saturday morning instead of Sunday. I'd appreciate it if you could make the flight change for me."

"Sure thing. I'll text you the new itinerary as soon as I have it."

"Thanks." Chase stepped inside his office. He touched the computer, bringing up the screen. At least the program had finished loading. Saving the information, he shut down his laptop and slid it inside the protective sleeve of his briefcase. Grabbing the itinerary, he shoved it in the front pocket. Hayden had gone too far. And one way or another he planned on getting to the bottom of this ridiculous mess— even if it meant losing his job.

* * *

Wearing a comfortable pair of jeans and a graphic tee, Chase jogged up the Caldwell porch steps. Already packed for his trip, he planned on spending as much as time as possible with Addie before he left for the airport.

After the sensational kisses they'd shared last night, he knew their relationship had changed. Chase admitted to himself that he might be falling in love with her. In spite of all the obstacles, he wanted to tell Addie how he felt. He knew she liked him, he just didn't know how much. Would it be enough to make her consider living in Tennessee?

One good thing that came out of this last minute trip to South Carolina was confiding in his parents. As soon as he left work, Chase went home and found his mom and dad were both there. It felt good to tell them about the potential job in Nashville. Both of his parents were supportive of his desire to pursue his music career, but he could tell they were skeptical about how successful he'd be. Their concerns seemed to stem more from the industry, and not because they didn't believe Chase had the talent to make it.

When he'd told them about the conversation with Mr. Barclay, he received some good advice from his dad. "Son, you be completely honest with both Hayden and her father so there are no more misunderstandings. After that, you just have to trust in the Lord."

His mother had reminded Chase of a mother bear protecting her cub. She wanted to go over to the Barclay's and give them a piece of her mind, especially Hayden. In the end, his dad had convinced her Chase was a big boy and could take care of things himself.

Placing one hand above the door for support, he knocked lightly and waited. Janie swung open the door and smiled. "Come on in. Addie will be down in a minute." Furrowing her brow, she looked over her shoulder to the stairs. "She's having a little trouble this morning."

"What kind of trouble?" Chase asked, hoping it wasn't something serious.

Before she could reply, he heard a grunt and the sound of someone coming down the stairs with heavy, slow steps. Between each step he heard, "Ow-ow-shoot-ow."

The two of them watched the stairs expectantly. "She's a little sore this morning," Janie whispered.

He wasn't sure if he should rush to her aid or laugh. "Does she need help?"

Janie grinned and shrugged her shoulders. "Sweetie, Chase is here. Do you want him to help you down the stairs?"

The footsteps and moaning ceased. "He's here?" Her voice sounded alarmed.

"Yep. He's standing right beside me."

Another pause ensued. Then Addie let out a long breath. "It's okay. I'm coming." The heavy slow steps resumed, but this time without the complaints.

The telephone rang and Janie picked up the handset in the foyer. Glancing at the caller-ID, she hollered, "Sugar, I need to get this. Y'all have fun today."

"Um-hmm," Addie murmured.

Janie winked at Chase before going into the kitchen. A second later Addie emerged, dressed in jeans and a butter-yellow T-shirt. Her hair hung in ringlets, glistening under the light of the chandelier. "Hey." She held onto the railing and gingerly took the last step. "I thought you weren't coming until eleven thirty?"

Chase fought back a grin and looked down at his watch. "It is eleven thirty."

The little lines between her eyebrows creased. "Oh. Well, I thought I could make it downstairs and loosen up my muscles before you got here."

"Are you okay?" His voice was full of laughter, despite his efforts to restrain himself.

She met his gaze, her lips turning up on the ends, carving the dimple in her cheek. "Don't you dare laugh," she scolded. "I am *so* sore this morning. I had no idea it took so many muscles to pedal a bike."

"I'm sorry," he said, unable to mask his amusement.

She put her hands on her hips and squinted. "You're laughing at me, I can tell."

He grinned. "I'm laughing *with* you, not at you."

"Uh-huh."

"I really am sorry. I had no idea the bike ride was going to be—" He paused, trying to decide the best way to finish the sentence. "—so strenuous.

I promise no more torture dates from here on out." He took a step toward her. "Are you sure you still wanna talk with Mr. Hanks? We can just hang out here if you want."

"If I don't get up and walk today, I'll never walk again. Just give me a second and I'll be fine."

The scent of her flowery perfume tickled his senses. Standing this close, he couldn't resist touching her. He reached for her hand, her skin warm and smooth. "If it gets bad, I can always carry you," he teased.

Amusement beamed in her soft brown eyes. "I don't think so. But maybe tonight we can watch a movie or play games with your family."

His stomach clenched, knowing he wouldn't be around tonight or the next. "Let's go and I'll tell you all about my morning."

As they made their way to his truck, he hoped and prayed Addie would understand, and maybe even give him some indication of how she felt. Somehow he needed to broach the subject of having a long-distance relationship, and the possibility for more.

Chapter Eighteen

Addie thanked Mr. Hanks again for showing them his house. "I'll probably come back this evening or be here early in the morning when the lighting is good to take the pictures."

"Any time, young lady." Mr. Hanks winked at her. "I ain't planning on goin' anywhere."

"Thank you, sir," Chase said, shaking the older man's hand. "It was nice talkin' with you again."

"You can stop by and talk any time you want to, sonny." He pointed at Addie. "Just make sure to bring this pretty gal with you."

Chase led her toward his truck on their way out. She could tell Mr. Hanks was lonely, and didn't want them to leave. When she did return with her camera, she knew Mr. Hanks would want to talk so she should just plan on an extra hour or so to talk with him.

As it turned out, Mr. Hanks was only a few years older than her own father. It made her miss her dad, especially after talking with him this morning. He'd sounded as lonely as Mr. Hanks, and mentioned more than once how happy he'd be once she returned home.

Chase helped her into the truck and quickly rounded the front of the vehicle to climb into the driver's seat. She could tell he was agitated about going to South Carolina. Before coming over to talk to Mr. Hanks, Chase told her all about the circumstances of his last-minute business trip, and the part Hayden played.

"He's really nice," she said, once Chase started the truck and backed out.

Chase shot her a wry grin. "He was pretty grumpy when he first opened the door. The minute he saw I was with a pretty girl, he turned on the charm."

"He's lonely. With both of his kids living in Alabama, and all those "no trespassing" signs, I doubt he gets very many visitors." Again, she thought about her own father. "He's been a widower longer than my dad. I need to talk to Aunt Janie. Maybe she can include him in her weekly coffee and sweet roll get together."

Chase reached across the seat and took her hand. "You're really sweet. I think you made his entire year when you told him how much you loved his house."

"I wonder why his kids don't visit him, or even call him that often? I'm so glad my dad has me and Chellie so close."

Chase was quiet for a few seconds. He gave her hand a squeeze before letting it go. "I'm sure your dad appreciates having y'all close by."

Addie glanced over at Chase. His jaw was tight, and his voice sounded strained. He had to be stressed about his job.

"Are you worried about your trip to Hilton Head?"

"More stressed than worried." He came to a stop sign, and looked her way. "I've got a lot on my mind right now."

Addie wanted to lighten his mood. "We should make a stop at the fudge shop. Chocolate cures all kinds of stress."

He smiled and returned his attention back to the road. "We can stop by if you want to."

Shifting in her seat, she studied him. He was so tense. "No that's okay. This is about helping you. If chocolate doesn't work, what does?"

He shot her a quick look, a wicked smile on his lips. "Kissing."

Instantly, her entire body flooded with heat. "Kissing, huh? That would sure be a lot less fattening."

"And so much more fun."

"I could probably help you out, if you want," she teased.

He reached across the seat and took her hand again. "You'd do that for me?" His mood had definitely improved.

"It might be a sacrifice, but that's just the kind of person I am."

He laughed. "Yeah, you are pretty awesome. Let me just find a secluded place to pull over."

Addie didn't know if he was joking or not, but judging how her body was reacting, kissing him in a secluded area probably wasn't the best idea. "Isn't making out in a truck a little cliché?"

"Maybe. Where do you suggest we go?"

"I don't know. I wasn't a big make out so I don't have that much experience."

He looked over at her and winked. "We can always go to my house. My mom's home, but she's pretty cool."

"I'm not going to your house to make out!"

He laughed again. "Maybe we should just go to the candy store."

"If you buy me fudge, I promise you'll get a kiss."

"Deal."

He headed for downtown Mitchel Creek. They didn't talk about kissing, but it didn't mean she wasn't thinking about it. It was a little scary that Addie might prefer kissing Chase over sugar. In fact, her feelings for him were more intense than she'd ever felt for Brandon. And that thought was even scarier.

What good would it do to fall in love with him? Chase had so many plans that didn't involve relocating to a small town in Idaho. Addie couldn't leave her father. Yes, Chellie lived close by, but she was a busy mother of three. She never wanted her dad to be as lonely as Mr. Hanks.

After they bought a half a pound of fudge, they drove to a pecan orchard owned by Sydney's parents. They walked hand in hand, nibbling on the fudge and talking about Addie's ideas to use Chase's sisters as models for the photo shoot at Mr. Hanks' house. Nutshells littered the ground, and crunched beneath their feet. Finally they came to a shaded area with a bench.

"My dad would love me forever if I brought home Georgia pecans to make him a pie." She sat down on the bench. "Do you think Sydney's parents would let me buy some?"

"You don't have to buy any." Chase took a seat next to her. "We can stop by the caretaker office and grab this roller tool that picks up nutshells on the ground."

"If I check my luggage, I should be able to take them on the plane, right?"

That frustrated look immediately darkened his features. "Yeah."

He turned and looked across the orchard, staring at...trees. As far as she could see, there was nothing else to look at. Not sure what the problem was, she didn't say anything, but watched him gaze off into the distance.

After at least thirty seconds had passed, he turned back toward her. He eyed her with an intensity she could almost feel. "We need to talk."

"Okay. What about?" She liked Chase. A lot. But she wasn't ready for a serious relationship. At least that's what she kept telling herself.

He took her hand and threaded their fingers together. "Addie, I don't want this to end when you go home."

She swallowed and looked away for a few seconds. He didn't want what to end? Their friendship? What else could it be? They barely knew each other, and then there was the whole risking-her-heart-again thing.

"It doesn't have to end." Her eyes flitted back to meet his. "We're friends. We can keep in touch by phone and the internet." She ignored the perplexed look he gave her. "Maybe sometime you can come out and I can show you around Daisy Springs." *Lame, Addie. You know that's not what he meant.*

His eyes remained serious. "I think we have more than just a great friendship, don't you?"

Yes, she said in her mind, but she couldn't vocalize it. She captured her bottom lip between her teeth. "Well, sure." She lifted her shoulder in a shrug. "But I live in Idaho and you live in Georgia. How could there be anything more?" She didn't want things to get complicated. She knew it was shallow and wanted to apologize, especially by the pain reflected in his green eyes.

He studied her for a few heartbeats. "Do you want there to be more? Because I know I do."

Addie's breath tangled in her throat, her chest tight with apprehension. She wanted to run away. Wanted to avoid the question. Tugging on her hand, she scooted back away from him. "Why do we have to talk about this now? You have a plane to catch."

Frustration flickered in his eyes. "Yes. And in a week, so do you." He ran a hand through his hair. "Please, Addie. I need to know where we stand."

"I…" Her eyes darted away from his while she tried to collect her thoughts.

This wasn't supposed to happen. She never expected to feel this way about him. Anxiety twisted her gut as somewhere deep inside her another thought arose. What if he was the one? If she walked away, would her chance at a happy marriage be gone?

Tentatively, she met his gaze. The tenderness and longing she saw loosened the knot in her stomach. "Yes. I do want more. But how will it work out?"

Tension drained from his face. "I don't know how it will work out, but I'm willing to try."

She didn't want to put any unreasonable stipulations on him, but after meeting Mr. Hanks, and after the conversation with her dad this morning, how could she leave her father alone?

All her worries dissipated in a flash when Chase's mouth met hers, and he kissed her long and slow. He tasted like chocolate, the combination proving to be more potent than all the sugar in the world.

When he drew away, both of them were a little breathless. For a few seconds they just stared at one another. Then his face grew serious again and emotion darkened his eyes. "We'll make it work. Okay?"

A spark of hope fluttered behind her breastbone. She wanted to believe him. And she would—for now.

"Okay." She leaned forward and gave him a lingering kiss. "Now, just remember what you've said when Hayden is trying to lure you away from me."

"Don't remind me," he murmured against her mouth.

She gave him one last quick kiss, then stood up and pulled him with her. "Come on, big guy. The sooner you go, the faster you can come home." She raised her eyebrows mischievously. "And I made you something last night when I couldn't sleep. If you promise to call me every day, I'll let you take your present with you."

Chapter Nineteen

Loosening his tie, Chase swiped his keycard to open the door to his hotel room. After tossing his stuff on the bed, he reached for the gift bag from Addie and pulled out another cookie. Taking a big bite, he closed his eyes, savoring the chocolate chip cookie. She also had made oatmeal chocolate chip and pumpkin chocolate chip. All three of his favorite kinds of cookies.

He missed her.

Taking a seat on the edge of the bed, he popped the rest of the cookie in his mouth and fished his cell phone out of his pocket. There were several messages from his coworker Kyle, apologizing for being sick. Chase wouldn't wish food poisoning on anyone. Well, maybe on a certain conniving woman. Still, Kyle's illness had provided the perfect excuse for him to avoid any contact with Hayden. Not that she'd tried to even talk to him.

Yet.

At the airport, he showed up with just enough time to get through security and board the plane. He and Kyle sat in coach, while the Barclays occupied first class. When they landed in South Carolina, Chase and Kyle hung back, waiting for the plane to empty before getting their carry-on bags. By the time they made it out, the Barclays had already taken a cab to the hotel. Once he and Kyle arrived at the hotel, they had a late-night supper, which resulted in Kyle's illness.

As predicted, Whit Barclay spent all his time on the golf course. Since Chase had to fill in for Kyle, his boss had yet to invite Chase to join their family for any "fun and relaxation."

He sent a quick message to Kyle, letting him know the meetings had gone well and asked if he felt well enough to go to dinner with him.

Kyle replied. *Done being sick but don't feel like eating. Think I'll sleep. Talk to you in the morning.*

Scrolling down, he opened a message from Addie. He immediately pushed the speed-dial for her number. While he waited, he flipped his wrist and checked the time. No wonder he was tired. It was past seven-thirty. He'd been in meetings since eight this morning.

Her phone rolled over to voicemail. "You've reached the personal cellular device of Addie Heywood. Leave a message and hopefully I'll remember to check my voicemail. Bye."

He left a message, missing her even more than before. He grabbed another cookie and kicked off his shoes. The separation had confirmed the depth of his feelings. He was in love with her. It had happened so quickly, and the timing was all wrong. He still hadn't told her about the potential job in Tennessee, which only complicated things more.

He unbuttoned his shirt and debated about ordering room service. Being cooped up in meetings for most of the day, he longed to take a walk on the beach. Rising from his bed, he moved to the sliding glass door and opened the blinds. The silvery moonlight illuminated the water as the rolling waves crashed over the beach.

Needing the fresh air, Chase changed into a pair of jeans, sweatshirt and flip-flops and slipped his phone and wallet in his pocket. Just as he placed his hand on the doorknob, a knock sounded from the other side.

Maybe Kyle had changed his mind.

He pulled the door open. "Hey, I'm—" The rest of the words caught in his throat. He narrowed his eyes at his visitor. "Hayden, what're you doing here?"

Hayden smiled and tipped her head to the side, her dark hair brushing against a bare shoulder. "I came to take you to supper." She took a step toward him. "Can I come in?"

Chase blocked the entrance to his room. Hayden wore a white halter sundress that revealed far too much skin. Besides that, he wasn't stupid enough to invite her inside his room.

"My mama taught me never to have a girl in my room. I'll just bet your daddy feels the same way."

One perfect eyebrow arched up as her lips parted in a slow smile. "Your mama and my daddy don't have to find out."

He snorted and stepped out into the hallway, pulling his door shut. "I said no." The strong scent of her perfume overpowered him and he moved a few paces away. He knew they needed to talk and clear the air, but his head hurt just thinking about it. He studied her for a few seconds, wondering how he'd ever found her attractive. She reminded him of his little sisters' Barbie dolls—beautiful but hard like the plastic they were made from.

"Hayden, why are you doing this?"

"Doing what?" she asked, appearing completely innocent. "Inviting you to supper?"

"Not just supper." He blew out a big breath. "Everything. Coming on to me…telling your father we've been seeing each other for the past month." He didn't want to bring up the hypothetical proposal.

Her jaw clenched tight and anger sparked in her blue eyes. "Because I know deep down I'm what you want." She closed the distance between them, slid her arms around his neck. "I know you miss me."

Her persistence astounded him. Reaching up, he took her by the wrists and pried her arms from around his neck and stepped back. "I want you to listen to me. I. Am. Not. Interested."

She blinked a few times. Then her eyes turned as hard as flint. "Is it because of that girl from Idaho?" Her voice was taut with irritation.

His personal life was none of her business. There was no way he was getting into this with her. "Does it matter?" Frustrated, he ran his hand through his hair. She couldn't be this hung up on him. "Come on, Hayden. The entire time we dated you were seeing several different men." He chuckled dryly. "You didn't want me then and I *know* you don't want me now."

Silence filled the corridor for a few heartbeats, her gaze locked on his. Slowly, the hard lines of her mouth lifted into a sardonic smile, and her eyes narrowed to thin slits. "You're right—you were never enough."

Her words didn't inflict any pain. Frankly, he doubted one man would *ever* be enough for her. "So you'll clear this up with your father?"

"Yes," she said, taking a step backward and tilting her chin up. "He never thought you were good enough, either."

Tell me something I don't know. "Fine."

She gave him one last look, her eyes filled with disdain. "I think I'll mention your job application with Nashborough while I'm at it."

With that, she pivoted on her heels and walked away, her hair swaying across her shoulders.

After she disappeared, he stood there for a second, wondering what would transpire after she talked with her father. Maybe this was all part of the plan. If he got fired, the only thing holding him in Georgia was his family. He didn't want to think about where his and Addie's relationship fit into the equation.

He walked over to the elevators and pushed the button. A ding sounded and the doors slid open. He stepped inside and pressed the button for the main floor. As he descended, he lifted a hand and rubbed the back of his aching neck. Sometimes life seemed so complicated.

The elevator came to a stop and Chase exited into the hotel lobby. He looked around, seriously expecting Hayden to be waiting for him. Some of the tension left his shoulders when he saw the coast was clear.

Crossing the lobby, he made his way outside. As his eyes scanned the enormous body of water, he greedily drew in a deep breath of the salty, ocean air. The soothing sound of the waves rolling in eased the stress from the day. He slipped off his flip-flops and hooked them with his fingers, letting them dangle at his side. As he stepped onto the beach, the cool sand oozed between his toes.

The full moon cast a beam of light over the water, and onto the shore. Lights from the resort lined the walkway, lighting the area in soft tones. He walked along the beach, his mind filled with so many things.

Hayden, his job, Nashville, and Addie. He wished she was here and missed her so much his chest ached with longing.

The lyrics to the song he'd been writing popped into his head. Earlier, he'd changed the first verse slightly, but now the rest of the words came so fast he wished he had a pen and paper with him. Pulling out his phone, he opened his notes app and quickly typed.

It was only supposed to be make-believe, but nothing's felt more real.
Your laugh, your touch, the kisses we shared.
I know what they make me feel.

So baby don't leave me, please don't go.
What we have is forever, and I can't let you go.
Yeah, what we have is forever, and I can't let you go.
I never believed in fairytales, but with you I know they're true.
Just give me a chance; we'll write our own happy ending.
A legendary love between me and you.

So baby don't leave me, please don't go.
What we have is forever, and I can't let you go.
Yeah, what we have is forever, and I can't let you go.

No this isn't a fairytale, it's not make believe.
Our love is forever, baby please don't leave.

He stared at the words as a melody wove its way through his mind. He'd never written a song so easily. Wishing he had his guitar with him, he wrote down the chords for when he returned home.

For him, the tune came easier than the lyrics, and once it was in his head, he wouldn't forget it.

There wasn't a reason to analyze the meaning of the song. It was simple. He was in love with Addie, and he wanted forever with her. The rest wasn't so easy. He couldn't expect her to make all the sacrifices. She had dreams of her own. Dreams which didn't include moving away from her aging father or her sister.

Feeling stressed, he palmed the back of his neck again. How could it be that last week he felt like his life was moving in the right direction, and now he had no idea what he really wanted.

Needing to talk to Addie, he slid his finger across the screen. As if on cue, his phone played, *I Wanna Kiss a Girl*, the new ring-tone he'd downloaded just for Addie.

"Hey," he said, "I'm glad you listened to your messages."

"Messages?" Laughter laced her voice. "I just saw I missed your call." He heard someone talking in the background and she giggled into the phone. "Just a second, I need to tell Taylin good-bye."

She was hanging out with his little sister? It seemed like one more sign they were supposed to be together. Taylin and Ashlee never liked any of his previous girlfriends. He heard Taylin thank Addie for taking the glamour shots of the girls at the youth center.

"It was fun," Addie said. "Thanks again for coming with me to Mr. Hanks this morning. The pictures are gorgeous."

Addie laughed at something his sister said, but Chase couldn't hear it. She came back on the line. "Sorry, Taylin just dropped me off at Aunt Janie's."

"You and Taylin have been hanging out?"

"All day. She is such a sweetie."

That was a new one. "Taylin is sweet?"

"Very, and she told me so many cute stories about you. I could totally blackmail you for anything I want."

He chuckled as he walked near the waves. Just hearing her voice washed away all the loneliness, like the incoming tide erased the tiny bird footprints in the sand. "So, what *do* you want?" To him the question had a double meaning.

"I'm thinking about it. I'll let you know when I come up with something."

He misjudged the water and gasped when it rushed over his bare feet, soaking the bottom of his jeans. "Yikes. That's cold."

"What's cold? Wait a minute, do I hear crashing waves in the background?"

"Yeah. I was thinking how much I wished you were here—the full moon is amazing."

"Stop. I love the ocean, and I'm kind of partial to full moons."

A grin stole across his face at her reference to their first kiss. "Maybe we can make a trip to Savannah. You could bring your camera and get some beautiful pictures."

"I'd love that. Promise you'll take me?" she asked playfully. "Just so you know, I'm batting my eyelashes right now."

The mental picture made him laugh. "I promise, but you have to do that eyelash-batting-thing for me when I get back."

She snickered. "Right. So, how did your day go?"

As he walked back to his hotel, he proceeded to tell her about Kyle's illness, his meetings and his run-in with Hayden. Now would be the perfect opportunity to tell Addie about the potential job in Nashville. "I need to look for another job."

"I have a great idea," Addie said before he could say anything further. "Daisy Springs needs a good web designer and graphic arts guy. Our company had to get someone out of Boise, which is about an hour north."

Chase gripped the phone tighter. She might be teasing, but he sensed there was a little fishing expedition going on to see if moving to Idaho was even on his radar.

It wasn't.

"That's a possibility," he lied.

"We have a great little historic downtown area, kind of like Mitchel Creek, minus all the antique shops and the best candy store in the world." Her voice was animated, and Chase didn't have the guts to stop her, and tell her about Tennessee.

"There's this vacant building I wish I could lease for my studio. It's perfect for a startup company, and has a two bedroom apartment on the second floor."

Chase's hopes of Addie relocating to the south died by the optimistic tone of her voice. Just yesterday he assured her it would all work out, but the truth was that it would work out if *she* was willing to move wherever he went.

"If you win the contest, do you plan on leasing the building for your business?"

"I don't know. I might have to wait until I build up my clientele before I invest in my own building." She sighed, not realizing what her words meant for them. "Dad said I could turn the basement into a studio. It would take a little work, but be much more cost effective."

He swallowed, and fought back the panic surging inside him. Their relationship was just developing. It's not like they were going to marry any time soon. He just needed to relax, and do what his parents continually advised—trust in the Lord.

Kicking at the sand with his toe, he gently cleared his throat. "So, tell me how it went at Mr. Hanks' house? It sounds like Taylin helped you out."

Addie told him all about the photo shoot with Taylin. The girls didn't have school since it was a teacher prep day for the upcoming new term, and Taylin willingly got up with the sun to be a model for Addie. Not surprisingly, Ashlee opted to stay home and sleep.

"Mr. Hanks, or I should say Oscar was really cute and followed me around. Can you believe he even let me get a few shots of him sitting on the porch playing his harmonica?"

Chase smiled. Addie charmed everyone she met. "Yeah, I can believe that. He was completely smitten with you."

He began to relax as he listened to her talk about the girls at the youth center. He felt a twinge of jealousy when Addie mentioned Pastor Dave was there. As Chase walked the length of the beach, the conversation flowed and they talked about everything and nothing until his phone beeped low-battery.

Forced to say good-night, he slipped the phone in his pocket and slowly made his way back to the hotel. He felt a little better about things. They would just take things one day at a time.

He entered the lobby and walked toward the restaurant, hoping it was still open. An older lady greeted him. "How many, sir?"

"Just me," he said, following her into the dimly lit room.

There were only a few people having a late-night dinner. Most of them were couples. Wanting to have a view of the ocean, he requested a booth by the window.

Chase slid onto the high-backed seat as the waitress placed a menu in front of him. "Can I get you something to drink?"

"Coke, please." He pointed to the card on the table with a picture of a steak. "And I'll have the special. Medium rare." He offered her a tired smile and handed back the menu. "Thank you."

She winked. "Be back shortly."

He stared out the window and tried not to think about his problems. Well, at least not all of his problems. He still had no idea what would happen once Hayden told her dad about Nashborough. Maybe the man would be so thrilled Chase was moving away from his daughter he wouldn't care where he went.

Hayden's tenacity still astounded him. Hopefully, she got the message once and for all that he wasn't interested.

The waitress delivered his food quickly, allowing him to focus on something else. Halfway through his meal, he heard someone being seated behind him.

Just as his fingers curled around the glass of soda, he froze when the person behind him spoke in a harsh whisper.

"Barb? This is Hayden, can you talk?"

Chase didn't know what to do. Staying meant another possible confrontation, but if he got up to leave, she would definitely see him. The only thing he could do was wait it out. He took another bite of his dinner, but nearly choked when he heard more of Hayden's conversation.

"I tried, but Chase refused to see me alone." Her voice broke on a sob. "What am I gonna do?"

The food in Chase's mouth turned to lead. He grabbed his Coke and washed it down. Eavesdropping was never a good idea, but as he listened to Hayden talk, everything became crystal clear.

When he had heard enough, he scooted out of his seat to confront the woman who was intent on dragging him down with her.

Chase stood in front of her and watched the color drain from her face, leaving her skin as white as the dress she wore. They stared at each other for a few seconds before she ended her call.

He saw her swallow as he sat down across from her. "You're...pregnant?"

Fear flashed in her eyes before she dropped her gaze to stare at her phone. "I guess you heard everything."

Yeah. He'd heard every word about how she planned to lure him into her bed so she could make him the father of her baby. She was desperate, and needed it to happen quickly in order for it to be plausible.

His gut twisted with anger, his hands clenched tightly into fists as he took in a slow breath. "Call your father. Right now."

Hayden lifted her eyes and shook her head. A bitter smile twisted her lips. "No."

"Then I will." Angrily, Chase grabbed his phone, hoping it had enough juice to make one more call.

Her blue eyes hardened with cool disdain. "And who do you think he'll believe?"

"Hayden, I am not taking the blame for this." Chase's fingers clamped down on his phone in frustration. She was right, though. Even if he did call her dad, he probably wouldn't believe him. But he wasn't giving up that easily. "You know, once the baby is born there are tests that will prove my innocence."

"True. But in the mean time, I wonder what your new little girlfriend will think?"

The subtle threat made his chest constrict. He had no idea Hayden would stoop this low. "Why are you doing this?"

"Hmm, guess I just don't like the other possible candidates."

"Sorry." He ground his teeth together. "But I'm not in the running." He held out his phone. "Either you call your father or I will."

She blew out a big breath. "I'm not ready to announce…um, my news just yet, so what exactly are we callin' my daddy about?"

Okay. His sisters were angels. He would never complain about them again.

"How about the truth?"

"Tell you what." She leaned in close. "I'll make sure my daddy knows we aren't an item anymore if you keep my problem to yourself." She smiled. "As a bonus, I'll even forget about the Nashville job."

Yeah, like he was going to broadcast her predicament. The sooner he could distance himself, the better. "I promise. I won't tell a soul."

"Good." She traced her finger across the rim of her water glass. "I'd hate to think what Adrianna or whatever her name is would think if rumors started flying."

Hayden wanted him to react. He wasn't going to give her anything. "Right."

She eyed him for a few seconds before pressing a number on her phone and lifted it to her ear. "Daddy, I need to ask you a favor." A lock of her dark hair fell across her shoulder as she leaned back into the booth. "Promise me you won't fire Chase just because I've decided to end our relationship."

Some of the tension melted away. It was decent of her to at least allow him to keep his job. For now.

Her mouth pressed into a pout. "No. It was all me." Her gaze flickered to Chase. "Let's just say I think I can do better." After a few seconds of silence, Hayden laughed and said, "Thanks. I love you too."

She ended the call, the cold calculating look back in her eyes. "Happy?"

Ecstatic. He scooted out from the booth. "Thank you."

"Anytime."

He stared at her for a moment and actually felt sorry for her. "I hope everything works out with…your situation." He didn't ask how this would affect her acting job.

She smirked and took a drink of her water. "Don't pretend like you care."

Chase didn't respond. Talking with her was a no-win situation. No matter what he said, she'd find a way to turn it on him. He gave her a brief nod of the head, then turned and left the restaurant.

Immediately, Chase went to his room and packed for his return trip home. At least some good things had come out of being forced to come on this trip. He now knew why Hayden had been after him so persistently, and since she wouldn't want her predicament broadcast, he believed she'd keep her end of the bargain and not say anything to her dad about his potential new job.

With this stress no longer pressing down on him, he could pursue his music career, and figure out a way to have Addie too.

Chapter Twenty

"They want to interview me?" Addie sat down at the table. "Why?"

Aunt Janie grinned and took a seat next to her. "Because of the letter you discovered! At my United Daughters of the Confederacy meeting yesterday, I shared the letter and picture with the group. The women were so excited, and Vera called her granddaughter who is a reporter for the *Telegraph* newspaper. Susannah is interested and wants to write a story for the paper."

Addie wasn't sure she wanted to be interviewed by a reporter. If it was scheduled at the same time Chase was getting home, there was no way she was doing it. "When is the interview?"

Janie glanced at her watch. "At ten."

Darn. She didn't have an excuse to say no. Chase was picking her up around noon. Addie pushed back from the table. "I better go finish getting ready."

An hour later, Susannah left with a promise to let them know when the story would run. If they had room it would come out in Sunday's paper, otherwise it would be in Wednesday's edition.

The reporter had done her homework and discovered that Lydia and Marianne had married brothers. What had probably seemed like a dream come true for the close sisters, turned into an ugly nightmare once the Civil War started.

When the war ended, Lydia returned to the house, caring for her wounded husband until he died a few years later.

Her sister, Marianne, died from an unknown illness, never setting foot in the house again. Lydia's posterity claimed she never found her sister's hidden valuables.

Janie was excited with all this information. "This means the treasure could still be buried. Wouldn't it be fun to find it?"

Addie nodded her head. "Sure, but I thought every inch of the property has already been searched?"

Her aunt walked over to the little computer desk in her kitchen. "That was years ago. And I don't think anyone ever used a metal detector. I wonder if I could rent one?" She jiggled the mouse and opened a browser to start her search.

The image of her aunt using a metal detector brought a smile to Addie's lips. "I guess they can't be that hard to operate."

Grinning, Janie raised both her eyebrows. "I'm gonna do it. This is so exciting!"

Addie laughed. "Go, Aunt Janie." She glanced at the clock. "Oh, wow. Chase is going to be here soon. I need to change my clothes." She started to run upstairs, but paused by the doorway. "By the way, what do I wear to a bar?"

Janie chuckled. "Sugar, don't think of it as a bar. Dress like you're going to a nice place for dinner."

Addie grinned, knowing just the thing to wear. After touching up her makeup, she pulled on a pair of dark-wash skinny jeans and a moss-colored, fitted peasant top. She slipped her feet into black, peep-toe heels, and accessorized with a pair of silver hoop earrings and several bronze and silver bangle bracelets.

She spritzed on perfume, excited to see Chase perform again. Since the guys had missed Friday night's rehearsal, they were meeting this afternoon to go over their music before setting up at Gracie's Haven, giving Addie a chance for a little preview of the band's show tonight.

Grabbing her purse, she went downstairs. Chase stood in the foyer talking with her aunt. He looked incredibly hot in a white V-neck tee, worn jeans and his boots.

He glanced up and she felt a jitter in her belly as she watched the slow curve of his mouth lift into a sexy smile. "Wow," he said. "You look prettier than I remembered."

"Thanks. So do you."

He quirked a brow. "I look pretty?"

Aunt Janie giggled like a school-girl, watching the interchange with pure delight.

Addie gave him a coy look with half-lowered lashes. "You know what I mean." Although, she still did think of him as a "pretty boy."

Grinning, he reached for her hand and pulled her close. He smelled unbelievably good as he drew her in for a hug. "Are you ready to go?" he asked, setting her back from him.

"Yes." She turned to say goodbye to her aunt. "Don't lock me out, I'll be home late."

Chase took her hand. "I promise to have her home before two."

Janie smiled. "I'll take a nap and skip my sleeping pill so I can wait up for you." She shooed them with her hands. "Y'all better get going. And have fun."

They said goodbye and walked to his truck. Instead of opening the passenger door, he led her around to the driver's side. "I want you to sit in the middle." He opened the door and helped her climb up.

She scooted across his seat and settled in the middle. Bench seats were a total plus when dating someone you really liked—and she really liked Chase.

He slid in next to her. The scent of his tangy cologne and the touch of his shoulder against hers made all her nerve endings tingle. A tiny sigh escaped her mouth as he looked over and gave her a crooked smile.

"You really do look gorgeous."

"Thanks." She lifted her face to his as he leaned down to kiss her. They were only a breath away when his phone blared out *Start a Band*.

Chase groaned as he withdrew his phone. "I swear Jackson must have some kind of radar."

He gave her a quick kiss and answered the phone. "Sure, no problem. We'll just swing by a store on the way."

Ending the call, he started the truck and backed out of the driveway. "Drew had to bring his three girls for the practice. I guess he forgot to bring diapers and he doesn't want to bother his wife." Chase pulled out into the street and then reached for her hand. "You don't mind if we stop at the store, do you?"

"Of course not." She leaned her shoulder into his, loving the way it felt to be with him again. Like the last piece of a missing puzzle being put in place, completing the picture.

On the way to the store, he asked her more about the mystery letter she'd discovered, and the interview with the *Telegraph* reporter. She made him laugh when she told him Aunt Janie planned to rent a metal detector to look for the buried treasure.

"If anyone can find lost treasure, it's your aunt," he said, pulling into the Kroger parking lot.

"So," Addie said, climbing out of the truck. "Do we know what size of diapers Drew's daughter needs?"

Chase took her hand and looked at her sidelong. "They have different sizes?"

"Yes," she said with a laugh. "If I remember right, several different sizes. How old are his girls?"

The automatic door slid open and they entered the grocery store. "I'm not sure. Something like seven, five and two."

Addie saw a sign for the baby aisle and she headed in that direction, pulling Chase with her. "It has to be for the two-year-old."

"Whoa. You weren't kidding," Chase said as the stood in front of the shelves containing a vast assortment of diapers.

Addie's maternal side unlocked as she stood next to him in the baby aisle. Everything looked so cute and fun to buy. Even the little jars of baby food. She picked up a package of number three diapers. "Is she a small child?" she questioned, noting they sized by weight not by age.

He lifted a shoulder in a clueless shrug. "She's little, like most kids."

Her lips twisted into a smile. "Maybe you should call and find out so we get the right ones."

After conferring with Drew, they selected the appropriate size and then Addie picked up a container of diaper wipes. This part of having a child wasn't as appealing as the little jars of baby food or the entire section filled with lotion and soap. She wondered if Chase was the kind of guy who would change a dirty diaper.

As the checker scanned the items, Addie couldn't help thinking the clerk probably assumed she and Chase were buying diapers for their own child. Secretly, she liked the idea.

Chase paid for the diapers, giving Addie time to study his handsome profile. A sweet emotion filled her chest and swelled with each breath. She knew she had to acknowledge her feelings. She was falling in love with him. Really in love.

It was time to stop her think-about-it-tomorrow attitude. She had to figure out a way to either live without her family or talk Chase into leaving Georgia.

* * *

Drew stood out on the porch, holding his crying daughter as Chase pulled into Jackson's driveway. He looked relieved to see them. "Y'all are lifesavers." He took the bag from Addie. "I'll be back in a second."

Chase could smell the telltale signs that Lauren definitely needed a diaper change as he and Addie followed him inside the house. He admired Drew's stamina. Would he be that kind of dad? A flash of panic hit him for a few seconds when he thought about Hayden and her plan to make him the father of her baby.

He turned to find Addie watching him, a flicker of a smile played across her lips. All thoughts of Hayden left him as he pulled her into his arms and gazed into her brown eyes.

"Guess he really did need the diapers."

"Guess so." Addie wound her arms around his neck, her bracelets jangling with the movement. "Are you gonna be the kind of guy who'll change a diaper?"

"Is that a trick question?"

Her dimple appeared. "No."

"Why do you wanna know?"

She played with his hair around the back of his neck, making it hard for him to concentrate.

"Just curious."

Curious as in if we had kids would she be the only one changing diapers?

"Uh-huh. So that's a question you ask all the time?"

"Well, sure," she said playfully. "Are you telling me nobody has ever asked you that before?"

Not exactly. But he was certain Hayden would not be the kind of mother to *ever* change a dirty diaper.

Intent on pushing Hayden and her predicament far from his mind, he gave Addie a teasing smile and then slowly lowered his head to kiss her. The second his mouth touched hers, something inside him shifted. His fingers pressed into her waist, pulling her closer. "I missed you," he said, temporarily leaving her lips to trail kisses across her jaw.

"I missed you more."

He smiled, and found her lips again.

A throat cleared and he reluctantly ended the kiss.

Drew held his now happy daughter, an amused grin on his face. "Hey." He held out his free hand to Addie. "I'm Drew."

"Oh." She took his hand. "It's nice to meet you. I'm Addie."

"Well, Addie, Lauren and I appreciate you and Chase bringing the diapers."

"You're welcome." She reached out and touched Lauren's button nose. "She's beautiful."

"Thanks."

Lauren suddenly lunged forward, holding her arms out for Addie. "Well, hello there," she said, cuddling the little girl close.

The sight of Addie holding a baby did something to Chase. It was like his senses were sharpened and everything came into focus. This was the woman he was going to marry.

Drew gave Chase an I'm-impressed look. "Wow," he said to Addie. "She's usually really shy. She must like you."

The little girl played with Addie's bracelets. "Or she just saw something shiny to play with," Addie said with a laugh. "Do you want me to watch her while you guys practice?"

Lauren squirmed, wanting Drew to hold her again. "That'd be great." He took back his daughter. "Syd has the other girls in the studio. I didn't mean for y'all to be babysitters, but my wife's blood pressure has been elevated and the doctor doesn't want her up and around too much. Her mama couldn't watch the girls until later on tonight."

"It's no problem at all. I'm glad we can help," Addie said as they walked into the studio.

Chase captured her hand and held her back. He leaned over and whispered in her ear, "You're good with kids. And yes…I'll change diapers."

She turned her head and stared at him with an intense gaze. Grinning, he leaned in and gave her a quick kiss. "Just wanted you to know." He winked and jogged away, laughing at the stunned look on her face.

Chapter Twenty One

Addie climbed out of Sydney's sleek car and slipped the strap of her purse over one shoulder. Gracie's Haven stood before her, the rustic-pine lodge looking nothing like the skanky bar in Daisy Springs.

She glanced back at the car to see Sydney still seated in the driver's seat, talking with her mother. Addie wished Chase would come out to escort her in, but knew he was busy setting up their equipment.

She was anxious to see him. Anxious to hear them play. Watching Drew's girls had proved to be a little challenging. While the band warmed up, Sydney decided to take the active girls to McDonald's. Addie didn't have a choice but to help her. By the time they returned, the guys were loading up their equipment.

Glancing around her, she noted a large marquee out front. Lit up like a beacon, it read: *Live Tonight—Chasing Dreams.* The place seemed popular as more vehicles pulled into the already jam-packed parking lot. The Saturday night crowd, dressed in tight wranglers and cowboy hats, were winding up for a night of entertainment.

At last, Sydney climbed out of her car. "Sorry. My mother doesn't understand why almost every weekend I need to hear my husband play. According to her, if I've heard him once that is more than enough." She rounded the car and beamed at Addie. "But you know what? I never get tired of hearing them play." She locked her car and gave her a grin. "Ready?"

A rush of adrenaline coursed through Addie. "Oh, yeah."

They stepped inside the crowded entrance and waited in line behind a boisterous group. Addie surreptitiously studied her surroundings, feeling a little out of place. She'd never been a party girl, or hung out with those kind of kids. Obviously, she'd led a sheltered life. The vibes she got from this place weren't like any restaurant she'd been to back home. It felt a little like the frat party some guy had taken her to her freshman year in college. Needless to say, she left early and never went out with the guy again.

Sydney confirmed their table reservations with a beautiful blonde who wore a tight black T-shirt with the words *Gracie's Haven* stretched across her chest in silver letters. She pointed them in the right direction and Addie followed Sydney through double doors. The lighting dimmed as cigarette smoke swirled around in a heavy fog. Crinkling her nose, she surmised not all restaurants had embraced the new smoke-free-environment like most places.

Addie's heels clicked against the wood floor as she trailed behind Sydney through the crowded bar. The place was buzzing with loud laughter and the low hum of voices, sounding as if someone had tried tuning into a radio station but couldn't quite find the right channel.

She felt a little uncomfortable as a couple of guys let out a low whistle as they passed by. Without thinking, Addie turned to see where the sound had come from and met the stare of more than one man watching them intently.

Before turning away, one good-looking cowboy raised his glass and winked at her. Her face burned hot and she quickly averted her eyes. The place was crawling with men. Where were all the girls?

She soon found the women…scantily clad and drooling over Chase and his fellow band members.

Seemingly oblivious to his audience, Chase sat on a stool strumming his guitar. Drew stood nearby stroking his instrument while Beau knelt in front of the amplifier, fine-tuning the sound. Jackson was at his keyboard, playing a few notes and then making some last minute adjustments.

Sydney stopped at a small round table near the front. "Here we are," she said, sliding into one of the chairs.

Addie pulled out a chair and slid in beside Sydney. Three women occupying the table next to them were laughing and making catcalls at the guys on the stage. She was pretty sure they were already drunk. Addie narrowed her eyes at the brazen women who—judging from the way they were dressed—could give a hooker some stiff competition.

Chase raised his face and his eyes skimmed over the crowd, then landed on Addie. His mouth lifted at the corners, warming her right down to her shimmering toenails.

One of the women turned, following his line of vision. She glowered at Addie and scanned her up and down. A feral grin tipped her painted lips, like she just realized Addie wouldn't be any competition.

A waiter stepped in front of Addie, blocking her line of sight. Good thing. She was just about to stick out her tongue. "What can I get you ladies to drink?" he asked, winking at her.

She sure hoped they served something other than alcohol, but seriously doubted it. The place was one rip-roaring party and the night was young. Sydney leaned over and whispered, "I always get a strawberry-lemonade. And the food here is really good."

"Sounds great," Addie said and Sydney ordered for the two of them, requesting a menu as well.

The waiter left to fill their orders just as Jackson played a few chords of music. Chase grabbed a hold of the microphone and spoke over the noisy crowd. "Hey, y'all, we're gonna start the night off with a song for all those guys out there who…" He paused and he looked directly at Addie and winked. "Wanna kiss a girl."

The familiar Keith Urban tune started and the crowd went wild, especially the three loose women sitting close by. Their seductive dance moves made Addie uncomfortable. She glanced over at Sydney to see what she thought. With a look of pure adoration written on her face, Sydney watched her husband, her fingers tapping against the table in rhythm to the music. She didn't even seem to notice what was going on around them.

Addie shifted in her seat and focused on Chase, trying to ignore the crowd of people. This was their song. Sort of. And he was amazing.

A feeling of pride and ownership gripped her. Smugly she got to her feet and started clapping to the beat of the music. At the end of the night she would be riding home with Chase and—unlike everyone else—getting a sensational kiss good-night.

The song came to an end and Chase spoke into the microphone over the applause. "How y'all doing tonight?" he questioned in his soft southern voice. He seemed completely at ease in front of the rowdy crowd.

The patrons responded with a few enthusiastic comebacks that said they were all feeling pretty good. Addie ground her teeth together when the brunette who had given her the evil eye, yelled out, "Much better if I get to go home with you, sugar." She added on another invitation that wasn't so innocent.

Addie came very close to throwing something at the back of the woman's head. Too bad she didn't have any fruit handy.

Chase didn't pay any attention to the brazen invitation and announced the next song they were going to sing. "A few years ago, Jackson, our keyboard player and I wrote this song. It's entitled *Dreams*." He looked up and gave the audience a boyishly charming smile. "I hope y'all enjoy it."

The minute Chase started to sing, the audience actually quieted. Addie sat spell-bound, unable to take her eyes off of him. He was incredible. His voice smooth with a slight, raspy-rocker sound to it. Both Jackson and Drew harmonized perfectly to the ballad, telling a story about what they wanted to be when they grew up.

Chase seemed to lose himself in his music, he and his guitar becoming one. Addie watched his fingers move effortlessly over the strings, his muscles rippled with the movement. It was easy to tune out the rest of the audience and focus on him, his instrument and his amazing voice.

When the song ended, Addie stood up and clapped with enthusiasm. Then she put her fingers between her lips and gave a loud whistle. Chase looked her way and smiled. She mouthed, "You were great." His smile widened and he gave her a wink before pulling his eyes away.

Sydney touched her on the arm. "What'd you think?"

"The song was amazing," Addie said, her eyes sliding back to the stage as she sat down.

Chase was amazing. Not only could he do fantastic covers, he also wrote great original music. She could easily see him having a successful music career, and hoped the talent scout showed up for tonight's performance.

That thought made her pause, and, for a second, panic seized her heart. If Chase was discovered, what were the chances he'd be moving to Daisy Springs to set up a new graphic arts business?

Zero. Addie already knew the answer.

When they'd talked last night, she'd been kidding about him moving to Idaho. Deep down, though, she really wanted to know if that was a possibility. If he could make a career out of entertaining, his graphic arts days were over.

She swallowed, and tried not to let her anxiety show as the band started the cover of another popular country song. The upbeat music kept rhythm with her heartbeat, and soon Addie's concerns about the future dissipated. Either that or she was using her old tactics of stuffing away her worries so she didn't have to think about them.

Honestly, she had so much in common with the heroine from Gone With the Wind—well, at least the I'll-think-about-it-tomorrow motto part.

The waiter brought them their drinks and a menu, stating he'd give them a few minutes to decide what they wanted to order. In the meantime, the band started playing another original song. The contemporary tune had most of the female patrons up dancing. Judging from their provocative moves, nearly all of their inhibitions had to be long gone. It was a little embarrassing, so Addie tried to ignore them and focus on the band.

After ordering fried shrimp and fries, and downing most of her strawberry lemonade, Addie needed to use the restroom. Syd gave her directions as the band started another song. The path to the bathroom took her directly past a horseshoe shaped bar.

Feeling a little nervous, Addie smiled and said hello to several people as she made her way to the ladies room. Most of them were men and she felt completely out of place, wishing Sydney would've come with her.

Her nose wrinkled with distaste as she pushed open the door to the bathroom. Apparently it also doubled as a smoking lounge. Didn't these people read the reports about tobacco and secondhand smoke? Addie didn't waste any time and finished up in the bathroom.

On the way back, she passed the same bar. It was a mistake. Her face burned with embarrassment at the whistles and invitations she got to have a drink with some of the men. Although nobody actually groped her, it felt like she was being mauled by the not-so-subtle comments. She rushed back to Sydney and vowed not to leave her seat for the rest of the night.

The guys were in the middle of an upbeat song she'd never heard before. It must be another one of their originals. They were good and looked like they were having a great time. She scooted the chair back and sat down just as the waiter delivered their food. Despite the smoky environment, it smelled incredible. "Mmm. This looks good." She picked up a jumbo fried shrimp.

"I told you," Sydney said, taking a piece of shrimp for herself.

The flavor popped in Addie's mouth and she stopped herself from moaning out loud. How come everything tasted so much better fried?

Just as she took another bite, a new waiter came by with a tray of drinks. "For you, little lady," he said, placing a tumbler full of amber liquid in front of Addie.

She almost choked on her food. "Uh, I didn't order that." She felt slightly alarmed at having an alcoholic drink placed in front of her.

The man winked at her and grinned. "I know. It's from that man over there."

Addie looked over in the direction the waiter pointed. An extremely handsome man, wearing a brown cowboy hat and white-button down shirt, smiled at her and touched the brim of his hat. She swallowed and turned around, gripping the edge of her chair. She was pretty sure he was one of the guys she'd smiled at on her way to the bathroom.

The waiter disappeared with his tray, leaving the drink in front of her. Panicked, she turned to Sydney. "What should I do?"

Sydney gave her a sympathetic smile and pushed the drink away from her. "We'll get someone to take it away."

When a waitress passed by their table, Sydney lifted a hand and waved at her. The woman stopped and placed another drink in front of Addie. This one had a cute little umbrella sticking out of it. "Hey, sugar," the waitress said. "The cowboy who sent this wants to know if you'll join him at his table."

What the heck! "Uh…" she didn't know what to say.

The waitress tapped her on the shoulder and pointed to a table across the room. Another man she definitely recognized from her trip to the bathroom gave her a smile and raised his drink. The only way she remembered him was because he resembled the syndicated sportscaster, Jim Rome.

Addie shook her head, and whirled back around. She took a shaky breath as another waitress swooped in with another alcoholic drink, telling her a man in the back sent it to her, along with an invitation to join him.

This was so embarrassing. Chase was going to think she was a complete idiot.

Full of exasperation, she turned to find Sydney staring at the drinks. Her eyes flickered back to Addie. Slowly her lips stretched into a smile and a puff of laughter escaped. "*What* did you do on your trip to the bathroom?"

"Nothing," Addie whispered. "I just said hello to a few people as I passed by."

Sydney covered her mouth with her hand, trying not to laugh any louder. "Oh, Addie. I should've warned you not to make any eye contact or talk to anyone."

Now she tells me. One by one, Addie pushed the drinks away from her, careful not to slosh any over the rim of the glass. If the men took her nervous hellos as a hey-I'm-available-and-want-to-get-to-know-you-better invitation, she might be in a lot of trouble. She was from Idaho. Everybody said hi to everybody! And she'd said hello to quite a few men.

She sunk low in her seat, wishing she could disappear. Sensing her despair, Sydney scooted over and patted her on the back. "Don't worry about it. We'll send them back with the next server that comes by."

"What if they bring more drinks? I didn't know that giving a simple greeting would be misconstrued as flirting."

Sydney reached for a big fat French fry and handed it to Addie. She obviously knew her well. Food always helped. "It's not your fault," Sydney said, taking a fry for herself. "Men here take any eye contact as a sign of interest. You didn't do anything wrong."

Maybe not. Still it was humiliating. She might as well be wearing a shirt that said: *Naïve, sheltered girl from Idaho.*

Chapter Twenty Two

Chase tried not to focus on Addie as yet another drink was placed in front of her. In total, six men had sent her a drink. He could see the distress written all over her face. There had to be a story behind all the unwanted invitations. At least Sydney seemed to understand. She pushed each drink away, and would pat Addie on the back.

It was almost time for a break, but Chase wanted to play the song he'd written for Addie. He hoped it would convey how he felt about her, and possibly put a smile back on her face.

"Hey, y'all," he said into the mic. "Before we take ten, I wanna play a new song I wrote just last night."

His eyes flickered to Addie and he could see he had her attention. "It's called *Make Believe*."

He started the ballad, and his talented band joined in. They'd only played through the song twice today, but they picked it up easily. After razzing him about writing a love song, they told him it was good and could go on his first solo album. Chase had no idea if the rep from Country Sounds Music showed up tonight, but if they did at least they'd know he could write music.

Strumming the last note of the intro, Chase began singing. "It was only supposed to be make-believe, but nothing's felt more real. Your laugh, your touch, the kisses we shared. I know what they make me feel."

When he started in on the chorus, his eyes locked on Addie. "So baby don't leave me, please don't go. What we have is forever, and I can't let you go. Yeah, what we have is forever, and I can't let you go."

A look of wonder and love radiated from her face. She smiled, and put both of her hands over her heart. In that moment, she was the only girl in the room. The crowd, particularly the obnoxious drunk women in the front, all faded.

Their eyes held throughout the song. His voice trembled slightly as he sang the last lines. "No this isn't a fairytale, it's not make believe. Our love is forever, baby please don't leave."

The crowd went wild, like he'd just announced drinks were on the house. Addie's reaction was all he cared about. The tender smile she gave him indicated she liked it.

Chase waited for the applause to die down a little before speaking into the mic. "Thank you. Y'all have been a great crowd. The boys and I are gonna take a little break now."

He slipped off his guitar strap, disregarding the dark-haired woman in the front, offering to help him take his break. Chase had learned a long time ago to ignore women—drunk or sober—and their comments.

A Luke Bryan song blared over the bar's sound system, and cut out some of the lewd comments coming from the same brunette. Chase made the promise to Addie that he'd never take a lady to a sleazy bar, yet that's exactly what he'd done.

"Hey, man," Beau said as Chase laid his guitar in its case. "It looks like your date is popular tonight."

Chase glanced over at Addie. She looked uncomfortable with all the raucous action around her. "Don't tease her about it. I already feel bad enough for exposing her to all of this."

Jackson arched an eyebrow. "Exposing her to what? Secondhand smoke?"

"No," Chase said. "The environment. Drinking, lewd comments and, yes, the cigarette smoke." Somehow, after singing in bar after bar, Chase had become immune to the skanky atmosphere.

"Dude," Jackson said. "This place is nice compared to some of the places we've played before."

"I know, but she's not into this kind of scene. Just don't tease her, okay?"

"Okay, bro. We promise not to say anything." Jackson clapped a hand to his shoulder. "By the way, your new song killed it."

"Thanks." Chase could hardly wait to ask Addie what she thought about the song.

He kept his eyes focused on her as he stepped down from the stage. He and his buddies were immediately swarmed by women looking for companionship.

Jackson held up his left hand and pointed to his ring as he pushed through. "Sorry, ladies. I'm happily married to that gorgeous woman sitting over there."

Chase tried to stay close behind Jackson, but the obnoxious brunette had other plans. She stepped in front of him, flattening her palm against his chest. "Hey, sugar. C'mon over to my table and I'll buy you a drink."

Beau and Jackson made it through the obstacle course, leaving Chase to fend for himself. "No thanks. I'm meeting my girlfriend."

The woman pouted and pressed closer. The overpowering scent of her perfume and the smell of alcohol assaulted his senses. "Oh, c'mon. She won't mind." One of her fingers made a circular motion on his chest as she attempted to be coy. She failed miserably.

Chase looked over the top of the persistent woman's head, and searched for a path to Addie. He found her standing by the table with her eyes zeroed in on the brunette in front of him. She minded all right. Even from here, he could feel the spark of jealousy radiating from her.

"Excuse me, ma'am." He removed her hand. "My girlfriend's waitin' on me."

The woman grunted and said something under her breath, but at least she moved out of the way. Chase turned sideways and squeezed through the crowded barroom floor. The smell of alcohol, tobacco and a variety of colognes and perfumes, mingled with the scent of warm bodies. The combination made him feel slightly nauseated.

As he neared Addie, a big brute of a guy stepped in front of him. "Hey, baby, I sent you a drink. So what happened?" he questioned, his words slurred.

Chase hoped he wasn't talking to Addie.

"I don't drink alcohol."

Oh, man. It was Addie. And she was having to defend herself against some drunken cowboy.

"That's okay, sugar. I can make you feel just as good without it."

A hot flush seared his neck as Chase pushed past another person. He did his best to get to Addie, but it was like every time he got close enough to reach her, someone else would get in the way.

"No thanks. I've got a boyfriend," she said, sounding a little bit intimidated.

The man gave a low chuckle. "I don't see a boyfriend."

"That's because I'm standing right behind you," Chase growled, trying to squeeze around the guy. "And I believe the lady told you no."

The guy slanted him a glance, his lip curled up in a sneer. "That right?"

Chase now stood in front of Addie, trying to protect her from her assailant. He had to look up. The guy had him by a few inches and at least a hundred pounds. "Yeah. That's right."

The man leaned down and spoke close enough for Chase to smell the alcohol on his breath. "Then I suggest you tell that…" He called Addie an ugly name, along with a few other expletives which included a reference to her bra size.

Chase didn't think about what happened next. It was an automatic reaction as he drew back his arm and drove his fist into the man's mouth. Sharp pain engulfed his hand, shooting up his arm. He was pretty sure he just busted a few knuckles. The guy was drunk enough his reflexes were pretty slow. His head snapped back and he staggered, trying to gain his footing.

Chase turned and looked into Addie's face. Her eyes were wide with shock.

Before he could apologize, she said, "Did he just call me what I think he called me?"

Chase shook his hand in an effort to ease the pain. "Unfortunately."

"And you hit him for it?"

He eyed her with caution, wondering if she found his actions heroic or thought of him as some hothead. "Yeah."

She surprised him by giving him a soft smile. "Thanks. Nobody has ever hit someone for me." She squinted and pursed her lips. "Of course, no one has *ever* called me that before."

"I'm—" He didn't get another word out as he was yanked around, coming face to face with the cowboy he'd hit. He heard Addie scream and Beau yell for him watch out as the man took a swing at him.

Chase pulled his head back, the man's knuckles just grazed his face. A string of profanities flew from the man's bleeding mouth and he caught Chase by surprise with a sneaky left hook.

He fell back into Beau's arms. "You just had to go and hit the biggest guy in the bar, didn't you?" Beau said, helping him stand upright.

Chase shook his head, hoping the double vision would go away. The next thing he knew a barroom-brawl broke out.

Between the two of them, he and Beau did pretty well holding their own. But when the cops showed up to break up the fight, Chase *knew* Addie would never talk to him again. Not only had he exposed her to this deplorable environment, she also heard words no lady should ever have to hear. And on top of that he was probably going to be arrested.

In the end, they lucked out. Because Chase and Beau hadn't been drinking and because they were the hired entertainment, the cops let them go with a warning.

"I better not catch you boys in another fight, ya hear?" Officer Jenkins said, trying to hold back a grin.

Chase held his ribcage with one hand and a wet washcloth to the side of his face with the other. "Yes, sir." He swallowed back a little blood from his split lip.

The officer lifted his face and winked at Addie. She stood next to Chase, holding a glass of ice-water that she would periodically dip the washcloth in. "And you, little lady, keep this one out of trouble, okay?"

"Yes, sir," she said, sending a worried look Chase's way.

Chase tried to smile, but winced from the split lip. He couldn't believe Addie was still speaking to him, let alone caring for his wounds. And she was the one responsible for the light reprimand. When the cops showed up trying to figure out who to arrest, Chase had been targeted as starting the whole thing. Addie had stepped forward and said something to Officer Jenkins. Then she rose up on her tiptoes and whispered in the cop's ear.

The man's face turned as red as a lobster and he immediately arrested Bubba. That was seriously his name. Bubba was outraged and let loose another string of profanity. Officer Jenkins had actually gagged the man before hauling him away to the police station.

Beau moaned and Chase turned to see Sydney helping him. His friend looked worse than Chase did. One of his eyes was already swollen shut.

Jackson and Drew came back in after loading the last of their equipment. The two of them hadn't gotten caught in the foray. Drew had still been out back talking to his wife when he heard the sirens. Jackson had tried to help, but he ended up protecting Sydney and Addie, getting them safely outside. By the time he got back in, the police had broken everything up.

"Okay, boys," Jackson said with a smirk. "Let's get you both home."

Home. Chase dreaded going there. That was the problem with being a twenty-eight-year-old man living at home. He still had to answer to his parents. Particularly his mother. He winced as he stood up. "Sorry we couldn't help. Do you have my keys?"

Jackson pulled them from his pocket and dangled them out in front. Addie snatched them out of his hand. "I'll drive Chase home. Can you guys get poor Beau home?"

Beau grunted. "Yeah, since I don't have a girlfriend or a mother to coddle me." Beau's family had relocated to Florida. Beau had stayed behind, mainly because of the band.

"You can come home with me," Chase said. If he had Beau with him his mother might not get as mad. "My sisters will take care of you. Taylin volunteers at the hospital, so she sort of knows what she's doing. And we all know Ashlee would jump at the chance to take care of you." He liked teasing Beau about his little sister's crush.

"I think I'll pass. Your kid sister is cute, but way too young."

Sydney helped Beau up. "You're coming to our house. Jackson and I will take care of you."

Beau didn't protest as the McCalls helped him out to their truck. Addie put her arm around Chase's waist. "Ready?"

He nodded his head. "Yeah, although I can't believe you're still even talkin' to me."

She paused and looked up at him with troubled eyes. "Why would you say that? I'm the one who got us into this mess."

He snorted then winced from the pain. "You know that's not true."

Her chin went up defiantly. "Maybe you don't know the whole story?"

Oh, he knew the whole story all right. She was a nice girl from Idaho who thought she was in a "nice restaurant" and said hello to a few men who were waiting for any kind of signal. He met her gaze. "Are you telling me you wanted those men to hit on you?"

Her eyes widened. "Of course not."

"My point exactly."

"But—"

He rested his forehead against hers. "Baby, please don't argue with me. My head hurts and I need to save my strength for when I get home. My mama is gonna yell at me the second she sees my face."

Addie brought a hand up and gently cupped his jaw. "Don't worry about your mother. I plan on telling her she raised a pretty wonderful man who defended my honor."

Despite the split lip, Chase grinned. His mother wouldn't be able to refute that kind of talk.

Addie reached up and kissed him on the uninjured side of his mouth. "By the way, I never got the chance to tell you how much I loved the song you wrote. It was beautiful."

Suddenly, his injuries didn't hurt as much. Addie loved his song. The way she gazed at him right now, he dared to hope she might love him too.

Chapter Twenty Three

Addie hung up the phone after telling another person they couldn't come and search the property for the buried treasure. The newspaper article in the Sunday paper had generated a lot of interest, particularly to those with metal detectors.

Aunt Janie hadn't had time to rent one and didn't want other people digging up her yard. She wasn't in any hurry to make the discovery, especially this week as the Macon Cherry Blossom festival kicked off its nine-day event. Aunt Janie had volunteered to help with the Senior Center float, and would be riding on it with some of the other members in today's parade.

The newspaper article also sparked Addie's renewed interest to solve the mystery. She'd spent all morning thinking about the letter, wondering if she'd missed any obvious clues. Focusing on the letter served as a great distraction, keeping her mind off of her last few days in Georgia.

She felt the week closing in on her just like the crowd of men at Gracie's Haven on Saturday. Only this time Chase and Beau couldn't fight off the bad guys. She had to return to Idaho—to her job and her family. She and Chase hadn't really talked about what would happen after she went home. Neither of them had any answers. So, by some unspoken rule, they'd decided not to talk about it.

The one thing they did know was the music rep hadn't been able to make it to the performance at Gracie's Haven. Chase didn't feel too bad, especially since the second half of the show was cancelled after the fight broke out.

She slid the plate of fresh-baked goodies toward her and took another chocolate chip cookie. They were for the parade today, but she'd already eaten two. Telling herself this was the last one, she took a bite and savored the taste, wishing it would take away the anxiety she felt as her time in Georgia grew short.

Popping the rest of the cookie into her mouth, she reached for a copy of the letter she'd discovered behind the photo. The clue had to be in this letter. She scanned over the spidery writing, searching for a key word. Nothing jumped out at her. Except the scripture reference. Her eyes flickered back up to the middle of the letter. John 4:11-14. Addie had looked it up before and assumed Marianne was trying to remind her sister of eternal life. But maybe she had missed something.

She scooted the chair away from the table and went in search of a Bible. Once in the living room, Addie pulled an oversized Bible from the bookcase. She sank down into the couch and carefully turned the pages until she came to the fourth chapter of John. Her fingers skimmed down the page until she came to verse eleven.

The woman saith unto him, Sir, thou has nothing to draw with, and the well is deep: from whence then hast thou that living water?

Unable to glean anything from the words, she moved on to the next verse. Before she could get very far, she was interrupted by the doorbell. Glancing at her watch, she grinned. Chase was thirty minutes early. It was perfect timing. Maybe between the two of them they could come up with something.

Laying the Bible down on the coffee table, she jumped up from the couch and rushed to the foyer. "You're early," she squealed, flinging the door open wide.

She just about launched herself into his arms when she realized it wasn't Chase. Not even close.

The man standing before her had dark, long hair pulled back in to a ponytail. His face was covered with a full beard that looked like it could use a trim. He wore a pair of denim overalls, emphasizing his protruding stomach.

The man grinned and revealed yellowed teeth, stained with tiny black flecks of something gross. "Howdy. Is Ms. Janie Caldwell at home?"

Addie was alone and she was getting some major bad vibes from this guy. Instinctively, she took a step backward, and remembered what she'd been taught as a child. "My aunt can't come to the door right now. May I help you?"

The man's eyes took on a gleam of expectation. "I hope so. My name is Ernie Claxton and I'd like to offer y'all my services to help Ms. Caldwell locate the family's buried treasure. I've got my equipment with me and could get started right away." He grinned again, as if trying to win her over with his charm.

Addie could now see a slight bulge in the man's bottom lip. He confirmed her suspicion he was chewing tobacco when he turned and squirted a stream of black spittle on the porch. She swallowed, trying not to throw up the cookies she'd just eaten.

"I'm sorry. Several people have already called and my aunt has told everyone the same answer. No."

The man's beady eyes darkened and he spit again. She was appalled but didn't want to call him on it. "I'd like to speak to Ms. Caldwell. I'll wait until she's *available*." He said the word to let her know he was calling her bluff.

She swallowed again. He knew she was alone.

Still, she tried not to show her growing alarm. "My aunt is busy getting ready for the Cherry Blossom festival in Macon. She won't be coming to the door. If you leave a business card, she can get back with you when she has the chance."

Janie wouldn't call this man and he knew it. He took another step toward her. Addie didn't know if she should try and shut the door or run past him so she was at least outside. He bent forward, bringing him close enough that Addie caught a whiff of his unkempt body.

"Why don't you just let me have a look around," he said in an intimidating voice. "If I find anything, Ms. Caldwell can have seventy percent." He stared at her intently, almost daring her to refuse him access to the yard.

Frozen in place, Addie offered a silent prayer. She wanted Chase to come and rescue her again. She felt her heart rate accelerate and the air felt thinner. She absolutely could not hyperventilate. The other night at the bar Bubba had scared her, but she hadn't even come close to having a panic attack. This guy was scarier because, for one thing, she was all alone.

Maybe she should just let him start looking. She could call the police. Maybe even Officer Jenkins would show up.

Before she could say anything, a car turned into the driveway and stopped. Addie squinted to see who it was, but didn't recognize the car. She raised her hand as if she knew them, hoping Mr. Claxton would leave.

Ernie spit again and looked over his shoulder at the idling vehicle. Then he turned and gave her another greasy smile. "Well, I guess I'll just try'n come back when your aunt can come to the door." He backed away. "You have a nice day now, Miss."

The stairs groaned under his girth and Addie let out the breath she'd been holding. Her heart rate returned to normal as Ernie started his truck and backed out. The unknown car at the end of the drive backed out as well. Either they were lost and just getting their bearings or her guardian angel drove a four-door sedan.

She watched Ernie's truck disappear from her view before going back inside the house. Her fingers shook slightly as she locked the door. Then she grabbed her cell phone and called Chase. He didn't answer so she left a message and then sent him a text. *Can you come early? Some creepy guy was here and I'm alone.*

Right after she sent the message, she felt guilty. He was going to get the text and probably think she was a basket case. Ernie Claxton was probably a harmless, but uncouth treasure hunter.

Five minutes later Chase called. He definitely sounded anxious. "Hey, I just got out of the shower. Is that guy still there?" He sounded a little out of breath, like he was dressing while running.

"He's gone. I probably just overreacted. I'm fine now."

"I'm on my way over. Did you lock the doors?"

Addie wandered back toward the front door. She reached out and pulled the curtains to the side, peeking outside to look for Ernie's truck. "I did and I'm looking out the window right now and he's gone." She shivered. "I didn't mean to alarm you, he just gave me the creeps." She went on to explain the many phone calls they'd received since the article had come out in the paper.

Chase made her talk to him as he drove over to get her. While she waited, she went back into the kitchen and ate another cookie. "You better hurry. The cookies are dwindling fast."

He laughed. "I better not speed. I have a record now and the police probably won't go easy on me again."

"You do not," she said with a giggle. "But I don't want you to speed." She pushed the plate of cookies away. "I promise not to eat anymore."

A few minutes later the doorbell sounded. Just to be safe, Addie checked to see who it was before she opened the door to let Chase inside.

"Hey," she said, feeling her mouth go dry. Chase wore a pink, V-necked tee that stretched across his broad shoulders. It was tradition for cherry blossom festival goers to wear pink. "I like your shirt."

"I like yours too." His eyes skimmed appreciatively over her matching pink T-shirt they'd bought for the parade. Always the gentleman, he brought his gaze back up to her face. The snug fitting tee felt a little too tight, but Aunt Janie hadn't agreed. She said if she had a figure like Addie's she'd show it off too.

"Thanks." She studied his handsome face, relieved to see he didn't look as bad as he had yesterday morning. In the two days since the fight, the swelling was gone, leaving a dark bruise on the outside of one eye. The split lip had healed quickly with only a tiny crack at the corner of his mouth.

"You should see the other guy," Chase joked.

"I was there, remember?"

"I remember." Chase tugged on the bottom of her T-shirt, bringing her close enough to thoroughly kiss. His phone chimed an incoming text, ending the kiss too soon.

While Addie collected her thoughts and got her breathing back under control, he glanced at his phone and rolled his eyes.

"We're meeting my parents in Macon for the parade, but Ashlee wasn't ready on time and my parents actually followed through with their threat to leave her. She's begging me to come and get her."

"What are you going to tell her?"

"I should tell her no." He started typing a reply.

Addie grinned, knowing full well he would rescue his sister again. "Let's go get her then. I don't want to miss Aunt Janie's float. She actually dyed her hair pink this morning and I haven't seen her yet."

Lifting an eyebrow, Chase looked up at her. "What makes you think I said yes?"

"Because you're a good big brother, and I've noticed that every time your sisters get into some kind of trouble, they always turn to you."

She wanted to add, "That's one of the reasons I fell in love with you." But couldn't bring herself to say it out loud. It would break their silent agreement to avoid the defining the relationship talk.

Instead, she gave him a quick kiss and moved toward the kitchen. "I just need to grab my purse and the cookies."

Chase followed her into the kitchen. Before leaving to get his sister, he stole another unforgettable kiss, and then he stole a cookie.

* * *

Cradled in Chase's arms, Addie sat on the curb of the sidewalk with her back pressed against his chest. The last float of the parade slowly passed by, and the MC announced a number of upcoming activities.

"You smell good," Chase said, nuzzling the side of her neck. She shivered when he placed a kiss just below her ear.

"What was that for?" she asked, tilting her head to look at him.

"Do I need a reason to kiss you?"

"Absolutely not." Her eyes darted from side to side. His family seemed to be engrossed in watching the last float pass by. She leaned in and kissed him on the mouth.

Now it was his turn to grin. "What was that for?"

She twisted and lightly skimmed her fingertips across the fading bruise next to his eye. "For coming to my rescue again."

"The guy was already gone."

She shrugged. "Okay, let's go with because you look so hot in pink."

Grinning, he leaned in and gave her another kiss.

"Okay, you two," Taylin said, standing over them. "Enough kissing. It makes me miss Ryan."

She and Chase laughed as his father's face contorted into a scowl. "Taylin," Charles said. "Don't ruin my fantasy that my girls are still ten and think boys are disgusting."

Ashlee stood up and patted their dad on the back. "They are disgusting. Especially hot drummers."

Charles groaned. "Stop it. Beau is too old for you."

"But, Daddy," Ashlee said, laying her head on his arm. "That's why he is the perfect guy for me to fall in love with. He sees me as his little sister so nothing will ever happen."

A smile lit Charles's face. "You have a good point." He put his arm around Ashlee's shoulders. "Now, who wants pulled pork? I'm buying."

"Me," Addie said as she popped out of Chase's arms.

It was no secret now how much she liked southern food. They stayed at the festival until it grew dark. She and Chase trailed behind his family all evening, holding hands and stealing kisses.

Later, when he took her home, he gave her another long kiss good-night. As the moon cast its silvery glow over them, Chase drew back and peered into her eyes. "I have to work in the morning, but I'm planning to get off early so we can go to the concert in the park."

Their hands were linked, neither one wanting to break the connection. "Sounds good." She gave him a playful grin. "Then you can buy me another barbeque pork sandwich."

He tugged on her hands and wrapped his arms around her. "Deal." He placed a kiss on top of her head. "I better go before I start kissing you again."

They both knew her aunt was waiting inside. "All right. See you tomorrow."

"Have a good night, and dream of me."

"You and the barbeque pork."

He laughed and opened the door for her. "Whatever it takes."

Addie couldn't dream about Chase because she couldn't fall asleep. Maybe she should've asked her aunt for one of her sleeping pills. Aunt Janie was dead to the world and wouldn't wake up if a freight train went through the house. Addie knew this because the other night she had tripped on a rug and fell against a table, smashing a vase full of silk flowers. Aunt Janie hadn't heard a thing and it was right outside her door.

Climbing out of bed, she took her cell phone and sneaked down the stairs. The wood floor creaked under her feet as she crept into the kitchen for a midnight snack. She also wanted to send Chase a text he would get first thing in the morning.

The moon illuminated the kitchen well enough for her to navigate without having to turn on a light. Somehow eating coconut cream pie in the moonlight seemed a lot more fun. She took a seat at the bar and sent Chase a message. She almost choked on her pie when he texted her back.

What are you doing up?

She grinned and sent him a message back. *Eating coconut cream pie.*

Holding onto the phone, she waited with anticipation for his reply.

Hey, I want some.

Come over and get it.

Stop tempting me.

She giggled and took another bite of pie. They continued with the banter for another twenty minutes. It was surprisingly fun to flirt via texting. Maybe they really could have a long-distance relationship until they figured things out.

After sending him a picture of the empty pie tin, Addie heard a strange noise outside. Keeping a hold of her phone, she went to the kitchen window and parted the curtains. The night was dark, the moonlight casting an eerie glow over the yard. But she couldn't really see anything suspicious.

Her phone chimed with another incoming message from Chase. *You're making me hungry. I'm going to the kitchen to look for food.*

Before making a reply, she glanced outside one more time and saw a light flickering between the trees. It looked like someone was waving a flashlight around, searching for something.

A prickle of fear worried her stomach. Who was out there?

She sent Chase a text. *I think someone is in the backyard. I see a flashlight.*

Instead of replying, he called her. "What do you see?"

Making sure the back door was locked, Addie peeked out the window, watching as the light made a slow arc across the yard. There was definitely someone outside. "It looks like someone has a flashlight and they're looking for something."

"Maybe you should call the police to come and check it out."

Addie could just see it now. She'd call 9-1-1 and the cops would show up and find nothing. "I don't want to. What if I'm just seeing a really big firefly?"

He laughed. "Did you really eat all of the pie?"

"What does that have to do with an oversized lightning bug?"

"Nothing," he said, laughing again. "I just want a piece of pie if I come over there to check things out."

She had saved three slices and put them back in the refrigerator. "If you come over, I promise to feed you coconut cream pie."

"I'll be there in a few minutes."

Addie glanced at the clock. It was forty minutes past midnight. "You really don't have to come over." She peeked out the window. Only the moon illuminated the yard. "I don't even see the light anymore."

"I still want to check things out. I'll be there in a few minutes."

"Are you sure?"

"Yeah, but my phone is almost dead. Don't do anything until I get there. And don't eat all the pie."

Addie ended the call, then went upstairs to put on her bra. She kept her pink lounge pants on, along with a black Tinker Bell tee that said, *Pixie's Just Wanna Have Fun* in hot pink letters.

Ten minutes later, Chase pulled into the driveway. Addie opened the door and waited for him to come inside. He looked adorable, wearing a pair of silky basketball shorts and a Mercer T-shirt that fit him snuggly. But the cutest thing was the glasses he had on. With his messy hair, the dark colored frames added to his overall hotness.

"You look cute," she said as he stepped inside the house.

He eyed her clothing, a wry smile tipped one side of his mouth. "So do you."

She closed the door and pulled him into the kitchen, feeling a little sneaky. But Aunt Janie was home and all they were going to do was eat pie—and maybe have one kiss.

Or two.

"Do you want to check out the yard first or eat?"

Chase peered out the window. "Let's check out the yard."

As Addie leaned in close to him, she caught the lingering scent of his cologne. "I haven't seen the light again."

He held up a small flashlight and unlocked the back door. "Show me where you think it was."

They held hands as they crossed the yard. The air was a little chilly and she wished she'd pulled on a sweatshirt. She wasn't exactly sure where the light had been, but they stopped near the gazebo and looked around with the bright flashlight. "I don't see anything," Chase said, holding the light so a beam shot across the rest of the yard.

"It probably really was just a big lightning bug."

He gave her an impish grin, shining the light above her so it cast her in its glow. "Or Tinker Bell."

A light breeze rustled the trees above and a lock of her hair blew across her cheek. Chase stepped toward her and combed her hair back with his fingers, tucking it behind her ear. "Do you think your aunt will kill me if we sit in the gazebo for a few minutes?"

"Hmm," she teased. "I sure hope not."

Behind the glasses, his eyes sparkled with mischief. "Good." He tugged on her hand, leading her toward the gazebo. "Because this is just too good of an opportunity to pass up."

"What do you mean?" she asked as they sat down on the bench.

Chase circled his arm around her shoulders and looked down into her eyes. "I mean the moon. You." He gave her a lopsided smile. "Me."

"I see." Her heart bumped around inside her chest as he slowly lowered his head. "I've never kissed a guy with glasses before," she said in a low whisper.

Man, she could say the stupidest things.

A puff of minty breath feathered against her mouth as he let out a low chuckle. Then he kissed her, stealing her breath and making her forget about anything else. Her head felt all floaty and light as his fingers tunneled through her hair.

Okay. This wasn't the first time he'd kissed her, but it seriously felt like she'd never experienced anything like this. Not even a couple of hours before. She brought her hand up and cradled his jaw, feeling the rough whiskers against her palm. Everything about him felt so right. So perfect.

It was perfect—until a twig snapped and someone grunted. They jerked apart, both looking toward the sound. "What was that?" Addie whispered, digging her hand into his bicep.

Chase removed his arm from around her and pulled out his flashlight. "I'm not sure." He stood up and stepped out of the gazebo.

Addie shot out of her seat to follow him. An owl hooted and she swallowed back a startled scream as she grasped onto his arm again. "Hey, don't leave me." She looked around, wondering how the romantic night had just turned creepy.

He made a sweeping motion with the beam of light as they stepped further back into the yard. They heard another twig snap and what sounded like a curse word. Someone was definitely out there.

"You need to go back inside," Chase said. "Go call 9-1-1."

Addie didn't want to leave him, nor did she want to venture back across the yard with only the moon for her light. "Let's both go back." She tugged on his arm.

He shook his head. "Go back and call the police. And wake up your aunt."

No sense mentioning her aunt was out for the night. "Okay." She scanned the area one last time before making a run for the house. She had only gone a few steps when she remembered her cell phone was in her pocket. Relieved she could join Chase again, she pivoted on her feet and ran right into something big and solid.

A hand came over her mouth. A dirty, smelly hand. "Don't make a sound, sweetheart."

Despite the warning, Addie tried screaming. But without much success. Pure terror rocketed through her and she squirmed, trying to get away. The man held her tightly—so tight she couldn't breathe. With her elbow, she jabbed him in his protruding stomach. He grunted and his hand loosened, allowing her to scream for all she was worth. "Help!"

"Shut up," the man said, pulling her back to his chest and clamping his hand back over her mouth. He dragged her out of the path, deeper into the shadows of the trees. "Just calm down."

Calm down?

She wiggled without making any progress as Chase's footsteps pounded against the ground. He yelled out her name, the light from his flashlight bouncing wildly as he sprinted toward her. "Addie! Where are you!"

He zoomed straight ahead, passing right by her. "Chase!" she screamed, only it came out muffled and lacking any kind of volume. Having a hand over your mouth tended to do that.

It made her mad.

She twisted and squirmed but the man kept a solid grip on her. A surge of adrenalin shot through her and she thrust her chin up and bit down. Her teeth only caught a little flesh, but it was enough to make him release her mouth. "Chase! Help me!" she cried out.

Her captor swore, shaking his hand. "I don't wanna hurt you, but if you can't shut up—"

The beam of a flashlight shone in their direction, making him stop talking. There was enough moonlight to show the shocked expression on Chase's face as he came to a halt.

"Hold it right there, son," the man holding her said. "I don't wanna hurt no one."

Oh, yeah? Then let me go. Addie thought as she tried to break away. The guy tightened his grip.

"Just let her go," Chase said, holding out an imploring hand.

The man grunted and then spit over Addie's shoulder. Suddenly she knew who was holding her captive. "Ernie?" she asked, trying to look at him.

He swore again. "Why can't you just shut up?"

His arm clamped around her neck, cutting off her airway. She closed her eyes and tried to concentrate on breathing as Chase tried reasoning with the guy. "Look, Mister. I know you don't want to hurt her so just let her go. We won't call the police and we'll forget this ever happened."

Ernie spit again. "I sure ain't wantin' to hurt no one, but y'all startled me."

Um, can't breathe, here! Addie caught at the hand around her neck, but he only tightened his hold. Unable to catch her breath, she felt her fingers start to tingle. Her respiratory rate increased as she desperately tried to suck in enough oxygen. She started to panic, a feeling of doom crushing her just as much as the arm around her neck.

Ernie and Chase continued their discussion. Her breath came in short gasps until finally her head began to spin. The men's voiced faded as Addie felt her world go completely dark.

Chapter Twenty Four

Chase tried to think of what to do next as he pled with
Ernie to let Addie go. He wasn't dealing with the
sharpest tool in the shed. The guy was stuck on the
fact he thought he was all alone and they had *intruded* on
him.

Holding the flashlight in one hand, Chase took a small
step forward. His gut clenched at the sheer look of panic on
Addie's face. Her eyes were wide and she was gulping for
air. The stupid guy had her in a chokehold. "Hey, man,"
Chase said. "You gotta let her go. She can't breathe."

Ernie glanced down just as Addie's eyes fluttered shut
and her body went limp. She slipped through the man's arms
and fell to the ground. "Well, shoot," Ernie said, looking
completely dumbfounded. "That ain't good."

Chase let out a growl as he lunged forward, knocking
the big man to the ground. Then he turned to Addie and
grasped her by the shoulders. Rolling her onto her back, he
pressed his fingers against her throat. Her heart beat at a fast
and steady pace, her chest rising and falling with each
breath.

Knowing she was safe, he twisted around to take care of
Ernie. The big oaf lay as still as a statue. Chase found his
flashlight on the ground and aimed it at the man's face.
Ernie's head lolled to the side, his arms flailed out beside
him.

Tobacco-stained saliva dribbled out of the corner of his mouth, disappearing into the unruly beard that covered his face. Scanning the light down, he noticed his chest expanding regularly as he inhaled and exhaled without a problem.

Just to make sure he was really out, Chase shone the flashlight directly in Ernie's eyes. There wasn't the slightest twitch in his eyelids. It could be a trick but he seriously doubted Ernie had the brain cells necessary to fake it this well.

A soft moan coming from Addie drew his attention away. He quickly knelt by her side, the moist grass cool against his knees. Taking her hand he leaned close. "Addie?"

Her eyes popped open, a wild look in them. She gasped, attempting to sit up. Chase kept her down. "It's okay, baby. You're okay."

"Where...But...I..." She licked her lips and took a steadying breath. "Ernie?" she finally said, giving up on anything more complex.

"Out like a light."

"You hit him?"

One side of his mouth lifted. "In a round-about way."

Her forehead puckered. "The grass is wet."

He helped her sit up and she threw her arms around his neck, knocking his glasses askew. "You saved me."

Holding her close, he drew in a deep breath of relief and smiled. She couldn't seem to form more than a three or four-word sentence. "Actually, you passed out." He buried his face in her hair. "Ernie wasn't expecting that." Neither had he. He would never forget how he felt as he watched her slump to the ground.

Behind him, Ernie groaned. Chase stood and Addie huddled behind him. "Addie, go into the house and call the police."

She pulled her phone from her pocket and held it out. "I'm not leaving your side again."

This time he agreed. Seeing her held captive by that man—not knowing what would happen to her—had been a wakeup call. In that moment Chase realized how much she really meant to him. How much he loved her.

He took the phone and dialed 9-1-1 and then reached behind him to find her hand. He held on, determined to never let her go.

The police arrived just as Ernie came around. Chase kept his hands to his side in an effort to keep from shutting up the guy with his fists. He wasn't typically a violent person, but when it involved the woman he loved, Chase found out he wasn't opposed to hitting someone in order to protect her. He glared at Ernie and admired the patience of the cop arresting him. The officer was more in control than Chase was.

"This ain't right, y'all. I didn't mean to hurt no one," Ernie said for the hundredth time as the officer hauled him away. "I'm telling ya…they startled me."

Gage, the paramedic attending Addie, snorted and rolled his eyes. "That boy's two bricks shy of a full load."

"I think it's more than two bricks," Chase said, shaking his head in disbelief. Apparently Ernie didn't see anything wrong with trespassing on private property. Or holding a girl in a chokehold.

Chase crouched down by Addie and took her hand. "You okay?"

She squeezed his fingers and nodded. "Yes. Much better now that I don't have to listen to that sorry excuse for a man complain anymore."

Gage chuckled. "For someone who isn't from the south, you sure got spunk."

"Hey," she said. "I've got southern blood running through my veins."

Both Chase and the paramedic laughed at her poor attempt at a southern accent. Addie was tough, and had been joking around with the police and the ambulance crew, but Chase could hear how shaky her voice was whenever she talked.

She narrowed her eyes. "What? I do. Not everyone loves pulled pork and coconut cream pie, ya know."

"Speaking of the pie," Chase said in a low whisper. "You still have a couple of slices, right?"

Her hand trembled slightly as she held up three fingers. "One for each of us if we're quiet about it."

Gage removed the blood pressure cuff. "Y'all knock yourself out." He patted his rounding stomach. "The wife's got me on a diet."

Addie grinned. "I have dibs on the third piece then."

"Hey," Chase said wryly. "Let's not forget who came over to rescue you."

"True." She batted her eyelashes playfully. "Even if I was held captive, you still deserve the third piece."

Gage laughed and picked up his chart to write on it. "I think the girl wins."

Chase leaned in and kissed her on the mouth. Then said, "Nah. I'm definitely the winner here."

* * *

Staring at the phone, Chase couldn't decide if he felt excited or panicked. Nashborough wanted him to fly in for an interview tomorrow.

In one way it couldn't have come at a better time. Whit Barclay decided to stay in South Carolina a few more days, so Chase wouldn't have to worry about him. As for Hayden, for once it appeared she'd kept her word. He knew she did it to protect herself, but this time around her selfishness actually benefitted him.

In matters of the heart, the timing was terrible. Addie only had a few more days in Georgia before she flew home. He still hadn't talked to her about the potential job and move to Tennessee.

His eyes scanned the rest of the email. He'd be flying on a private jet owned by Nashborough, and had the option of staying the night in a hotel, or returning that same evening by the same plane. Either way, the company needed his reply by the end of the day.

Placing the phone on his desk, Chase stood up and walked over to look out his office window. If he'd gotten the offer last week, he wouldn't be having this dilemma about what to do. He'd prayed so fervently about working for this company. He believed if he got an interview, and then subsequently offered the job it was an answer to his prayers.

Now, he wasn't sure what to believe.

Last night, when Addie fainted, Chase knew he was in love with her, and wanted to marry her. No fear. No second guessing. His doubts returned this morning the minute he read the email.

He groaned, and ran his hand through his hair. "Please, God. Tell me what to do." He waited for a few heartbeats, praying for divine guidance. Closing his eyes, he prayed more sincerely about what to do.

The only impression he had was to talk with Addie. He grabbed his phone, and sent her a quick text, telling her he missed her, and asked if it was okay if he came by right now.

While he waited for her answer, he exited his office and strode purposefully to Shanna's desk.

"What's up?" she asked.

He wished he could share the exciting news about the interview with her, but decided it would be better to wait until he and Addie talked.

"I've had some things come up that need my attention so I'm taking the rest of the day off."

She lifted a brow. "Anything I can help with?"

"No, but thank you for asking." He started to walk away, but paused. "If anyone calls and needs to speak to me, just text me and I'll take care of it."

She opened her mouth, then closed it, simply nodding her head. Chase waved and hurried out to his truck.

Addie replied just as he started the engine.

Sure it's okay. Just looking through my picture files for the contest. I've narrowed it down to three photos. Maybe you can help me decide?

I'll do my best. Be there in a few.

Chase shifted the truck into gear and started for the Caldwell's house. How ironic that he needed Addie's help making a decision that affected his career, and she wanted the same thing from him.

Chapter Twenty Five

Aunt Janie hadn't left Addie's side all morning long. Still in shock about what happened the night before, she hovered around Addie like one of Chase's groupies.

"Chase is coming over," Addie said, unable to hide her delight. "You should go meet your quilting ladies for lunch. I'll be fine."

"What if he can't stay very long? I don't want you here by yourself."

"He's going to help me decide which picture to send in to the contest. After, we'll warm up some of your Brunswick stew you pulled out of the freezer this morning." Addie grinned mischievously. "He said his boss is still out of town, so I'm sure I can persuade him to skip the rest of the day."

Aunt Janie smiled, but the worry remained in her eyes. "You two seem to be getting along quite well. Have you talked about anything serious yet?"

Addie's stomach tightened. Her sister had asked her the same thing this morning when she told her all about her close encounter with Ernie. Chellie recounted the past week, and Addie realized she and Chase had spent almost every day together since he'd picked her up.

"No, we haven't. We've only known each other eleven days."

"But you've been with each other ten out of those eleven days, and that's only because Chase had to go out of town."

True.

"We're taking things one day at a time. Besides, long-distance relationships are a lot easier these days with all the technology."

While her aunt considered this, Addie stood up and gave her a hug. "Don't worry about it, okay?"

"Okay, sugar." Aunt Janie squeezed her hard before releasing her and standing up. "I promise not to be so nosey."

Addie laughed. Her aunt would always be nosey. "Now go have fun with your friends, and I'm going to run upstairs and change into something cute."

"It's too bad that pink tee is ruined by grass stains. It hugged your figure perfectly."

Another laugh bubbled out of Addie. "You and Daddy couldn't be more opposite. He liked my shirts to do anything but hug my figure."

"That's because he's your father. You don't have any clothing that's indecent, and I wouldn't let you out of the house if I thought you looked like a loose woman."

"Thank you. I appreciate that."

Grabbing her purse, her aunt waved goodbye. "If Chase can't stay, just text me and I'll come home directly."

"Okay." Addie had no intention of ruining her aunt's luncheon. "Have fun."

As she climbed the stairs to her room, Addie thought about how loved she felt by her aunt. Because of that love, Addie realized that if she ended up living in Georgia it wouldn't be completely horrible. She'd have Aunt Janie.

Of course she still worried about her dad.

Chellie assured her everything was fine, and that he'd come out to her house a few times. He rarely left home, unless Addie drove him somewhere, so she'd been surprised by that news.

More than once, Chellie told Addie to stop coddling their dad. Maybe she was right.

After changing into a pair of denim capris and a teal colored tee, she brushed her teeth. Chase pulled in just as she peeked out the window.

Warmth spread through her entire body just watching Chase approach the door. At some point they needed to talk about their relationship, but right now she just wanted to kiss him.

She opened the door before he could knock, and threw herself into his arms. He smelled so good. He tasted good too.

"Did I do anything special to deserve such an incredible hello?" he asked when their lips finally parted.

"I'm just happy to see you." She tugged on his hand and led him toward the kitchen. "I thought I'd have to wait until this evening."

"Where's your aunt? From what you said a couple of hours ago I didn't think she'd let you out of her sight."

"She wouldn't have if you hadn't come over." Addie directed him onto one of the bar stools. "Are you hungry? I've got Brunswick stew we can warm up."

Chase didn't answer right away. In fact, he kind of looked a little pale. "I'm not that hungry right now."

Addie expected him to be playful and maybe try kissing her again. She hoped he wasn't getting sick. "Are you okay?"

Again, he waited a few seconds before answering. "Yeah, but I have to talk to you about something."

A cold feeling of dread snaked through her. Brandon had said those exact words to her when he broke off their engagement. "Okay." She slid onto the bar stool next to him. "I'm listening."

He drew in a small breath. "I have a job interview tomorrow."

She smiled in relief. "That's awesome. Now you won't have to work for Hayden's father anymore."

"The interview is in Nashville."

Confused, she sought clarification. "Is this for your music?"

"In a roundabout way." He swallowed hard, making his Adam's apple bob. "I'd be doing the same thing I do at Barclay, only the clientele at Nashborough are mainly those in the music industry.

It sounded like the perfect set up, except for one problem. That cold feeling enclosed around her as she drew the fateful conclusion.

"You'd move to Nashville if you got the job, right?"

He nodded. "Yes."

Addie might be able to reconcile living in Georgia, but Tennessee? Assuming the two of them did end up together, that is.

"Wow." She licked her lips, unable to say anything else at the moment.

Her brain whirled with the information. Naturally, she figured if he got picked up by a record label there was a good chance he'd spend a lot of time in Nashville. She just didn't think he'd have to live there.

Had that been wishful thinking? Of course it had. Somewhere in her subconscious it allowed her to justify falling in love with him.

"Well, congratulations." Her voice wobbled, and she popped out of her seat before she did something stupid like start crying.

"Addie, I'm sorry." She heard him scoot the barstool away and walk toward her.

She blinked rapidly, and kept her back to him. *Do not cry. Do not cry.* "There's nothing to be sorry about. This is a fantastic opportunity for you."

Ha! She'd gotten out an entire sentence without losing it. She moved to the fridge to get the stew out.

Then he touched her. Stupid chemistry. One touch and she was ready to follow him anywhere, including Tennessee.

"Addie." He gently turned her around to face him. "I'm not sure what I'm gonna do. I never planned on falling in love with you."

Those words nearly stopped her heart. He was in love with her. She pressed her back up against the refrigerator, grateful to have something to keep her upright.

"You love me?"

"Yeah, does that scare you?"

Not as much as it should.

"A little." She managed to give him a tremulous smile. "But I think I love you too."

He grinned. "You only think?" He placed both his hands against the fridge, trapping her in place.

"Um…"

She couldn't utter anything else as Chase took his time lowering his head until their mouths touched. The kiss was achingly slow and tender, making it feel as if the floor disappeared from beneath her, and she floated on air.

Too soon, he pulled away and gazed into her eyes with a passion that appeared to be able to start a fire. "Change your mind?"

If she said no, would he kiss her like that again?

"Okay, I *know* I love you too."

Miracle of miracles he kissed her again.

She slid her arms around him, pressing her palms into his muscled back. Chase cradled her face in his hands and deepened the kiss. She lost track of time. When both of them knew it was time to stop while they still could, they mutually drew apart. Their rapid breaths mingled, and she had to force herself not to instigate another lengthy kiss.

"So what does this mean for us?" she whispered, her breath still erratic.

"I don't know." He took her hand and led her to the dining table. He sat down on one of the chairs and pulled her onto his lap, wrapping his arms around her. "I don't even know if I should go to the interview."

Addie melted into his embrace, wishing she had an easy answer for him. "If you go to the interview, it doesn't mean you have to take the job, right?"

"Right."

She pulled back so she could look at him. "I think you should go. We've got time to figure things out."

His green eyes immediately filled with gratitude. "All right. The company is flying me out in one of their corporate planes in the morning, and I'll be home in the evening."

"Sounds fancy."

He smiled. "They're an incredible company. Whit Barclay hates them, if that's any indication of how successful they are."

"You better not let him find out then."

His eyebrows knitted together. "It wouldn't be good, that's for sure." He kissed her lightly and then helped her stand up, following right behind her. "Let's warm up that stew and take a look at your pictures. I think you have a shot at winning that contest."

Addie pushed away the negative thoughts creeping into her happy mind. She would worry about whether or not starting a studio in Georgia or Tennessee was feasible when the time came.

* * *

The next day Addie sat on her bed and glanced at the clock. Chase's interview should be getting under way any moment now. It would be the perfect time to make a call to her dad. She hadn't called Chellie yet, mainly because she didn't want to hear her glee over being right about Addie falling in love with Chase.

Denying her feelings adamantly the past few days would only make her confession harder. But she couldn't deny how she felt any longer, especially after what happened the other night with Ernie Claxton. Life was short and you never knew how much time you had left on this earth.

Her fingers shook as she slid her finger across the screen and touched the phone icon. In Idaho it was a little after eight in the morning. Her dad should be up and dressed by now and was most likely eating his hot cereal in front of the television, watching the news.

She pushed the speed dial for home. Her stomach threatened to throw up her breakfast as she waited for her dad to answer. She shouldn't be so nervous. Her dad would support her in whatever she decided.

Playing with the edge of the quilt, she listened as the phone rolled over to voicemail. Dad had a phone right next to his easy chair. He should've answered it. She tried calling a few more times without much success. Although worried, she figured he might have had one of his sleepless nights and was catching a nap. He often didn't hear the phone ring when he was so tired.

She stood up and paced around the room, debating about calling Chellie. Her sister might know where their father was, and then Addie could tell her all about her love life. That should be a fun conversation. Chellie would gloat, then she'd switch into mother mode and want to know answers she and Chase didn't have.

Walking to the window, she frowned. If it weren't raining outside, she'd go out into the garden to make the calls. Since Aunt Janie and Hazel were in the kitchen having a bake-off, or so it seemed the way they argued who did what better, Addie had retreated to her room soon after breakfast. She and Chase texted back and forth until he arrived at Nashborough headquarters for the interviews. Apparently, he'd be interviewed by several different managers, including the CEO.

Returning to the bed, she sank down on the yellow comforter and tried calling home again. A tiny spark of fear worked its way inside her chest when it rolled over to voicemail again.

After trying one last time, she made the decision to call her sister. Chellie picked up on the second ring.

"Good morning," she answered cheerfully.

Addie relaxed. If anything had happened to Dad, her sister wouldn't be so perky. "You're such a morning person."

"It's called exercise, sister. You should try it some time."

"Ha ha."

"You're date must have been good last night if you're calling me this early in the morning."

"That's not really the reason I'm calling, but, yeah, it was pretty memorable."

"Oooh," Chellie teased. "This sounds good. Don't leave anything out, especially the kisses."

"How did you know there was more than one?"

She laughed. "I didn't, but now I do."

"Well, before I give you any details, I want to know where Dad is. He's not answering the phone."

"Hmm," Chellie said. "I tried calling him last night and couldn't get a hold of him, either. I wonder if he lost the handset."

Their dad always put the phone right back in the base. Plus there was one in his room and in the kitchen. Her fear mounted with each word. "Chellie, maybe you should go over to the house. What if something happened to him?"

Chellie assured her everything was okay, but still agreed to drive over to check on him. Addie decided not to say anything about her feelings for Chase until she knew her dad was okay. "Call me as soon as you get there, okay?"

"I will, but please don't worry. I'm sure he's fine."

Knowing it would take at least twenty minutes for Chellie to get to her dad's house, Addie opened her laptop and brought up the picture she, Chase and Aunt Janie had picked. It was of Mr. Hanks sitting on the aged porch, playing his harmonica. Somehow she'd managed to capture a feeling of nostalgia, of simpler days gone by. The photograph was timeless and could have been taken in another era. She couldn't wait to see it in print.

Addie had sent her entry in late last night when she couldn't sleep. Now she had to wait and see, just like everything else right now. Typically not a patient person, all this "wait and see" would test her stamina.

Like right now. Chellie should already be at the house. Why hadn't she called back?

Minutes ticked by. Just as Addie was about to call her sister, Chellie called back with the news. All the blood rushed out of Addie's head, making her dizzy.

Her sister found Dad lying on the floor in his bedroom, unconscious and having difficulty breathing. Chellie had called the paramedics and she was following the ambulance to the hospital.

Addie hung up and ran out of the bedroom, yelling for her aunt. She had to get home. As she raced down the stairs, she couldn't help thinking if she'd been home, none of this would've ever happened.

Somehow Addie held it together long enough to pack while her aunt made flight arrangements for both of them, packed a bag for herself, and found someone to take them to the airport. Since Chase was gone, and Hazel didn't drive distances, Aunt Janie called Mr. Burns for a ride.

Although the arrangements had been made quickly, the ride to the airport seemed to take hours. Mr. Burns actually drove ten miles over the speed limit, but it wasn't fast enough. Addie's panic mounted with each second that ticked by. She prayed, asking—no begging—God to spare her father's life.

About fifteen minutes from the airport exit, Chase called. Addie was too sick to answer her phone, so Aunt Janie did it for her.

"Chase, Addie's father has had an accident and is in serious condition. We're heading to the airport right now."

Just hearing the words again froze her breath. She could hear Chase talking, but not enough to pick out any words.

"I know, honey," Janie crooned, "but our plane leaves in an hour. We're fixin' to take the exit in a few minutes. We can't wait."

A tear slipped down Addie's cheek. She could imagine how helpless Chase felt right now. The way she felt was indescribable. What if she got home and it was too late? What if it was already too late, but Chellie hadn't told her the truth since Addie would be on a plane and couldn't do anything about it?

Her stomach knotted with panic, and she sucked in quick breaths until Aunt Janie put a hand on her back. "Slow down your breathing, sugar. We can't have you passing out or they won't let you on the plane."

While Addie concentrated on taking slow, deep breaths, she listened to her aunt talk to Chase. "She's okay, just very worried."

There was a lengthy pause and then Aunt Janie touched Addie on the back again. "Baby, do you think you can talk to Chase?"

Addie shook her head vehemently, her respiratory rate increasing as rapidly as her heart rate. She couldn't talk to Chase ever again. It would be too painful, and it would be better to end things now. She could never move away from her father, and Chase was well on his way to Nashville.

He probably aced his interviews and would get the job. He'd move to Tennessee, start work at his new company and wow the crowds at the open mic clubs. Next, he'd get a music contract, and then he'd meet someone else, fall in love with them and forget Addie Heywood ever existed.

Chapter Twenty Six

As the Learjet ascended higher, Chase gripped his phone in frustration, listening to Janie ask if Addie would talk to him. He waited, wishing he could magically transport himself to be with her. He might have just been given the most incredible job offer he could've ever hoped for, but it didn't mean he could ask Nashborough's pilot to veer his course from Macon to Atlanta.

"Now isn't a good time, Chase," Janie said softly. "She's really struggling with her emotions. We'll call as soon as we land in Boise."

"Okay," he said, although it wasn't okay. He wanted to be there and comfort her in person. "Tell her I love her, and that I'm going to take the first flight I can get on to Boise."

He listened to Janie relay the message. For the first time, he heard Addie speak, and it wasn't what he expected.

"No. Tell him he doesn't need to come."

"Addie, he's concerned about you and wants to help you."

"Then tell him to stay in Georgia, or wherever he's going to live. It's better that way for both of us."

A sharp pain of fear stabbed Chase's heart at the biting edge to her voice. There was a rustling sound, and he could only hear muffled tones of conversation. The rustling sound resumed, and Addie came on the line.

"Chase, thank you for calling and for your concern, but you don't have to worry about coming to Idaho."

"I love you, Addie. Of course I want to come to Idaho."

There were several heartbeats of silence, and for a moment he thought they'd lost connection. Then he heard her draw in a stuttering breath.

"Don't come, Chase. This will never work, anyway, so it's better if we just forget it."

Forget it? Anger and fear battled inside him as he listened to her cold words. She sounded mechanical, and he had to remind himself what she was going through right now.

"I'm not going to forget it, Addie."

"What's the point, Chase? You're getting ready to move to Tennessee, and I can't leave Idaho. I should've never left in the first place."

Despite the panic welling inside him, he tried to keep his voice calm. "I'm sorry this happened, Addie, but you can't blame yourself."

"Don't tell me not to blame myself!" she snapped. "If I'd been home, my dad wouldn't be lying unconscious in the ICU right now."

He wanted to tell her the accident could have happened while she was at work, or out taking pictures, but knew it wouldn't do any good. "I'm sorry, and I want to help you in any way I can. Just please don't shut me out."

"I can't think about this right now." She sniffed. "All I can think about is my dad. If he dies…if he dies before I get home, I'll never forgive myself."

She started crying uncontrollably, making Chase ache to take her in his arms and comfort her. He could hear Janie consoling Addie before she took the phone and came back on the line.

"Chase," Janie said in a quiet voice. "Don't listen to what she's saying right now. It's just fear talkin'."

He knew it was fear. It didn't make her rejection any easier. "I want to come and be with her, but it sounds like I'm making it worse."

"How about you hold off on making flight arrangements until we get to Boise? Chellie's husband is picking us up at the airport, and I'm sure he'll have an update."

Left without a choice, Chase conceded. "All right." His voice cracked, and he cleared his throat. "Y'all have a safe trip, and I'll be praying for you."

"Thank you. I'll be in touch."

She ended the call, and Chase sat back in the chair, and closed his eyes. He prayed for Addie's father to be healed. He prayed for Addie and Janie's safety, and he prayed Addie would let him love her. But trusting in the Lord was much easier to do when things went your way.

The pilot announced they'd reached their cruising altitude and would be landing in Macon in approximately an hour and ten minutes. It might as well be one hundred hours.

Needing to do something to occupy his mind, Chase opened his laptop and connected to the inflight Wi-Fi. Even though he wouldn't purchase his ticket now, he'd at least like to know his options.

He selected a redeye flight leaving tonight. After a series of clicks, he found the plane had plenty of seats open. He ignored the exorbitant ticket price, and saved the information without actually going through with the purchase.

Since finding the flight information only killed ten minutes, he opened his email and read over the job offer from Nashborough.

He'd been so excited to talk with Addie about the interviews and the potential opportunity to work for such an amazing corporation. In every way, it was completely opposite of Barclay Industries, including how the CEO operated. Although the workplace atmosphere came off much more relaxed, it still maintained an impressive level of professionalism.

Chase knew he'd nailed every interview and felt qualified for the position. The last interview with Brett Morgan, Nashborough's CEO, was something he'd never forget. Brett, about the same age as Mr. Barclay, ushered him into an office very similar to the ones his managers occupied. No lavish wet bar occupied the space, nor did it have a putting green like Whit's office.

Reminding him a little bit of his father, Brett put Chase at ease, and complimented him on the quality of his previous work experience. He asked Chase how he dealt with new clients and how he would pinpoint their needs. Chase easily answered the questions, but was uneasy with the next request.

"As you know," Brett said, suddenly turning serious. "Barclay is one of our major competitors. If the opportunity to bring some of your current clients along with you came up, how would you go about doing that?"

Chase took his time before answering. Whit Barclay had no problem with a new hire bringing over their former employers clients. In fact, he encouraged it, stating it was a tough business and you had to take every advantage you could. Did Brett Morgan feel the same way?

Swallowing, Chase knew it didn't matter what the man wanted. He knew right from wrong, and the bottom line was if a client decided they wanted to follow Chase to his new company, he had no control over that.

But since most of the time the ad campaign and web design was a team effort, Chase wouldn't feel honest about taking other co-worker's ideas with him.

Not sure if Mr. Morgan wanted an employee who was willing to be unethical or not, he decided to answer truthfully. Looking Brett in the eye, Chase explained his position, and ended with, "Integrity means everything to me. I won't compromise my integrity, even if it means losing a promotion, a bonus, or even my job."

A wide grin spread across the man's face, and he leaned forward and held out his hand. "Son, that's the answer I was looking for." He gave Chase a firm handshake. "Even better, I know you meant it."

The plane hit an air pocket, and rattled Chase's laptop. He steadied the computer, until the bouncing stopped. The pilot came over the speaker again, apologizing for the bumpy ride and hoped a change in altitude would help avoid any more turbulent air.

Nothing could be more turbulent than what Chase felt right now. His music career, his job, and Addie.

If only it could be as easy as simply changing altitude.

After pursuing the dream of becoming a successful country music singer for so long, Chase needed to face reality. His chances of ever getting a recording contract were about as good as Hayden giving up her acting career to become a nun. It was time to grow up. Music was a part of him, and he could play and write music wherever he lived. It just wouldn't be his career.

He was lucky, because he loved his job as a graphic artist, he just hated the corporation he worked for. It only took a few minutes of being in Nashborough's offices to know working for them would be a fantastic opportunity.

Yes, he would have to leave Mitchel Creek, but it didn't have to be permanent. Chase wanted to work for Brett Morgan, and learn everything he could about how to run an honest, fair, and successful marketing business, and then maybe one day start his own company.

Then there was Addie. He loved her. She said she loved him. But she would never consider leaving Idaho now, not even for a few years. How could they make it work?

The plane leveled out, and the ride became noticeably smoother. A thought entered Chase's mind, making him pause. His course, just like the pilots, wasn't set in stone. He could make alterations with the direction, altitude and even the timing. Possibilities about the changes he could make flooded his mind.

He opened his laptop again and opened a blank document. He started typing, listing his goals and prioritizing them by importance.

Marrying Addie Heywood was number one.

Chapter Twenty Seven

Ready or not, Addie was going back to work today. She slipped on her shoes and pushed back her shoulders, pasting on a smile. Her dad was awake and she had to keep up the front that she was happy to be home. He could never know how truly miserable she was.

That first week she'd been home, Addie had refused to talk about Chase with either her aunt or sister, and made them both promise not to say anything to her dad. Her focus had been on her father and his injury.

He'd broken a couple of ribs which resulted in the pneumothorax in the lower lobe of his right lung. Addie had quickly learned this essentially meant his lung had collapsed. Along with the respiratory problems, he'd broken his right arm, had a slight concussion, and bruised his hip. The doctor said it was a miracle he hadn't broken his hip, and wanted to know what kind of milk her dad drank.

Now, three weeks after her return from Georgia, Dad was finally home. Aside from being stiff and sore, her eighty-year-old father was healing.

If only Addie's heart could heal as easily.

Aunt Janie had called Chase after they'd landed in Boise, and Derek gave them the update on her father. Addie still refused to speak to him, knowing she wasn't strong enough to make him stay away. She'd felt horrible, but hadn't wanted it to be any harder than it already was for either of them.

Chase honored her wishes and didn't call. He did, however, send her a text every morning. They were pretty much the same thing.

Short and sweet, basically telling her to have a good day. He never said anything about missing her and he never mentioned love again.

But why should he? She'd pretty much slammed that door closed when she'd left for home. Her stomach tightened with pain and she forced herself not to think about the colossal mistake she'd made. Once again she'd forged ahead without thinking to pray about what she was supposed to do. First getting engaged to Brandon, and now driving Chase away.

By the time she realized it, too much time had passed and she lost her nerve to call and tell him. She figured the text messages were just the southern gentlemen in him. Eventually he would grow bored with her and stop texting.

As much as it hurt to think, Addie was probably just another girl to him. How could she be anything else? They'd had a whirlwind romance. Sometimes it didn't even seem real. Besides, was it even possible to fall in love with someone in less than two weeks? She told herself no. But she knew she had.

Letting out a deep breath of disappointment, she flipped off the light and stepped out of her room, making her way to the family room to say goodbye to her dad. The sight of him in his recliner watching the morning news was comforting. He looked more alert now that he wasn't taking the pain medicine on a regular basis. He glanced over and grinned, his eyes crinkling at the edges. "Don't you look pretty this morning."

She forced her smile to brighten with the compliment. The truth was she looked terrible. There were dark circles under her eyes from the lack of sleep. And her clothing hung loosely on her due to her nonexistent appetite.

And that included anything with sugar. "Thanks." She leaned down and gave her dad a kiss on the cheek. "You sure you're gonna be okay today?"

She worried about leaving him home alone, especially since Aunt Janie had returned back home to Georgia.

His wrinkled hand patted her face. "I'll be okay. Chellie is coming over to check on me, and the church ladies have someone coming over with lunch."

Trying to ignore the knot of anxiety coiling in her stomach, Addie straightened up. "I don't have to go back to work, Dad."

Her father gazed at her with a worried expression. "Addison, I'm doing so much better. What happened before was an accident. I got tangled up in the sheets and fell. Had you been home, it still would've happened."

They'd had this conversation several times, but Addie couldn't help feeling guilty. If she'd been home he wouldn't have lain there for hours waiting for help to arrive. It was something they agreed to disagree about.

"I know, Dad. I just worry about you."

She started to pull away, but her father caught her by the hand. His grip was surprisingly strong. "I'm worried about *you*. And I don't think you're telling me everything about the young man you spent time with in Georgia."

Addie felt her lower lip start quiver. *Oh, no.* She couldn't fall apart now. "Daddy, I told you. Chase is a really good friend. We had a lot of fun together, but things just…didn't work out."

He kept his eyes focused on her and gave her hand a gentle squeeze. "I've been praying and have made a decision about the house. I'd like to put it on the market and move into that new assisted living center near Chellie's. I took a tour while you were in Mitchel Creek, and it'd be like living in a five-star hotel."

She stared at him in disbelief. Her dad had talked about this long before his accident. A couple of Mom's friends had moved into the elegant assisted living place. They had their own apartment with a kitchen and small living room and claimed they had so many fun activities they were never bored.

"Dad, you don't have to move. I'm not going anywhere."

His mouth turned down into a frown and he let out a long sigh. "That's what I'm worried about. You're not going anywhere."

He was kicking her out? Tears welled in her eyes. "Where am I supposed to go?"

A tender look crossed his features. "I think we both know where you *want* to go."

What she wanted might not matter anymore. How could she fix things with Chase? "Even if you do move," she said, wiping at the wetness on her face. "I blew it with Chase."

"Baby girl, I don't think it's as hopeless as that. You have a phone. Give him a call and just talk, see where things lead."

"What if he doesn't want me anymore?"

Her dad let out a deep chuckle. "I don't think that'll be a problem. According to Janie he was smitten from the very first time he saw you."

Addie knew her aunt couldn't keep quiet about Chase. She just bet Chellie had talked as well. Still, for the first time in weeks, hope flared in her chest. "But if I move, I won't get to see you or Chellie that often. Maybe once a year if I'm lucky."

He smiled and raised both of his eyebrows. "But you'll have your young man. And even if y'all end up moving to Nashville, you'll still be close to Janie, as well as your new in-laws."

"Wow, Janie and Chellie have been telling you everything, haven't they?"

"Yep."

She let out a shaky breath. "I'm scared, Dad. But I think I might really love him." She wiped away another stray tear. "I must. I can't eat and we both know nothing has ever affected my appetite. Not even Brandon calling off the wedding and marrying someone else."

Her dad's bushy brows drew together. "I really wanted to ring that kid's neck." He grinned and gave her a playful wink. "Now I might have to give him a hug the next time I see him. The entire time you dated him, you never once lit up the way you did just now."

"Oh." She smiled and blinked away the last tear.

"Addie, I want you to be happy. I believe you can be if you'll let yourself. I'm a big boy and I'm okay with another man taking care of my little girl."

She leaned down and hugged her father, careful of his broken ribs and arm. "I love you, Daddy." She drew in a deep breath, finding comfort in his familiar musky aftershave.

"I know you do, sweetie." He patted her back. "I know you do."

Tonight she would call Chase and tell him how she felt. As much as she'd miss her dad and sister, life without Chase would be miserable.

* * *

Addie sat at her desk and read over the email she'd just opened. Her hopes of winning the contest were dashed by the news she'd taken second place. She couldn't feel too sorry for herself. Her photograph of Mr. Hanks would be featured on the website, and a check for fifteen hundred dollars had been mailed out to her.

It wasn't enough to buy the expensive camera she wanted to start her own photography business with, but it would give her the option to buy a few more accessories.

Before leaving her desk to head home, a new email from her Aunt Janie popped up in the inbox. It was entitled: Infamous or Famous?

Curious, she immediately opened the message. A link for the Hollywood gossip website *Celebrity Weekly* was attached with a simple sentence from her aunt. "I always knew that girl would wind up on the cover of some tabloid."

Addie's eyes widened as a picture of Hayden Barclay appeared on her screen. Beautiful, and wearing a revealing red dress that left nothing to the imagination, Hayden smiled for the camera, clutching the arm of a man who looked to be at least twice her age. The headline read: Former Georgia Beauty Queen Reveals the Name of the Father of Her Unborn Child.

What? Hayden was pregnant? Unable to stop herself, Addie read the article about Hayden's affair with a married man who was the director and producer of the new television series she was starring in. A quote from Hayden made Addie snort a disbelieving laugh. "I knew he was the one from the first moment we met. We're so in love and couldn't be happier about the baby."

Right. Just a few weeks earlier, Hayden, already pregnant, had been after Chase!

Wanting to talk to him more than ever, Addie dug her phone out of her purse and checked to see if Chase had texted her. The inbox was still empty. A knot of dread formed in her stomach as she left work and made her way to her car.

Why would he pick today not to text her? Here she'd made the decision to call him and confess her feelings. Now she wasn't sure what to do.

After starting her car, she placed the phone on the passenger seat, staring at it, willing it to do something. Her eyes started to burn and she rapidly blinked, determined not to cry. Again. That's all she'd been doing since coming home.

"Please, let him call me," she prayed. "Or should I call him?" She waited, hoping for a definitive answer.

Letting out a deep breath, she reached out and picked up her phone. Her finger hovered over the preset button programmed with Chase's number. Call him now? Or maybe wait until tomorrow? If Chase texted her in the morning it would be a sign she was supposed to call him. Stupid, she knew, but right now even plucking petals from a flower and playing the he-loves-me-he-loves-me-not game sounded reasonable.

Depressed and tired, she set the phone back down and put her car in gear, anxious to get home to check on her dad. Chellie called her from the house earlier, assuring her Dad was fine and enjoying a nice lunch with some friends. Friends who were eager to have him move into the assisted living center.

How pathetic would it be to have her dad move out, getting on with his life, while she was stuck...where? Chellie's basement? Or worse, trying to move back in with her dad?

She rubbed her forehead with her hand, needing something else to think about. *Music.* That's what she needed. She'd turned into a country-music freak in the last three weeks.

Reaching out, she pushed the radio on, knowing it was already set to one of the three stations dedicated to country music. It was torture when she heard a song by Keith Urban or Tim McGraw, but it was one way to make her time in Georgia seem real.

A traffic report ended and the DJ announced the next song by Darius Rucker. She reached out again, turning up the volume. A few measures into the song, she realized it wasn't his usual upbeat kind of song. She frowned and her heart twisted with pain as the words filled the car. It was a love song. She definitely shouldn't listen to this right now.

She stretched out her finger to find another station when the words from the song jumped out at her. "Baby, this could be our last first kiss…the thought of forever."

Last first kiss? The line was so familiar. She listened intently, the words so sweet and sentimental. When the chorus started again, a memory flashed in her mind. *"You know what? I think I just had my last first kiss."* Chase had said that right after he'd kissed her for the first time.

Could that mean what she thought it meant? Excitement, hope and a whole bunch of other positive emotions rushed through her. A tiny giggle bubbled out and then more tears! Happy tears as she listened to the lyrics. "What if this was that moment…a chance worth taking …"

Calling Chase—telling him how much she loved him, needed him—was definitely a chance worth taking. And she wanted to call him. Now.

Grasping tightly to the steering wheel, she looked for a place to pull over. She turned on her signal and eased into the parking lot of a convenience store. Her hands shook as she picked up the phone and pressed the speed dial for Chase.

What would she say? What would *he* say? Her hope fell when the phone rolled over to voicemail. There hadn't even been any beeps, letting her know he was just taking another call. It was like his phone was turned off.

Maybe this was her sign. She shook her head and smacked the steering wheel with her palm, frustrated and feeling a little grumpy. This just hadn't been her day. When she got home she was going straight to bed. She did not want to talk to anyone about anything.

Fifteen minutes later, she pulled into the garage, her head ready to explode, her stomach empty and her heart breaking. Reaching over, she grabbed her purse and climbed out of the car. As she entered the kitchen, she heard her father laughing. Then she heard another voice. A male voice with a smooth, tenor southern accent. Her heart seized in her chest and then started pumping again as she set her purse down and tiptoed across the floor. It couldn't be…could it? Holding her breath, she peeked around the corner, her gaze colliding with a pair of soft, green eyes.

He stood up and gave her a slow, lazy grin. "Hey, Addie."

Chapter Twenty Eight

Chase watched as Addie's eyes widened, her mouth hanging open in shock. He'd forgotten how beautiful she was. Well, not really, but seeing her again in person was so much better than a photograph or his memory.

"Chase?" she finally said, her voice just above a whisper.

He tried to determine if the incredulous look she had in her pretty brown eyes meant she was surprised, but pleased to see him. After spending the past two hours talking with her father, he'd felt confident Addie would be more than happy to see him. Now he wasn't so sure.

He held her disbelieving gaze and squirmed a little, hoping his trip to Idaho hadn't been in vain. "I, uh, was in the neighborhood and thought I'd stop by and say hey."

After a few heartbeats, the slightest grin tipped one side of her mouth. Then her eyes lit up with such an intense love that Chase felt the sparks flare and ignite inside his chest. "Well," she said, taking a tiny step toward him. "You said hey."

Chase felt himself relax and gave her a smile as he took one step forward. "I also got a chance to talk to your father."

"Oh?" She arched an eyebrow playfully and took another step toward him.

At this rate, they'd be here all night before he got to touch her again. Chase glanced over at Mr. Heywood, catching the broad smile on his face. Turning back, he met Addie's eyes again.

"Yeah. I was just tellin' your daddy that I'm crazy in love with his daughter and I can't live without her."

She hiccupped a tiny gasp, her hand coming up to clasp her stomach. "You can't?"

He shook his head. "I can't. I love you, Addison Mae Heywood, and I'll live anywhere you want as long as we can be together."

Her light brown eyes were filled with love, joy and a tiny bit of fear. "What exactly are you saying?"

Flashing another smile, he moved toward her, unable to stand the separation one more second. He stopped in front of her and cradled her face with his hands, the warmth from her soft skin seeping into his palms. Slowly, he stroked his thumb across her bottom lip and gazed into her eyes.

"Marry me, Addie." Then he kissed her softly, hoping Mr. Heywood's permission to marry his daughter also allowed for a few kisses. "Please, marry me." He kissed her again. "Pretty please, with sugar on top." His lips brushed hers once more. "I'm beggin' you—"

Addie giggled and put her fingers over his mouth. "Be quiet so I can answer you."

He stopped talking and held her gaze, waiting for her response. "I love you, Chase Jefferson Nichols." She gave him a smile that just about knocked the wind out of him. "And, yes, I'll marry you."

"Yeah?" he said with a grin, feeling like his world had just righted itself again. "Okay, then." He leaned down and gave her a long, slow kiss, conveying the depth of his love and making up for the past three weeks. His fingers slid between her silky hair as he deepened the kiss. *Ah, man.* He had missed her.

Chase honestly forgot they had an audience until he heard her father clear his throat. "I'll just leave you two alone for a second."

He and Addie broke apart, breathless and dazed. Mr. Heywood had already disappeared down the hall. "He's not going to get his shotgun, is he?" Chase asked, wondering if he'd overstepped his bounds.

Addie giggled. "The only gun he owns is a BB gun."

Chase grimaced. "It'd still hurt. Should I be worried?"

Eyes sparkling, Addie didn't answer him. Instead she pulled his head down, kissing him again. After a few minutes their lips drew apart, but they remained very close. He touched his forehead to hers. "I think we've almost made up for the three weeks, seventeen hours, and twenty-two minutes you were gone."

"Maybe," she said, twining her fingers through his hair and giving him a look that made him glad she'd agreed to marry him. "I'll let you know." She reached up to kiss him again.

Chase held her back, knowing her daddy could come back any second. "Addie," he said, looking over his shoulder. "Stop tempting me." He tried putting a little space between them. "Besides, I have something for you."

"A cinnamon bun?" she asked hopefully.

With a laugh, he shook his head and released his hold on her. "Sorry. I finished the last one somewhere around St. Louis."

"St. Louis?" she asked, furrowing her brow. "How did you get here, anyway? And why didn't you answer your phone?"

"You *missed* my truck and the U-haul trailer parked out front?"

She bit her lower lip and blushed. "I decided to call you but when you didn't answer, it kind of threw me off balance. I wasn't really paying attention."

"I see," he said with a smile. "Well, my phone and a Dr. Pepper collided early this morning right after leaving Wyoming. Neither one survived."

"Oh. I'm sorry." She tilted her face up and gave him an impish smile, making that adorable dimple of hers crease her cheek. "Now, what did you have for me?"

Chuckling, he reached into his pocket and pulled out a black velvet box.

Her eyes went as round as the O she formed with her mouth. "I hope you like it," he said as he nervously opened the lid. His little sisters had gone ring shopping with him and both had oohed and ahhhed over this one.

"Oh, Chase," she whispered. "It's beautiful."

His hand was surprisingly steady as he removed the ring and placed it on her left hand. "Do you like it?"

The princess cut diamond sparkled in the light as she held it up. Tears filled her eyes and spilled over her bottom lashes. "I love it." She threw her arms around him, burying her face in the hollow of his neck. "I love you so much," she whispered against his skin.

Suddenly, she jerked back. "Wait, if you moved out here, what about your job? What happened in Nashville, and what about your music career?"

Knowing they had a lot to talk about, Chase gave her a shortened version. "I quit my job at Barclay, turned down the job offer from Nashborough, and found another way to share my music." He grinned, still not believing what his agent had done for him. "The song *Make Believe*, the one I wrote for you, I sold it to Phillip Jacobs. It'll come out as a single in a couple of months."

Addie stared at him dumbfounded. "I've been crying for three solid weeks and you did all that?"

He laughed and pulled her back in for a hug. "So you missed me?"

"So much." She buried her face against his chest.

"I missed you too." He held her tight against him, catching the scent of her clean hair. "Don't ever leave me again."

"I won't," Addie said and looked up at him.

Chase decided to risk kissing her again, but Addie thwarted his intentions when her eyes went wide, and she stepped back.

"I almost forgot. Did you hear about Hayden? She had an affair with a married man, and is pregnant."

Later, Chase would tell Addie all about Hayden's scheme to snare him as the father of her unborn child. If the man she actually named was smart, he'd require a paternity test. "Yeah, let's just say her news made it pretty simple to leave Barclay without Whit giving me any trouble."

"I'll bet." She bit her lower lip. "But what about Nashborough? You turned the job down?"

"I did. Mr. Morgan, the CEO, was very understanding when I told him why I couldn't accept the job. He wished me luck with my new business venture, and even said he'd be willing to mentor me."

Curious brown eyes met his. "What's your new business venture?"

"You're lookin' at the new owner of Daisy Spring's very own photography and graphic art design studio."

"Daisy Springs doesn't have one."

"They do now." Chase pulled out a business card and handed it to her.

"Nichols Photography and Graphic Art Design Studio."
Addie's voice shook as she read the words out loud. He
watched her eyes scan to the bottom of the card, and she read
the names he'd listed. "Addie M. Nichols, photographer, and
Chase J. Nichols, graphic artist."

She looked up at him and smiled. "You were pretty
confident I'd say yes, huh?"

He grinned. "Your sister has been very helpful."

"You've been talking to Chellie?"

"At least every day."

Addie looked back down at the card. She pointed to the
address and gasped, "This is the property I wanted to buy for
my business."

"I know." When she met his eyes again, hers were filled
with moisture. He touched the side of her face, wiping away
a tear that had escaped. "We won't be able to afford a house
for a few years, but the lease includes the two bedroom
apartment upstairs."

"Are you sure you'll be happy? What about getting a
recording contract?"

"Addie, I've never been more sure about anything.
Music will always be a part of my life. My agent said Phillip
is interested in looking at some of my other songs I've
written or co-written with Jackson." He kissed her forehead.
"Besides, this is Idaho, and country music is pretty popular
here. I've done a little digging and found a few clubs nearby
that like to feature new artists. I can still play and sing
whatever I write, whether I sell them or not. I promise it will
be enough."

"I'm sorry I was so stupid. I love you more than
anything, and I'll gladly move to Tennessee if that's what
you want."

"I know. Chellie said she caught you a few times looking at jobs in Nashville."

"I did. I even called on a few, but nothing seemed right." She hiccupped a laugh. "I can't believe how happy I am. We need to celebrate with chocolate or something."

"That reminds me, I have one more surprise." He walked over to his duffle bag and pulled out a pink and white striped candy box.

Addie squealed. "You brought me fudge?"

"Yes. A whole pound."

Closing the distance between them, she tossed the candy box on the couch. "I love you," she said, curving her arms around his neck.

Chase couldn't help it. He kissed her again.

Epilogue

Addie gazed up at her husband as Steve, the
photographer they'd hired, captured another
moment of their wedding day. This afternoon, four
weeks after Chase moved to Idaho, they were married. It had
taken a lot of work to pull off the wedding in such a short
time, but neither of them wanted to wait. It had all been
worth it and in two hours they'd leave for their honeymoon.

"Okay," the photographer said. "Go ahead and kiss
her."

Chase complied, ignoring the groans from Beau and
Jackson. "Enough, already," Beau said. "When is it my turn
to kiss the bride?"

"Never," Chase said, giving Addie another kiss.

The camera flashed and she and Chase separated just in
time to see Ashlee sidle up next to Beau. "You can kiss your
own bride in about a year," she said, winding her arm
through his.

Beau raised an eyebrow. "A year?"

Ashlee gave him a coy smile, her eyes smoldering. "I'll
be eighteen, and we can get married."

A red flush colored Beau's face and he choked out an
answer. "I'm too old for you." He backed away, and tugged
at the collar of his white dress shirt. "And you're forgetting
I'm a military man now. I'll probably be stationed
somewhere overseas next year."

Ashlee pouted, crossing her arms in front of her.
"Why'd you have to go and do that, anyway?"

Beau was saved from answering when Steve called him
over. "Groomsmen from Georgia, I need you right now."

Surrounded by Beau and Jackson, Addie smiled as they leaned in and kissed her on the cheek. They were good friends—supporting Chase and his decision to move to Idaho, even though it meant the end of Chasing Dreams.

Drew couldn't make it to the wedding. He had his hands full with his three girls and a new baby boy born two weeks ago. Incidentally, he'd also given the guys notice to start looking for another base player. He wanted to focus on his growing family, and the band took up too much of his time.

Soon after, Jackson announced he was done with the band. Sydney's father was letting him take over running the multi-million dollar horse farm Sydney's parent's owned. It would require a lot of his time coming up to speed with his new responsibilities, and there wouldn't be time for playing in clubs every other weekend.

The biggest surprise had been Beau. He had a college degree and a great career as an architect, but he wanted to serve his country. After praying about it, he joined the army. His basic training would start next week.

"That should do it for now," Steve said with a wink.

Aunt Janie flitted over, smiling as bright as the chandeliers lighting the room, and announced people were lining up for the reception. The rest of the evening was a blur as a steady trickle of people Addie had known all her life, congratulated her and her new husband. Chase charmed the women with his sexy southern accent, and Taylin and Ashlee had every unmarried male asking for their numbers.

After the cake was cut and Addie had tossed her bouquet, she and Chase were finally ready to leave. Outside, a limo sat waiting to take them to a bed and breakfast in Boise. They held hands as their friends and family stood in a line, blowing bubbles at them as they passed by.

While Chase said goodbye to his family, Addie hugged each of her family members, saving her dad for last. "Thanks, Daddy. For everything." She leaned in and kissed him on his wrinkled cheek.

"You're welcome, baby girl." His voice cracked with emotion as he gave her a tight squeeze. "You two have fun. Call if you need anything."

"Okay," Addie said as she slid into the seat.

Chase climbed in and shut the door just as everyone yelled out their good-byes one more time. He held a small package, wrapped in silvery paper with a big bow on top. Before she could ask who the gift was from, he leaned over and gave her a soft, but very passionate kiss, turning her insides to jelly. She was vaguely aware of the limousine pulling away.

When he drew back, she was too dazed to question him about the gift. Chase raised a hand, skimming his fingers down her cheek. "I think I'm gonna like having you for my wife."

"You only think?"

"I *know* I'm gonna like having you for my wife."

"That's better."

He chuckled and leaned in, kissing her again until she could hardly breathe. The car suddenly jerked to a stop and without the restraint of a seatbelt, they separated and held on to the seat to keep upright. "Sorry, folks," the limo driver said through an intercom. "A truck didn't see the red light."

The voice invaded their privacy and Addie wondered if the driver could see them. When Chase pulled her close again, she pointed to the package, trying to divert her husband in another direction until they were truly alone. "Who is that from?"

He gave her a crooked grin. "Are you trying to distract me?"

Addie's eyes flickered to the dark window that separated them from the driver. "Just temporarily." She gave him a playful smile. "Plus, I like opening presents."

* * *

Curious about the gift himself, Chase chuckled and handed the present to his wife. "Your aunt gave this to me just before I got into the limo. She said we should open it now."

"Maybe it's a piece of cake," Addie said, ripping the paper. "I can't believe I only got that tiny little bite you fed me."

"I could've given you a bigger piece," Chase said with a laugh. "In fact, Beau encouraged it."

She peeled back the paper and looked at him sidelong. "I know what Beau and Jackson wanted you to do. And if you had, I seriously would've started a food fight. If I got cake shoved in my face. They would too."

Chase grinned as she lifted the lid off of the white shoe-box sized box. A strong musty odor filled the air, making Addie wrinkle her nose. "Ooh. Definitely not cake." She handed him the box. "What's in there?"

He peered inside to see a small weathered wooden chest. "It looks like a treasure chest."

Leaning over to take a peek, Addie gasped, "It does. Can we open it?"

Chase reached in and fingered the old wood, warped by the elements and time. He lifted the lid, and set it to the side. Inside the box lay a white envelope with their names written on it.

Addie snuggled into his side as he lifted the envelope out. He slid his finger under the flap to open it. Inside were several tattered pieces of old paper currency, an antique sapphire ring and an old picture of the Caldwell house.

"Do you know what these are?" Chase asked, taking a closer look at the money. "It's old Confederate notes from the Civil War."

"You're kidding," Addie said, slanting forward. "Where do you think it came from?"

"I don't know." He pulled a note card out of the envelope and said, "Maybe this explains it."

With their heads close together, they read the note from Janie, explaining about the contents of the gift. Addie squealed in delight to find out her aunt had finally solved the Caldwell mystery. Having come across another photograph of the house, she'd placed it next to the others and made an exciting discovery.

... Addie, you were right. The clue had been the scripture verses Marianne gave to her sister. This photograph I found shows that where the gazebo now stands there had once been a well. A man I hired found the capped well and opened it. Buried deep inside, he found this small wooden box. Miraculously it survived the elements. The Confederate money isn't worth much as it is stuck together and badly decomposed. The sapphire ring, however, is still valuable and my gift to you. Sapphires symbolize long-lasting love and the ring itself reminds us of eternity. No beginning and no end...

Chase circled his arm around his wife and pulled her close. "*Mmm*," he said, brushing his lips across her ear. "I like the sound of that. Eternity. Infinity. No end."

She tipped her face up, her gaze filled with absolute love. "Forever," she whispered. Then she wound her arms around his neck and, regardless of the driver, gave him a long, sweet kiss.

Oh, yeah. Eternity was going to be *so* good.

About the Author

Cindy Roland Anderson has always had a penchant for chocolate and reading romance novels. Naturally, romance is what she loves to write—usually with chocolate. Cindy has won several awards for her writing, including first place with her bestselling novel *Fair Catch*. She hones her writing skills by attending workshops and conferences, and is active in a couple critique groups with some awesome ladies. Cindy is a registered nurse and works in the newborn intensive care unit. She loves to bake, not cook (there is a difference!) and enjoys spending time with her family. Cindy and her husband John reside in Farmington, UT. They are parents to five incredible children. Over the past few years their family has expanded by adding a son-in-law, a daughter-in-law and four adorable grandchildren. To contact Cindy or to see other projects she is working on go to www.cindyrolandanderson.com

Acknowledgments

I love the South and love my southern roots. My mother, who incidentally is from Idaho, fell in love with my dad, who happens to be from Georgia. They graciously let me tag along with them on one of their trips to Georgia to visit my dad's family. Thanks to my sweet husband and kids, I got to spend nearly two weeks exploring Georgia for this book.

A special thanks to my Aunt Barbara and Uncle Jack Burns. I had so much fun staying at their house, eating Brunswick stew, coconut cake and trying my first fried pickle. I loved reconnecting with my cousins and meeting their families. It was fun naming some of the characters in my book after them.

I need to thank my neighbors Keith and Juelle Sorensen for allowing me to use their beautiful home and yard for the cover pictures. And an added thanks to Kambria Johnson Smith for being the cover model. She is so adorable and a lot of fun to work with.

Thank you to my daughter, Nicole Harbertson, for helping with the cover photo shoot. Although very pregnant, she took the time to help get the perfect picture. Thank you Casey for, once again, transforming that perfect picture into another amazing cover!

I want to also thank Sadie Anderson, my talented editor, typesetter and formatter. You're the best!

Thank you to my beta readers Stephanie Fowers, Lisa Ferguson, Valerie Drollinger, and Valerie Bybee. Your honest feedback is invaluable. I also want to thank Cami, Sherry, Amanda, Cindy, Susan, Jenny, and Angela, the awesome women in my critique groups, for their input and for catching little things I completely miss.

Fair Catch
By
Cindy Roland Anderson

Chapter One

Ellie Garrett's feet pounded rhythmically against the
pavement, her anger growing with each step as her mind
replayed the frustrating phone call she had received thirty
minutes ago. Sweat trickled down her back as she made
another loop around the jogging trail. She wiped her hand
across her forehead and slowed her tempo. She needed to
cool down—in more ways than one.

Thomas Garrett, her ex-husband, had done it again.
He'd managed to make her angry, disappoint their son Cade,
and place the blame on Ellie's shoulders. She already had
too much weight on her shoulders. Raising her four-year-old
son by herself was more than enough.

Decreasing her pace down to a brisk walk, Ellie slowly
blew out her breath and looked around the affluent area
where she now resided. She was definitely the little fish in
the big pond. Six months ago her dad, a professor of ancient
history at the University of Colorado, fulfilled a life-long
dream by taking a position in England for the next two years,
teaching at Cambridge.

When her parents left, Ellie and Cade moved from their
tiny condo in Boulder, Colorado to her parents' house in
Pleasant Wood, a suburb of Denver, allowing her to quit her
part-time job.

So now, according to Thomas, she was rolling in the
money and could take Cade to Disneyland herself. She

added delusional to his list of defective qualities.

Glancing at her watch, she noted it was almost time to pick up Cade from preschool. Inevitably, he would ask about going to Disneyland with his dad. How was she supposed to explain to her little boy that his father had another pressing obligation and wouldn't be coming?

"Father. Right," Ellie muttered. She wished for once in his life Thomas would try to be a father. Currently, he lived in Australia, enjoying the life he'd always dreamed about. Translation: Single with zero responsibilities.

A derisive puff of air escaped between her lips when she thought about his lame excuses. Ellie couldn't relate. Cade—their son—was her only obligation. More than likely, Thomas's urgent business involved a woman.

Pulling the band from her ponytail, she finger combed a few blonde strands of her long curly hair away from her face. The mild breeze sifted through her curls and cooled her off. A young couple, pushing a toddler in a stroller, walked in front of her. When Cade had been that size, Ellie had been all alone.

Twisting the band back around her hair, she set off at a slow jog toward home. She needed a shower. And chocolate.

Coming up behind her neighbor's house, tiny branches and pebbles crunched beneath her shoes as she veered off the paved trail. As she entered the secluded cul-de-sac, Ellie saw a large moving truck parked at the enormous two-story house across the street from her parents' home. She stopped running and stared at the gorgeous French Country manor. Made of gray stone, it resembled a small castle, complete with a stone turret bordering the left side. On the market for nearly two years, everyone was anxious to meet the new owner, especially since the sale was confidential.

Ellie squinted against the bright May sun, looking for any kind of evidence the new owners had children. She couldn't tell, but maybe her friend would know something.

Betsy Stewart stood on the sidewalk, no doubt trying to be the first one to welcome the mystery home-owners before anyone else. Her husband, Owen, was the pastor of Pleasant Wood Community Church, and knew the identity of the anonymous buyer. He wasn't allowed to say anything to anyone—including his wife. The suspense was killing Betsy.

Cutting across the road, Ellie headed toward her neighbor. Betsy's short, auburn hair swayed as she whirled around, a wide smile stretched across her tanned face. "Ellie, can you believe we'll finally get to meet the new owners?"

Ellie wasn't as intrigued as Betsy. She just hoped the new neighbor wouldn't mind a precocious four-year-old who, on occasion, wandered into houses without his mother's knowledge.

"It'll be nice to meet them. If I'm lucky, Cade will get a playmate."

While she watched the movers carry in an entertainment center, Ellie pulled at the front of her sweat-dampened T-shirt, allowing cool air to pass through. Sure, having the empty house occupied would be a good thing, but as far as Ellie was concerned, the cul-de-sac she lived in was perfect just the way it was. The Stewarts lived on one side. The Colemans, a nice jet-setting retired couple, lived on the other.

The gorgeous house across the street was flanked by a huge yard. The entire property actually consisted of the other three lots that had been available when her parents had built their home. The asking price was astronomical, and she felt a little intimidated by the kind of people who could afford such a home.

Images of Thomas flitted through her mind. He loved money and expensive things. He also hated parting with that money to pay alimony and child support. At twenty-seven, the last thing Ellie had ever dreamed about was being a divorced, single mother. She'd married Thomas right after her twenty-first birthday. Eighteen months later, she gave birth to Cade. When Cade was only three weeks old, Thomas told her he had a girlfriend and wanted a divorce.

Betsy nudged her with her arm, cutting into the dark memories. "I'm baking bread right now, and then I'm planning on taking over a welcome basket. Do you want to come with me?"

Ellie's mouth watered just thinking about the fresh-baked bread. "I can't. After I pick Cade up from preschool, I'm taking him into Denver to the children's museum." She gave a deep sigh when she remembered what she had to do. The forty-five minute drive to the city would probably be a good time to tell Cade about the canceled trip to Disneyland. "We won't be home until this evening."

"Hey, you sound like you're a little upset. Is everything okay?" Betsy asked. Although Betsy was twice her age, she was Ellie's best friend.

Shaking her head, Ellie heaved another defeated sigh. "No. Thomas called this morning—he's not coming to take Cade to California."

"What?" Betsy's naturally happy face clouded with anger. "You know, if I ever meet that man face to face …well, maybe the next time he's here, I'll sic all four of my boys on him."

Ellie grinned. The Stewart boys were as mild mannered as the pastor. "Don't worry, my brothers told me to call them the next time he pulled something like this. They'd like a

little time alone with him, and I don't think it's just to talk."
Really, her big brothers wanted a chance to knock some
sense into him. Too bad both boys lived out of state and
were never around when Thomas did make a visit.

Betsy chuckled. "Your brothers are just looking out for
their little sister." She patted Ellie on the back. "Honey, we
just need to find you a man."

Ellie grimaced. "Please don't! The last thing I need is a
man." Having been thrown back into the dating world, Ellie
hated being back on the market, so to speak. She hated how
everyone seemed to think she needed help dating and finding
another husband. She didn't want anyone else—not after
what Thomas had done to her. It would be a struggle to trust
a man ever again. The wounds he'd inflicted still hadn't
completely healed.

Betsy smiled at her knowingly. "Ellie Garrett, you are a
beautiful woman, and I know the Lord is preparing someone
special for you."

Why did everyone think that? She'd already had a
husband, thank you very much. As for her beauty…it wasn't
enough to keep him from leaving.

"Hey, I'd better go inside to shower." She avoided
Betsy's eyes by looking at her watch. "Cade's class is out in
thirty minutes."

Betsy laughed and nudged her in the shoulder again. "I
get it. You don't want to talk about it right now."

Ellie took a couple of steps backward. "That's why I
like you so much."

"Yeah," Betsy said with another laugh. "I said right
now. You and I need to have another talk, young lady."

"Did I just say I liked you?"

Betsy grinned and waggled her finger. "You *love* me.
By the way, I made an extra loaf of bread for you and Cade."

"You're right. I do love you."

Ellie decided to leave while she had the chance. She turned toward her house and waved goodbye. "Have fun today."

Fifteen minutes later, Ellie left to get Cade. As she drove out of the cul-de-sac, she passed a white Denali. At the stop sign, she glanced in her rearview mirror. The SUV turned into the driveway next to the moving truck. It was probably the new owners.

Ellie paused as she debated about whether or not to wait and see who the new neighbors were. When they didn't immediately get out of the vehicle, she pressed on the gas and made a left turn.

Her curiosity could wait. Cade couldn't.

* * *

Nick Coulter grinned as he made the last turn toward his new home, and the GPS declared he made it to his destination. His phone buzzed just as he pulled in beside the moving truck. Grabbing the phone from its cradle, he saw the name on the screen and thought about declining the call. His manager, Alec Lawson, would put a damper on his good mood.

Nick's thumb hovered over the decline button. He probably should answer it, especially since he had promised to return the call a couple of hours ago. He pressed to accept. "Hey, Alec. Sorry I didn't call you back."

Alec snorted. "Yeah, right."

Nick leaned back in his seat and stretched out his legs. "No really. I've been busy driving. And thank you for asking, but yes, I made it safely."

"Wonderful. How is Pleasure Garden?"

Nick rolled his eyes. *"Pleasant Wood."*

"Whatever."

He glanced out the window at the tall maple shading the driveway. "It's beautiful. Retirement is going to be awesome."

Alec let out another sarcastic laugh. "Don't get too relaxed. You've got a packed schedule and a few proposals to look over. Incidentally, I still think we should do a press release right away about your move to Colorado. The news would get your name out there and boost your revenue."

Nick thought about having a few days without the media knowing about his new location. That would be better than the Colorado Smashburger he hoped to have for dinner. "Nah, let's keep it until next week like we planned."

Alec let out a deep breath. "I still can't believe you opted for Podunkville instead of L.A. Do you know what you're missing?"

Yeah. Life in the fast lane. At thirty-four, Nick, a recently retired pro-football player was ready to settle down. The rural community outside of Denver had been home to his best friend and college roommate, Jared Huntsman. Whenever Nick had needed a break from his crazy life in California, Jared's house had been like a refuge.

Then, six years ago, Jared and his wife had been killed by a drunk driver. Their deaths had changed Nick. Suddenly, he hadn't felt as invincible. He had taken a good, hard look at his life, and didn't like what he had found. All the money and fame he'd gained over the years had filled every part of him, leaving no room for his Christian faith.

Days after the funeral, Nick had gone home to stay with his parents for a few weeks. There he'd found the solace he was seeking, and had come away with a renewed commitment to his faith.

Although Nick loved his parents, when it had come

time for him to retire, Pleasant Wood, Colorado had sounded more appealing to him than staying in California. Plus, it was where he was supposed to be. A decision confirmed by prayer.

"I won't be missing anything, Alec."

"I really don't get you."

"Yeah, I know."

"Nick, ABC sent over another request. Are you sure—"

"I'm not doing it. I can find a wife on my own." ABC wanted Nick to be their next bachelor. Having seen previous episodes of *The Bachelor*, Nick had declined the offer. Despite what everyone thought, sitting in a hot tub with more than a dozen scantily clad women vying for a rose was not his idea of having a good time. No amount of whining on Alec's part was going to change Nick's mind.

"You're kidding?" Alec said sharply. "Do you have any idea how much money this could get you?"

"We've already talked about this. I'm not doing it."

"Fine. Make sure you read the email with your schedule for the next month. Call me if anything comes up."

The phone went silent. It wasn't the first time Alec had hung up on him, so it didn't offend Nick. His relationship with his manager wasn't exactly symbiotic, but Alec did play a valuable part in Nick's life. He had saved Nick's reputation a few years ago, making him forever in his manager's debt.

Nick slanted forward and propped his hands and chin atop the steering wheel, his eyes sliding over the beautiful home. He purchased the house sight unseen because it fit the needs he'd requested. In all honesty, it was too large a house for a single man. However, he needed the square footage to host the mandatory parties required to maintain his charity foundation which helped underprivileged kids throughout the United States.

Anxious to be out of the car, he climbed out of the Denali and made his way to the front door. He stepped into the large entryway and looked around. It was a beautiful home—sparsely decorated, though. Why hadn't he listened to his mother and hired a decorator before moving in? He made a mental note to call his mom later. She'd said something about having a friend who could help him.

The two men from the moving company came down the stairs. Larry grinned and stuck out his hand. "All done, Mr. Coulter."

"Thanks." Nick gave him a firm handshake. "You guys were fast."

He pulled his check book out of his back pocket and had the men follow him into the kitchen where he wrote out the check. As he handed it to Larry, he reminded both men about the bonuses they'd receive if his move wasn't leaked to the press.

Offering the men the extra money was one way to ensure his privacy until his new location was revealed. His realtor valued word-of-mouth references and wouldn't dare to jeopardize his reputation. The only other person who knew his identity was Pastor Stewart. He happened to live across the street and, like everyone else, vowed to keep Nick's confidentiality.

After thanking them again, he stood on the sidewalk and waved goodbye as the truck turned the corner, disappearing from his sight. With his hands on his hips, he glanced around and took in his surroundings. The neighborhood was beautiful and secluded. Just what he'd wanted.

It appeared to be empty right now. Really empty. And

quiet. Despite what he'd just told his manager, part of him had kind of hoped for a welcome-to-Colorado party.

As the former quarterback for the Sacramento Defenders, he was used to the media and the fans. He hated to admit if he'd gone ahead with the press conference, he'd definitely have a welcoming committee. But that was not why he'd moved here. Instead, he wanted peace and quiet. Normal.

He looked around again and felt... *lonely?* No. He was just a little tired. As he turned to go back inside his house, he heard a door slam. Looking across the street, he saw a woman coming toward him. She wore a big smile and carried a basket on her arm. As she drew closer, he could see she was probably about his mother's age. He wondered if this was the pastor's wife.

"Hello!" She waved with enthusiasm, crossing the street.

Nick raised his hand to wave at her. At least somebody was going to welcome him to the neighborhood.

"Hello," she said again as she drew closer.

"Hi. I'm Nick, your new neighbor."

"Well, I'll be." The woman stopped dead in her tracks. "Owen is in so much trouble."

Discovering Sophie
by
Cindy Roland Anderson

Chapter One

It was love at first sight. Those baby blue eyes captured
Sophie Kendrick's heart the minute she looked into them.
"Hi, handsome," she said running her fingers through soft
brown curls. "How are you feeling today?"

The only answer she received was a firm tug on the
stethoscope that hung around her neck, bringing her face
close to warm skin, scented with one of Sophie's favorite
smells—baby lotion.

She smiled and couldn't resist pressing a gentle kiss
against the baby's curly hair. "Mmm. I wish I could take you
home with me."

"Yeah, you say that now," Jenny, the baby's mother
said. "Just wait until he wakes you up every three hours to
eat."

Sophie gently reclaimed her stethoscope, only to have
the chubby little fingers grasp onto a chunk of her chin-
length dark brown hair. Laughing, Sophie freed her hair and
passed the little boy back to the young mother. "He's
beautiful, and perfectly healthy."

"Thanks, Dr. Kendrick."

"You're welcome."

"We love him so much." Jenny cuddled the little boy
close. "I really don't mind the middle of the night feedings."

"I'm glad you brought him by."

Sophie watched mother and child leave the Denver
Children's Hospital multipurpose room, grateful that a mere

five months ago her steady hands had successfully repaired the baby's defective small intestine a few days after his birth. She felt such a joy to see some of the children she had helped over the past year and half since she had come to Denver.

The hospital was celebrating the opening of a new wing by throwing an open house for the public. Some of the guests attending were parents of children who had previously been patients at the hospital. Working as a pediatric surgeon, Sophie usually only saw very sick children. Today was a special treat for her to see so many happy, healthy kids.

Stifling a yawn, Sophie turned and saw her boyfriend, Peter Elliot, standing in the corner. He was busy with his iPhone—something that was not unusual—and something he had been doing since he'd arrived nearly an hour ago.

As always, whenever she looked at Peter, she couldn't help noticing how incredibly handsome he was. Dark wavy hair styled to perfection and a strong jaw line made him stand out in any crowd. The way his shoulders filled out his Armani suit, Peter fit the image of a successful attorney, which he was.

Everyone always thought they were the perfect couple. A doctor and an attorney. Since both of them had dark hair and brown eyes, they were bound to have beautiful dark-haired, intelligent children.

If only it were that simple. While Sophie loved Peter, she wasn't *in love* with him. She longed to get married and start a family. Peter was a very sought after bachelor, but when he'd asked her to marry him a couple of weeks ago, she'd told him she needed more time, hoping that once life settled down she would find her feelings had deepened.

Before she looked away, Peter met her gaze and gave her an impatient look then gestured toward his watch. He had wanted to leave thirty minutes ago. Knowing she'd made him wait long enough, she nodded her head and stooped down to pick up her purse.

A wave of dizziness made her start to lose her balance. Slowly she stood back up, drew in a long, cleansing breath and waited for the dizzy spell to pass. The weeks of sleepless nights were finally getting to her.

The nightmares had started nearly three months earlier. At first they only came once or twice a week. Now, each night when Sophie closed her eyes, the recurring dream would awaken her, remind her that her father was still missing, and that she had no idea what had happened to him.

Sophie crossed the room, hoping she didn't look as bad as she suddenly felt. She finger-combed the wispy layers in her hair, hoping it helped restore some of its style. Reaching inside her purse, she pulled out her tinted lip gloss. What she really needed was a shower, but she didn't want to miss having dinner with the Elliot family.

As she approached Peter, a twinge of guilt pricked her conscience. She might not be madly in love with him, but she was completely in love with his family. His parents were wonderful people who loved being surrounded by their children and grandchildren.

The fact that she loved Peter more for his family than for him troubled her. But at the same time while Peter had said he loved her, Sophie had a feeling his affection had more to do with her looks and her chosen profession. He had often said that dating a beautiful doctor was good for his image and he loved having a girlfriend men envied him for.

Meeting his gaze, Peter's brown eyes no longer held irritation. Now he watched her with concern. "Are you okay?"

"Just a little dizzy." She gave him what she hoped was a confident smile. "It's been a long day."

He reached out and took her hand in his. "Mom delayed dinner. I'm sure you'll feel much better once you can sit down and eat."

"She didn't need to do that, but I appreciate it." Mrs. Elliot's consideration warmed Sophie's heart.

Sophie leaned into Peter's shoulder as they stepped onto the elevator. Maybe she did love him enough to marry him. He made her feel safe and protected.

She'd already been in a long-term relationship where passion had been the pervading element. That had ended four years ago when Sophie had finally realized her boyfriend David never had any intention of marrying her. She'd given everything to David, much more than just her heart. In the process she'd distanced herself from God by letting go of her Christian faith and the values she'd always adhered to in her youth. When she had reaffirmed her faith and resumed attending church again, David hadn't liked the changes in her—or their relationship. He had walked away without looking back.

How ironic for her to now be dating a great guy who shared her faith and wanted to marry her, yet she was the one who couldn't commit. It didn't make sense. She was an only child and after her mother died when Sophie was eight years old, it was just her and her father. That's why she loved being with Peter's family. He had his parents, two sisters and two brothers—all of which were married—and nearly a dozen nieces and nephews. She wanted that for herself.

The first time Peter had taken her to a family dinner at his parents' house, Sophie had been awestruck. She'd felt like Lucy—the Sandra Bullock character in *While You Were Sleeping*—when she had celebrated Christmas with her pretend fiancé's family. Like Lucy, Sophie had taken everything in that day, loving the family interaction between the adults and children, the laughter and the incredible food. Peter's parents and siblings had welcomed her with open arms, expressing how glad they were that he was dating someone like Sophie.

If she didn't marry him, what were the chances she would find another guy with an amazing family who loved and accepted her like she belonged?

She was so conflicted inside and desperately wanted to fall head-over-heels in love with Peter. Part of her believed that if she stayed with him long enough, those feelings would come.

For the time being, she could hold off on her answer to Peter since her father had gone missing in the Costa Rica jungle a few months ago. To not hear from her father for a month or even two months was not unusual, but when three months had passed, Sophie had grown concerned.

Then, about four weeks ago, the recurring nightmares had started, and she knew something had happened to him. The bad dream was virtually the same almost every night and felt like some sort of omen. Sophie ran frantically through the jungle, calling out for her father. She would always catch a glimpse of him right before someone grabbed Sophie around the throat and pressed a hand against her mouth. Her terror filled scream would awaken her, leaving her shaking and unable to fall asleep again.

Peter tugged on her hand as the elevator door slid open. They reached the main lobby and exited to the parking garage. Sophie pulled her keys out of her purse. "I'll just follow you in case I get a call for an emergency."

"I thought you weren't on call?" Peter's voice had an edge to it, letting her know he didn't like the way she ran her practice.

Sophie was one of the few doctors who wanted to be notified if there was an emergency with one of her patients. They always called her first and she would then decide whether or not she deemed it necessary to follow up herself or allow the on-call doctor to take care of it.

"I'm not, but you know I like to be available if a child needs me."

He let out a deep sigh as he continued to lead her toward his car. "If you really need to return to the hospital before our evening is done, I'll bring you back."

"Thank you." She glanced up at him. "Sorry I made us late for dinner. Every time I started to leave, another mother or father would stop me."

Peter didn't look at her or make a reply until they had made it to his black Mercedes. Instead of opening her door, he leaned her against the car and kissed her. She kissed him back, wanting to feel something beyond contentment and security.

After a minute, Peter pulled back and stared at her. His dark eyes blazed with passion, making Sophie feel even guiltier for not feeling the same way.

"If you agree to marry me, I won't mind how much you work."

She bristled at his comment. He worked more hours than she did, but since her job required her to be on call, a lot of their time in the evenings or on weekends was cut short. "You could've stayed by my side tonight instead of hiding in the corner with your phone." It wasn't like Sophie to be so sharp-tongued, and she almost apologized. Then she thought about how irritated Peter would get if they were at a social gathering and she would have to take a call.

He took several seconds to respond to her terse comment. Finally, he nodded his head. "You're right. While I did have some pressing issues with the Van Buren case, I shouldn't have used the added time I had to wait for you to conduct business. I apologize for not being more considerate." He leaned down and gave her another lingering kiss. "Forgive me?" he whispered against her mouth.

She'd been with him long enough to note his apology was couched by pointing out that *he* had been waiting for her, but she was too tired to say anything about it right now.

"If you'll forgive me for making us late," she said, turning her head so his lips brushed against her cheek.

"Of course." He gave her a brief hug before he stepped back and opened her door.

Sophie caught the scent of his expensive cologne as she slid into the immaculate car. He climbed in behind the wheel and started the engine. Deciding to touch up her makeup, she pulled down the visor and almost gasped at how bad she looked. While Peter was always put together, she frequently looked like she had been wearing a scrub cap all day long. It didn't matter that she actually *did* wear a scrub cap all day long—or at least part of the day—she should have done something with her hair before going to the open house. She flipped up the visor, knowing the only thing that could help her look better was a good night's sleep.

"You look tired, Sophie," Peter said. "Have you heard anything about your father?"

"No." Her voice quivered as the constant worry she felt bubbled to the surface. "The man I hired to find Daddy changed his email address and his phone number once I sent him more money."

"You should've asked me before you issued additional funds. I could've advised you to never send anyone more money until you have some kind of results from the first payout."

Sophie bit back another biting reply. Lashing out at Peter wouldn't help anything. "Probably," she said, glancing out the passenger window.

"So, now what happens?" he asked, reaching over and taking her hand.

"I need to decide what I should do next." A decision she would make once she heard back from her friend Camille.

"If I have time this week, maybe I can do a little research and find someone else to search for your father." He gave her fingers a gentle squeeze before releasing them. "Someone a little more reputable, like a private investigator."

Sophie *had* hired a private investigator. Peter must have forgotten that little tidbit. Sometimes it seemed like he never listened to anything she said.

"That's not necessary, Peter. I'll figure something out."

"But I want—" His words were cut off when Peter's phone beeped an incoming call. "I need to get this." He didn't wait for her to respond before answering the call with his Bluetooth earpiece.

While Peter was deep into his conversation with one of his clients, Sophie leaned her head against the back of the seat and closed her eyes. She didn't need to hire another private investigator. What she needed to do was go to Costa Rica and look for her father herself. A plan she had already set in motion. A plan she knew Peter would never support. So Sophie had simply decided not to tell him. Yet.

She had already requested the time off for the end of the

month and was just awaiting the contact information for the guide she hoped to hire.

Sophie recalled the telephone conversation she'd had with her best friend, Camille Campbell, two weeks ago.

"I have a brilliant idea!" Camille said, her voice bubbling with excitement. "I can't believe I didn't think of it earlier."

Sophie had just finished with a four hour surgery and she desperately hoped Camille's idea involved chocolate. "What is it?"

"Did I ever tell you about Jack Mathison?"

"No," Sophie said, pulling off her scrub cap. "Who is he?"

Camille went on to explain that when she was in high school her older brother Tyson had just graduated from college and had gone on a youth service mission trip with their church to Central America. He lived in Costa Rica for four months, and Jack Mathison, another volunteer, had been one of his roommates.

"I had the wildest crush on the guy," Camille said on a sigh. "He came home with Tyson and stayed with us for a week and then burst my seventeen-year-old fantasy bubble when he introduced me to his fiancée."

"Okay," Sophie asked, glancing at the clock. She had an hour break before she needed to get to her office to see patients. "But how does this all amount to a brilliant idea?"

"I'm getting there. Anyway, the twins were taking a nap this morning so I decided to watch TV while I folded laundry. The first channel I turned to was that movie *Dragonfly* with Kevin Costner. He plays the part of a doctor who goes into the Amazon jungle to the place where his wife died. I totally got sucked into it when all of the sudden it reminded me of Jack!"

Sophie rubbed her eyes, wondering where Camille was going with this. "Jack looks like Kevin Costner?"

"No. Jack was way better looking."

"Camille, you have totally lost me."

"That's because you won't let me finish." Camille blew out a big breath. "Anyway, Tyson and Jack had lost contact with one another, but about eight years ago Tyson had run into one of the other guys who had also gone on the mission trip. He told Tyson that Jack had never married and had permanently relocated to Costa Rica. The last he'd heard Jack took medical outreach groups deep into the Costa Rica jungle so they can provide medical services for the natives in some of the remote villages."

A spark of interest ignited in Sophie as she finally got what Camille might be trying to say. If this Jack Mathison still did that, it would be the perfect setup. Sophie could search for her father while doing humanitarian work.

"You could go look for your father while at the same time be doing your doctor stuff and Jack can be your guide!" Camille said, confirming they were on the same page.

Sophie sat down on a chair, her mind going a million miles an hour. The logistics of her traveling to Costa Rica seemed insurmountable, but the warmth inside her chest confirmed this was exactly what she was supposed to do.

"Sophie, you still there?" Camille asked.

"Yes. It *is* a brilliant idea."

"I know, right!"

Camille's enthusiasm made Sophie smile. "Does your brother know how I can get a hold of Mr. Mathison?"

"I'm not sure. Tyson and his wife just left for a Caribbean cruise. I've emailed him, but I have no idea when he'll get the message, or what he can do until he comes back."

A chime alerted Sophie of an incoming text, bringing her back to the present. Peter was still engrossed in his conversation, and she hoped the text wasn't the hospital calling her in for an emergency. He wouldn't be very happy about turning around and taking her back right now.

Reaching down to get her purse, she slipped her phone from the outside pocket. A tiny smile curved her lips when she read the message from Camille.

Houston, we are go for launch. Call me ASAP.

Before Sophie could reply, Camille sent her another text. This one made Sophie want to roll her eyes at her friend's impertinence.

FYI: JM is still single!

Made in the USA
San Bernardino, CA
06 September 2016